The Price of Innocence

Also by Lucy Kidd

A Rose Without Thorns

LUCY KIDD

The Price of Innocence

Heinemann : London

First published in Great Britain 1994
by Mandarin Paperbacks
and William Heinemann Ltd
imprints of Reed Consumer Books Ltd
Michelin House, 81 Fulham Road, London SW3 6RB
and Auckland, Melbourne, Singapore and Toronto

A CIP catalogue record for this title
is available from the British Library

ISBN 0 434 39040 2

Phototypeset by Intype, London
Printed and bound in Great Britain by
Mackays of Chatham PLC, Chatham, Kent

For Colin, with love

Author's Note

Some of the places in this book are real, and some – notably Manangwe and the town of Stadhampton – I have invented. Similarly, all of the people and companies in this book are fictitious; any resemblance they might bear to actual companies or real people is purely coincidental and unintended.

I would like to thank all the people who have helped this book along the way: Linda Neshyba, for information on geology; John McConnell, for talking with me about law and American law schools and giving other last-minute assistance; my mother, for sharing her memories of travelling in Britain in the 1950s; Ginger Barber, Octavia Wiseman and Abner Stein, for their encouragement; Caroline Upcher, for being an enormously helpful and inspiring editor. Last of all, I would like to thank my husband Colin, whose good humour has cheered me throughout my writing.

Lucy Kidd
May, 1993

1989

Again Holly lifted the receiver and tapped the long sequence of digits, known by heart, into the phone. And again she stopped before the last, before it could ring. *Go on*, she thought, *finish or give up*. Corinna herself would never have been so indecisive.

It would be 1 a.m. in England, in Oxford. The college porter would pick it up, as he had before, gruff at being disturbed: would shout, 'What?' and 'Eh?' down the receiver in a tone that left Holly rattled – so used was she to calm subservience in most of the people with whom she dealt. Sometimes the porter would go in search of Corinna, as she had no phone in her room; usually he was only willing to take a message.

And then dutifully Corinna would phone back the next day, not bothering to hide her annoyance. 'But you *said* it was an emergency! Well, that's what the note says. So why did you call, Mom?'

As usual, the words would freeze in Holly's mouth. Corinna sounded the same as ever. Nothing had happened . . . .

'Listen,' Corinna would say, 'is there anything else? Because there's a queue – ' She would break off then, momentarily stranded between British and American English – 'I mean a *line* for the phone, Mom, and I've got this meeting to go to – '

Corinna was always going to meetings. When she wasn't

studying, she was debating or running for president of some class or club or society; she had been running for offices, and winning most of them, ever since she was fourteen.

Her first high-school election. Lanky, blonde, dazzlingly beautiful even then – her metamorphosis from girl to woman seemingly completed in a matter of months – Corinna had run into the kitchen waving a sheaf of emerald posters. 'VOTE,' they said, 'FOR SECRETARY.'

'I'm running!' she announced. 'And I know I'm going to win, Mom. I've got it all figured out. . . .'

Holly smiled, with a warm rush of love, still, as she thought of it. The receiver resting, still silent, against her ear, the long, distant number incomplete, she put the phone down.

Her face lay dimly reflected in the plate glass of her window, which looked out over Park Avenue. Scattered lights shone in the tall buildings up and down the street, filling the blue-black night with haze. As Holly stood and stretched, the familiar long sweep of the avenue, down to the towers of the Pan Am and Helmsley buildings, twinkled with slow-moving beads of red and white light as cars and taxis made their way home.

Or perhaps not home, thought Holly. She was in no hurry to go home herself. The pale oval of her cheeks and jaw, the wavy shoulder-length red hair, the slim hands, elongated further by the glass, all showed in the imperfect mirror of her office window. The wrinkles didn't. Perhaps at forty-nine she was lucky that they ran no deeper than thin traces around her eyes; slightly deeper furrows in her forehead, around her mouth. *Worry lines.*

Once, there had been someone to call them that: to belittle them by kissing them away.

Not any more.

And so, as on many other nights, she lingered at the office when almost everyone had gone. Often the rooms around her felt more like home to Holly than the converted town house where she actually lived. She could remember

2

how, newly promoted to partner, she had chosen the office's rose-coloured carpets and curtains: the dark panelling which had helped transform it from the nondescript fourteenth storey of a midtown glass box into a series of interconnected, hushed chambers radiating timeless probity. She had searched through the dusty drawers of a print shop for the sixteenth-century maps which hung in her office and the hall, in token of the firm's speciality: international law. And more than one client had told her that these offices reminded him, more than anywhere else, of London. . . .

Slowly she snapped shut the hinges of her briefcase. There was only one file folder, a heavy one, inside it. When she walked into the hall she could see the light still burning in Abe Kravitz's office.

'On your way?' called Abe. He was a father: a worrier, like herself, round-cheeked and wrinkled.

Holly stood in his doorway and gave him an answering smile. 'When are *you* going home? You'll get lonely.' *Lonely*, she thought: who am I to talk?

'Hey, what about you? You've been here every night this week.'

'I wasn't working.' Once, Holly reflected, she would have been loath to admit that.

'Then what were you doing? Nah, don't tell me. I know. Top secret.' Abe smiled.

Truer than you think, thought Holly. 'Hardly. I was just . . . fooling around. Thinking about phoning Corinna.'

'Again?' Abe's eyebrows shot up.

Holly shrugged helplessly.

'Give the girl a break! She's twenty-four. You people with only children . . .' Abe himself had six.

'I didn't phone her,' Holly interjected, half smiling. 'I held off.'

'Well, good.' Abe's eyes – anxious, beady, familiar to her now for more years than she could count offhand – fixed on her again for a moment. 'Are you OK, Holly?'

'Yes.'

3

For a moment Abe's concern hung, unspoken, between them. Holly gripped her briefcase tighter and turned.

''Night, Holly.' Abe sounded worried, unfinished.

'Good-night.'

Holly was glad of the empty elevator: of the space that surrounded her when, once outside in the cold winter air, she began to walk. The Christmas lights had come down from the trees along the middle of Park Avenue: she was glad of that, too. Corinna had spent Christmas in Morocco with a group of other Rhodes scholars. Holly had worried about her, so far away. When she told her so, they had argued.

They argued too much. Perhaps Abe was right, and she ought to let go. But then, Corinna was young, still, in so many ways.

At the same age ... thought Holly, ignoring the DON'T WALK sign to cross an empty 60th Street. At the same age, she had been married – pregnant. Corinna wanted none of that. Not now. She wanted a life of her own first: a career, as Holly had taught her to. Corinna would put herself first, because no man could be depended on. Had Holly taught her that, too?

At fourteen, at eighteen, Corinna had had all the ambition that had seized Holly so much later in her own life: but Corinna's was a pure ambition – idealistic, ever-confident. She wanted to be a lawyer, like her mother, or an investment banker. Eventually a senator. She thought she could be all of these: fit many lifetimes in one.

Her toe catching on a crack in the pavement, Holly stumbled and thought, *I should know.*

She passed the building where she had grown up; it was massive and Victorian in appearance, at Park and 65th. It seemed to her, not for the first time, that she had travelled an awfully long way to end up only a few blocks from where she had begun.

And yet, all the same, she had travelled.

The sidewalks were empty; here and there, doormen regarded her as she passed under the awnings of their

4

buildings. Still she did not wave for a cab. She crossed 68th Street, still deep in her thoughts.

For a moment, again, in her mind, she stood in the misty dawn light of Key Isotro. And knew. Again, she was twenty-five and felt her future forming: a determination, wrapping itself around a terrible hate. *I will get even.*

'Why don't you ever go back to England?' Corinna had asked her once, innocently. How old had she been, then? Twelve, thirteen?

'Because,' Holly remembered answering calmly, 'I didn't have a very pleasant time there.' She had smiled – a plastic smile – both to appease her daughter and to indicate that the subject was closed.

Because, she thought now, *I was nearly destroyed there.*

When Corinna had run home and thrown her arms around her, ecstatic, screaming, 'I got the Rhodes! I'm going to Oxford!', it had taken all the self-control Holly could command to steel her mouth, her face, and breathe, 'That's wonderful.' Which it was. For Corinna. 'I'm very – happy for you.'

Holly had seen Corinna off at Kennedy Airport. She had played the perfect mother. She had let go. And why?

Because the only other choice was to tell her.

Perhaps, she thought now, it really would be all right. *They* did not know Corinna was there. In a year and a half she would come home. They would not have touched her . . . .

Holly could not, would not think of the alternative. For she had come so close now. *Revenge.*

The depositions from Africa and South America gathered weight in her file, in her briefcase. The case accumulated – her second conscience. Yet she could not pretend that she was entirely altruistic. She sought justice, yes, but for herself she sought victory. A triumph over the past. . . .

Once she had triumphed, she might be able to tell: to sum up, coolly and dispassionately for her daughter, all the lost years of her life.

But would she dare then, even having won? Corinna

5

was, after all, a feminist. A child of her own times. Deep down, Holly wondered if she would ever understand: or if, knowing the truth of her mother's past, she would only despise her.

Holly's feet, in their narrow kid pumps, ached as she turned the corner of 73rd Street.

The doorman in the building next to hers nodded a friendly good-night.

'Good-night.' Holly unlocked the front door of the town house, wreathed in grimy city ivy, and reached into her mailbox. Catalogues, bills. Nothing from Corinna. Still she lingered, shuffling paper mindlessly, putting off the moment when she must go upstairs and open her door on darkness, knowing that after all there had been no miracle: no reprieve. She was alone.

II   *Oxford*

Two short taps sounded on Corinna's door. That would be Justin, come to fetch her for the speech at the Union. She threw a hasty glance around her attic room, littered with clothes, and decided not to let him in.

As she skittered past him, down the worn steps, she asked, 'What should I know about this James Carr?'

They emerged into Pickwater Quad: the compensation, Corinna often thought, for her eight-by-ten-foot quarters with their musty furnishings and lack of running water. Majestic eighteenth-century façades – the library, the art gallery – rose up all around her. She had not quite learnt yet to keep her eyes to the ground and take them for granted.

'Carr's fairly impressive,' said Justin lackadaisically. 'Less so in person, of course, than on the hustings.'

'You've met him?' Corinna's interest was piqued, even though she knew Justin Lucas-Jones was a show-off.

'Met him once. Don't know why my father bothers with wets like Carr when it's the PM's ear he wants to bend.' Justin took Corinna's arm as they ducked through the porter's lodge; out in the street Corinna gently freed herself.

'Life's so un*fair*!' she said. 'I've never met *any*one important.' Which was a bit of an exaggeration, if you counted Supreme Court justices and Attorneys-General.

Justin's face, she noted, registered a flicker of amusement. He was not handsome, exactly: too thin for her taste, with long wolflike teeth and a slouch. But he possessed the wardrobe and air of self-assurance that, she had learnt, in this country, belonged only to the anciently wealthy.

'I forgot,' he said, 'you were underprivileged. You only went to Harvard.'

Annoyed, Corinna tossed her blonde hair and walked faster. It was starting to rain, which irritated her more than anything Justin could say. Her suede boots would be ruined.

The Union was jam-packed, cameras and television lights crowding the back wall, and Corinna and Justin had only just found seats when the Union president came on to introduce the speaker.

Corinna leaned forward to listen. She hadn't had time this afternoon to read up on James Carr.

The Union president mouthed the usual platitudes. Tonight's speaker, the Minister for the Environment, had served for thirty years as MP for Stadhampton, surviving the vicissitudes of party politics, as well as personal tragedy. . . .

What personal tragedy? Corinna tapped her foot in annoyance as the Union president went on without explaining, as if everyone in the room already knew. People were always doing that here: assuming previous knowledge. . . .

And now James Carr himself walked on stage. Tall, broadshouldered, he grasped the podium and leaned forward as he spoke, his hair – still fairly thick, though he must be in his late fifties – shining red-gold in the light.

'Tonight,' he said, 'I am going to take you on a tour of this country in the year 2010. Now, before you jump to the conclusion that this is going to be some personal utopia, let me warn you. It's just the reverse.'

Justin, beside Corinna, rolled his eyes. She ignored him: after all, he was a hard-line Thatcherite who regarded anyone whose career had flourished before the Great Lady's as worse than useless. And he might well resent Carr's good looks. It was unfair but true that in the political game, faces counted. And Carr's was the right kind. With the contours of his face hollowed by time and fine lines etched in his weathered, slightly ruddy skin, he had shaken off most traces of the pretty boy Corinna guessed he must once have been. Yet he was still undeniably handsome. And that, she had no doubt, accounted for part of his magnetism.

A veteran of student politics and political speeches herself, Corinna tried to discount that magnetism: but she couldn't. Not completely. She did not know when, exactly, she began to be drawn into James Carr's speech so that everything else in the room, the extraneous noises and lights, vanished. Was it when he talked about the 'disenfranchised', the poor, who no longer believed it was worth voting because governments could make no difference? Was it when he leaned forward and seemed, for a second, to look into her eyes with his own piercing sea-green ones? And said, 'It's not *other people's* job to change that future. It's yours.'

For her body grew taut then, and she felt a cold sweat break on her skin. She thought at once, *Yes, it is my job, and I will*; and, with a queasy fluttering deep in her chest, *I know him*. She did not know which thought came first, or which drove her to her feet when Carr stood back and the president of the Union called for questions.

She could not possibly know him. She had never seen

him before in her life, except in the papers. He was an MP, a member of Cabinet. The name was only a coincidence.

What could it mean, anyway? *Carr.* In this country there must be hundreds – thousands – of Carrs. Even to her, for whom it should, by rights, mean something ... it said little. A name. An incompletely familiar name, connected only with the distant past, with her mother's years in England.

She wondered for a second if this Carr, James Carr, might have known her mother then – and quenched the thought. *A minister ... a member of parliament. ...* It was impossible.

And now he was nodding at her, telling her to go ahead. The deep-set green eyes met hers for certain this time. She knew the whole audience was listening; and with that knowledge a familiar calm suffused her.

'You seem – ' she spoke as loudly, and in as low a tone, as she could – 'to agree with Mrs Thatcher that to speak of an underclass is to create one. But isn't it equally fair to acknowledge that there is a growing group, in both America and Britain, which is effectively cut off from personal advancement?'

She felt the flicker of hot light, now, on her, and heard the click and snap of cameras; she felt for a moment that she shared the spotlight with James Carr – the almost unbearable, yet exhilarating, pressure of steady scrutiny. And then he spoke, and she fell back into the shadows.

'We must not,' he said, 'deny anyone the opportunities which exist for a majority in our society. You spoke of America, where, interestingly enough ...'

He talked about studies in the United States; she longed to ask him another question, but the president of the Union was shouting out, 'One question only! No follow-ups – '

And so it was other people's turn. Corinna was glad she had been first. The tension was always greatest before the first question: now it dissipated into the routine back-and-forth of queries and answers.

As James Carr backed down from the podium – to loud

applause, Corinna noted, despite the fact that he was a Conservative minister in front of a student audience – her eyes remained fixed on him. Even as she was pulled along with the crowd towards the back exit, she longed to break away and run after him. But she had had her question: her moment's attention. What more could she say?

Justin teased her after that. 'I see,' he said, in his laconic way, 'that the last of the great Tory wets still possesses his renowned attraction for women.'

Corinna denied it, of course. How could she explain, anyway, that what she had felt inside the Union was not really attraction, in the conventional sense – but something deeper, more instinctive. *Recognition?*

Justin asked her to two parties in the next two weeks. The first invitation she turned down, because it was only a boat club dinner. But the second she could hardly bring herself to refuse: the Royal Chelsea Armoury Ball. It excited her just to think of it. Maybe she'd get her photograph in *Tatler*.

On the night, she wore a black crushed-velvet dress, not too short. She didn't want to be ostentatious. For decoration, there were pearl earrings and the necklace her mother had given her – or rather, let her have, when Corinna came across it in the bottom of a drawer. It was made up of five twisting strands of baroque pearls, in all different sizes and shades of white: like a spray of sea-foam. But when she had shown it to her mother, Holly had only said, 'Oh, that. Yes, take it if you want it.'

Now, as she walked into the ballroom ahead of Justin, shaking hands with the line of matrons at the door, she congratulated herself for her find. Her sea-foam necklace looked far more original than their heavy gemstones.

The ladies, who all, evidently, had known Justin since childhood, looked her over curiously; and she saw the relief in their faces when they heard her American accent. *Just a bit of fluff, then, a passing fancy,* she could imagine them thinking. *I'll show them*, she thought, and clutched Justin's arm as they walked in under the chandeliers.

Justin nodded to the left and right, in his element. Corinna could easily see him as an MP in a few years' time. Knowing no one here herself, she felt obscurely jealous. 'Why don't you introduce me?' she demanded.

'All right,' said Justin mildly, swinging round. 'Will the Earl of Stadhampton do?'

Suddenly Corinna was facing a tall, blond, elegant man, whose level gaze met hers; whose long hand shook hers, as he nodded at her name; and who looked so familiar that she could only stare.

'James Carr's elder brother,' Justin explained.

'What a humbling form of introduction.' The earl gave a wry smile.

For once, Corinna had to struggle to recover her composure. She could not meet the earl's eyes now: they reminded her so much of his brother's. Though, in fact, they were darker, nearly brown, and narrower. Just as his face and body seemed slightly elongated versions of James Carr's, and his movement, as he stepped back from her now, had a more feline grace.

'I'm sorry,' she said – for it was the first thing that came into her head – 'I'm still not used to the way people here can come from the same family, and have different names.'

'Ah,' said the older man. 'I'm also known as Tyrconnel Carr. Carr, or Stadhampton. Whichever you prefer.'

Justin, touching her elbow, excused himself with a look that said, *so there*. Now she was left all on her own with the earl. Who already – or so it seemed to her – was scanning the room for a means of escape.

Corinna did the only thing she could. 'I think,' she said rapidly, 'your brother's wrong about America being in economic decline.'

'Well, you would, wouldn't you?' The earl's eyes crinkled, and now his attention settled on her for a second. 'Why?'

Corinna talked. She talked as if her life depended on the

earl's attention – and she did not even know why. She talked about the industrial base, taxes, the money supply; she talked – as she often had before – about matters of which she had only the faintest knowledge, gleaned from *Time* and *Newsweek*. And, as she had before, she seemed to convince.

The earl smiled and fixed her in his benevolent, catlike gaze. When she finished talking, she realised – absurdly – that she did not even know whether he was interested in politics, or what he did for a living, at all. She knew only that, through the earl, she might make an impression, however faint, upon his brother.

'What a striking necklace,' he said, when at last he spoke.

Corinna was startled. 'Thank you.'

'Tell me, if you don't mind – where did you get it?'

'It was my mother's.' The earl, Corinna realised, was staring down at it in a way that, for a second, unnerved her. But then he flashed her a conspiratorial smile.

'And what part of the States do you come from?'

'New York.'

'Would you like to have lunch?'

Corinna could not remember, later, how she managed to answer him. But somehow she had ended up with an appointment to meet at the Ritz at 1.30 next Thursday. She turned, blank-faced with amazement, to Justin, who had reappeared beside them – and then did not tell him.

She decided she did not want Justin – who, after all, was *not* her boyfriend – to know every detail of her personal life.

All the following week, she had to suppress the excitement – the rising feeling of expectation, hope and mystery. The earl had seemed to know her. As, for a few fleeting seconds, his brother had.

That Thursday morning she changed and rechanged clothes five times. It seemed important to look exactly right. At last she settled on the same outfit she had worn to James Carr's speech: silk scarf and blouse, tweed jacket, cords, suede boots. She looked, she hoped, casual: student-like. As if this meeting did not mean too much to her.

Her legs even trembled as she walked past the Palm Court and into the restaurant. It was crowded; she did not recognise the earl at first, so accustomed had she become, in less than a week, to thinking of him as someone larger than life. Standing up, he regained the stature she remembered; he must be well over six feet. But he looked thinner, more angular and older. Wine was waiting in a cooler by the table, but he was drinking mineral water.

'I'm glad you came,' he said formally, as the waiter pulled out her chair.

She did not know what to say.

'Perhaps,' he said, 'you are wondering why I asked you here. I should be flattered if you thought I were in the habit of meeting young ladies like you every day.'

Corinna smiled; it seemed politic not to answer that, either way. She wondered how old the earl really was. At the ball she had thought he looked no more than forty-five. Whatever age he was, he was well preserved. There were streaks of grey in his waving hair, which almost matched the dove-grey of his waistcoat. When he smiled, his eyes crinkled.

'I don't suppose,' he said, 'you wonder about the past a great deal. At your age, I certainly didn't. I took my parents' lives for granted – '

Here he broke off, for the waiter had reappeared. He gestured for Corinna to order first. She focused on the menu and chose, unthinking.

'What do you mean,' she said, finding her tongue again when the waiter had gone, 'about the past?' Her heart pounded.

'Wait.' The Earl of Stadhampton smiled and sipped. 'Give me time, and it will all become clear to you, Corinna. Why else do you think you are here?'

England, 1958–1965

Hollis Clayton stood at the edge of the ballroom of Stad-hampton House and knew that she was in love.

Although, at eighteen, she had never yet fallen in love with a person, she was sure now that it was possible to fall in love with a country. She had felt the first pangs – an uncomfortable ache, a kind of longing – on the cab ride into London, past Buckingham Palace, past Nelson's Column: the sense that a long-imagined and yearned-for place had come to life. She had felt it again among the stone houses of Warwickshire and then, at its strongest, as the cab from Stadhampton station juddered up the long drive towards this house: an enormous golden mansion of Cotswold stone, its pilasters and window-frames slightly nicked and crumbling with age. Climbing out, she had gazed up in awe at the two long wings and the Regency dome rising far into the sky. As her father fumbled, red-faced, for change for the driver and her mother adjusted her bolero jacket over her bosom for the ninth or tenth time, Hollis ignored them to stare at the butler, expression-less as a statue, who held open the great door so that their hostess, Lady Carr, could rush forth.

'Oh, I *am* pleased you could come,' Lady Carr had cried. She had short-cropped black hair and gave Hollis's father a kiss, which evidently surprised him. Her hands fluttered; she alone was smaller, livelier, *newer* than anything Hollis had imagined.

For Hollis had come to England for the first time filled with dreams and imaginings. In London it had been she, uncharacteristically, who ordered her parents about: 'Can we go to the Old Curiosity Shop, and Chancery Lane, Daddy, *please*?' She had torn through the sites of every Dickens and Austen novel she had ever read; she had dragged her parents through sooty lanes until they found the site of Blake's print-shop in Poland Street.

Joe Clayton had been happily indulgent. 'Whatever you like, honey,' he always answered. 'Nothing's too good for my chickadee. You're going to see all over England and be one up on those college girls.'

Hollis's mother had shot her husband a withering look, at that. She was too much the Yankee to endorse any form of showing off.

Oddly enough, she did not seem to be paying much attention to her own rules now. Her voice, a slightly raucous amalgam of Boston and Manhattan, drifted back to Hollis from the fireplace of the ballroom, where her mother was standing in the middle of a crowd of elderly Englishmen.

'I said to Barb – Barb Hollings, you know, at the Embassy, she's an old school chum of mine – "Barb," I said, "you must have the most marvellous friends." Before I knew it, we were at tea with Lady Carr, and I *knew* she and I were going to get along just like a house on fire. . . .'

Please, please just shut up, thought Hollis. She wished her mother wouldn't overdo absolutely *everything*. Hoping to escape the drift of her voice, Hollis edged away along the line of French windows: as ever, acutely aware of the upper edge of her turquoise-blue evening gown. It was the first strapless her mother had let her wear, and two layers of boning sustained it. Hollis creaked when she moved too quickly.

But right now, alone in the gentle breeze drifting in from a sweeping lawn, where a rococo fountain played and beyond which the sun had not yet set, Hollis didn't want to move any further. She wanted to close her eyes and make time stop: right here, on this warm July night at Stadhampton House, so very near the centre of England. *England.*

Yes, she decided: I am in love.

'Miss Clayton. I do hope you aren't bored.'

Hollis jumped. The voice was masculine, vaguely familiar. She felt the beginning of a blush begin to creep its way up her neck to her face.

'I must apologise for the band. My mother insisted – to appease the older generation. But soon we shall be able to put the gramophone on and do as we please.'

Twice. Now it was twice he had spoken to her, and she had still not answered him. She edged round to look at him, feeling the blush expanding, flourishing. What could she say to him now? Her host: Lady Carr's son Tyrconnel, the ravishingly handsome young Earl of Stadhampton.

'I think – the band is good,' she blurted out.

'Do you? Then will you join me?'

Hollis could not believe her ears. Such things simply did not happen to her. Plain, gawky, too-tall Hollis, for the last two years the permanent wallflower of every school dance on the upper east side of Manhattan.

He was being polite, she decided. Yet that made her feel no less elated as, taking her silence for a yes, he guided her out towards the centre of the room. She felt his touch on her elbow with a terrible intensity.

He moved easily into position, one hand on her waist. She could feel her palms sweating. She wanted to run away. Instead, she started, stiffly, to move with him.

'I couldn't find you till now,' he said. 'Have you been dancing?'

'No,' she said abruptly.

'I can't imagine why not.' Tyrconnel Carr smiled. A lock of dark gold hair slipped loose and tumbled down by his left eye. He did not seem to notice it.

Because I'm a wallflower! Hollis wanted to shout back. Anyone can see that. Nobody asks me to dance. I'm too tall.

But she didn't feel too tall now. Even though she was five foot nine, Tyrconnel Carr stood a good six inches above her.

She looked bravely up into his dark brown eyes and smiled. 'You have a very beautiful house. Do you live here all the time?'

Silly, she admonished herself immediately: of course he does. She thought she could feel her dress creeping down, and stole a peek at her bosom.

'Only at weekends.' Tyrconnel swept her through a smooth turn. In the flash of a second, the room seemed to revolve around them. 'During the week,' Tyrconnel explained, 'I live in London. But I am indentured to Stadhampton.'

'Indentured?'

'A sort of slave, you might say. Stadhampton is a very exacting mistress.'

There was a curious twist to his voice, and his words, that Hollis could not identify. It made something quicken within her – a dim sensation of things unknown – and she jerked back.

Tyrconnel's grasp on her hand and her waist hardened.

'I think – Stadhampton is really lovely,' Hollis said, trying to return to their former conversation. Her voice sounded unnaturally high.

'Indeed,' was all Tyrconnel said. His fingers loosened.

'Is it very old?'

'Eighteenth century.'

Hollis looked around, so as to avoid looking at Tyrconnel. The ballroom – a vast double cube of perfect proportions – looked more magnificent by candlelight than by day, when its sparsity of furniture and the dullness of its olive-green paint were more easily visible. But Hollis saw no need to notice the house's dilapidations when the whole of it was so splendid.

Her mother's eagle eye, of course, had quickly detected the stained wallpaper in the bathroom and the brown marks on the dining-room ceiling: the result, Lady Carr had explained, of water fights by the soldiers who had been housed here during the war.

The chain of formal chambers surrounding the great domed hall on the first floor had, for Hollis, the air of a museum: worn antique carpets and brocade chairs faded by sunlight. Walking through them, she could imagine the ghosts of long-deceased Carrs wandering, scarcely noticed, among the living. Thinking of it, she felt the past, again, with such an urgency that she wanted to explain it to Tyrconnel.

'I think your house is magical,' she said; but her words couldn't convey what she felt. 'It's so different from any other place I've been. It's as if the past is always around you, and I think you must be so lucky – ' She was talking animatedly now: as she always did whenever she managed to break the bounds of her shyness. When she realised it she flushed. She thought she felt her dress creeping down, and gave it a quick glance.

Tyrconnel smiled. 'You don't need to keep checking on your bosom, Miss Clayton. I feel sure it will stay where you put it.'

He propelled her through another turn. This time both the room and Hollis spun.

I didn't hear that, she thought. He *couldn't* really have said that. 'You can call me Hollis,' she spluttered, 'not Miss Clayton. Everyone calls me Hollis.'

'Don't they call you Holly?'

'It'd be too confusing.' Hollis smiled broadly – then drew her lips together to cover her big teeth. 'You see, my mother is called Hollis, too. It's a family name. My grandmother was called Hollis, and so *she* was Holly, and my mother only got to be Holly when she got married and was living away from the family. And so – '

'*You*'ll become "Holly" once you get married,' Tyrconnel Carr said gravely. Hollis wondered if he knew how beautiful he was. Perhaps English earls counted such looks among their birthrights: burnt-gold hair, unblemished skin, perfect bones beneath. With its hawklike nose and straight brows, Tyrconnel's would almost have been a harsh face, except for the slight fullness of his lower lip and the dents in his cheeks which, when he smiled, matched the cleft in his chin.

The eyes too, seemed softer than the rest of his face: deep-set, shining. When she gave them a wary second glance, Hollis could see that the brown was flecked with green. It seemed that minutes had passed since the earl last spoke.

'I think,' he said, 'I shall call you what I like.'

'OK,' she breathed out, childishly. It was so unfair, she thought: she hadn't a hope in the world of such a man. With her height, her big hands and feet and teeth, and her red hair, she knew herself to be ugly. Plain, at best. Oh, there were good points: her eyes, with their blonde lashes, were an inoffensive hazel. Her hair, when curled and sprayed into an obedient bob, took on the rich shade of a worn penny. Her legs were good – if only her mother would let her wear shorter shirts.

She wondered if Tyrconnel Carr had even seen her legs, from his great height. Most likely not. No, the dance would end, and he would leave her, his duty done. Probably he had only danced with her to be a good host.

Without realising it, she sighed.

'Don't be *sad*.' Tyrconnel looked down at her with a mystified smile. 'I know I'm terribly old, Holly, but you might at least *pretend* not to be bored with me.'

'Oh, no. I'm not – '

Tyrconnel only chuckled and pulled her closer.

Two dances later, the band was still playing. And he was still with her. They moved rapidly through the thickening crowd, oblivious of all the others: the men in tailcoats of indeterminate age, the women in dumpily cut crumpled taffetas. And some in tiaras. They made Hollis think of a costume party whose participants were middle-aged rather than young and did not realise quite what dowdy figures they cut.

She did not think it was an impression to voice to

Tyrconnel. Her mother said the English were all terribly poor since the war. And that even before it they had never been known 'for their food, dear, or, I'm afraid – their sense of style'.

'Do you do this every weekend?' Hollis said to Tyrconnel now. She was getting hot, and the combined boning of dress and underclothes was starting to dig hard into her ribs.

'What? Dance?' Tyrconnel tossed the question back.

'No. Have so many guests.'

'Oh, yes. Especially in winter. We stack them together, like logs. The warm bodies are a good source of heat.'

Hollis giggled. The ballroom *was* chilly, even in summer with a fire.

'The closer together,' continued Tyrconnel, 'the better.'

Except that Hollis didn't think she and Tyrconnel could be much closer together and still have room to dance. 'Maybe,' she said, looking around at the floor full of dancers, 'we're generating heat here now.'

'I expect so.' Tyrconnel looked into her eyes with a knowing smile.

'I didn't mean – ' *Oh, no*, thought Hollis. She had made it worse. 'You must have an awful lot of friends,' she said, to change the subject.

'They're Mother's friends mostly. She wasn't allowed to entertain much while Father was still alive.'

'There's your mother now.' Hollis glanced past Tyrconnel's shoulder with a little rush of – what? Curiosity? Envy?

No matter how hard she looked at Lady Imogen Carr, she just couldn't make it add up. Tyrconnel must be near thirty. Yet his mother looked no more than ten years older. If it were to do with dyes and makeup, it could be explained. Yet there were streaks of grey in the Countess's black hair, waving back from her temples, for all to see. They made no difference.

She could see Imogen Carr bending back, willowlike, against her father's arm as they danced. Her hair was slicked back from her face, as short as a boy's, displaying neat pearl-studded ears. An unusual necklace of twisted baroque pearls set off her simple black dress. Narrow and short, the dress followed the lines of her body loosely; there was a violet sheen to its fabric, and the back of the neck dipped so low that Joe Clayton's hand was resting against bare skin.

'Your mother's very beautiful,' breathed Hollis.

'Yes. I suppose she is.'

Of course, Hollis realised, Tyrconnel wouldn't really notice. He would take her for granted. Yet it was impossible not to compare Imogen Carr with her own mother, who, with her bleached hair, in her bouffant-skirted Balenciaga, looked every one of her fifty-six years as she chattered and blew puffs of smoke at her diminishing audience. Impossible, in fact, not to compare Lady Carr with every other woman in the room. Including herself. Suddenly turquoise seemed so . . . naive.

'Dollar for your thoughts?'

Hollis cocked her head, puzzled. 'You mean a penny.'

'I know,' said Tyrconnel. 'But as you're American. . . . One thing you ought to know about me, Holly: I don't deal in small change.'

'I fear you've exhausted me, Mr Clayton. I must beg you – '

'Aw, d'you really mean it, Lady Carr? I haven't had such a good time in years.'

Joe Clayton was puffing; his heart was thumping hard, sporadically, in his chest, the way the doctor had warned him about.

'I'm afraid – ' Imogen Carr flashed him a brilliant smile, and her long lashes shaded her eyes for a moment – 'that, as you know, the saying goes, "A horse sweats. A woman perspires, and a lady *glows*" – and I am already past the point of mere glowing.' She paused for significance. 'Far past it.'

Joe Clayton's eyes widened as he offered his arm. 'Whatever you say, Lady Carr. Where now?'

'Now, you really mustn't monopolise me, Mr Clayton. What will my other guests think?'

'Your other guests can come back again. I'm only here once.' Joe Clayton grinned. His skin, naturally inclined to redness, had turned a deeper shade than usual; the bald dome of his head shone, and what was left of the gingery hair behind it was wild and tousled. He was a robust man, his short, stocky frame still hard as a rock – as he was often proud to demonstrate.

'What do you do, Mr Clayton?' Imogen had reached for a cigarette from the butler stationed in the doorway. Now she inclined her head towards Joe Clayton, who, with some fumbling, proffered a light.

'Metal alloys. It's like – supposing you want the flexibility of aluminium, and the hardness of steel, and yet you want to keep – '

'I see.' Imogen nodded. It might have been said that she cut him off, but Joe Clayton was so dazzled by her smile that he wasn't sure.

'What do *you* do?' he said, to tease her.

Imogen laughed. 'Nothing. I manage.'

'A house like this? Must be a lot of work.'

Imogen laughed again, inexplicably. 'Let's go next door. It should be quieter there.'

Next door proved to be a dark connecting chamber, half parlour and half passageway. The air was blissfully cool. 'Imogen – ' Joe said. His voice was husky. He reached out with one arm, but she was not there.

She had glided a few steps away; she was looking out the window. 'So dependable, moonlight. It's becoming a bit clichéd. Every time one throws a party, one thinks, "Moonlight would make it just perfect" – and there it is. Tedious, isn't it? I think next time I shall summon a thunderstorm.'

Joe Clayton moved hopefully forward. 'Imogen,' he tried again. His hand slid along the smooth fabric that covered her arm, towards her bare back.

'Now, don't go all sentimental on me.' She threw him a half-smile in the darkness – or he thought so. 'Please.'

He pulled her against him. He did not expect a struggle.

Her mouth was muffled at first by his. But her hands reached up and tugged his hair down, hard. She wriggled back from him. '*Let me go.*'

Joe Clayton gasped. 'Hey, I didn't – ' He let her go, and reached up to pat the injured place on his scalp where she had pulled. 'If you didn't want it, you shouldn't have brought me in here and made out as if – '

'I made out as if *nothing*.' Imogen walked in a wide circle around him, to the door. 'You will excuse me, Mr Clayton, if I return to my other guests.' She strolled back into the ballroom, past her younger son Jamie and his wife Daphne, who were perched by the windows on two frail *chinoiserie* chairs. 'Heavens,' she said, smiling brightly down. 'Don't you mean to circulate? All these people are your constituents, now.'

'Not these people, Mother.' Jamie grinned good-naturedly: his face was broader than his brother's though just as handsome. 'They're all your friends, down from London.'

'The *country* is your constituency, James.' Imogen gave him a roguish smile and strolled on.

Daphne smiled. 'I think she really means it.'

'Of course.' Jamie tightened his arm around his wife's slender shoulders. Even relaxed, she sat erect, as if on horseback. Jamie's thumb traced a path to the nape of her long neck, with its down of mouse-brown hair. Daphne had the blank eyes and quiet watchfulness of a woodland creature – a mouse, a fawn – combined with the simplicity of a schoolgirl, which, at twenty-one, she was still not far from being. It astonished Jamie still that she was carrying their second child.

'I'm sorry I don't feel like dancing.' Daphne looked down mopily at her feet, in their flat ballet slippers. 'I've gone all queasy.'

'It'll pass.'

'I wonder . . .' Daphne's voice was a gentle gust: nearly a sigh.

'What d'you wonder, Daph?'

'I wonder . . .' Daphne's sentence trailed off again, as hers had a way of doing. 'That American girl . . . dancing with your brother.'

Jamie glanced up towards the dancers. Earlier, briefly, he had taken note of Hollis Clayton. Tall and a little awkward, with good legs and interesting hair. Now his eyes wound their way back to Daphne. 'What about her?'

Daphne looked wistful. 'She seems so – *dramatic*.'

'*You'll* be dramatic, Daph, a few months from now. You'll be enormous.'

'That's not what I mean!' Daphne gave him an injured look, then melted and laughed. 'When can we go?' she said.

'How about now?'

'*I* think your brother's a dish.'

Tyrconnel's mouth gave a wry twist. 'A "dish". Now what is that?'

'You know! Choice. A dreamboat.'

'All that! Should I be jealous?'

Hollis glanced away and bit her lip. 'Well. You said he's married. So I shouldn't really notice him anyway.'

The band had gone: they were dancing at last to the long-promised gramophone records. By the time they had finished the twist she had been ready to collapse with exhaustion. Thank goodness it was Sinatra now.

'You haven't answered me.' Tyrconnel's breath was close to her ear. 'I'm not married. So can I be a "dreamboat"?'

Hollis giggled nervously. 'I shouldn't tell you!'

'Why not?'

'It'll make you vain.'

'Then I am one.' Tyrconnel grinned.

'For heaven's sake!' Hollis spluttered. 'I'm sure you know. You must know it!' She was glad she could hide her face against his shoulder. She felt the lean length of his body, barely touching hers.

'Then,' Tyrconnel half-whispered, 'I am lucky indeed.'

'It's only – ' Hollis went on nervously, 'one of those silly things people say. I didn't mean I thought – '

'Didn't you?' But then, like a fisherman toying with his catch, he decided to let her go. 'You American college girls seem to have a language all your own. Tell me some more.'

'Well, I'm not a college girl yet.'

'Where is it you said you're going?'

'Smith. I'll be studying English – the metaphysical poets. You know, Marvell and Donne – oh, and also Dr Johnson and Blake.'

'But what is the point of it for girls?' Tyrconnel extended his arm suddenly, sending her through another turn. 'You'll get married afterwards, anyway.'

'Don't girls go to college here? What do they do?'

'Have coming-out parties, learn to cook. . . .' Tyrconnel shrugged. 'Heaven knows.'

'So you think I'm strange,' said Hollis. 'Again. First you said I was odd not to go to boarding school . . . I know I would have hated it, getting sent away at – how old was it?'

'Eight.'

'Didn't you miss your family?'

'It's just what one does.'

Hollis shook her head in amazement; then, at last, allowed herself to look straight up. The music had slowed.

'Cultural collision.' Tyrconnel's eyes flickered at her. His long, narrow nose curled down slightly above his smile. She wanted to reach up and brush away the lock of hair that fell in his eyes. But she was not brave enough, or drunk enough.

'I want to stay here,' she said suddenly. 'I wish I could stay here. Six weeks isn't very long.'

Tyrconnel's hand pressed against her waist, pulling her closer. The other loosened itself from her and brushed against her cheek. 'I know.'

26

He caught sight of his mother watching him. Imogen twitched her head impatiently.

A few seconds later the song ended, and Tyrconnel excused himself. 'Back in a moment, Holly,' he said.

He was gone before Hollis had quite awoken from the dreamy state in which he had left her. She drifted towards the side of the room.

'Hey!' Her father stretched out both arms to block her path. 'How 'bout a dance, chickadee?'

'OK,' said Hollis, with less than her usual enthusiasm. She felt as if her legs were going to give way. Joe Clayton box-stepped briskly, heedless of his collisions with other dancers.

'Tired, honey?' He pinched her cheek.

'Ow. Don't, Daddy.'

'I'm just glad I can get in a dance with my girl. You been having a good time tonight?'

Hollis's smile spread across her face. 'Oh, yes. I'm so glad we came, Daddy. I really am.'

'Guess you're an Anglophile, just like your mother. Hey, if you two are happy, so am I. I only want the best for my chickadee.'

'But don't you think – ' Imogen Carr flicked the lid of her lighter open, and touched a flame to her cigarette – 'you ought to cast your favours more widely, Ty?'

'I do.' Tyrconnel gave her a lazy grin.

Imogen frowned as she drew in her first puff of smoke, but even that could not eclipse the look of nicotine satisfaction that suffused the rest of her face. Her nose – thick, almost masculine, and a fraction too long for perfection – flared for a second, and her long artificial lashes veiled her eyes.

'In any case, Ty,' she went on determinedly, 'you shouldn't give that girl *hopes*.'

'You asked me to dance with her.'

'Once. Not fourteen times.'

'Oh. I thought it was fifteen.'

27

'Stop it, Ty.' Imogen glared. 'I am beginning to revise my opinion of the Claytons. The man's a dreadful bumpkin, no connection to anyone important at all. And his wife's a lush.'

Tyrconnel gave a mischievous grin. 'Well, I think Holly is sweet. I'm going to get myself a drink and then go and find her again.'

Imogen half-snorted, half-sighed. 'For heavens' sake! Don't waste your time, Ty – '

Her son was already gone. Again, she drew on her cigarette and smiled. She thought she had played that rather well.

Joe Clayton gave Hollis a low bow, as always, when the song ended. She was too embarrassed to try her habitual curtsy: an old, jokey habit. No one else here did that kind of thing.

They went in search of her mother, and found her slumped, drunk and sleepy, on a chair by one of the windows.

'C'mon, honey,' said Hollis's father. 'Time for bed.' He put an arm around her and started to haul her up.

'Joe?' His wife's voice was hazy.

It was an old routine. Hollis knew it well. They flanked her mother – like an armed guard, she thought wryly – and made their way across the emptying ballroom. She was relieved that Tyrconnel was nowhere in sight. But then, maybe he hadn't meant that about coming back to her. Men said things like that, didn't they? When they wanted to get away. . . .

Not that she knew very much about men.

Maybe Tyrconnel is even dancing again, she thought, as she made her way up the dark stairs to the first floor, her arm around her mother's waist.

Maybe Tyrconnel was with some other girl now, and glad to be rid of her. She made herself face the thought: like sticking herself with pins.

In her parents' bedroom, she took off her mother's

jewellery. The Balenciaga would be crumpled by morning. At home on Park Avenue, one of the maids would have been able to remove it discreetly. Here, they just had to make do.

Hollis left the lamp off as she undressed in her own room next door. Moonlight shone in through the cracks in the tall curtains, and she imagined for a few minutes, again, that she was dancing.

Tyrconnel Carr, she thought. A magic name. She would not be surprised if, by the next morning, he had vanished like Cinderella's coach. A magic prince.

Or if he were right here, and simply never bothered to speak to her again.

Never seek to tell thy love, she thought, *love that never told can be*. In the morning she would wake up and it would be gone: the magic.

She had thought that falling in love with a place and a person were much the same thing. Now, she was beginning to suspect they were very different.

II

Lunch the next day was sparsely attended. Lady Carr and Tyrconnel were nowhere in sight; Jamie and Daphne huddled, whispering, at a corner of the table, until halfway through her cold roast chicken Daphne announced, 'I feel better. I think I shall go for a ride.'

Jamie patted her on the rump as she went away, and an elderly gentleman – Farnham, or Farnborough? Hollis had never caught his name – gave them both a momentary leer.

Since her mother was still asleep upstairs, her father buried in the *Financial Times*, Hollis was left to her own devices after lunch. After blundering into a few locked doors, she found her way out on to the terrace, and wandered across the vast rectangle of green lawn beyond.

The fountain, with its dancing circle of nymphs and cupids, was silent today; beyond a waist-high hedge at the bottom of the lawn she could see Daphne riding across the fields – a broad stretch of olive green dotted with bushes and hillocks. Hollis breathed in the scent of mown grass and felt almost perfectly happy; except that she wondered where Tyrconnel was. No one had mentioned him at lunch. He might even have gone back to London. But hadn't she warned herself he would probably vanish?

She sighed as she watched Daphne guide her horse expertly out of sight. Hollis didn't ride. Her mother had vetoed lessons even though there was a school near the Claytons' summer house in upstate New York, claiming that all that sun would give Hollis freckles. The truth, Hollis suspected, was that riding lessons would have interfered with her mother's summer routine of gin and tonics by the pool at the country club, where occasionally she might stroll over to watch Hollis play tennis or practise her diving.

Hollis adored both water and sun. Now she tilted her head back to try to absorb more of the mild English sun as she walked along the gravel path past the Victorian wing of the house. This was an oddity: tacked at a right angle to Stadhampton's splendid south façade, its stone a mustardy yellow rather than the gold of everywhere else, it looked a failed attempt at Gothic, with its squinting pointed windows. Beyond, on a scruffy patch of grass, a woman in a sun hat was wheeling a pushchair whose occupant flailed for freedom.

'All right, my love. On you go.' The woman bent to undo the straps of the pushchair, and as Hollis walked past, called out, 'Fine afternoon, dear, isn't it?'

She smiled up and caught Hollis's eye; but it was the baby girl who made Hollis's heart melt, all golden-red curls and searching blue eyes.

'How old is she?' said Hollis.

'Eighteen months. She'll be getting a little brother or sister soon – won't you?' The woman addressed the child in a flat, half-cockney accent the sound of which was quite new to Hollis. She looked Hollis up and down. 'You a visitor?'

Hollis nodded. The woman's manner surprised her, as did her evident self-absorption as she studied her red-polished nails, then smoothed a hand over her hair: a smooth chignon of an artificially rich red-brown.

'Miss Laura –' the woman gave a cursory nod in the direction of the little girl, now crawling around on the grass – 'is Master Jamie's. I raised Master Jamie himself from a sprig, and Master Tyrconnel too. They were the darlingest boys.'

She smiled and Hollis blinked. So this woman was a nanny. She certainly didn't look like Hollis's image of an English nanny; she was not at all plump or motherly look-ing, though an apron covered her dark blue dress, which might conceivably pass for a uniform.

She seemed to read Hollis's mind. 'You can call me Nanny. Nanny Walters,' she said. 'Everyone does. I don't suppose you have any little ones yourself?'

Hollis giggled. 'I'm not even married.'

Nanny Walters chuckled in return. 'I think she likes you,' she said, nodding at the little girl, who was making faces at Hollis.

'May I?' Hollis knelt down on the grass and crawled towards the little girl, who retreated, giggling. She could hear the hooves of Daphne's horse thudding rhythmically through the field, and briefly she wondered how Daphne could bear to leave her baby all day with a nanny.

If I had a baby like this, she thought – not to mention a handsome husband like Jamie – *I* wouldn't let either of them out of my sight.

'Hollis!'

She heard a sharp voice and climbed hastily to her feet. But it was only Imogen, Lady Carr, smiling from the garden steps in smooth tan jodhpurs and a riding hat. 'I see you're not at too much of a loose end, you've found Nanny. Would you like to come up to my rooms for tea?'

Running to catch up with Lady Carr, Hollis felt wonderfully honoured.

Imogen strode along a downstairs passage, peeling off her gloves. 'You'll have to excuse me. We shall be very casual if you don't mind. Whenever I'm in from riding I feel so beastly and hot.' She glanced back at Hollis. 'What lovely hair you have! *I* always wished I had red hair when I was young.'

'Thank you,' said Hollis, thinking, *Why?* Imogen's smooth black cap of hair didn't even need brushing now, as she took off her riding hat.

'I do hope your parents are enjoying themselves,' she was saying as she reached the door of her sitting room on the first floor. 'I've always been partial to Americans, you know. My own mother, in fact, was an American – '

She stopped in mid-sentence as she opened the door. Her two near-identical sons sat grinning up at her from the sofa.

'*You* two,' she said in feigned displeasure as she walked through to her bedroom beyond. 'You'll have to take yourselves off somewhere. Hollis and I are having a *tête-à-tête*.'

'Well, you'll just have to wait till later to corrupt her morals,' said Jamie. 'Do you want some of our tea?'

It was sitting on a damask-covered table in an elaborate silver pot.

'No, thanks,' said Imogen. 'It'll be cold by now. So you two can send for some more, and then bugger off.'

Hollis gaped. Her own mother would never use such language.

'You'll have to excuse Mother,' said Tyrconnel, his dark eyes meeting Hollis's. 'She wasn't properly brought up.'

Hollis smiled back, her eyes wide as an eager puppy's. She was so relieved that Tyrconnel hadn't disappeared that she didn't know what to say.

A few seconds later Imogen emerged from her bedroom in what looked like a man's dressing-gown, gold with black lapels, tied with a black cord.

'If you two are going to stay,' she said, running a silver-backed brush over her hair, 'you shall have to entertain me. Any news?'

'Daphne had Laura up on horseback last week,' offered Jamie. His skin, Hollis noticed, was slightly redder than Tyrconnel's, and the broadness of his face gave him a look of greater innocence.

'It's a wonder your wife doesn't grow four legs,' said Tyrconnel, 'and start braying. Or perhaps she already does.'

Jamie was frowning and looked about to retort, when Imogen said smoothly, 'I'm so glad Daphne has time to exercise the horses, Jamie – I'm much too busy. *And* I'm getting too old. Do you know, Hollis, I shall be sixty on my next birthday.'

Tyrconnel rolled his eyes. 'Don't fall for it, Holly. She's fishing for compliments.' As he lit a cigarette, Imogen turned round, stretching out a hand towards him.

'*Thank you,*' she said pointedly, as belatedly he lit a second cigarette for her, from his own. 'My sons,' she sighed, 'have the manners of barrow-boys. Do you smoke, Hollis?'

Hollis shook her head. *Sixty*! she thought. She still could not believe it.

'Good for you. Such a dirty habit,' said Imogen.

But as the tea was brought in, Imogen directing the maid's movements, cigarette trailing elegantly from her fingers, Hollis almost wished she had not promised her father never to start smoking. It looked so elegant.

Jamie sniffed and threw her a conspiratorial smile. 'Foul polluters, both of them.'

'Don't get preachy, Jamie.' Imogen poured and sipped. 'You do have a tendency to the holier-than-thou.'

Jamie reddened but said nothing. Hollis smiled and tried to catch his eye, in sympathy.

'Remember,' murmured Tyrconnel, watching her, 'what you said last night about dreamboats. And married men.' Hollis met his gaze and her teacup shook in her hand. She could feel herself beginning to flush under the attention of both brothers – however short a time it was destined to last.

'I believe,' Tyrconnel continued, 'I do have first claim.'

'Whatever are you mumbling about?' broke in Imogen.

Tyrconnel's answer was interrupted by a rapid knock on the door.

'Yes?' Imogen called.

The maid, Clare – the same one who looked after Hollis's room – was panting, her eyes full of tears.

'What is it?' said Imogen. She sounded impatient.

'Oh, my lady, it's Eduardo – '

The butler, who had been standing quietly by Clare's side, took over. 'Not to alarm your ladyship,' he said, 'but the emergency services have been called. There's been a slight mishap in the kitchen. . . .'

Imogen leapt up, and Hollis soon found herself hurrying downstairs with all the others: Imogen businesslike, her sons concerned, Clare wailing.

The kitchen – a vast, whitewashed basement room – was silent, the servants circled around the slumped body of the cook, Eduardo, who had stabbed himself with a kitchen knife while boning a leg of lamb. Blood was seeping from a gash in his white apron.

Hollis felt faint. Strong arms took hold of her around the waist as she stumbled. 'Look the other way,' Tyrconnel murmured. 'Hold on. I'll take you outside.'

Imogen was kneeling beside Eduardo, rolling up her sleeves. 'Eduardo?' She spoke to him, slapping his face. 'Eduardo! Yes, look at me. You must try and stay awake. . . . Blankets!' she shouted at the servants behind her. 'Bring me blankets. At once. He'll be in shock. And whatever fool pulled the knife out? You've only made it worse.'

Blood was slowly soaking one of Imogen's gold satin slippers. Hollis could only stare at it in horror from the doorway. Tyrconnel still held her. 'We don't seem to be lucky with Italian cooks,' he said with deliberate casualness. 'The last one walked out after a month.'

Hollis shuddered, but Tyrconnel continued to talk to her in the same soothing tones. 'Mother's always had Italian cooks,' he said, 'even before it was the fashion. She grew up on the Riviera, you see. It was a terrible bone of contention with Father. He liked his roast beef a healthy shade of grey and his puddings of a consistency to sink a German gunboat.'

Hollis gave in to a feeble giggle.

By the time the ambulance came, the cook was fully conscious, thanks to Imogen's ministrations. She saw him on to a stretcher, then washed the blood from her hands in the kitchen sink. 'Dinner,' she said to the assembled staff, 'shall be at 8.30. I do hope everything's in order.'

And it was. Dinner, despite everything, was delicious. Joe Clayton frowned down at the *tagliatelle al pesto* that appeared on his plate for the first course, but helped himself twice, as did old Farnham and his wife, to the butterflied leg of lamb that had nearly been Eduardo's undoing. Fortunately the hospital had reported a few hours ago that he should make a complete recovery.

Talk of the accident kept conversation humming; Imogen didn't seem to mind it. Indeed, as she presided at the end of the table, radiant in a lilac cocktail dress, it would have been hard to guess that two hours ago her hands and feet had been soaked in blood.

'Your mother,' said Hollis to Tyrconnel, 'is amazing.'

He had seated her beside him at the end of the table – perhaps out of kindness, to spare her the worst of the gory speculation which was now surrounding Imogen. 'I suppose she is,' he answered her drily. 'She has a strong stomach. Which one needs here. People often make the mistake of assuming that running an estate is all hunts, bills and garden parties.'

Hollis nodded. She had little experience of the country, and she didn't want to say the wrong thing.

'Horses and *enormous* bills, I can vouch for those.' Tyrconnel smiled as he forked lamb into his mouth, red juice trailing down his full lower lip. Hollis watched with a certain aesthetic fascination as he mopped it up with his napkin. 'Those who choose to live in such demanding piles as this one run a fine line between honourable debt and penury.'

'I don't believe you.'

'It's true.' Tyrconnel's eyes met hers, mischievous, over the rim of his glass. 'I told you, I work night and day to keep this place.'

'But what do you do?'

'I own a newspaper. The *Courant*.'

Hollis's eyes widened. 'I've seen it.' She was surprised both to hear that Tyrconnel owned a newspaper, and that it was that one: a cheap broadsheet with lots of hazy pictures and headlines like 'Vicar and Nanny in Village Love Triangle'. But she did not say so to Tyrconnel. 'Does it make lots of money?' she blurted out.

If the question was crass, Tyrconnel didn't seem to mind. 'It will.' He leaned back, looking satisfied, as a footman came to take away his plate. 'The *Courant*'s my foundation stone, so to speak. I hope eventually to break out of Britain, to invest in more basic industries. . . . Good God, don't let me ramble on this way, Holly. I'd rather hear about some of those poets of yours. Donne, or Marvell.' Tyrconnel glanced across the table at his mother, who nodded up at the butler, who in turn began his route around the table bearing dishes of strawberries and zabaglione. Hollis couldn't help admiring the wordless synchronisation of it all.

'I'm afraid I – can't talk about Donne,' she mumbled. 'I'm hopeless at talking about things I care about, like poetry.'

'Well, then, do as the English, and talk only of what you *don't* care about.'

Hollis laughed nervously. Across the table, her father caught her eye and winked; her mother was too busy lecturing an old lord on the deficiencies of the Cunard

Line's transatlantic service to notice what anyone else was doing.

'So who's better,' said Tyrconnel lazily now, 'Presley or Sinatra?'

'Oh, Elvis!' said Hollis instantly. 'Everyone knows that. He's got *beat*. But do you know who else I really like? He's got the best lyrics – you're going to cringe, because you'll think I'm so old-fashioned. Cole Porter.'

'The John Donne of our day?' Tyrconnel raised an eyebrow. His knees, across the corner of the table, were disconcertingly close to hers.

'Oh, no. But maybe . . . Someone *lighter*, like Herrick, or Andrew Marvell. Do you know "To his Coy Mistress"?'

Tyrconnel shook his head, bemused. Hollis's strawberries still sat, untouched, in front of her.

Her gaze rose high above the heads of the others at table, towards the green and white cornice whose stains had already faded, in her eyes, to the etchings of dignified age. She whispered the words: 'And though we cannot make our sun/ Stand still, yet we will make him run.'

Below the table, Tyrconnel's hand reached out for hers. She clutched his fingers, hard, but could not bear to look into his face.

A few minutes later, the company at table broke up.

'Come outside,' said Tyrconnel. Hollis saw her father watching her again, but she shot him a reassuring smile and followed Tyrconnel through the dark, empty ballroom out on to the terrace.

'Come this way,' he said, and took her hand, his long legs swinging down the steps and across the gravel. They came to a door in the garden wall. 'Take a deep breath,' he said, as he took both her hands lightly in his and pulled her in. The door creaked shut behind him.

The walls surrounded them, enclosing and heightening the damp scent of summer roses. And Hollis, always preternaturally sensitive to scents, wondered how he knew.

As she let her breath out at last in the dark, she thought

she could hear it stir the leaves around her. Above, the first stars twinkled in a lavender sky.

'Now,' said Tyrconnel, pulling her closer, 'say those words again.'

'I can't.' She was afraid.

'Then I will.' There was a moment's silence: and then his voice, mellow-timbred and easy:

> 'Let us roll all our strength and all
> Our sweetness up into one ball,
> And tear our pleasures with rough strife
> Thorough the iron gates of life:
> Thus, though we cannot make our sun
> Stand still, yet we will make him run.'

'You lied,' said Hollis. 'You knew it all along.'

Tyrconnel's head tilted down in agreement. 'Come closer,' he murmured.

But she could only bring herself to inch forward. His hands slid up the length of her arms, and he bent down, kissing her hair where it sprang from her forehead in a widow's peak.

'You're so young,' he said musingly. 'So innocent.'

With those words all her young girl's yearnings for experience fell away; and she wanted to be exactly as he saw her. 'I don't mind it – any more,' she stammered.

He smiled. 'Why should you?'

Suddenly it seemed too much to explain. Holly only shook her head. She thought she ought to step back – although it was the last thing in the world she wanted. Would he think she was fast, for lingering on, so close to him?

But when she tried, hesitantly, to move, he seized both her shoulders again.

'Not yet.' He leaned down and at once she knew this was the moment: the one she must hold and treasure for ever. The first kiss of her first love. In trying so hard to think, to remember, she almost missed the sensation itself

– the feel of his lips on hers, velvet soft, tobacco scented. She held still and breathed in that scent even after he had let her go.

'Come and visit us when you get back to London,' he said.

'Yes,' she breathed; it was all she could manage.

'Do you promise?' His voice teased her and now he swung away, leading her back to the garden door.

All she could think that night was that it had happened at last: she had fallen in love, and not with England any more. No: this was something sharper, harder, more elating, more painful. All that night, long after her parents snored and wheezed in the next room, she squirmed, overheated, beneath the sheets – sometimes leaning up on her elbows to look out through the crack in the curtains towards the moon, the better to remember.

Tyrconnel's kiss had been so perfect, so pure and sweet, that she wished she had saved herself for him completely. In truth, she had been kissed before, twice during a game of spin the bottle at her friend Beth's sixteenth-birthday party. But those kisses had been the efforts of mere boys: wet, unskilled and slobbering.

At least, she thought, the rest of me is pure for him. She wondered now if Tyrconnel had had lovers. He must have: he was much older than she, probably nearly thirty. But that did not matter. He would be her first. If. . . .

She tried to stop herself thinking of *if*. She might mean nothing, or very little, to Tyrconnel. After all, he was so handsome. Perhaps he was even a womaniser – a Don Juan. How could she know? She must be careful.

She arrived late and red-eyed at breakfast, just as the footmen were trundling her parents' luggage down the back stairs. She had had no time even to put on lipstick, but was careful to dab some Yardley's Tea Rose behind her ears, in the hope that – should she get close enough to Tyrconnel – it would remind him of last night.

Imogen, her hair and skin sleek as ever, was pouring tea

with smooth efficiency; but Tyrconnel, to Hollis's immense disappointment, was not there.

It took her mother a good half-hour to say goodbye. Between shouting orders to the men who were loading her trunk into the boot of her hosts' Daimler and tripping back to Imogen Carr to apologise – '*All* my best dresses are in there.... *Must* travel the right way up' – Mrs Clayton delayed her family's departure until they had only fifteen minutes to make their train. Hollis's heart drummed ever faster, more anxiously. Soon they would be gone: on the train all the way up to Scotland. Tyrconnel had not come to say goodbye.

Just as Hollis's mother was climbing into the car, Tyrconnel sauntered down the steps. He ignored the older Claytons. 'Goodbye, Holly,' he said, extending a hand. A dark gold lock flopped over his left eye.

'Goodbye.' Hollis's voice was nearly inaudible. Behind her, the car's engine revved.

'Remember what I said about coming to visit.'

Hollis smiled weakly. 'Did you mean it?'

'Of course I did.'

'Because – ' Suddenly it seemed too much to explain. Hollis took a deep breath. 'I have to go back to America so soon. When I go, I don't want to miss you – too much. I want to be *happy*.' She knew what she said made no sense; her eyes darted wildly around Tyrconnel's face.

Briefly he touched her chin with one finger, as he had the last night, lifting her face up so that she looked into his eyes. 'Cheer up, Holly,' he said gravely. 'I want you to be happy, too.'

Hollis felt her heart go still, and then beat frantically.

'*Bon voyage*,' Tyrconnel called softly as she ran across the gravel and slid into the back seat beside her mother.

III

It rained all the way from Glasgow to Fort William, while Joe Clayton struggled with the Morris Minor he had rented.

'You need five hands to drive this thing. British engineering,' he grumbled as he ground through the gears up yet another narrow pass where clouds obscured the peaks of the hills.

'Never mind, darling,' Hollis's mother would answer absently. 'It's so romantic.'

For her part, Hollis could think of nowhere more romantic than London, where they would be again in just over a week's time. She was counting the days.

The weather cleared and she walked, daydreaming, along the shores of the loch at Glenfinnan. The night before, her father had blundered his way, by sheer good fortune, into a hotel with dusty stags' heads in its massive baronial hall and, even better, private bathrooms with unlimited hot water. This morning Hollis's mother had refused to budge.

Damn, thought Hollis: we'll never get to Edinburgh on time, and if we don't we'll be late to London. Which meant less than a week there before leaving England. Less than a week to see Tyrconnel. . . .

Tyrconnel Carr had become her obsession. Hollis's nature, she knew, was such that she would fix on an object, sometimes for weeks on end, work at it solely and think of nothing else. In school, she had been able to focus on her hated physics course until she had acquired the last of the string of As that probably got her into Smith. Even on vacations down at Key Isotro she would spend so long out on the water with her miniature sailboat that her father would have to remind her, 'Take it easy! It takes years to learn to sail, chickadee.'

But when you fell in love, she thought – and it frustrated her – there was nothing you could *do*. She could not shift her parents any closer to London until they wanted to go; nor could she tell them the reason for her urgency.

She did not even notice the mist clearing over Loch Shiel, or the faint sun lighting the column at the water's end commemorating Bonnie Prince Charlie. She stared out absently at the water, and her father's voice startled her.

'Can I catch you up?'

She glanced back and nodded. His arms goosepimpled under his golf shirt because he was too proud to put on a sweater in August, Joe Clayton strode up and fixed his hands stolidly in his pockets, bouncing on his heels to create some warmth.

'Beautiful view. Maybe your mother's right about the Highlands.'

'Maybe.'

Joe studied Hollis. 'Have you been down to the monument?'

Hollis shrugged. 'I'll go some time.'

'Getting homesick?'

Hollis looked up sharply and tightened her face into something close to a smile. 'No. I like it here, really.'

Her father glanced at her for a moment, but, to her immense relief, said nothing. He had seen her talking to Tyrconnel. And she would not for a moment imagine him as oblivious as her mother. If her face, or Tyrconnel's, had given anything away, her father would have noticed. She knew she must change the subject. 'Will there be dancing tonight?'

'Hey, that's my girl.' Joe sounded relieved. 'Always ready for a quickstep. I'll tell you what, if there's no dancing here tonight, we can drive somewhere else and find some.'

'I doubt there's anything for about forty miles.' Hollis smiled. 'I could just see us breaking down in the Morris

Minor in the middle of nowhere. Thanks, Daddy. But it's OK.'

Joe Clayton gave an abrupt, accepting nod and started back towards the hotel. Hollis didn't follow him.

From further on he looked back at her lanky figure, stooping slightly by the lake, her red hair frizzed by the damp into a woolly pyramid. She was wearing a brown cashmere twinset – one of about twenty that she owned in various colours, he supposed – with a brown checked circle skirt, bobby sox and loafers. He had thought often before that it was too bad no one ever seemed to think her pretty – except him. And then of course he was partial. He didn't know what it was about clothes and hairstyles that managed to do down whatever beauty she possessed. For he had seen her, sometimes, coming to kiss him and her mother good-night in her white nightgown, her face pale and scrubbed clean, red hair brushed any which way, and thought how fresh and lovely she looked: how fine her full mouth was, and her big hazel eyes. It was too bad, he thought, that the boys at the dances couldn't see her like this. Any girl her age wanted a boyfriend. It was only natural.

Walking back, now, to his wife, who was lounging in her second hot bath of the day, he remembered Stadhampton; and a shadow of worry cut across his thoughts. Hollis had said nothing about that young man, and he wasn't going to force her. He just had a feeling that if she were going to fall in love for the first time, this – with a sophisticate who would pick her up and drop her – would be the worst possible way.

With much grinding of gears, Joe Clayton manoeuvred the Morris Minor into Edinburgh, dropping his wife and daughter, with their luggage, at the North British Hotel.

His wife, relieved to be near shops again, headed immediately for Princes Street. Hollis, her spirits lifted by the thought that they were now only a day's train journey from London, was happy to follow in her wake. She even spent a few shillings of her pocket money on a bottle of Chanel No. 5 at Jenner's. Her mother, of course, disapproved. She wasn't sure perfume, real perfume, was proper for someone Hollis's age; but, her eye caught by the tiers of fashion beyond the circular railings above, she did not argue too long.

Hollis was chattering blithely to her mother as she swung her shopping bags through the glass doors of the hotel lobby.

She nearly missed him.

'I couldn't wait till you came back to London,' said Tyrconnel, ambling forward from the wall, where he had been standing talking to Joe Clayton.

Oh, my God, she wanted to cry out, but held her tongue. 'Hello,' she managed. Her eyes widened. 'What are you doing here?'

'A fine thing to ask when I've come all this way.' Tyrconnel looped his arm through her free one. 'Your father has invited me to join your family for dinner.'

Joe Clayton hadn't known what else to do. There was something about the Britishers, he realised, that put him off his stride: all those much-bragged-about good manners. He didn't think much of them himself, especially after his run-in with Lady Imogen; but still, when Tyrconnel Carr had knocked on the door of his hotel room he had been so taken aback that he had seen no way out of his momentary impasse other than to invite him to join them.

All through the meal Clayton was uncharacteristically silent. Watching his daughter and Tyrconnel together now, at close range, he was filled with foreboding. Hollis's eyes kept drifting back to Tyrconnel as if pulled by an invisible magnet. She virtually ignored her food – and Hollis usually adored smoked salmon. And when, as Tyrconnel poured the wine, his hand brushed hers – Joe had to suppose accidentally – she looked down and flushed pink.

Mrs Clayton made up for her husband's silence, and her daughter's lack of appetite. 'Tell me,' she said coyly to

44

Tyrconnel, winding a sliver of Hollis's salmon round her fork, 'what is this "business" of yours that brings you up here?'

'Nothing very entertaining. A few meetings with my brokers. I like to keep some of my business up here, as they tend to take a longer-term view of investment.'

'*Oh.*' Mrs Clayton's eyes widened and she gave a knowing nod. 'All our money's in United Alloys. I'm always telling Clay it's not very well distributed – '

'Honey.' Joe Clayton spoke suddenly, loudly. 'I'm sure Mr Carr isn't wanting to hear about our money.'

Hollis cringed. *Lord* Carr, she wanted to tell him. Didn't he know? A waiter came to take their plates.

'Holly tells me you haven't been sightseeing yet,' said Tyrconnel amiably.

Clayton looked confused for a moment and Hollis's mother spluttered, 'I don't remember – '

Tyrconnel smiled. 'Forgive me. I mean *Hollis*. I've fallen into the habit of calling your daughter by a nickname – which I gather will only be hers when she marries.' He surveyed the table, brows slightly raised.

Clayton only cleared his throat, tucking into the steak which had arrived at his place.

'Yes.' Hollis's mother gave a mincing smile. 'An old family tradition. I was named after the Hollises – ' she looked questioningly at Tyrconnel – 'on my mother's side. A very old Boston family.'

'I see.' Tyrconnel chewed his steak thoughtfully; then began to entertain the Claytons with the histories of various names in his family. The Carrs went back at least to the fourteenth century. Richard Talbot, the Earl of Tyrconnel, no relation, had been the hated Catholic Lord Lieutenant of Ireland in the seventeenth; the less famous Anglo-Irish Tyrconnel who was the Carr's own ancestor had been remembered in the middle names of succeeding generations of earls, down to the present one, whose parents called him Tyrconnel to distinguish him from his father, whose first name, John, was also his own.

45

Hollis was glad he was talking, for it meant her mother could do no more than interject some approving 'Ahs' and 'Ohs'. By the time dessert came, Hollis thought with relief, *We've made it*. But she wasn't quite sure whom she meant by 'we'. Her family? Or – herself and Tyrconnel?

'Well, good-night, Tyrconnel,' Joe Clayton said a little too heartily as they all emerged from the restaurant and passed through the bar.

'If I might just detain your daughter,' said Tyrconnel. His voice was low but carried easily over the background noise.

Joe Clayton turned, his thick brows beginning to hood his eyes. 'Now, I'll be frank with you. We don't approve of our daughter spending time in bars. I'm sure you'll understand – '

Tyrconnel drew up. 'I wasn't thinking of the bar, Mr Clayton. There is a room next door where we could have coffee. It's quiet and, I promise you, perfectly safe.'

Clayton acceded, with a gruff nod. Before he turned away he caught sight of his daughter arching her neck up to Tyrconnel Carr and saying something in a delighted whisper.

'Really, Clay.' Mrs Clayton took her husband's arm. 'Come on. Let them be.'

They walked to the lift, and once they were alone inside it, she began. 'I can't believe you acted so suspicious of that nice young man. It's not as if he's some troublemaker we'd be ashamed to have seen with Hollis.'

Two passengers entered the lift on the first floor, interrupting her. On the sixth floor they disembarked in silence.

'Well? Are you planning to ignore me?' Mrs Clayton said testily, once inside their suite. Her face was pink and puffy, as always when she drank. She reached in her crocodile bag for her cigarettes, then lit up, pacing and wobbling on high heels. 'If Tyrconnel Carr is interested in our daughter, why on earth do you want to spoil things?'

'*Why* should he be interested?' Joe sank on to the chintz sofa, realising too late the tactical advantage of the height he had lost. 'A guy who looks like that, the girls should be flocking around him. So why is he bothering with Hollis?'

'Really, Clay! She's not as plain as all that.' His wife, who considered a slight on her daughter's looks an equal slight on her own, fluffed her hair in agitation. 'I think it's splendid – and perfectly appropriate – that Lord Carr has decided to take her out.'

'So what's this about business here in town? Sounds pretty fishy to me.'

'Why shouldn't he have business in Edinburgh?' Mrs Clayton's voice rose to a high pitch. 'You know, Clay, I don't think you want what's best for our daughter. A chance like this comes her way and all you want to do is spoil it.'

'What chance?' Clayton's voice was loud and flat. He could see his wife give a shudder, for she detested it most when he sounded like that: 'at your most Midwestern', she would say. 'I don't want to see my daughter screwed around by some Romeo, that's all.'

'Romeo,' said his wife, 'was perfectly faithful to Juliet.'

'Christ! What do I have to do to get through to you?'

Clayton's wife gave him an icy look. 'Stop interfering.' The narrow skirt of her emerald-green suit wrinkled as she perched on a chair-arm. 'This could be a very good chance for Hollis.'

'I don't want to see Hollis marrying some Brit!' Clayton half rose, leaning forward. His wife's smoke was clouding the air; he detested her smoking but had been unable, in twenty-one years of marriage, to stop it: just as he had made no dent in her patrician confidence that in every situation she knew what was right. Hollis Heyward had been thirty-five and decidedly on the shelf when he married her, and he, having built up his own Ohio company from scratch, was far richer than her parents, the idle third-generation heirs to the Heyward shipping fortune – but none of that made any difference. Holly had borne the first eight years of their marriage, out in Cincinnati, on sufferance; when their daughter reached school age, she had insisted on moving to New York, even if that meant Clay had to commute between his company and his family. Fortunately, aeroplane travel had made that easier, and he was increasingly able to manage United Alloys by phone. Despite the fact that he paid all the bills, Holly had always kept careful tabs on 'her' money. 'I bought that table with *my* money,' she would announce, or 'I used my money to buy a few new dresses for Hollis.' It was, he supposed, her way of reminding them both that her money, if lesser than his, was older.

'What do you have against Hollis marrying an Englishman?' she demanded now.

'Why should she?' said Joe gruffly. 'She could marry an American in a few years' time – I'd give her my blessing. But why should she bury herself in this dump? England's had it. They've got *old* buildings and *old* streets and *old* cars – you can't even get a hot bath or a decent cup of coffee! You look at a family like the Carrs, and they *look* well off, but they're probably scraping the bottom of the barrel just trying to keep that huge place of theirs going. I'm not saying Tyrconnel's not a bright guy, but he'll go bankrupt keeping up a house like that and paying the taxes – and why? I guess because the Brits basically refuse to live in the twentieth century.'

'Honestly, Clay.' His wife stubbed out her cigarette and her voice was a near-whisper of disdain. 'Sometimes you can be *so* provincial.'

It was lunchtime. Hollis looked curiously around at the dark, smoky room with its beer taps, and long row of men lined up at the bar. Then she peered doubtfully down at the pile of mashed potatoes and brown sauce on her plate.

'Remember,' said Tyrconnel, 'you were the one who said your parents never took you into a pub. *You* asked to come here.'

Watching him digging with some relish into the heap on his plate, Hollis decided she had better do the same. It tasted better than it looked, especially after a morning spent tramping all the way from the Castle to Holyrood-house, where all the portraits of the Scottish kings on the walls, with their long, distinguished faces and noses, had reminded her of Tyrconnel. 'Could be,' he had shrugged, when she mentioned it. 'They're all fairly obviously portraits of Charles II, and he is a distant, though not quite legitimate, ancestor.'

'This shepherd's pie's OK,' she volunteered now.

'Just like at Eton,' said Tyrconnel, who had nearly cleared his plate.

'What was it like there – ghastly?'

'The food? Not much worse than this. The first years I was there, the war was on, which meant Woolton pie three times a week. Potato covered in mashed potato.'

Hollis giggled. 'That sounds like what Sanna likes to make. Our cook. She's from Finland.'

'From the sound of it your mother's running an English-language school. Can't you get any American servants?'

'Americans don't want to be servants. Besides, my mother teaches our maids lots of useful English. They sure learn how to chew each other out.'

Half an hour later they came out again into the sunlight. Hollis felt giddy. Perhaps it was all the ale Tyrconnel had urged her to drink – most of one of those huge pint glasses. 'We can't go back,' she said. Her voice sounded fuzzy.

'Why not?' Tyrconnel took her hand and swung their arms between them as they walked out of the alley and on to the Royal Mile.

'We can't meet my *father*,' said Hollis. 'We can't! He'll know I'm . . . funny.' Suddenly she let out an enormous burp. 'Oh, no.' She came to a halt, stricken with embarrassment.

'Poor little Holly.' Tyrconnel gathered her close for a second and kissed her head. 'I've got you drunk!'

She looked up. She wished he would kiss her again, like he had at Stadhampton. His body felt warm and welcoming: big, lean and hard all at once. But he only smiled down, running his fingers through her unruly hair. The

49

green in his dark eyes seemed to glow, and his blond lashes caught the light.

'No,' he agreed. 'I mustn't take you back. Not yet.'

It was seven o'clock when he dropped her off at her hotel room, and she barely had time to change for dinner with her parents. To her disappointment, he wasn't going to be able to eat with them again: he had a dinner meeting with his brokers. 'You can come and see me later,' he said. His room was on the seventh floor.

'Oh, no.' Hollis shook her head, abashed. 'I couldn't.' Her parents would never let her.

'Then I'll see you tomorrow.' Tyrconnel bent down to give her a quick kiss on the lips. 'I'll come for you after breakfast.'

Their second day of sightseeing passed much like the first, except that Hollis's feet by now were so sore from two days in high heels that pain stabbed her at every step, and she was too ashamed to admit to Tyrconnel why she kept wanting to sit down. It was glorious to be able to wear heels without feeling toweringly tall. When she caught sight of her reflection in shop windows – walking in long, happy strides, her hair flying – she almost didn't recognise herself.

Halfway through the afternoon, the cloudy sky broke into a downpour. Tyrconnel flagged a cab in Charlotte Square which whisked them back to the hotel.

'What'll we do now?' said Hollis. 'It's only three o'clock.'

'You could,' said Tyrconnel carefully, 'come to my room for a drink.'

'In the middle of the afternoon?' Hollis looked shocked.

'Tea, then.' Tyrconnel smiled and clasped his hand over hers. 'And I promise I shall behave like a gentleman.'

'So you should.' Hollis laughed as she looked up and down from the black polished tips of his shoes to his charcoal grey suit and pale silk tie. 'You *are* a gentleman.'

In every sense of the word, she thought: in their two days here, he had not tried to take the least advantage of her. In truth, she wouldn't mind if he tried to take just a little more.

They rode the lift up, hand in hand. The sky outside the window of Tyrconnel's sitting room had turned nearly black. As he phoned room service Hollis watched lightning crackle down over Arthur's Seat, that vast lifeless dark hill contrasting with the bright lights of the town nestled around it.

The waiter brought a bottle of whisky as well as tea, and Hollis didn't refuse when Tyrconnel offered her a splash of whisky in a crystal tumbler. Emboldened, perhaps, by her first, harsh swallow, she said, 'My father thinks your family's secretly poor, but I don't believe him.'

'Does he really?' Tyrconnel came to the window to stand beside her. 'Well, I'll tell you the truth, Holly. I'm working like the devil so that we won't *ever* have to struggle. I aim to make the Carrs an international power.'

Hollis stared. She almost wanted to laugh.

'You don't believe me,' said Tyrconnel. 'But money can do it. It can buy anything: influence, whatever sort of power one needs. I'm sure your father would understand my feelings when I say I don't intend anyone in my family ever to lack for anything.'

'How do you make so much money?'

'Buy cheap and sell high.' Tyrconnel's mouth twisted into a smile. 'Really, that's about all there is to it.' He reached down and his fingers laced through Hollis's. 'Your tea is getting cold.'

'That doesn't matter.' Hollis took a last, quick gulp of whisky and turned to face Tyrconnel. His gaze shifted down to her, the green glow in his dark eyes stronger than she had ever seen it. *Kiss me*, she thought.

He traced a line with one finger from her forehead, down her slightly turned-up nose, to the tip of her chin. She arched her back and stood on tiptoe, and at last his hand clutched the back of her head and he drew her close, his lips warm and moist. She strained to press closer to him, but he drew away. 'All in time,' he said. 'Are you a virgin, Holly?'

The words startled her so that she fell back on her heels and gasped. 'Yes.'

'Good.' Tyrconnel laid his glass down and placed both his arms around her shoulders. 'I want my wife to be a virgin.'

Out over the hills, the lightning crackled and the thunder brought down a fresh onslaught of rain. Hollis thought she had never felt so safe: so warmed and surrounded by love.

'You understand what I mean, Holly.' Tyrconnel laid his chin on top of her head. 'I want to marry you.'

'I do too,' Hollis gasped, before she realised how forward that might sound. She drew her head back so she could look at Tyrconnel.

'Then – ' he was smiling – 'the only question is when?'

Hollis's heart thundered, and she could not think of *when*, but only repeat to herself, overwhelmed by the wonder of it, *He wants to marry me. He wants to marry me.* Her impossibly beautiful dream had come true. She saw herself as a bride, as beautiful as any of the brides on the pages of any glossy magazine; he saw herself standing with her proud husband, posing for a portrait outside Stadhampton, while around them three or four children played. *We'll have children right away*, she thought, and only realised her thoughts had run away with her when she heard the end of something Tyrconnel was saying:

' – mind very much about missing university?'

'University?' she repeated.

'Your college. Smith.'

'Oh, no, I don't mind,' Hollis breathed. She had not even thought of it. And now – what would she want with college? A lot of silly courses, a dormitory full of girls, weekend dates. . . . Why should she want that, when she could become Mrs Tyrconnel Carr? Or – she corrected herself – *Lady* Carr. Her friends at home would be amazed. And jealous.

'I can't believe it,' she murmured, and laid her head against Tyrconnel's chest. She could hear his heart beating.

'Believe it.' He pulled her even closer, stroking the back of her neck and kissing her hair. 'Your life is about to change, Holly, in more ways than you can imagine.'

They went down to dinner hand in hand. Hollis's eyes were aglitter, swimming with tears of disbelief. Tyrconnel had wanted to run right out, in the middle of the downpour, to choose an engagement ring; she had only dissuaded him by promising that they would do it as soon as her father gave his blessing.

She saw her parents waiting, and burst out with it at once. 'Mother, Daddy! We're getting married.'

'What?' gasped her mother.

Tyrconnel's voice overrode them both. 'With your permission, Mr and Mrs Clayton, I should like to marry your daughter.'

Joe Clayton swayed in his seat a moment, his face reddening, frozen as if by the shock. Then he rose, smiling stiffly, and extended a hand.

'Congratulations. Well . . . we shall have to see if congratulations are really in order. But I'm sure my daughter's honoured – '

His wife couldn't wait for him to finish. 'Oh, darling!' She ran forward to embrace Hollis. 'This is wonderful, wonderful news. Lord Carr . . . may I call you Tyrconnel now?' She gave him a wet kiss and clung to his and Hollis's hands. 'Oh, Clay. I think this calls for a celebration. Why don't you cancel the wine you ordered and get us some champagne?'

As they all sat down at the table, a strange silence fell.

'Well,' said Joe Clayton.

'Oh, Daddy. Are you happy for us?' Hollis was anxious.

'Now, honey,' said Joe, 'of course I am. But this is going

to take some thinking. You don't want to rush into things, after all. You're only eighteen.'

'Really, Clay.' His wife patted his hand with an anxious flutter of painted nails. 'All kinds of girls are marrying young these days. It's quite the thing to do.'

'I don't care whether it's the thing to do – ' Clayton was gruff – 'but only whether it's the right thing for my daughter. Now, Hollis. I know you haven't started thinking seriously – ' Hollis was saved by the arrival of the champagne, and the obligatory toasts. But when they were over her father returned to the subject as if nothing had intervened.

'If you two could be patient,' he said, 'you could have a long engagement while Hollis finishes college. I'm sure, honey, Tyrconnel would understand – '

'Oh, Daddy, please!' Tears filled Hollis's eyes. 'Four years is so *long*.' She couldn't even bear to think of it.

'I'm afraid I must agree.' Tyrconnel took her hand, comforting, under the table. 'Chance was against my ever meeting Holly. And now I've found her, I don't want to let her slip away.'

Joe Clayton looked uncomfortable, and his wife filled the gap in the conversation with speculation about the wedding. 'Will it be over here? I suppose it'll have to, unless you want to wait till after Christmas and have it in New York. . . . Oh, but Tyrconnel won't want to go on all that long trip just to get married, will he? He's a busy man. So I suppose it'll have to be here. A wedding in England! How exciting. . . .'

With Tyrconnel's and Hollis's help, she carried them through till the end of dinner. Before the coffee came, Joe Clayton rose abruptly. 'I'm going back to our suite for a drink, Tyrconnel. Would you care to join me?'

It did not sound, to Hollis, as if he had much of a choice. Instinctively she rose when Tyrconnel did, wanting to go along with him, to protect him.

'No, Hollis,' said her mother. 'Let's just stay down here for a minute and let the boys talk.'

Tyrconnel shot Hollis a comforting smile, but still she fidgeted in her seat, left alone with her mother, who was going on again about wedding dresses.

What could her father and Tyrconnel be saying?

'You understand,' said Tyrconnel, 'I would not have made such an offer to your daughter unless I felt sure I could support her in the style of life to which she is accustomed.' He took two long strides to the window, aware of his advantages over Joe Clayton in height and sobriety: the long-drawn-out dinner had served him well, giving him time to measure the degree of the American's opposition. 'As you know,' he said, 'I own a newspaper, the *Daily Courant* – '

'One newspaper, and a pretty junky one, too, doesn't seem to me like – '

'Excuse me,' broke in Tyrconnel. 'If you would let me finish. I see the paper as no more than a foothold in Britain: a training-ground, if you wish. I've owned it for nearly five years and I think I've learnt a great deal there. The main lesson has been that no serious profits are to be made in this country alone.'

Clayton stared at him. He was silent only because he agreed. 'Well, go on,' he said finally, gruffly.

Tyrconnel sipped his whisky. 'As you may know, I have contacts in Africa through my brother-in-law Hywel, who is in the Foreign Office.'

'Your brother-in-law – '

'The husband of my half-sister Esmé. You haven't met them; they are living in Manangwe. With their help – and provided I am convinced of the stability of the Manangwean government – '

'Aren't they all having revolutions down there?' Clayton's knowledge of Africa was vague.

'I should think you would know – ' Tyrconnel's tone was momentarily icy – 'being in the metal trade yourself, that Manangwe, which contains ore deposits almost as large as South Africa's, has been under the control of a white, Conservative government for the last ten years. Willem de Vriet – '

'The President. I know,' said Clayton, anxious to get his own back.

' – aims to stabilise his country's economy, and an injection of foreign capital could well determine his success. Capital to take the mines in hand, employ workers and ensure exports.'

'And you think you can provide this capital.' Clayton trod heavily to the window. *Capital*, he thought. Good God, he had piles of it: factory space, machinery, half of it rotting away because his suppliers couldn't get him metals fast enough to keep up with his orders. 'Where are you going to get the money you need?' he said now, evenly.

Half an hour later the two men were on their third drink, the coffee table of the suite covered by the market pages of the *Financial Times* and the sheets of hotel stationery on which Tyrconnel had scrawled out his calculations. Joe Clayton could feel the sweat standing cold in his pores, his skin tingling the way it did only when he knew he was on to a sure and daring proposition. He hadn't felt the sensation, not as strongly as this, for years.

Still he wasn't sure. *Africa*. If he were to trust Tyrconnel, it meant relying on his knowledge of countries whose shifting politics Joe Clayton himself barely understood.

'I see the world economy,' said Tyrconnel, 'dividing. In the next twenty years, the gulf between producer and consumer countries will grow larger. All those colonials one reads about, fleeing Africa, may be right. It's a gamble. Ghana's gone; the Central African Federation is shaky. The whole continent may be in upheaval for at least the next decade.'

Joe Clayton nodded, recognising truth, even as something inside him recoiled at Tyrconnel's vision. The politicians, the newspaper leaders, were optimistic about Africa. Tyrconnel wasn't. He saw faction fighting, poverty, room for dictators. And for himself: because, as he said, 'One can't change situations. One can only . . . make use of them. We all know the British political empire's finished. The world *economic* empire's the one that counts. And it's barely begun.'

Joe Clayton tossed in his bed that night, his mind over-heating. Only a few times in his career had he met a man who could make him look at business in a totally new light: and Tyrconnel was one of them. He had the guts, Clayton realised now, and the instincts to found a fortune.

Yet mistrust still lurked in his mind. Why would such a worldly-wise man want to marry Hollis? She had no money of her own: Clayton had made that clear. On his death, for want of a son, she would inherit a great deal; until then, everything was tied up in the business.

'I understand,' Tyrconnel had answered him crisply, per-haps affronted. 'I shall be quite able to provide for her. I hope you realise . . .' He had choked slightly. 'I love your daughter deeply. I should be happy to delay our marriage if you prefer a long engagement, but in the circum-stances. . . .'

The circumstances, thought Clayton, as Tyrconnel prob-ably knew, demanded that he get back to Cincinnati. A month was the longest he liked to be away; this six weeks' vacation was an exception.

In the end, he knew, he had to leave it up to Hollis. If she were a hundred per cent certain. . . .

'Oh, Daddy.' Hollis paced up and down her parents' hotel room, which had already been emptied of luggage by the porters. 'How can you ask? Of course I want to marry Ty.' She had started using his family nickname now, since they were engaged.

'And you understand,' said her father, watching her care-fully, 'what you'll be missing? You can't get back your college education.'

'Oh, Daddy, what would I need it for once I was mar-ried, anyway?' Hollis looked up at him, her blue-edged hazel eyes full of yearning, her unpowdered cheeks flushed.

Love, he could see now, showed in her face, and even in the quick, excited way she moved.

'I always expected you to get married,' he said heavily, putting an arm around her shoulders. 'Of course, that's what every dad wants for his daughter. I guess I just didn't expect to lose you so soon.'

'You won't be losing me.' Hollis wrapped her arms around him. 'You'll see. We'll see lots of each other. You can come visit – '

'You know you're going to be far away from home.' Joe Clayton felt a lump in his throat. 'You've never even lived away from home before.'

'Oh, but I love it here! I've always loved England, from the day we first got here. And just think – if we had never come, I would never have met Ty. Think of the luck of it, Daddy! Say you're happy for me?'

And Joe knew then, hugging her tighter, that he could do nothing else.

The front door of the house at Chester Square banged shut behind Tyrconnel.

'Mother? I'm back.'

'Where have you been?' A disgruntled voice. Tyrconnel made his way through to the sitting room and bent down to give his mother a peck on the cheek. She was watching the news on television, which he switched off.

'I've been away on business,' he said, his eyes glowing enigmatically. 'One might say, the most important business of all. I'm getting married.'

'The Clayton girl?' A half-smile lightened Imogen's face.

'Are you angry?'

'No.' Imogen shook her head. 'I suppose I should be pleased. I *am* pleased. Congratulations.' She stood up, kissing him on the cheek, and he noticed for the first time that she smelt strongly of Joy and was wearing a long indigo evening gown.

'Waiting for someone?' he said.

'Mm-hm.'

Tyrconnel was used to his mother's seldom explaining her men friends or her destinations. Now she gazed at him, smiling broadly, her eyes burning coals beneath their thick lashes.

'She's very young,' she said. 'Do you think you can carry it off?'

'As far as I'm concerned,' said Tyrconnel, 'I already have.'

IV

For Hollis the month that followed was a heady round of dressmakers, department stores and *coiffeurs*. She had never in her life felt so important.

As soon as they arrived back in London, she and Tyrconnel went to Garrard's for her engagement ring: a pear-shaped sapphire set off by four clusters of diamonds. She thought she would never dare wear it out of doors, but soon she did every day, because Imogen Carr had lent the Claytons her chauffeur, who picked her and her mother up at Claridge's every morning and drove them into Knightsbridge or wherever they decided to shop.

They picked out a dinner service at Harrods; it wasn't really needed because Hollis and Tyrconnel, it had already been decided, would live in the Carrs' house at Chester Square, Belgravia. 'The house is *yours*, Ty,' Imogen had insisted. 'I shall hardly be here. When I am, I shall fly in and out so fast you'll scarcely see me.' At Stadhampton the attics were stuffed with the accumulated linens and dinner services of seven generations of Carrs; all the same, both Hollis's mother and Imogen thought there was always room for gifts.

Sometimes all three together, they shopped at Woollands and Harvey Nichols for Hollis's trousseau. Imogen's dressmaker was already working on the wedding dress, ivory satin with a smoothly fitting bodice and five-foot train. But Hollis also needed a going-away suit: three or four new suits at least to be safe, thought her mother. Not to mention new shoes and evening dresses for the sociable life she would now be leading.

Hollis, whose idea of material bliss until now had been to possess a collection of grown-up perfumes and a cashmere sweater in every colour, revelled in shopping with Imogen, whose very presence opened up whole new vistas of glamour. No cash ever slipped through her hands; she seemed to have accounts at every store. And her taste in clothes was far more sophisticated than Hollis's mother's. Still, Hollis sometimes had to suppress her disappointment when she turned to the mirror and saw that the crimson satin which would have looked so splendid on Imogen only made her look pale, or that a black and white striped sheath, so snappy on a petite figure, only made her look like what her mother called 'a long drink of water'.

There was all the business of the ceremony to settle, too. Imogen debated with herself over the church. St Michael's, Chester Square would be too small, she finally decided; besides, she was friends with the vicar at St Margaret's, Westminster.

'Westminster!' Hollis's mother cried. 'That sounds perfect. So ancient – '

'Not Westminster Abbey, Mother.' Hollis had to make sure she understood.

Through it all, Tyrconnel remained tolerant, gentlemanly and slightly aloof. Hollis's only complaint, during the busy weeks in London, was that she didn't see much of him. She longed for his touch, for his company – for the mere sound of his voice on the phone. At the *Courant* they were busy with a redesign, which he wanted to see finished before the wedding. Still, Tyrconnel managed to dine with her, or with her family, every few nights, and sometimes to kiss her good-night afterwards. She yearned for more, but her parents were never far away. Perhaps Ty guessed how she felt. 'Just you wait,' he would say, brushing her cheek or her hair with silken fingers. 'Not long now.'

A week before the wedding, during a lull in the preparations, both families decamped to Stadhampton. As Imogen said, Hollis deserved to see the house properly, from top to bottom this time – spare bedrooms, dusty cellars and all – 'because it will really be yours now'.

Hollis could not help wondering, though, observing Imogen's proprietorial air as she showed her around. It didn't matter, she told herself: Stadhampton House was big enough to accommodate any number of family members. Jamie and Daphne already used the top two floors of the east wing.

'He needs a home in the constituency for weekends,' Imogen explained, tapping on the door of the room Daphne had made into a parlour. 'No one's there.' She opened the door. 'For heavens' sake! What's the baby's cot doing here? Oh, well. You see Daphne's Stubbs – her father's present when little Laura was born.'

The room, with its cosy proportions, yellow walls and the portrait of an eighteenth-century stallion above its mantelpiece, had a comfortable, lived-in air lacking in most of the rest of the house. Perhaps it was because of the cot, and the litter of Laura's clothes and toys. 'Daphne *is* rather careless,' Imogen sighed, closing the door.

But Hollis thought secretly that she would love to fill just such a room with a baby's clutter.

The bedchamber that would be hers had walls covered in dusty rose damask; Tyrconnel's, adjoining, was sternly masculine with its massive desk and scroll-backed Regency bed. Both looked out over the south lawn, with its fountain, unfortunately bordered by the Victorian wing. Tyrconnel and Imogen took Hollis there, too, but they did not stay long. The downstairs rooms had been scientific laboratories for Tyrconnel's great-grandfather, the eighth earl, and still held tables and shelves covered with dust-clogged, murky vials. Upstairs had once been servants' quarters, but those were no longer needed.

'A monstrosity,' summed up Tyrconnel. 'And before we know it some Department will have slapped a preservation order on it so we won't even be allowed to let it decay. Too bad Grandfather's chemicals can't produce some long-delayed explosion.'

After lunch Tyrconnel had business in the town, so he drove Hollis and her mother in to wander about while he saw his solicitors. Stadhampton was a medium-sized market town, with a sleepy High Street, a few alleys of half-timbered buildings and limited outskirts of what Hollis thought rather mean-looking, identical semi-detached houses.

'Solidly Tory,' Tyrconnel explained. 'Always will be. They're rich enough here, and insular enough, not to worry unduly about their fellow men. Fortunately for Jamie.'

'Is that what they mean by a safe seat?' asked Hollis.

Tyrconnel, she supposed, was too preoccupied with his business to answer; and as it turned out, later in the day the source of a good many answers appeared as she was walking in the gardens.

'Nanny Walters!' she cried and gave a wave.

'Miss Clayton! Why, don't you look radiant. To think the last time I saw you, you was just here for a quick visit. . . . Well, imagine.' Nanny Walters was wearing no hat this time, only her own russet hair in a French roll that was shiny and motionless in the breeze. 'I always said Master Tyrconnel'd marry, one of these days – No! Laura.' She hurried after her small charge, who was trying to eat a handful of moss from the fountain. Deprived, Laura started to scream. 'Headstrong,' said Nanny. 'Like everyone in this family.'

'It must be hard sometimes,' Hollis ventured.

'You just have to be firm. Lady Imogen, when she made me nanny thirty years ago, told me I wasn't to lay a hand on her children. And to this day I haven't.'

'Really?'

'Those days, mind you, not many nannies were having that. 1928 it was. Lady Imogen was that big with Master

Tyrconnel – Master John he was, but you know how they always called him Tyrconnel – and she couldn't find a nanny as'd take her rules for love nor money. So she hired me. I was just a chambermaid here, only eighteen. Maybe that put her at her ease, because she said to me, "I want you to understand, Walters, you're never to hit my son." See, she was sure even then that she was going to have a son.' Nanny Walters broke off, as Laura had crawled to the far hedge, and was pulling at leaves. 'Oh, no, miss. You're not eating *that*.'

She came back winded, Laura gurgling in her arms, and while Hollis stretched out a tentative hand to the baby, who grabbed it, she said, 'Now, where was I? Well, she had her plans, did Lady Imogen. Once the boys were six and three, she had it all set. One was going into business, the other to the law. They both were reading by four, but she used to fret with me. "Now, you're not making 'em work too hard," she'd say. "You've got to be careful of their eyes." But, like I told her, they *wanted* to read. All the time.'

'So they were clever?' said Hollis eagerly.

Nanny Walters nodded. 'When it came time to send them away to school, there was the most enormous row. Old Lord John and all the men in his family before him had gone to Astonbury. But Lady Imogen said she wanted her sons taught with the best in the land, at Eton. They fought like cats and dogs. For days.' She gave Hollis a meaning nod. 'And so Master Tyrconnel went off to Eton, and that was that. What a treat it was when he used to bring his friends home. Always such handsome young men. . . .' Nanny Walters's face was rosy with recollection.

Hollis reached out for the baby. 'Can I hold her?'

'All right. You hold on tight.' Nanny shifted her dozing burden, with some relief, into Hollis's arms. Laura was unexpectedly heavy. But she felt so warm, and smelt so sweet.

'Do you know Tyrconnel's half-sister, Esmé?' Hollis asked now. 'She's too far away to come to the wedding.'

'Poor little tyke,' said Nanny Walters with surprising feeling. 'Not her fault, after all, who her father was.'

'What do you mean? Who was her father?'

'Rutherford, he was called.' Nanny Walters's lips tightened into a narrow line. 'I don't know much about him. He and Lady Imogen was divorced. At the time, everyone said it was a shocking scandal, her getting to marry the Earl of Stadhampton.'

Hollis's eyebrows leapt. 'She was divorced?'

'Not that *I* ever thought she was a scarlet lady or anything. But you should have heard some people talk.' Nanny Walters gave Hollis a knowing look. 'No one believed he'd actually marry her. He was a bachelor, after all, nearly fifty, keen on his hunting and his clubs. We was all shocked when he came home with a wife. Though you might say we adjusted quicker than he did. He'd got set in his ways, the way a single man will. When he didn't get what he wanted, he'd roar like a lion – '

They were interrupted by the brisk approach of Daphne in riding clothes. Her jodhpurs were streaked with mud, and strained where her waist was thickening, but she looked flushed and happier than usual. 'Mandarin's jumping wonderfully,' she announced. 'Really shaping up well.' She peered down at Laura, who was still in Hollis's arms. 'Isn't she heavy for you?'

'I don't mind. She smells so good. I didn't know – '

Daphne cut her off, without seeming aware that she was doing so. 'Imogen tells me dinner's early tonight because of Jamie's meeting. Blast it, he always wants me to go along.' Her horseback-induced energy rapidly fading, she drifted away. Hollis thought she had never heard such a strangulated voice as Daphne's in all her life. It sounded as if it came from way down in her throat, her vowels strained to their outer limits. Hollis also found her hard to talk to – although, figuring that they were close to the same age and soon to be related, she had tried. Somehow Daphne never really seemed to try in return.

That night when Jamie and Daphne trooped off to their

constituency meeting and Tyrconnel retired to his room with papers from his solicitor – something to do with leases on estate cottages – Hollis went to bed, too, with the copy of *Forever Amber* she'd been unable to finish for the past six weeks, so much more exciting than fiction had her own life become.

She had no better luck with it tonight. *Five days*, she thought. The wedding was only five days away. She would be married next Saturday, and on her honeymoon, and. . . . The suspense was unbearable. She longed to creep down the corridors to Tyrconnel, except that he had kissed her good-night quite firmly and said, 'Sorry, I've got all this to finish tonight, darling. See you in the morning.'

She didn't want to disturb him. Her mother maintained that there was a necessary space between husbands and wives. That was why they sometimes kept separate bed-rooms – as the Carrs seemed to expect her and Tyrconnel to do. Though surely that was a bit absurd for newlyweds, who would spend every night together.

Of course, before the wedding she and Tyrconnel couldn't be properly alone – not with their parents all around them, keeping watch. Still, she had hoped that during their brief engagement they would get to know each other more. That hadn't happened. So often, Tyrconnel was elusive: not that he avoided her, but simply that he avoided confiding. Perhaps that was simply British reticence. It would go away after the wedding. Then, she would know everything. . . .

She luxuriated between the smooth sheets, thinking of her wedding night. Beyond the double bed, her white lace nightgown and the first, delicious embraces she had little idea what to expect. Biology class in school might tell you what frogs and pigs did, and even, in a very theoretical way, what humans did; but they couldn't *convey* it. Even *Forever Amber*, which she had to hide from her parents, didn't really say –

Someone knocked on her door, putting an end to her mildly shameful thoughts. 'Come in,' she called.

It was Imogen. 'Sorry to disturb you, dear,' she said, 'but I didn't think you'd be asleep yet. I've brought something for you.'

She handed Hollis a velvet drawstring pouch, which Hollis opened and emptied on to her lap: a spill of shimmering white. Hollis remembered now: it was the baroque pearl necklace Imogen had worn on the night of the ball. Its five strands untwisted as Hollis held it up, then rewound, as if of their own volition.

'It's not especially old,' said Imogen engagingly, 'or new, or borrowed, and certainly not blue. But I wanted you to have it.'

'Thank you.' Hollis smiled, her cheeks glowing.

'To tell the utter truth – ' Imogen's voice was low and lazy – 'I bought it from Tiffany's in New York at the end of the war. So it's American, like you. It seemed appropriate. You know my mother was American.'

'Yes, you told me.'

'She was a Hancock. Not the founding-father ones – the bankers.'

Hollis had heard of them: they were still tremendously rich, in the same league as the Morgans and Vanderbilts.

'So one might say,' Imogen continued, 'Americans run in our family. Only my mother was rather less lucky than you will be. She married a sweet young viscount who ran utterly out of money. My father died before he could even inherit his title! My mother was heartbroken – fled to Europe. So that was how I grew up, you see – flitting from one hotel to another. How I longed for a home . . .' Imogen's eyes crinkled in a smile, and she squeezed Hollis's hand. 'Though I must admit, the Riviera was very beautiful then. Unspoilt. Sanary, Ste.-Maxime, St. Raph . . . Those days were brilliant.' Her eyes, so brown they were nearly black, glittered with tears. 'Anyway. I want you to be very happy, Holly. Do you mind if I call you that now, since Ty does?'

A few minutes later, Imogen slipped back down the hallway in her gold silk dressing-gown. She felt a little hollow, having given up her favourite toy pearls: but virtuous, too. Where the hall opened out into the moonlit doomed gallery, she paused, observing the dark portrait of her late husband at the top of the stairs. Thankfully, the darkness obscured it. By daylight, it gave her the shivers. She avoided looking at the broad planes of cheekbones and jaw: the deep-set blue-green eyes, like Jamie's. John had broadened out by the time he knew her, and lost much of his youthful handsomeness. Yet his features had retained their strength even into his seventies, and his gaze, despite his habitual heavy drinking, never dulled. When his heart gave out, death had come mercifully quickly.

She had not run him: that might be what some people thought, but it was not true. Her occasional affairs after the boys were born had been conducted in perpetual fear of discovery. She had known, then, that she was putting her security at risk; yet perhaps she had not been able to shake off the lingering inclinations of the gambler.

John hadn't gambled. He had simply failed to face facts. Stadhampton was poor. John's father, Ty's grandfather, had been forced to sell off a good deal of land; then came death duties. There was no compensating fortune in stocks and shares to pay for upkeep.

Imogen wondered, now, what John would think of Ty's marrying an American. John hadn't liked Americans. But he had married Imogen despite her ancestry. She had not dared to lie to him – pretending that she had money, or that Errol Rutherford, who still racketed noisily around the casinos of southern France, was conveniently dead. Nor had she lied when, a lone divorcee, she announced herself pregnant with John's heir. For it was true. She was pregnant; although she could not be sure that it would be a boy.

Though Errol, the stunningly handsome card shark she had married at eighteen, had taught her never to take an unfixed bet, she had done it, that once: estimating that

John Carr, the perennial bachelor, still wanted an heir enough to marry her. And she had won.

She smiled at the dim portrait now. After all, she had borne one son after another. She had not deceived him.

Hollis fastened the pearls around her neck and looked in the mirror. Even worn over the lacy top of her nightgown, they gave her, she thought, a sophisticated air. She would treasure them especially because Imogen gave them to her.

Imogen had called her Holly. *I really am Holly now*, she thought. From now on she would be Holly: grown up, married and loved. She had been baptised.

V

At the reception in the Hyde Park Hotel ballroom, there where white orchids on every table. Tommy Kinsman's band played. The receiving line took an hour to snake through the door, and all the while Imogen's pet photographer, a young man called Armstrong-Jones, took pictures.

Joe Clayton didn't regret a penny spent. Tyrconnel Carr was a promising young man, and if it made Hollis happy, it made him happy. That was what he finally decided.

He remembered how she had looked, at the church. Her gown was of the heaviest ivory satin, and her veil swept all the way to the floor. As she had spoken her vows, in almost a whisper, her face had flushed pinker than the bouquet of roses she was holding; and her father had seen beauty dawning in her face. He had been so proud.

As the vast *faux*-rococo room filled with guests, Holly's face began to ache from smiling. So many: four hundred. That was how many Imogen had invited. Holly felt ungrateful for wanting to get away.

Yet that was how she had felt, ever since she and Tyrconnel joined hands at the altar. Nothing else mattered now: the rest of the ceremony, the reception, the gifts. When the organ pealed, they walked out into the autumn sunlight; strangers on the street stood grinning, watching, waving.

All these guests, as far as she was concerned, might as well be strangers. She kissed Barbara Hollings, her mother's friend, from the Embassy. She would have given anything, just now, for one of Tyrconnel's encouraging smiles. But he was too busy speaking to Barb's husband, the ambassador, to notice her.

Soon, she told herself, they would be alone, on a boat to France; a train to Switzerland. Tyrconnel had planned their trip. *Anything you want*, she said. She had never been on the Continent before.

The thought of the honeymoon sustained her through the long wedding breakfast, and the dancing. She danced with her father, Lord Astor, Lord Farnham, Jamie. Occasionally Tyrconnel, too. *We will be going soon.*

Imogen and Joe Clayton danced stiffly.

'You know,' he began, once, 'Imogen, I – '

'Joe. Please.' She smiled rigidly. 'Let's not mention anything.'

'Are you mad at me? All this time we've never really been able to talk – '

'No. Because I don't want to. Do you see?'

As the music ended, Clayton extricated himself even before she could. He went in search of Tyrconnel and beckoned him, with a twitch of his head, into a corner.

'Something for you,' he said. 'Never got the chance to give it to you earlier.' He fished in his breast pocket for his chequebook and a gold-plated pen. 'I don't want my daughter catching cold over here. So this is to get central heating in your houses.'

'Clay, really. You've already been more than generous – '

Joe Clayton made a silencing gesture. 'I don't know exactly what things cost here, but this should about cover it.'

Tyrconnel opened his mouth again to protest, then fell silent. The cheque was for $100,000.

Across the room, Imogen observed them, her face wrinkling up with laughter. The gaucherie of it – right in the middle of his daughter's reception! She sought her son's gaze, but was interrupted.

'Imogen.'

She gasped with delight as she turned. 'Charlie! Charlie Moncrieffe!'

'The years are treating you well,' her old friend said as he led her to the dance floor.

'Not as well– ' Imogen smiled – 'as they've just begun to.'

At four o'clock, Holly changed into her dark green Dior suit trimmed in fox fur and stood in the doorway of the ballroom beside Tyrconnel, waving farewells. She could see her parents in the crowd: she wouldn't let herself cry. In the car to the station, she found herself surrounded by almost unnatural silence.

Porters helped her and Tyrconnel on to their train, and out again at Newhaven, where a cab took them to their boat.

'It'll seem easy when we get to the Continent – only a couple more trains!' said Holly nervously. Winding down from the wedding, she felt shaky and strange and unnervingly close to tears. Tyrconnel squeezed her hand.

She was surprised to discover that he had booked them two cabins, side by side.

'They're so very small,' he said, flashing her a comforting smile, 'and you, dear, have so much clothing.'

It was true. She hadn't been able to decide what to bring, so had filled three large cases. 'Sorry,' she mumbled through the door that joined their rooms. It slid open and closed like a medicine cabinet. She wondered if the bed in her room were meant to be a double one. It didn't look big enough for two.

'Never be sorry,' said Tyrconnel. 'You're my wife now.'

'Is that your family motto?' Holly managed a faint giggle. Her heart was pounding. ' "Never be sorry"?'

The porter had gone, closing the door to her cabin discreetly behind him. Tyrconnel moved close to her, his hands resting on her shoulders. *Will it be now?* she thought. *Even before dinner? Before anything? After all, we are married . . . .*

For one heady, terrifying moment, Tyrconnel remained: then moved on past her to the door. She breathed out in relief.

'Would you like to come out on deck?' he said. 'Lady Carr?'

Lady Carr. She sighed, this time with bliss, and smiled broadly. 'Yes. Yes, *my lord*, Lord Carr. I will.'

As she walked out she remembered that of course she knew the Carr family motto, from their coat of arms. It was only one word: *Floreamus*. 'Flourish.'

Halfway through dinner Holly began to yawn uncontrollably. She had hardly slept the night before, and now, though she was wearing wonderful new clothes and sitting in the ship's restaurant across from a man she still couldn't quite believe was really hers, she found herself longing for sleep.

'Do you want to skip dessert?' Tyrconnel murmured.

She nodded, her eyelids drooping.

Tyrconnel ducked through the door into his own cabin once he had unlocked hers. Holly collapsed on to her bed and could not move. She was still wearing everything: rings, stockings, suit, the same tight one-piece 'foundation', covering everything from her breasts to her hips, that had smoothed the line of her wedding dress.

Tyrconnel moved through the doorway in a dark red silk dressing-gown. She opened her eyes and for a second her heart thudded. It was going to happen now. She wished she could be more awake for it: that she desired it more.

'Poor Holly.' Tyrconnel spoke kindly as he sat on the

71

bed and began to undo the buttons of her jacket. 'You're completely worn out.'

She nodded. He continued to undress her, easing the jacket down past her shoulders; the blouse. He slipped the suede shoes off her feet and reached with delicate fingers to undo the zip of her skirt. It glided down over her silk slip; then he eased that, too, up over her head. For a moment she opened her eyes all the way, and to her surprise she saw that Tyrconnel was pale. His eyes were wide and there was a film of sweat on his upper lip.

So perhaps he was afraid too, she thought: despite the fact that men knew what to do. Perhaps he was afraid because he would have to initiate her. She reached up to kiss him, to comfort him, but as he caught her gaze he smiled with sudden confidence.

'Let's get the rest of these off,' he murmured, and now, with fingers more expert than she expected, he slipped open her garters and peeled down her stockings. If she were not so sleepy, Holly thought, by now she would be embarrassed. Tyrconnel rolled her on to her stomach and slowly undid the hooks and eyes down her back. Her breasts were free from their elastic prison; then her waist. She curled up gratefully.

He pulled the covers over her, smoothing her hair, and she reached up blindly with one hand, in thanks. He understood: he was letting her wait. 'I – love you.'

'And I love you, darling. Good-night.'

The next day, they travelled south by train, through Paris and on to Lausanne. The hotel Tyrconnel had chosen was on Lake Geneva, just beyond Vevey; they took a taxi from the station. Briefly Holly glimpsed a marketplace, bright in the sun; a row of trees, then the lake, a pure and deep blue beneath a crystal-clear sky. They pulled up the gravel driveway of the Hotel Bayern au Lac.

'Oh, Ty, it's perfect!' cried Holly as soon as she saw the long white façade, the flower-decked terrace. More flowers – begonias, pansies, chrysanthemums – formed a giant 'B' and 'L' in round beds on the lawn. A porter came for their bags, and inside the white lobby of the hotel the air smelt as clear and cool as water. This place was nothing like the slightly musty grand hotels she had visited with her parents. Everything was sparkling clean and fresh, and, as she was to learn, the hotel staff made sure it ran like clockwork.

Today, she decided, would be the first real day of her married life.

They had time only to take a quick walk down to the lakeside, then change for dinner. When they returned to their rooms their clothes were already hanging in the mirrored wardrobes, and a giant spray of flowers adorned the dressing table.

' "Best wishes",' Holly read from the card, ' "on this happy occasion. Gustav Meyer, Manager." Do you know him?'

'From other visits.' Tyrconnel had shed his dark suit and was stepping into his evening clothes. For a moment Holly could see the cordy muscles of his long legs; she observed the shape of his shoulders, perfectly sculpted, beneath his white shirt. She gave a shiver of admiration, which Tyrconnel did not seem to notice. 'Hurry up, then, darling,' he said cheerily. 'I know Gustav, for one, will want to meet you.'

Holly put on her pale pink chiffon and Imogen's pearls, and they went down. The broad windows of the dining room looked out over the lake, and mirrors on the opposite wall echoed the view, catching Tyrconnel and Holly in mid-motion as they descended a short flight of steps. Heads turned to watch them.

'Franz.' Tyrconnel nodded to the *maître d'*.

'Milord Carr.' The man bowed to both of them. 'Leddy Carr.'

Tyrconnel placed a proprietorial hand on the small of Holly's back. The *maître d'* led them to a central table,

73

smiling at Holly for a fraction of a second too long as he bowed again.

Still heads were turning, inspecting them; then turning back to their soup and talking. There were a great many old couples in the room, but some young people, too. Holly stared down, abashed. To think they were looking at her! Of course she knew they must really be looking at Tyrconnel. She was only an accessory.

'The curiosity of the idle rich, marooned at a waterside boarding-house,' murmured Tyrconnel as he scanned the wine list. The dining room was very quiet, those who talked doing so in hushed tones.

Holly felt constrained by the silence, and so whispered back only, 'Some boarding-house!' She realised how little she had to say to her husband – at least for public consumption. But he seemed content with silence.

She admired the way he divided the flesh of his trout from the bones: a few flicks of his knife and the job was done, nothing wasted, the skeleton removed to another dish. Her own fish, in its wine sauce, looked messier.

'I wish I could have seen more of Paris,' she tried. Of course, they were going there on the way home, for two days.

'Well, as I've said, Holly, it's not my favourite place.' Tyrconnel drained his wineglass. 'The French are inclined to dirtiness. I find one gets the best of all worlds here: a French chef and Swiss management.'

'I'm sure.' Holly smiled. She could think of worse evils than dirt, but did not want to start an argument. 'Have you been here lots of times before?'

Tyrconnel nodded briefly. 'On business. I think you'll like the *escalopes de veau*. They're very tender.'

He did not seem inclined to talk further. And by now, Holly was growing too nervous. She thought of their suite. There was only one bedroom, this time – one bed. She imagined Tyrconnel standing above her, loosening the black cord of his dressing gown. . . .

She shook her head.

'Are you sleepy?' Tyrconnel flashed her a smile before he divided up the rest of the wine, giving most of it to himself. 'You must have a dessert, then, Holly. And coffee. That will restore you.'

The thought of coffee made Holly's nervous stomach turn. She ordered a sorbet only because he pressed her to. It was sour and made her shiver inside. He would find it easier, she thought, undressing her tonight. She was wearing less underclothing than she had been on the boat.

Tyrconnel smiled – perhaps catching sight of the apprehension in her face – but he seemed in no particular hurry. When the bill came, he engaged in a long and scrupulously polite debate, in German, with the head waiter, over one of the charges.

Really, thought Holly. Her mother would have called that bad manners. She fidgeted in her chair.

At last Tyrconnel took her arm, and they moved slowly back through the lobby, then up the broad, red-carpeted flight towards the first floor. Waiters, bellhops and clerks all nodded good-night to them as they passed. Holly tensed. It was as if they *knew*!

It was early yet: only ten o'clock on the gold wristwatch she had left lying by the bedside table. Tyrconnel stood by the wardrobe, removing his jacket, loosening his tie. Nervously Holly peered out through the curtains.

'Do you have anything to read?' asked Tyrconnel.

Holly turned sharply. He was sitting down now, she saw, with his feet propped up on the bed. There was a book on his lap: *Diamonds are Forever*. She had never seen him read a book before, and that one seemed inexplicably out of character, like a prop in a play.

'It's too early for me to sleep,' he explained. 'If you want, I can read in the other room.'

'Oh – no,' Holly sat down. She couldn't really relax in her pink chiffon, but she felt too embarrassed to undress right in front of Tyrconnel. Besides, she had hoped – half expected, really – that he would undress her himself, just like last night.

She stood again. 'Maybe I'll write a letter.'

In their sitting room was a leather-topped desk with a drawer full of stationery. Slowly she took a sheet out and wrote, 'Dear Mother and Daddy,' but then couldn't think what to say next. She wandered back to the bedroom.

'I think I *am* tired,' she announced at last. Tyrconnel, chuckling at something in his book, did not answer.

She took her white lace nightgown out of the drawer where the maids had put it and went into the bathroom to change. She brushed her teeth extra hard, and then reapplied her lipstick. The nightgown was Empire line, the top all lace, transparent. She admired the effect for a moment in the mirror: more innocent, she decided, than naughty. Then she walked back into the bedroom.

Tyrconnel looked up and smiled. At last. His eyes ran up and down her. 'You look lovely. I won't be a moment.'

He emerged from the bathroom and began to undress, folding his clothes neatly over the back of a chair. Holly was torn between wanting to watch him and thinking that perhaps men were shy about their bodies, like women. In the end, she crept under the sheets and closed her eyes.

She heard Tyrconnel flicking light switches off. The sheets on the bed were smooth, cool, as she had imagined them. She could see his shadow coming towards her. She turned swiftly and held out her arms to him.

'Wait.' His voice was low in his throat. He crawled above her, his knees knocking against hers. He took hold of her extended arms.

'Can you see?' she whispered.

'I don't need to.'

With a quick, rough movement he stripped the sheets and blankets down off the bed. 'Turn over,' he said.

'Aren't – aren't you going to kiss me?'

Tyrconnel was silent, but now he drew her closer for a moment and pressed his lips to hers: warm, clean. His tongue darted inside her mouth for a second, but then he moved just as firmly away, disentangling himself from her arms.

She arched her back towards him, but her body could not find his: could not feel the warm length of him pressed close to her, the sensation she craved.

'Now turn over,' he said again, his voice admonishing.

She was kneeling on the bed by now. Obediently she turned, and Tyrconnel's hands glided up underneath her gown, against her bare legs. He tugged the nightgown up over her head in one motion, as quickly as he had stripped the bed. 'Now get down,' he said in a low voice. He pushed against her back. 'Stay there. Just – just do as I tell you.'

She felt foolish, kneeling, and she was glad now, so glad that the lights were out. Behind her Tyrconnel caressed her buttocks, then fumbled against her; she wondered if what she felt touching her sometimes was not his hand but his male part, which she hadn't seen. She pushed against him slightly.

'Don't move.' Tyrconnel's voice was tense. His fingers were groping, quickly searching. She felt a finger slip inside her and she shouted out with surprise.

'Shh.' Tyrconnel leaned forward and, with a hand that felt damp and cold, closed her mouth. For a moment his fingers clenched against her lips and chin. 'Keep quiet.'

She felt cold now and she wanted to move. Her knees ached. She longed to turn, to feel Tyrconnel against the front of her – to kiss him again. But then she thought, *He must know what he's doing.* Maybe he was doing this some special way, for the first time, to make it easier.

And as she was biting her lips and thinking this, something butted against her, then forced its way inside that female passage whose contours she did not herself know well. It was big, bigger than his fingers, bigger than she had ever guessed it would be. It slid and withdrew, then forced itself in further. She wanted to cry out – with pain? with a kind of strange pleasure? She did not know, but made herself stay silent.

Then Tyrconnel withdrew. His wet fingers were working at a different opening.

'Why – ' she began.

'Shh.' She could hear his strangulated breathing. 'It's harder – you know – with a virgin, Holly. Be patient.'

You wanted a virgin, she wanted to say – but didn't. Tyrconnel's fingers worked at her again, in that strange place. Then, breathing more heavily, he seemed to climb up above her. He took hold of her hips; then his hands slid up and encircled the base of her throat.

'Don't shout,' he said, before she could speak. 'Don't say anything.'

He moved one hand, to take hold of himself, she could feel his fingers grazing her buttocks – and then pushed.

She thought she would be torn in two. She had never felt a pain like it, searing and never-ending. She disobeyed Tyrconnel and cried out.

His fingers clamped over her mouth. He pushed against her again and she thought the pain, which had dulled, could not get worse, but it did. Her teeth clenched around one of his fingers, and now he yelped out too.

'You little bitch.' He wrenched his hand free, and now he put both hands around her neck again, too tight, pulling her against him. Her back arched; he forced it to; sometimes she thought it would break. He was heavy on top of her; finally her legs gave way and he straddled her, his hands still tight around her throat, grunting and thrusting like an animal.

Then finally he too collapsed.

His fingers loosened, and he slid back from her. Dully Holly felt something wet streaking her back and legs. She did not move. She heard the light click on in the bathroom, and water run. Some time later, she did not know how long, Tyrconnel came back and threw the sheet up over her.

Still she lay, afraid to move, with the same frozen feeling as if she had woken from a nightmare: as long as she kept still, nothing bad, nothing worse could happen.

She did not see the blood until the morning.

VI

She knew the old wives' tale about blood on the sheets, but she did not think there should be so much.

It had hurt when she first sat up, and stabbed her for a second, when she stood, with such raw pain that she wanted to scream. But then the pain faded and she walked carefully to the bathroom. A hot bath soothed her a little. She still had not seen Tyrconnel, only heard his newspaper rustling next door, and she was glad.

She did not know how she could face him.

She walked back to the bed wrapped in a white hotel bathrobe; the softness of it made her feel cosy and cared-for, as she used to feel, back at home, on the days when she had to stay home sick from school, and the maids would bring her cups of lemon tea. She wished someone would do that for her now.

And then she saw the streaks on the clean white sheets, dried red-brown and horrid. Quickly she pulled the blankets up.

'Have a good sleep, darling?' Tyrconnel called.

How could he dare ask that? Had he slept just the same as ever, after –?

'Would you like some coffee?'

'No thanks.' She decided to get dressed. Dress, and then go for a long walk. Alone.

'They've brought up croissants and jam.'

She did not answer.

A few minutes later, wearing trousers and no makeup, she grabbed her handbag and announced that she was going out. She was through the door before she could hear his reply.

An hour later, sipping coffee on a square in Vevey, she felt a little better. The autumn sky was a brilliant blue. She was in Switzerland, on her honeymoon; and she was sure now that if she tried to talk to Tyrconnel, he would understand. Last night must have been a misunderstanding. An aberration. She would tell Tyrconnel that it had made her . . . unhappy. That he must try to be gentler.

I will work on my French, she thought, and wandered from street to street reminding herself of words for things she had once learnt in school – *marrons, confiserie, chien méchant*. She looked at clothes in the shop windows, and ate *raclette* at another café for lunch, and by the late afternoon felt ready to catch the bus back to the Bayern au Lac, and face her husband.

She found him smoking on the terrace and reading a typed report. She peered at the title. *Mineral Study for Potential Development.* . . .

'Have a good day?' he asked.

'Yes. I went to Vevey.'

'Well, that's good.'

She squinted at him for a moment in the sun. She wondered if he felt at all awkward. He didn't seem to.

She changed into her dark grey taffeta for dinner: the one her mother had said she wasn't old enough for, when they had bought it. Well, she felt old enough now. She didn't bother with jewellery.

Tyrconnel wore the same dinner jacket as the night before; once again everyone looked at them as they descended the stairs. Once again, dinner was accompanied by a great deal of silence.

'I've been looking at a couple of reports on Manangwe,' said Tyrconnel over the oysters. 'I thought we might fly down there next spring.'

'Really.' Holly could not bring herself to smile politely. 'To see your sister?'

'Yes. Would you like that?'

Tyrconnel looked a little worried. His brows tilted, giving his eyes the anxiousness to please she remembered from the early days of their courtship. She thought it was a hopeful sign.

'What's it like in that part of Africa?' she asked. 'Have you been there before?'

He hadn't; but fortified by that afternoon's reading, he had a great deal to tell her. By the third course some of her appetite had returned, though it still hurt to stay sitting for so long. She let him talk.

But now, she knew, the worst part was to come. They would go upstairs again. . . . She dawdled as long as she could over her coffee.

'Would you like to go for a walk?' said Tyrconnel.

They walked down the drive and across the road to the shore of the lake.

It really is beautiful, thought Holly. *I must remember this. I must appreciate this.* . . . After all, she must appreciate what she could.

Tyrconnel looped his arm through hers. She wanted to draw away, but managed not to.

'I must apologise,' he said, 'about last night. Perhaps we should have discussed it.'

She stayed silent.

'It can be – difficult at first.'

'I didn't know it would be *that* difficult.' Now Holly drew her arm away. If they were going to have to talk about it, she thought, then she really couldn't touch him at the same time.

'I know.' Tyrconnel reached out – then withdrew. He cleared his throat. 'Perhaps – we should have gone more slowly.'

'Perhaps.' She was walking ahead of him now. It helped to have only the calm lake in sight. She could talk more easily that way. 'I know you must think I'm awfully naive.'

'There's nothing wrong with innocence. Truly, Holly.'

'I may be innocent – ' Holly's voice was tight – 'but I am not completely ignorant. I know something about . . . I mean, we learnt in school – '

Tyrconnel chuckled. 'Ah, Holly. What one learns in school and what men and women really do are such different things.'

She bristled at the way he was laughing at her. When he came up behind her and put an arm around her, she had to fight the urge to slap him off.

He stroked her cheek, and she relaxed a little. 'I don't think you understand,' she said. 'It really did *hurt*.' She had to turn her head, because she felt on the verge of tears.

'I had forgotten. That was my fault.' He reached to wipe her tears away, then kissed her gently below her eyes, where they had fallen. 'But it's true lovemaking hurts sometimes, Holly, especially at first.'

Though the words were kind, his voice had grown brusquer, reminding her suddenly of last night, and she jerked away. 'It wasn't – normal, what you did,' she said. 'It wasn't natural.'

Tyrconnel laughed: the same warm, low chuckle as always, yet now it burnt in her ears. 'There are all sorts of ways of making love, Holly. And that is one of them.'

'Then I don't like it.'

'You'll learn.' He caressed her shoulder, but she turned towards the lake again and flicked him away.

'I can't. Not now,' she said. The waters of the lake rose, wind-buffeted, in angry orange crests, reflecting the sunset.

'We don't need to do anything now,' said Tyrconnel gently. 'Nor for some time, until you wish to, Holly. But let us try to enjoy the rest of our time here.'

Holly sighed, then allowed herself to lean back against his shoulder. Tyrconnel's long, sinewy arm encircled her, and she tried to let his closeness give her comfort. When she looked at the waters of the lake now, the sun had faded and they seemed less angry.

For the next few days she managed to suppress her own inner turmoil. Tyrconnel slept beside her in the wide bed, scarcely moving the whole night long, not disturbing her. He woke very early most mornings, five or six hours of sleep seeming to suffice him, his face still clean, his hair only slightly dishevelled – never the matted mess she was used to seeing in the mirror after her own nights of tossing and turning.

In the mornings he would read the English papers, and she would walk along the lakeside or go into Vevey. In the afternoons he would hire a car to take them to Lausanne or Montreux, or up into the mountains. They walked along the well-marked paths or ascended the heights in the funiculars. Everywhere they went, Holly noticed proudly, people looked at them, struck perhaps by their youth, their height or their clothing – she made sure to wear a new outfit every day – or simply by Tyrconnel's golden handsomeness.

One day towards the end of their stay, Tyrconnel announced that he was going into Geneva on business.

'What business?' Holly asked instantly, curious. She still did not know what occupied him every morning, or why he was constantly making phone calls from their room. Something to do with the *Courant*, perhaps. She could hear nothing on his end but noises of agreement.

'Nothing to bother your head about,' was all he said now. 'Very tedious. I have to go and see a banker.'

'Let me come with you.'

'You won't have anything to do. I'll be in meetings for hours.'

'I want to see Geneva.'

Tyrconnel shrugged in resignation, then flashed her a faint smile. Her heart melted: not instantly, overwhelmingly, as it used to, but just a little. He was surely the most beautiful man she had ever seen, especially when his cheeks creased in that smile, the curve of his mouth accentuating the cleft in his chin, his hair falling over one eye, as if by accident.

She was not sure yet, but she thought she had almost summoned the courage to try again.

And so when they got to Geneva and she left Tyrconnel at his bank – an austere stone building marked only by a brass plate at the door reading *Banque Sanson* – she drifted almost automatically towards a department store, where on the top floor she found the lingerie.

'*Vous cherchez, mademoiselle?*'

She had never bought lingerie alone before. There were black lace underthings below the glass counter: silk, and expensive-looking, with no price labels. 'Those,' she said, pointing, meeting the eye of the matron guarding them.

The assistant, unruffled, asked Holly her size.

Holly walked out of the store overwhelmed by her own daring. She had spent nearly all of the money Ty had given her on a transparent lace bra and lace panties, and, naughtiest of all, a suspender belt. Her mother had always said no real lady ever went without a girdle.

She still had several hours to kill, wandering around the old town. When Tyrconnel emerged, looking pleased, from the Banque Sanson, he glanced at her shopping bag. 'What have you got there?'

She rolled it up in her hand to hide the contents. 'Nothing much.'

They ate lunch, then took the train back along the lake shore. *Black lace*, Holly thought to herself, *black lace*. The train's engines seemed to echo the words in her head as they accelerated. Like her anticipation.

She dressed while Tyrconnel was still down on the terrace having his evening drink. Black suited her pale skin and red hair rather well, she thought. Her breasts had never been big, only a tolerable medium size, but the expanse of black lace lifting them up made them look more spectacular.

She wore a dark blue dress to match, since she had nothing black. Its soft crêpe brushed against the bare tops of her legs: it was a delicious sensation. Soon Ty would be touching there, too. And then. . . .

A moment of fear paralysed her, then passed.

'You seem far away,' Tyrconnel remarked as he sank the point of his knife into his steak. Red juice pooled on his plate.

'No,' said Holly, 'not really. I was just thinking about –

84

tonight.' She looked at him, hard, for a moment. She could not bring herself to say anything more.

Tyrconnel's eyebrows lifted slightly, then he nodded. 'The châteaubriand's superb.'

It never ceased to surprise Holly how her husband could combine extreme outward fastidiousness with a gargantuan appetite. He would arrange his food slowly on his plate, and carve it precisely; then, in what seemed a matter of seconds, he would dispatch it all, dabbing his mouth clean with his napkin. She liked to watch him eat, to see his long smooth hands, with their moon-tipped fingernails, in motion.

Soon, she thought, and dug into her own steak with what she knew must seem messy abandon. She did not really like it that red, but Ty had ordered it for them both. Anyway – she shifted on her chair and felt her skirts drift against bare skin – it didn't matter.

They went for a walk; then Tyrconnel hung up his clothes and read in his dressing-gown, as usual. Holly stayed dressed and pretended to read a fashion magazine she had bought in Geneva.

He came out of the bathroom while she was still struggling with the zip at the back of her dress.

'Let me help you,' he said, coming closer. He undid the zip and eased the dress down off her shoulders.

Holly turned suddenly, wanting him to see her new underthings but too embarrassed to show him properly. She spun and smiled, flushing red, and covered her chest with her arms.

'New?' said Tyrconnel.

'Do you like them?'

'Does this mean what I think it means?'

She thought there was a smile in his voice, but could not see his face. He had moved across the room to bolt the door. As he came back to the bed, he shrugged off his robe. *That* hair, she noticed, was the same deep gold as the hair on his head. The member nestled in it looked smaller than she had expected.

He flicked off the light before she could see any more, and she was aware of a tremor of disappointment. He didn't seem to care to see her, despite all that black lace. He crawled into bed beside her, his arm brushing hers. 'Turn over.'

'No. I don't want to.'

He stroked her arm gently; spoke patiently. 'Then what *do* you want?'

'I don't know. Whatever you want – but not that way.' She waited. Tyrconnel's fingers combed through her hair, then slid down her back.

'All right. Then touch me,' he said.

She reached out tentatively, and he guided her hand. He felt soft. A few minutes later, his fingers took the place of hers.

'Wait,' he said. Then he climbed above her: entered her.

This felt better than before. Feeling brave in the dark, she arched her hips slightly against him. Her fingers wandered up, almost of their own accord, to skim the contours of his chest, with their fine golden hair.

He took hold of her wrists and removed her hands. A few seconds later he removed himself.

'Was that better?' he asked.

'Yes,' Holly answered in a whisper; but she would have liked it to go on longer. She did not think anything had come out of him. There was no stickiness between her legs, as there had been before. 'Was that – ' she began. 'Was that all? Did you finish?'

Tyrconnel grunted what sounded like a yes into his pillow.

'Are you sure?' she whispered.

'I'm tired, Holly,' he said. 'If you need to talk, can we do it in the morning?'

He knew perfectly well that she wouldn't want to, Holly thought. The next morning she folded away her new lingerie in a drawer.

The day after that they took the train to Paris. Tyrconnel had booked them a room at the Crillon: 'the best hotel in

Paris,' Holly's mother had informed her, nodding approvingly at his plans. From their windows Holly could see the gardens of the Louvre, and all around them were celebrated avenues with their long vistas of buildings, white, grand and ineffably French; the streets here even *smelt* different to those of London or Switzerland. Another of her dreams was coming true: she was seeing Paris.

Yet a longing overtook her to talk to Ty: to try to iron their troubles out. For surely all was not right. This was their honeymoon, and they scarcely even touched each other. Or rather, he never touched her. During their walks, she often gave in to the urge to take his arm or insinuate her hand into his. He never seemed to mind – but he never kissed her, either, the way he had before they were married. Or only if she asked him to.

They went out to a restaurant called the Méditerranée, where the walls were hung with Picassos. Tyrconnel was in good spirits. He ordered *langoustines* and kept up a high flow of talk amidst the other noisy customers.

'Perhaps I was wrong,' he said, 'not to bring you here for longer. Next year, when this Manangwe business is settled, we'll come back.'

'So you don't mind a little dirt?' Holly teased him.

He smiled. 'I exaggerated about France. Think I'll order some more of these,' he said, polishing off the last of her *langoustines*.

But it was all small talk, thought Holly, frustrated. Sometimes she wondered if her husband knew any other kind of talk. He certainly was not one to dwell on his feelings.

'What do you mean?' he said, when she probed him in that direction as they walked out into the night, 'the city makes you sad?'

Around them all the lights of windows and cars shone, flicked on and off, diminished. 'So much life,' said Holly, 'going on all at once. And so many people, and we can't even know who a few hundred of them are. Doesn't it make you think of all the other lives – the opportunities you might be missing?'

'No,' said Tyrconnel.

'It doesn't make you feel anything?'

'Like a good night's sleep.' Tyrconnel yawned. 'Shall we get a cab?'

So they had an early night. Holly longed to be out in the city doing ... she did not know what, but *out*, seeing the life around her. Of course, Tyrconnel had seen Paris before. That would explain it. He was willing enough next morning, once he had read his papers, to walk with her down the rue de Rivoli and everywhere else she wanted to go. He even took her out to Montmartre that night, where they sat in a café until, as he put it, she had seen enough of that ' "life" you were talking about.'

They went back to their hotel at midnight, but Holly could not sleep.

'Ty.' She spoke into the darkness. 'Do you think everything's – all right between us?'

'Of course, darling.' His back was to her.

She stroked his shoulder; then, tentatively, moved forward to kiss his neck.

'What?' he said.

'Nothing.'

'Do you want something?' he said. He turned on to his back.

'Do you really think everything is all right?'

'If you want something – ' his voice had hardened – 'I wish you'd come out with it, Holly. It'd save us both a lot of trouble.'

'All right, Ty. I want to try again.'

Silence fell.

'God almighty.' Tyrconnel's voice was low.

Holly's, by contrast, was wound up high by nerves. 'Well, is it so much to ask? We've been married nearly two weeks. I don't know what I'm doing, if I'm doing it right or wrong – '

'If you love me you'll have to stop making demands.'

88

'I'm not making demands. I only want to know –'

Tyrconnel sat up, and his shape seemed to Holly to loom in the half-dark, threatening. 'For Christ's sake! I took you out all day, I held your hand, I did exactly what you wanted. And now this.'

'I'm not making a demand, Ty, really.'

'Sometimes I think that's all I have in my life! Demanding women.'

Holly let the silence take hold this time. 'I don't know what you mean.'

Tyrconnel sighed and fell back against the headboard. 'Some women don't *like* sex, Holly. Has it ever occurred to you that you might be one of them?'

'I don't know.'

'Because if we try everything and you still don't like it, that's probably the answer. If it is, I'll understand. I'm a busy man, I don't know if you've realised – at least when I'm at home. So for my part I shan't expect to be overly – demanding.'

Holly let out a long slow breath; she did not know whether it was out of disappointment, or relief that Tyrconnel's anger seemed to have been defused.

'Have we really,' she said, 'tried everything?'

That way at least was painless, she reflected later. And if it seemed odd and unnatural at first, she sensed that it might grow on her with practice, might become almost pleasant. Since Tyrconnel kept so scrupulously clean, the only taste was a mild saltiness. He had instructed her in what to do: to use her tongue, to keep her teeth well away. He closed his eyes tightly the whole time, occasionally yelling out, 'Ouch! Damn it, Holly.'

After what had seemed an eternity but was perhaps only ten minutes he had made her stop. 'Was that all right?' she asked uncertainly.

'Fine,' he had said, but then he began to manipulate himself. She had watched, intrigued, until the white liquid came out: slowly – it surprised her. Like lava.

He went away to run a bath then, and she pretended to sleep. Only when he was back in bed, and sleeping, did she rise and go to the window. Distant lights flicked and danced in the deep blue night, tantalising her. She wondered if there were other women out there, at other windows, who loved and yet could not wrest happiness from loving. She wondered, in turn, if there were others who lived with their men – husbands, lovers – normally, peacefully oblivious that for anyone else it could be different.

She remembered how she had once thought this was a city of love: a place where one day, perhaps, she would career down long avenues at night in an open-topped car: like Cyd Charisse with Gene Kelly, Audrey Hepburn with Cary Grant. . . .

And yet if she told Tyrconnel these things, he would not understand. If she told him he was her perfect hero, handsomer than Cary Grant, a better dancer than Gene Kelly, he would laugh; her childish fantasies held no interest for him.

Silently she drew back the curtains until the light from the Place de la Concorde fell along his profile and edged his chest, tinting him silvery bronze, like a god of old. How she had dreamed about him: the passion with which he would take her. The patience with which he would slowly initiate her, not minding her shyness, covering her with kisses and gentle stroking. The feel of his arms around her, his body covering hers: she had been sure they would lie together, late into the mornings, entangled.

But in reality she could not touch him without his asking her why. She could not even gaze at his beauty in peace, so intermingled had his fine features, his opaque returning gaze, become, in her mind, with desire and disgust and fear. Only now, with his eyes closed, unconscious, could she admire him.

She knelt by the bed as he turned instinctively from the light, and traced the curved, smooth outline of his chest and shoulder with one hand, just above the tiny hairs, where she thought he could not feel her. He was so leanly, so perfectly sculpted. But now he turned, and muttered, 'What?'

His eyes were closed, so he was still asleep, but, afraid, she backed away.

They drew into Chester Square in the rain. Imogen, Jamie and Daphne were all waiting in the sitting room.

'Welcome back, Holly,' cried Daphne, who by now was visibly rounded. 'How I envy you. You look the picture of –'

'The picture of health,' Jamie finished for her, giving Holly a brisk kiss.

Holly turned to her mother-in-law, but Imogen was looking sombre as she addressed Tyrconnel. 'Darling,' she said, 'I felt I ought to warn you before any of the press got hold of you. There's been a terrible fire.'

VII

When they were all settled in the front parlour, with its sober green walls and ticking clock, Imogen and Jamie took it in turns to explain.

The fire had happened late last night, in Derry Street, just east of the City of London: a few miles away from Chester Square and yet sufficiently remote, in its own way, to cause Daphne to breathe out in relief, 'At least it's nothing to do with us, Holly.'

'But the people there are your . . . tenants?' said Holly. She did not yet understand British land law or the full extent of the Carrs' possessions.

'Yes.' Imogen sighed. 'We shall have to do something for them. I feel so wretched about it all, Ty.' Her forehead wrinkled.

He patted her hand. 'An electrical fault, Mother. These

things happen. You know the tenants aren't really our responsibility. I'm sure the council – '

'Mother has a point,' put in Jamie. 'This could be awkward for me in the House. You large landowners – ' He looked at Tyrconnel – 'aren't very popular these days.'

'Jamie!' Imogen reprimanded him. 'This land belongs to *all* of us.'

Jamie only raised his eyebrows.

Tyrconnel, Jamie and her mother now became engrossed in a discussion of what should be done. While Daphne quietly dozed off in her chair, Holly listened. It reminded her of the time a hundred men at her father's factory had threatened to strike over unsafe machinery. Negotiating, her father had seemed as concerned for their safety as they were; just as Imogen, especially, seemed concerned about Derry Street now.

'Dinner's at eight,' Imogen told her, breaking off. 'You and Daphne may want to change.'

Once Holly was gone, Tyrconnel turned to his mother. 'What on earth are you playing at? Talking about giving the tenants money. . . .'

Imogen laughed. 'For heavens' sake! You fell for it.'

'What am I supposed to think?'

Jamie's green eyes flickered from Tyrconnel to his mother, whose inside knowledge he had been, for once, the first to share. 'You know,' he added with mock sententiousness, 'you really should have seen to that wiring.'

'I gather,' said Tyrconnel slowly, 'someone did.'

'Top marks, big brother.' Jamie grinned.

'While you two were planning this minor conflagration, did neither of you think of informing me?'

'Your brother wasn't part of it,' said Imogen calmly. 'I did it. While you were out of the country. To keep you in the clear – '

Imogen's voice halted suddenly at the sound of a knock on the door.

'Sorry,' said Holly, reappearing. 'I can't find any towels.'

She shrank back at the way the others all stared at her – as if she were an unwelcome stranger.

The house on Chester Square – 'John's little cottage', Imogen liked to call it, for her husband had acquired it in his bachelor days – was narrow-fronted but deceptively large. Five-storeyed and white, with a columned portico and an iron railing enclosing a rarely used small terrace just above, the house extended a long way to the rear, allowing for two sets of rooms on each floor. Tyrconnel's and Holly's were on the first floor; his looking out on to the small park at the centre of the square, hers on to Eaton Mews at the back.

Holly liked the quiet of the square, a green oasis in the heart of Belgravia where cars scarcely ever ventured, probably because it was on the way to nowhere else. And she could see why Imogen, though she grumbled about being cramped for space, had never bothered to move. Tyrconnel, for his part, probably didn't mind where he lived, because he was never at home.

He had warned her that he worked long hours. But she had not expected that every morning he would be gone before she woke for breakfast, nor that half the nights of the week he would not even come home for dinner. Imogen was there, of course. Contrary to her predictions, she was not spending most of her time at Stadhampton. 'I'm always *meaning* to go,' she told Holly in the middle of that first week at Chester Square, 'but how things catch up with me! I've had invitations I simply can't refuse – how does one say no to Lady Bullenden? And of course, with this terrible business on Derry Street, I like to be near to help Ty if there's any way I possibly can.'

'Is there anything I can do?' Holly asked, not that she really thought there was. 'Have all the people living there found other places to stay?'

'Oh, yes. These people will have families, you know, in the neighbourhood. And Ty has positively had to *besiege* the council, but at last they're admitting it's their job to find new houses. . . . So, really, Holly, there's nothing you can do.'

That, Holly thought, was her problem. Nothing to do. She had been unprepared for the emptiness of life after marriage; for the unexpected privacy of her sunny yellow rooms. She supposed that she had always imagined a humbler sort of marriage, entailing a few duties: cooking, light housekeeping, a bare house to decorate, a husband to look after. But Tyrconnel – with the help of Reeve, who in addition to being butler acted as his valet – looked after himself perfectly well. And with a finished house full of antiques and attended to by a cook, maid and chauffeur, everything else was taken care of, too.

So she read and went for walks and tried to learn her way around central London; she met Imogen's dinner guests, and soon, Imogen said, she would take Holly shopping and to some of her charity committee meetings. Holly knew she could not blame Imogen if she was at a loose end.

Or Tyrconnel, she told herself; she tried to believe it. They had not slept in the same bed since their honeymoon, though he had come to visit her once: had requested the service he had last taught her to perform – had called her 'sweet Holly' once it was done, and tousled her hair and seemed satisfied.

A baby, she knew, would keep her occupied. Though she was still young, she felt almost ready for one. Daphne, after all, was only three years older, and already having her second. Babies followed naturally from marriage – or so she had always thought. In fact she had been seventeen before she learnt that you could go to the doctor and get means to stop them.

But however limited her knowledge of biology – and Ty, for one, was always laughing at her ignorance – she knew for a certainty that what he preferred to do, or have her do to him, was never going to give her a baby.

After dinner Imogen leafed through the papers. She never

actually settled down for long enough to read them, and in fact got most of her news from the television. 'Oh, look,' she would say to Holly occasionally, pointing at the sketch of a new outfit at Harrods or Woollands. Sometimes she would fold the paper down and hand it to Tyrconnel or to Jamie, if he were there, with a significant nod.

Ten days after the fire in Derry Street, she opened *The Times* and gave a start. Holly was the only one in the room.

'Would you read this to me?' said Imogen.

Holly supposed her mother-in-law might need reading glasses, and be too vain to admit it. ' "Numbers 110 to 113, Derry Street, before the fire",' she read from the caption. Then the headline: ' "Lord Carr dismisses arson query".'

'Oh, my God. It's Ty. Why didn't he say?'

'Do you want me to go on?' Already Holly was skimming the rest of the story. *Arson query.* It couldn't be. If it were, who would have done such a thing? Someone who lived there? Someone who hated the Carrs?

'Please,' said Imogen, in a shaking voice, 'do read on.'

' "Routine questioning as to the cause of the fire that gutted ten houses in part of the Carr Estate the night of 27 September has failed to allay suspicions of arson. Chief Inspector Donald Tooley of Scotland Yard – " '

'Scotland Yard?' Imogen whispered.

'I'm sure it's nothing,' said Holly. 'They must investigate all kinds of things.' She read on: ' "Lord Carr, chairman of the Courant Newspaper Group, had no comment on the investigation. Mrs Aurora Threadneedle, who had lived in Derry Street for thirty years – " '

'Is that all there is?' said Imogen. 'About Ty?'

'Yes. It's very short. If you want to look. . . . Here.' Holly handed the paper back to Imogen, who disregarded it. Her eyes were black and tearful; she played with her rings.

'I'm sure it'll be all right.' Holly leaned forward anxiously. 'I'm sure Ty can explain it all when he comes home.'

'When he comes home,' said Imogen, her eyes drier, 'he'll already be hours too late! *Damn!*' She twisted her rings again. 'I knew something like this would happen. They're hounding us, Holly. No one who owns land these days is safe. They won't stop until they've – kicked us all out.'

'What do you mean?'

Imogen sniffed. 'The government. The papers, Scotland Yard – everyone's against us. Never mind that we've scarcely made a penny from Derry Street in thirty years!' She paused. 'It makes me feel – dirty, even to be associated with such lies.'

'But, Imogen.' Holly looked at her earnestly. 'You shouldn't worry. It'll be all right. You haven't done anything.'

Imogen smiled faintly, partially reassured.

Tyrconnel said it was all a storm in a teacup. 'In a week it'll all be over,' he told Holly, patting her shoulder.

'It seems such a shame,' said Holly, 'that just because you own those houses, people accuse the family – the estate – of doing something wrong.'

Tyrconnel spoke grimly. 'There're a lot of Communists out there, just waiting for us to take one wrong step.'

'May I remind you,' said Jamie jovially – he had come over after his mother's distressed phone call – 'you are talking about quite a few members of Her Majesty's loyal opposition. Our comrades in the Labour party.'

'That's exactly who I mean.' Tyrconnel glowered. 'Loyal to the Kremlin, if you ask me.'

Jamie chortled. 'Don't be ridiculous.'

'Really.' Imogen shot Jamie an angry look. 'I don't think this is any time to bicker.'

'Sorry, Mother,' Jamie muttered.

'Now, Ty,' said Imogen. 'I ask you again. Is there anything I can do?'

'Oh, Monty.' A laugh bubbled up from Imogen's throat.

'You are the same as ever. All I can say is how *glad* I am you gave up silly old Scotland and came back to the Bar.'

Lord Charles Moncrieffe gave a cautious smile. 'I didn't know I'd been missed.'

A waiter approached with their menus. Imogen waved a hand helplessly at the long selection of dishes. 'Oh, you order for me, Monty. You'll know the food here so much better than I.'

'Hm. Do you eat oysters?'

Imogen's eyes glittered. 'Indeed I do.'

Three-quarters of an hour later, when the venison had come and Moncrieffe was munching contentedly, Imogen put down her fork. 'Monty,' she said, 'I must confide in you. I am so worried.'

'Oh?' said Moncrieffe warily. 'What about?'

'I feel so useless when this kind of thing happens . . . Ty tells me not to worry, but I simply can't stop myself. I know there's nothing to these charges! But they *stick* so, even if there's nothing proved. The suspicion always lingers. . . .'

'What's this? Do you mean – the arson business? In the papers?'

Imogen nodded heavily, and looked up through wide dark eyes.

'I shouldn't think it would come to anything.'

'Oh, but that's just what I don't know, Monty. The man in charge, you know, the director of what do you call it. . . .'

'Director of Public Prosecutions?' said Moncrieffe kindly.

'Yes! You know, the one who decides whether to bring a case. . . .'

Moncrieffe longed to reach out to pat Imogen's hand in reassurance, but a lifetime of reserve held him back. 'Don't worry. The DPP's a reasonable man. I went to school with him.'

'Did you?' Imogen brightened.

Thank goodness, she thought, for *Who's Who*.

97

'I'll talk to him,' said Moncrieffe finally: decisively. 'Now what'll you have for pudding?'

Two days later Imogen received a phone call which made her shout with joy. Holly overheard her in the hallway.

'Oh, Monty,' she heard Imogen cry. 'I *am* so relieved. It was such a burden, and I'm so glad it's all over. Thank you.'

Holly heard a blur of talk at the other end: then Imogen answering. 'Yes, I am glad, too. Oh, yes. For old times' sake.'

Holly closed her bedroom door quickly as Imogen came trotting up the stairs.

'Good news, darling!' she shouted. 'They've dropped the investigation.'

Holly heard the news with relief, and thought no more about it. Her mother-in-law was on the phone several times more that day, from her room up on the second floor, and only because the more comfortable bathroom was upstairs, adjacent, did Holly happen to overhear her.

Imogen's secretary, Miss Squires, had come that afternoon. A small, unimposing woman with grey hair in a bun, she came and went three afternoons a week, barely making her presence felt. She kept track of Imogen's invitations and bills and typed her correspondence.

Just before Miss Squires left, Holly overheard Imogen telling her, 'There's a number in my book under "Mechanics", Dolly, the first one. Would you ring it for me?'

Imogen really made full use of her servants, thought Holly laughingly as she climbed the stairs: she had them do the simplest tasks for her!

Miss Squires departed, leaving Imogen on the phone. Holly paused over the hot water tap.

'Dex?'

Holly heard Imogen's voice through the half-closed door: a brisk voice unlike the one she used for talking to her friends.

'You're all clear.'

98

There was a pause. 'No,' said Imogen then. 'Nothing else. Not now. It's not safe.'

Another pause. 'What?' Imogen gave a brittle laugh. 'Well, you know my policy, Dex. We agreed on that.' Her voice grew more heated. 'Well, perhaps Errol would have done things differently. But that was a long time ago. And now you're dealing with me.' Her voice was pleasant again, though still brisk. 'Yes, Dex. I'll remember that. Goodbye.'

Holly shut the bathroom door then and ran the hot water loudly. She did not want Imogen to think she had been eavesdropping. *Mechanics?* she thought. And hadn't Imogen mentioned Errol? That was the name of her first husband.

It was, by any reckoning, an odd conversation. But all Holly could deduce from it was that her mother-in-law kept in touch with some unlikely-sounding people.

'To us.' Imogen lifted her tumbler of whisky. Her eyes met Tyrconnel's, then Jamie's.

It was midnight, and they kept their voices low. The servants and Holly were in bed. The library, in any case, was a secluded room at the back of the house, its walls lined with leatherbound classics, Churchill's war histories and bestsellers from the 1930s that no one ever read. Cigarette burns marred the green leather tabletop where Imogen now laid down her glass.

'What about planning permission?' said Jamie. 'If you want, I can put in a word.'

Imogen looked to Tyrconnel for an answer.

'Let's see how it works through the normal channels,' he said. 'There's been no trouble with office-building lately. Broakes and the Sutton Estate have been speeding all their plans through. I thought we'd aim for a full-scale development involving all our streets in the area.'

'After all, Derry Street's a ruin,' put in Imogen. 'They can hardly say we should put back those dingy terraces just as they were.'

'So,' said Tyrconnel, 'within two years we should have four, maybe five twenty-storey blocks of corporate tenants. Derry Street pays for its keep at last. Well done, Mother.'

Jamie said nothing. He finished his cognac and looked edgily out the window.

'I'm glad,' said Imogen, smiling, eyes half-closed, 'I kept in touch with some of Errol's friends. Who would have thought the milieu of such a little crook could have proved so useful?'

Jamie gave a fleeting smile. 'Don't suppose you know any assassins, Mother.'

'What do you mean, Jamie?'

'To set to work on my political enemies.'

'Really, Jamie. Will you never grow up?' Smiling thinly, Imogen paused and looked at each of her sons again. 'How long do you think we should wait, before the other?'

'Not now,' said Tyrconnel, alarmed.

'Do you mean the wing?' said Jamie, his green eyes darting from his mother to his brother. 'Where Grandfather kept his laboratory?'

'Such an eyesore,' said Imogen, with a brief nod. 'And – insured.'

'Mother.' Tyrconnel moved back restlessly. 'Do you have any idea what I've been through this week? They'll come down on us like a ton of bricks if you – '

'Cash in hand,' interrupted Imogen, in a harsh voice. 'Have you any idea of the bills?'

'Just a minute, Mother – '

'Your fine fancies for Derry Street are one thing, Ty. But where's the money going to come from?'

Tyrconnel paced back edgily, rubbing the back of his neck. 'Just give me another few months.'

'You said the *Courant* would turn a profit last year. That was when I sold the Van Dyck at Christie's. Do you remember?'

Jamie watched his mother anxiously. 'It was an ugly old picture anyway, Mother.'

'And then we sold the Canaletto,' Imogen went on. 'And

do you remember the two Constables? They went on death duties. Great bare patches on our walls. When are you going to turn a profit?'

Tyrconnel slammed his glass down on the table. 'I don't need to listen to this. I work like a slave. D'you know – ' He laughed maniacally. 'That's what I told Holly once. I'm this family's indentured servant. I could walk out – '

'You'd have nothing left,' said Imogen coolly, 'without us.'

'Hold on,' said Jamie. 'Both of you. This is absurd.'

'Do you know,' said Imogen, turning to him now, 'we haven't paid the rates on this house for nearly a year? Do you know that I let three maids go last summer and we may have to get rid of Reeve and even Eduardo if things don't get better fast?'

'They will,' said Tyrconnel through clenched teeth. 'It's all a matter of cash flow.'

Imogen ignored him, still talking to Jamie. 'What about the cheque Holly's father gave him at the wedding? He won't use it to help keep us going because, he says, he needs it for his "plans". Which didn't preclude his spending a fortune on that honeymoon – '

'What else could I do?' Tyrconnel's voice was a near whisper, but contained all the suppressed power of a shout. 'Do you want my wife to think we're so near the bone we *need* her father's money?'

A silence ensued. 'Come on, Mother,' said Jamie. 'You know he's right. Holly's sweet. And she's so young. We can't let her know things are desperate.'

Imogen sniffed.

'By the way,' said Jamie, 'I forgot to tell you, Mother, I've just been promoted.'

'Oh, yes?' said Imogen tersely.

'To the whips' office.' Jamie grinned. 'Macmillan called me in the other day. Said he wanted me to be one of his heavies. Whip the Members into line.'

Imogen chuckled, perhaps causing her sons to reflect

briefly, gratefully, that at least they had a mother whom no *double entendre* could offend.

'Really!' She shook her head, in better humour. Then she shifted her gaze to Tyrconnel. 'It seems your brother will soon be in a position to help the family. How about you?'

Tyrconnel stared at her through narrowed eyes. 'I do my part, Mother. But you should know by now, I do it my way. And I don't want you bringing my wife into any of this. Do you understand?'

'Ty,' said Imogen, with all semblance of innocence. 'Of course I do. *I* think I'm taking good care of Holly, if I say so myself.'

VIII

'Don't worry,' said Imogen, patting Holly on the shoulder. 'I've always trusted André.'

The Dover Street salon reeked heavily of hairspray and a mixture of cloyingly sweet perfumes. Behind Holly, a row of women and girls sat reading *Vogue* and *Queen*, their heads cocooned by driers.

'After this,' said Imogen, 'we shall go to Harvey Nichols and have a look at that pink organdie I thought would suit you.'

'Oh, good.' Holly smiled. There was a big dance tonight at Lady Bullenden's: her twin daughters' coming-out, Christmas and the New Year combined. As Imogen said, this was the busiest season.

So when André approached, with his little squinting eyes, porcupine nose and endless, ingratiating patter, she bent this way and that as instructed. She nodded when he said, in his exaggerated French accent, 'Thees hair, we will straighten it on the beeg rollers, no?' He cut her fringe too short so that it fell in an unflatteringly straight line across her forehead, but still she didn't dare object. Perhaps the end result would be worth it. Another party tonight, filled with condescending ladies and nonchalant English débutantes. She wanted her looks, at least, to live up to her surroundings. For she rarely felt that her social skills did.

She wished that Tyrconnel would come along sometimes. Without him, she felt like an awkward single girl again, almost as if she weren't married at all.

'Nonsense,' Imogen had told her firmly. 'You're not the least bit awkward, Holly, just tall. All the fashion models are tall. Why, I expect most of the girls you meet envy you for it.'

But there was more to it than that. More that Holly couldn't explain, when Imogen meant so well and tried so hard to give her confidence. 'Just be *yourself*,' Imogen would urge her. 'So many girls try too hard to be witty. They've no idea what a jaded air it gives them.'

Imogen always made a point of mentioning, when she introduced Holly, that her daughter-in-law was American. 'It gives them something to start with,' she explained. But Holly wondered if it was always the bonus Imogen seemed to think. She had met with several suspicious stares: one, from an elderly marchioness, had lasted so long she had tried to joke to break the silence: 'I'm not a spy, really!'

The marchioness had only looked at her, mystified, and said, 'No, dear, I shouldn't have thought so.'

Other people had mentioned 'Suez', which she gathered was supposed to make her feel guilty. Once, Imogen had introduced her to a colleague of Jamie's from the Commons, adding significantly, 'Holly's father's very fond of sailing. He has a house in the Florida Keys.'

When, inevitably, Imogen drifted off, Holly, taking this as some sort of hint, had asked the man, 'Do you sail?'

'No,' he said, poker-faced.

'My father does,' Holly babbled, 'every time he can take a vacation. He keeps a couple of catamarans, and he's just bought a big new boat. . . . Have you been to the Keys?' she tried again.

'No. Never,' said the MP's wife.

Holly had managed a conversation with the couple but somehow they never really warmed up; and when a familiar figure, Lord Farnham, joined them and the couple disappeared, she told him about the confusion.

'Oh, dear,' said Lord Farnham.

'What do you mean? Why?'

'Why, their son died in a boating accident. In the Florida Keys precisely, if I recollect.'

Holly had felt stricken. How awful, she thought. The whole situation embarrassed her so much that she wanted to wipe it out of her mind. So she never asked Imogen whether she had confused the MP and his wife with other people.

'Thees way to the drier, Lady Carr,' André was saying now, and she followed him, trying to shake off the memory of that hideous encounter. Tonight was another party, another chance; she would wear the pink organdie dress. It had been Imogen who noticed that Harvey Nichols ad; Holly had to give her credit. Imogen had taught her, in the last few months, a very great deal about style. 'Always underdress' was one of her rules; another was that once you thought you were ready, you must take one piece of jewellery *off*.

Holly sighed. If only there were rules – such easy rules – for making small talk. . . .

Lady Bullenden's front windows looked out on Grosvenor Square. All around the vast salon, which had been cleared for dancing, clusters of débutantes teetered on their heels and giggled as they drank too much champagne; their escorts gathered nearby, evidently conscious of their duty but not enough so to intermingle. A Christmas tree hung with real candles filled one corner of the room.

'Holly!' cried Charlotte Bullenden.

'How seasonal,' chimed in her sister Charmian. 'Are you called that all year round?' She let out a high, meaningless giggle.

Before she had time to think up an answer Holly felt herself being passed down the receiving line to Lady Bullenden herself, formidable in blue damask.

'So glad you could come, Holly,' she boomed. 'Imogen! I was afraid you'd be up in the country.'

Even Imogen's answering voice, normally distinct, was drowned out by the elder countess's. 'Lady Bullenden,' she had confided to Holly that afternoon, 'could command five battalions, but I don't much like her trying to command *me*.'

Imogen was asserting her autonomy, Holly noticed now, by giving Lord Bullenden a protracted kiss on the cheek in greeting. Since she had already met the earl, she wandered on ahead into the room. The cut of her pink organdie dress, a copy of Dior, made her anxious; it followed the new 'arc' line, the waist barely below her bosom, skirt swelling out below. She wondered if people would think she was pregnant.

She recognised one girl in a group of debs, a friend of Daphne's who had been visiting at Stadhampton the last time she and Tyrconnel spent a weekend there.

'Hello, Emma.' Holly's hand, in its elbow-length white glove, spanned an awkward wave.

'Oh, hello.' The other girl gave her a brief smile, then turned to the others, explaining, 'This is Holly Carr. She just married Tyrconnel.' Her eyes widened into a significant look: Holly had seen it before, on the faces of girls about her age. *The lucky thing*, the look said, or perhaps, *How did she manage it?* 'Holly,' Emma introduced her, 'this is Mona, Catherine, Felicity, Annie. We were all at school with Daph.'

'At St Mary's?' said Holly. But the last girl introduced had interrupted her.

'You can't really say *I* was, Em. I got the boot.'

'Oh, yes.' Emma smirked. 'Annie was expelled. For, um – '

The other girls broke into giggles. One of them glanced

over as a group of men walked past. '*Look* who's here,' she said.

'*Is* he?' said Emma. 'The nerve.'

'He's not as bad as his brother,' giggled the girl who looked slightly cross-eyed: Felicity, Holly thought she was.

'Bonkers,' spluttered Annie. 'D'you remember?'

Holly scanned the line of windows in vain for the source of all this excitement, but she saw only a line of young men of varying degrees of chubbiness and baldness. 'Who are you talking about?' she asked Emma, but the girls' conversation had already moved on.

'Drambuie,' Felicity was saying.

'Yes! On a Saturday night . . . .'

It was like a foreign language. Holly wondered if she had once been like that with her schoolfriends at Spence: chummy, sharing in-jokes and secrets. She supposed she had. The other girls didn't seem in any rush to include her; eventually she turned away, in search of Imogen.

The party was full of strangers. There were no more familiar faces, like Emma's – not even Lord Farnham, who often turned up at these events, like a kindly uncle, to save her when she most needed it. She decided to explore the other rooms.

In the dining room, the servants were putting the final touches to the buffet, whose centrepiece was a huge pastry in the shape of the Bullenden coat of arms. The next room was a library, and nearly dark. Holly was turning away from it when she heard a voice call out, 'You can come in if you like. Don't mind me.'

The voice sounded female, and English, though some-how not so English, in that clipped, half-mumbling way, as the voices of Daphne and her friends.

Holly turned, and as she did, someone switched on a lamp: a girl, sitting eating a plate of hors-d'oeuvres from the buffet. The girl patted the space on the window-seat beside her. 'Come in. I'm feeling glum and antisocial, but you might as well join me.'

Holly didn't think the other girl sounded glum. She

looked about Holly's own age, but was, Holly noticed now, dressed very strangely for a party. A slouchy black sweater as big as a man's, decorated with sequins, hid her shape. She wore her straight, dark blonde hair in a pony-tail, and, most unusual of all, she wore trousers. They were black and close-fitting, and now largely hidden because her shoes were kicked off and her legs curled up under her.

It suddenly seemed to Holly that she herself was sitting very primly. 'I'm Holly,' she offered.

The other girl nodded. 'Helen.' She licked her fingers and offered her plate to Holly. 'So are you a refugee too?'

'Refugee?'

'I just couldn't take any more. Nigel's pillocky friends. . . . Sorry.' She looked Holly up and down. 'Do you know what a pillock is? You're an American, aren't you?'

'Yes – '

'I used to be American.'

'How can you "used to be"?' said Holly curiously.

The other girl shrugged. 'I was born in America, in New York, but my father moved us here on business.'

'Really? I'm from New York.'

'I lived there till I was ten. I used to go to a school called Spence.'

'That's where I used to go!' Holly knew she sounded ridiculously delighted. She had begun to think she would never meet anyone here with whom she shared something so simple.

'Really?' Helen sounded excited, too. 'I used to have a real Gorgon of a second-grade teacher. Mrs Weston. Did you have her?'

'No. But I had the other one. Mr Schiffold.'

They were off. It was amazing, Holly thought, how much they had in common. They had been at the same school – though, as it turned out, Helen was seven years older. But they knew some of the same girls; Helen had actually lived half a block away from the Clayton's apart-ment at 65th and Park.

107

Best of all, Holly realised when Helen stood up to fetch seconds from the buffet – Helen was just as tall as she was. Maybe even taller. She had big hands with bitten-off fingernails, broad shoulders and, Holly suspected, broad hips, although they were concealed by her floppy sweater. Helen moved with assurance. 'D'you want some?' she asked. 'We can get you a plate. No one else is eating yet but it's OK. I'm friends with the powers that be.'

Holly moved contentedly along the table while Helen chatted with the waiters; picking, as Helen had, one of this, one of that, straightening the canapés so that what she had taken wouldn't be noticed.

'Why you no sound American tonight?' one of the waiters was asking Helen. He sounded Italian and looked, Holly thought, besotted with Helen.

'I don't?' Helen grinned. 'All right. I'll be American if you want.'

And she did. She had switched accents effortlessly, though neither her Americanness nor her Englishness was extreme.

'I wish I could do that,' said Holly as they wandered back to the library with full plates.

'You'll learn, probably,' said Helen. 'Give it time. How long've you been here?'

'Six months.'

'You're married,' said Helen, unquestioning, 'to Tyrconnel Carr.'

'That's right.' Holly wondered how Helen knew that. Perhaps she had seen the wedding pictures in the *Queen*.

Helen rolled her eyes, which were dark and slanting. 'Lucky you!' She had gone back to her English accent. 'How'd you pull that one off?'

Holly shrugged, abashed, and laughed. 'I don't really know. Are you married?'

'Yes.' Helen licked her fingers. 'To Nige. Nige *English*, if you can believe it!' She laughed. 'I guess I wasn't sure of my nationality, so I had to marry it. Nige is an appalling socialite. Probably flirting with all the other girls in there. He'll say it's for the sake of business.'

'What's his business?'

'He's started up a magazine, called *New Review*. It sells art.'

'How exciting.' Holly half wished, then, that Tyrconnel ran a magazine like that, instead of the alternately boring and beastly *Courant*. 'Do you work for the magazine too?'

Helen laughed. 'Dear me, no. I'm colour-blind. I don't mean literally. Just that all that new art makes my skin crawl. For every ghastly piece Nige brings home, I buy a mezzotint. I like old things, from antique shops.'

Holly wondered if Helen's clothes came from an antique shop. She was just trying to think of a way to ask her that without being rude, when a tall thin man in black-framed spectacles appeared in the doorway.

'Nigel,' Helen welcomed him – or announced. 'Are we sprung? Can we go home yet?'

Holly's heart sank slightly at the thought that she was about to be thrown back into the mêlée of the party.

'Aren't you going to introduce me?' said Nigel, nodding towards Holly. He had a more reserved manner than his wife, and a quieter voice. Youthfully springy curls leapt out from behind the bald dome of his forehead.

'Nige – Holly,' said Helen offhandedly. 'Are we going on?' Then, 'Holly, are you coming with us?'

'I don't know –' Holly hesitated. 'I came with my mother-in-law.'

'Oh, but she'll understand,' said Helen. 'You *must* come. I'll explain.'

Imogen looked mildly amused as they took their leave, and a few minutes later they were roaring, or rather spluttering, out of Grosvenor Square. The Englishes' car was French, shaped like half a can of sardines, and painted a startling electric blue. 'We call her Baby Blue,' said Helen. 'She's not up to much, but she gets us around.'

They drove down quiet, lamplit streets into Soho, where Nigel pulled up in front of an unspectacular-looking coffee bar. 'The 2 i's', its sign said. A dull thump of music came up from below the floor.

'That's the basement,' said Nige, 'where the groups play. Tommy Steele, people like that. A bit too hep and loud for me.'

Nigel and Helen seemed to be regulars. The other people along the bar – mostly men with slicked-back hair and strangely formal, stick-legged suits – nodded and made way for them. A few stared at Holly's party dress and Persian lamb coat.

They settled at a formica-topped table, with three espressos. 'You'll have to excuse the informality,' said Nigel, tapping the tabletop. 'We're clinging to our youth.'

'You don't look exactly old,' said Holly, half-truthfully: Helen looked more or less the age she said she was, twenty-five, and about Nige she couldn't be certain.

'Ah, but that's our way. Always feeling the future closing in on us, chasing after that receding dream.'

'Nige is a beatnik,' said Helen, then wrinkled her nose and laughed.

'Are you?' said Holly, seriously, to Helen.

'Oh, no! I don't *aspire* to be anything, unlike my husband.'

Nigel got up to order more espressos. Holly had loaded her first with sugar, and was beginning to take to the strong taste. She felt that way, too, about the Englishes. She wanted to take them in, in all their strangeness.

When they had finished their espressos, they walked along the street to a jazz club. Inside, the air was thick with smoke. A mixture of men, black and white, including one trumpeter whose eyes stayed closed in a trancelike state, played rhythmically, captivatingly, nonstop.

'They're good,' said Holly, surprised, because her taste for rock music had never led her down the more exotic path of jazz.

'American.' Nigel nodded at the group.

'We're all *addicted* to America, you see,' said Helen, leaning across to Holly.

'Then why didn't you stay there?' Holly whispered, half teasing but also half serious.

Helen shrugged, and squeezed Nigel's knee. 'That's love.'

Holly smiled. Love had kept her in England, too. *But then*, she thought, *if it did, why isn't Ty here?*

When Nigel and Helen drove her home it was nearly three, but still she struggled out of bed early the next morning, because she hadn't seen Tyrconnel in two days. Helen had said she probably saw so little of her husband because they shared a house with his mother. 'Your mother-in-law!' she had cried, astonished, when Holly told her. 'I don't know how you *bear* it.'

'She's really very nice,' Holly had protested. But the more Helen talked, the more she had begun to wonder. Maybe it was true that Chester Square kept her and Tyrconnel apart. It was so big: even when Tyrconnel was home, half the time Holly didn't know where to find him. And then, they didn't share a room. Tyrconnel's, filled with his clothes, his books and austere furniture, seemed so very much *his* that Holly doubted she could ever insinuate herself inside it.

Perhaps the house was even too luxurious. Maybe if, like Helen and Nigel, they had a smaller house, without live-in servants, Holly could learn to cook for Tyrconnel – even iron his shirts! It sounded almost romantic. Especially when she imagined the candlelit dinners they would eat together, alone. . . .

As soon as she went into the dining room, Imogen asked about her evening. Tyrconnel was reading his paper.

Holly told her mother-in-law briefly about the jazz club as she helped herself to scrambled eggs from a chafing-dish on the sideboard. She was not sure it was the sort of place Imogen would approve of. 'Helen and Nigel have a house in Islington,' she went on, hoping Tyrconnel would notice.

'Do they?' said Imogen.

'In Canonbury. Helen says that's the best part of Islington, full of Georgian houses. She says lots of the houses there are going for next to nothing.'

'No wonder,' said Tyrconnel, munching his toast. 'Islington's a dump.'

'Helen says it's really nice.'

'The Englishes,' interposed Imogen, 'probably can't afford anything better, dear, so I'm sure they are making the best of it.'

Holly's momentary hopes sank. Still, she didn't give up. 'I was thinking, Ty,' she said, 'what if – we got a place of our own? It wouldn't have to be a big one. It might even be a sort of – investment.'

'This is our house,' he said blandly.

Imogen picked up her letters and excused herself.

'I think you've hurt Mother's feelings,' Tyrconnel said when she had gone.

'Oh, no! I didn't mean to do that. I only meant. . . .'

'Anyway – ' He smiled now. 'What would we want, Holly, with moving to some poky little flat in the suburbs? We have this house already.'

'It's only . . .' Holly felt her argument crumbling.

'Do you mind sharing with Mother?'

'No. Not exactly.'

Tyrconnel looked concerned. 'I'm sure she'll try not to intrude on you if you want to be alone.'

'That's just it! I don't want to be alone. I want to see more of *you*.'

'Is that all?' Tyrconnel swallowed the last of his coffee and stood. 'I'll tell you what. Have lunch with me. Meet me at my office at one.'

Holly met him; it was only the second time she had seen the grubby Fleet Street offices of the *Courant*, with their printing presses and typesetters working in a basement of near-Victorian grime. After lunch Tyrconnel took her to Derry Street, where the steel skeleton of his new office building was already planted in its foundations. The Courant Building, as they were going to call it, would be twenty storeys high, dwarfing the terraced houses around it.

'Soon,' Tyrconnel said, 'it'll all be skyscrapers around here. The way of the future.'

But none of this answered Holly's questions, or solved her problem; even when Tyrconnel came into her room that night. As ever, he seemed at his most remote when he took control of his climax, his pleasure.

Over the next few weeks, she began to look at the notices in the papers for flats and houses for sale or to let. She even found some in Kensington and Belgravia that did not seem, to her inexperienced eye, outrageously expensive, and when she did, she showed them to Tyrconnel.

'But we don't *need* to move,' he would say. His answer was always the same.

At the end of February Daphne and Jamie's second baby was born, a girl, and a christening was held in the church at Little Hampton, the village adjoining the grounds of Stadhampton House.

Little Laura was two now, and she scampered around the church garden like an untamed colt while the photographer took pictures. Holly chased after her, picking her up with a warm auntly hug. 'Do you remember me?'

Laura, whose stubborn face was now softened by a wreath of blonde curls, evidently didn't. But she smiled anyway. Holly held her close with a pang.

'Thanks, Holly.' Jamie flashed a smile at her. 'That one's turning into a little hoyden.'

For a second, then, Holly's heart ached for the normality, the solid family love, she saw in Jamie and Daphne. Daphne looked plumper after her pregnancy; her voice even sounded soft as she whispered to the new baby. No one would have guessed that this second was a small disappointment; that she and her husband had been hoping for a boy. They had named the little girl Davina, after Daphne's late mother.

Daphne's father, Major Mainwaring, had a firm arm

around his daughter, and the other around Jamie. He had given them another Stubbs from his sizeable collection, in honour of the birth. 'Let *go*, Daddy,' Daphne had to tell him, before the photographer could take his next shot.

Hollis missed her father then, not for the first time. Perhaps it was bound to happen, as the novelty of England and marriage wore away. Perhaps she would have missed her parents this much, wherever she was.

Laura became so heavy she had to put her down. *A baby*, she thought. That would make it all right. Her parents would come over for the christening. But when she looked up at Tyrconnel and smiled, hoping to transmit that wish, she could not catch his eye. A few weeks ago, when they heard about Davina, she had finally braved the subject.

'A baby?' Tyrconnel had said. 'Of course, darling. Me, too.' But that night he had done nothing any different from before; had stayed inside her for only a few seconds. Only twice – and she remembered those occasions exactly – had he ever managed to climax inside her. Often he never went there at all. She had tried to ask about that, too.

'I *can't*,' he had said through gritted teeth. 'Stop questioning me.'

While Nanny Walters, beaming in cerise, carried Davina, Daphne and Jamie strolled out of the churchyard, hand in hand. Holly wondered for a moment what they were like together; what they did when they made love. Then she looked down, embarrassed at harbouring such thoughts.

Not that she had anything to fear. Tyrconnel never said, 'Penny for your thoughts?' any more; or anything like it. He just didn't seem to care.

IX

Tyrconnel and Holly flew to Manangwe in March 1959.

It was Holly's first visit to Africa, and as she peered

down through the plane window at the cliffs jutting out into a deep blue sea, she tried to think of the walls of rock in the terms with which Tyrconnel described them – *layered intrusions, crystallisations, ore formations*. But she could see only something vast, impregnable, mysterious.

Tyrconnel said there were immense riches waiting to be tapped beneath the earth floor of Manangwe: copper, iron, gold. And he wanted to win the right to mine them.

His half-sister Esmé and her husband, Hywel Campbell, met Tyrconnel and Holly at the airport. They both wore short sleeves and straw hats and looked very brown: more, Holly thought at first, like big sister and younger brother than husband and wife, since Esmé was so sturdy and Hywel so small and thin.

Holly barely had time to adjust to the blanket of heat that had struck as soon as she climbed off the plane, or to look around her at the airport shops, with their signs in Portuguese, Dutch and English, and the Manangweans in bright-coloured clothes who swarmed everywhere, before Esmé hurried them out into the car.

'Home,' she boomed to the black driver. 'We've left a man to wait for your luggage, Ty. It can take hours. At least one thing we've no shortage of here is servants.'

'You two are lucky,' piped in Hywel. 'You've missed the worst of the heat. Foreigners always think the hottest month is January, but in strict terms of temperature *and* humidity. . . .'

Esmé turned to Holly long before he could finish. 'Let me explain,' she said. 'This is the main road to Manang, and over there's the warehouse. Useful place. Sells things like lightbulbs and six-week-old English biscuits.'

The main road grew narrower and more congested, until they arrived at what Holly guessed to be the centre of the capital city: a dense collection of metal-roofed wooden shacks. People carrying bundles and packages crowded the road, making way for the embassy car as it passed, sometimes with a friendly wave at the passengers, or a curious smile.

'They're lovely people here,' said Esmé.

Tyrconnel looked nonplussed. 'I see.'

They passed the capitol building, at one end of a European-style square erected by the Portuguese during their brief colonial tenure. Its white paint now peeled in the sun. Then they swept out of the city; shacks gave way to parched grassland and low hills. The embassy compound lay up a dirt drive, shaded by trees. Three children ran out to meet the car at the gate.

'Down!' shouted Esmé, as she might to a pack of dogs. 'All right! One at a time. Clara, little Hyw and Mungo. Do you remember your uncle Tyrconnel? And this is your new aunt, Holly. Mungo! Take that out of your mouth at once.'

A black nanny followed in the children's wake, with the youngest Campbell, a baby, in her arms; and now everyone moved together towards the long, low white house. There were others dotted around it, belonging to other embassy officials; the biggest, the ambassador's, sat on a further rise, screened by palms.

Esmé showed Tyrconnel and Holly their room, then took them out to the pool. The view was breathtaking: the green valley giving way to the sprawl of Manang, made picturesque by haze and distance, then the sea.

'I think,' said Esmé, handing Holly a cold drink, 'that the men, who have to go down into town, have the worst of it. While they work, you and I, Holly, are going to have an absolutely splendid time!'

By the next morning, when she was lying by the pool, Holly had decided she *absolutely* agreed. That was one of Esmé's favourite words, and Holly had begun to get the giggles every time she heard it. She had carefully shaded her face with a hat, to keep off the freckles; now, as the sun warmed her arms and legs and she opened to the first page of *Peyton Place*, one of a stack of bestsellers Esmé had left conveniently in the spare bedroom, Clara and little Hyw ran up.

'Aunt Holly. Want to play ball?'

'Now, you just pay no attention, Holly,' Esmé shouted from the veranda.

'That's OK,' said Holly. 'I'll play. Where?'

'In the water!' said Clara importantly: as if she ought to know.

So much, thought Holly, for getting a tan to look glamorous for Ty, as she dived beneath the cool blue surface of the water. She had always loved swimming much more than sunbathing anyway.

'You certainly made a hit with the children,' said Esmé after lunch, when the children had been forced inside for naps and lessons. She had insisted that Holly retreat to the shade of the veranda before she got completely sunburnt. Holly had just addressed a postcard to Helen and was wondering what to write; it still rankled with her that she had had to refuse two dinner invitations from the Englishes because Tyrconnel was always too busy to come along. The next time, Helen had told her, she must simply come on her own.

A servant brought out a pitcher of lemonade. Esmé poured two glasses and stretched back in her chair. 'Bliss,' she said, 'isn't it?'

Holly had searched, the other day, for any resemblance between Esmé and her mother, and couldn't find it, except in their dark hair. Esmé was tall and big-boned, with a long, wide mouth and thighs that sprawled comfortably out beneath the conservative black bathing suit that, like the other embassy wives who now dotted the poolside, she seemed to wear for most of the day.

'So how do you like London, Holly?' said Esmé. And, without waiting for an answer, 'Has Mother been difficult?'

'What do you mean?' said Holly, surprised.

'Oh, she's awfully possessive of Ty. Jamie, too, though to a lesser extent. Always has been.'

'Well – she's been very nice to me. . . .'

'Hm.' Esmé gave an unexplanatory shrug. 'Well. All I can say is I'm glad I'm far away.'

'It is lovely here.'

'Beautiful. And distance makes the heart. . . . Ah, well. I really shouldn't go into it.'

But Holly knew somehow, even before Esmé went on, that she would.

'The thing about Mother . . .' Esmé stretched back. 'Well, really I missed growing up with her. I suppose that explains it.'

'How's that?'

'Well, she sent me away to school when she remarried.' Esmé gave a short laugh. 'Can't say I blame her. An awkward five-year-old, always getting in the way. . . .'

'You were five?' Holly was shocked.

'There are some schools that take girls as young as that. This one was run by nuns. Although of course we weren't Catholic.'

'What about . . . your father? Did you ever see him?'

'He said he'd visit. Never came. I suppose the journey was too much for him. So many casinos along the way.' Esmé shifted in her chair, shading her eyes. 'I don't really remember much of him, only what Mother told me. Yet I suppose they must once have been very much in love.' She gave Holly a fleeting smile. 'Funny, isn't it?'

'Oh, I don't know – '

'Not that I can pronounce judgment now. Four babies rather take the edge off a grand passion.' Esmé gave a wry smile. 'But I shouldn't be telling you this. You haven't even had your first yet.'

'No . . .' said Holly. And then, she did not know what made her continue, 'But we hope to. Soon.'

Hywel brought Tyrconnel home that night, ready to celebrate. The President of Manangwe, Willem de Vriet, had agreed to a meeting the next day. Beaming in the reflected glory of Tyrconnel's coup, Hywel poured out some of his best Manangwean white. By the end of a long dinner,

Holly felt decidedly tipsy, and she wondered if it were her imagination that Hywel was fawning dreadfully on her husband.

'It takes vision – ' Hywel's voice pitched drunkenly – 'indeed, I would even say a certain bravado, to come into Africa in troubled times like these. Of course, what most people fail to appreciate is that Manangwe is not Africa. In terms of government. . . .'

'Hywel Campbell,' said Tyrconnel later, as he sank into bed, 'is one of the world's great bores.'

The President's office was stuffy, thickly curtained and carpeted, its white walls lined with photos of a young-looking Willem de Vriet in the company of other states-men: De Gaulle, Eisenhower, Khrushchev. Now he had fallen out with nearly all of them, whether over his support for the independence of fellow African states like Ghana, or for the racial policies of Manangwe's neighbour, South Africa.

'What they don't understand,' he told Tyrconnel now, in his slow and heavily accented voice, 'is that we are all Africans, white or black. I am an African first – my family has been here for centuries. Forgive me if I do not open the window, Lord Carr. Security.'

'I understand.' Nearly gasping with the heat, Tyrconnel loosened his tie.

'These walls are five feet thick.' De Vriet knocked on one of them. 'As tall as a man, ja? No one can hear through this. That is important. But for myself I keep every conversation – ' He tapped a wooden tabletop – 'on tape. I think you should know this.'

'I see,' said Tyrconnel. The height of the President had surprised him at first, and the sharp yellow of his hair. The ageless face – the same as it had been when, in the course of five years, in his forties, De Vriet had taken his country into the Commonwealth, and then, against strong British objections, to full independence. The hooded, steely eyes Tyrconnel already knew well from photographs.

'You work alone,' De Vriet was saying now.

'Yes.' Tyrconnel gave a thin smile. 'When it comes to matters of importance. I find there is no one else I can trust.'

'We have a saying here, "I trust him like family." Yet like you, there is no one I would say this of now. I have a son, he is twelve. So perhaps one day he will come to fill my shoes.' De Vriet chuckled indulgently.

'Of course Manangwe,' said Tyrconnel neutrally, 'is a democracy.'

'Ah, yes! But it is the same in our two countries, no? You have a brother, I believe, an MP. Is it not true that there are advantages to the families of those in power?'

'Quite.' Tyrconnel gave a wry smile.

'I like you, Lord Carr. You are not verbose. But is it true you have the money to do what you say? The evidence for this I have not seen.'

'My bankers will be happy to confirm – '

'And the experience,' interrupted De Vriet. 'You know the wealth of this country. But you do not know the workers. Some say it is the gift of the Portuguese. They left our blacks lazy, unwilling to work. Those who have owned the mines before have found this. That is why they now belong to the nation. The men will take a big cash payment to go out to the mines, and then – ' De Vriet made a fizzing sound – 'nothing. One can make them do nothing.'

'I am sure there are ways,' said Tyrconnel.

There was a knock at the door; it sounded muffled, because two further doors interrupted the passage between the outside corridor and this room. De Vriet pushed the button on an intercom. '*Ja?*'

A minute later a young black man entered. He wore a close-fitting English-style suit, and a film of sweat shone on his forehead as he deposited a locked briefcase beside De Vriet's desk, then laid down the tray that was balanced in his other hand, containing two glasses.

'Whisky and soda?' the President asked Tyrconnel. 'Sam,

here, has read my mind. He always does.' He smiled at the young black man, who stood very straight by the door. Sam was exceptionally handsome but incongruously dressed, his muscles perceptible beneath his dark suit as if in a moment they would burst through it.

'Sam is seventeen,' said the President. 'He is a clever boy. Sometimes I think I will send him to Oxford! Ho, ho!'

Sam did not flinch under De Vriet's gaze or Tyrconnel's newly interested one.

'Perhaps you should send him,' said Tyrconnel gravely. His eyes ran up and down Sam's figure. 'It would be a great opportunity.'

Suddenly Sam smiled and half-bowed. 'Thank you, sir,' he said formally. He stared back at Tyrconnel, almost in challenge.

'That will be all, Sam,' said the President. Sam turned and walked away, revealing the shape of tight buttocks beneath his trousers.

'You may think,' said De Vriet, when he was gone, 'it is unwise of me to trust a black as my personal servant. But he comes from a good family. He is not one of those – agitators.' His nose wrinkled in disgust.

'One has to trust one's own judgement.'

'We are not like South Africa, you know,' said De Vriet suddenly. 'In this country, I truly believe that the peoples can live in harmony. We do not need apartheid here. Each race knows where it belongs.' He walked to the window, which looked out towards Manang's Portuguese square. 'Of course, the whites will govern. We always have.' He paused. 'I am a patriotic man. I do this duty for the good of my country. Would you like to go up to Omumba with me now, to see the mines?'

Taken aback, Tyrconnel accepted.

'Good.' De Vriet grinned. 'We will go in my lorry. British-made. Sam will drive us.'

Holly was surprised when that night Tyrconnel called from

a hundred miles north of Manang, to say that he was going to see the mines, with the President himself. Even Hywel seemed surprised – but pleased. He said De Vriet was capricious.

Tyrconnel was away in the north for three days. He returned suntanned and exultant. He even hugged Holly tight, spinning her round in his arms in front of the others.

'We're nearly there,' he said. 'Pack your bags, darling. We're going to the President's palace.'

'I am glad,' said Willem de Vriet, smiling obliquely at Holly, 'to see Tyrconnel Carr has a wife so beautiful. A man of ambition, energy, needs this small pleasure.'

Holly forced a smile at this dubious compliment. 'You're very kind.'

The table was the longest one she had ever seen. It filled the state dining room, which itself ran along the whole eastern side of the presidential palace. Its outer wall was composed almost entirely of glass, giving a view through a shaded veranda straight out to the ocean.

Tonight the room was filled with guests. But she and Tyrconnel, seated on either side of the President, were the guests of honour. Old-fashioned ceiling fans spun overhead, and the food – several large fish courses followed by a strangely-spiced *boeuf en croûte* – made no concessions to the temperature. The white Manangweans who lined either side of the table, leathery-skinned and heavily adorned with gold and diamonds, did not seem to notice the heat. Most of the women had drunk their cocktails wearing elbow-length gloves.

Holly had worn her lightest summer evening dress, of pale rose silk with an off-the-shoulder neckline that showed off Imogen's pearls; she was not sure whether the colour made her look tanned or merely accentuated her freckles. But De Vriet was admiring; and his wife – reportedly a doughty Manangwean with little English – was nowhere in sight.

On Holly's other side was a businessman who tried

intermittently to elbow his way into conversation with the President. But De Vriet made it clear that this was unwelcome. 'Lady Carr is just telling me about America, about New York,' he would say, and then return to whatever he had been telling Holly. 'I believe,' he said, 'that in the land lives the real soul of the African people.'

He seemed to like to wax lyrical about 'the African people'. Holly wondered whether he meant the white people or the black people, who were not at all in evidence tonight, even as servants; but she did not ask. Tyrconnel had warned her to be diplomatic, as he was near to closing an agreement with the President.

At one point, however, a black man did come in: a handsome young man in a tight-fitting suit, who swept in from the terrace and leaned down to whisper something in the President's ear. Holly saw Tyrconnel look up at him, closely, and the black man glance back.

'My assistant,' De Vriet explained. 'Sam Hrere.'

The young man returned when the company had moved into a shady back room to drink coffee. This time he stayed, talking in a low voice to Tyrconnel; De Vriet steered Holly in the opposite direction.

'I think,' he said, 'you have not met Mr and Mrs Stergen. I will leave you to talk.'

A few minutes later, Holly glanced around in search of Tyrconnel but could not see him anywhere.

The next morning, when Holly and Tyrconnel walked down to the beach, they saw Sam Hrere again. Unlike the other servants here, he seemed to have the run of the place. He walked past them in his beach trunks, his bare shoulders gleaming. For a moment, he seemed to catch Tyrconnel's eye, but they acknowledged each other with only a small nod.

'It's funny,' Holly said, 'how he acts so superior, for a servant.'

'Hm,' Tyrconnel grunted.

*

The President and Tyrconnel met again in a high turret of the palace, overlooking the sea. The floor was tiled and bare; the wind blew through open windows; there was no tape recorder.

'You see,' said De Vriet. 'I come to trust you.'

'Or you don't want what we say to go on record.'

'*Touché.*' The President smiled. 'No one is safe.'

'You aren't worried, though.' Tyrconnel's tone was questioning.

De Vriet blew out a sigh. 'Who can say? There are the Communists, there are the revolutionary leagues – we cannot stop them completely. To tell the truth, we could not survive an uprising. We have not sufficient men, sufficient weapons. We are a rich country, yes, but with our debts. . . . One must be wary about selling what wealth we possess, do you understand this? To see our country in foreign hands. . . .'

Tyrconnel nodded.

'That, you see, is the reason our constitution declares that no more than 30 per cent of the mines can be foreign owned. I am willing to ignore this, in the current position. But I am sure you will understand. . . .'

'What do you want?' said Tyrconnel. 'A percentage for you? For the government?'

The President's face was hard. 'No. Guaranteed. Up front.'

'That's difficult. You know it'll take a few years just to break even.'

'You will be breaking my country's constitution.' De Vriet looked coldly out towards the ocean.

'Then tell me your terms.' Tyrconnel's voice was raw with frustration, aggression. 'How much?'

'We've done it,' Tyrconnel told Holly, collapsing into a chair in their room.

'What? You've got an agreement? That's great!'

'If it doesn't work,' Tyrconnel muttered, 'he'll bleed me dry.'

Holly had no idea what he was talking about. 'You've said there's iron and copper and gold in the mines. I'm sure it will work!'

Again, at dinner, Sam slipped in and out, speaking to the President; sometimes to Tyrconnel. Occasionally his gaze lit on Holly as he stalked, with stately grace, from the room. *What does he want?* Holly wondered, but she had no answer.

That night Tyrconnel sank into bed without speaking to her, exhausted, she supposed, by the afternoon's negotiations. He would be meeting the President tomorrow morning to sign papers, then wiring his bankers for funds. She did not know how much; he had never told her.

She drifted into a light sleep, and was surprised when she woke up, an hour or so later, to find Tyrconnel gone. She got up to check the bathroom and the balcony. Probably, she supposed, he was too wound up to sleep, and had gone out for a walk.

She went back to bed but now she couldn't sleep, either. Finally she got up and pulled on a dress and sandals. A full moon was in the sky, and the beach would be quiet. She would walk, too.

'What, do you not like it so?' Sam Hrere's smile flashed in the moonlit darkness as he fell back on to the sand. Carefully he brushed the fine grains from his knees.

'No,' said Tyrconnel gruffly. 'I like to be in control. I should have known you were too old.'

'De Vriet, he likes me to give it to him that way. He's just like a baby. He cries.'

'Well, I don't,' said Tyrconnel brusquely, shifting away. 'I never cry. Cigarette?'

The red flame of the match, shifting from one cigarette to the other, momentarily lit their two faces.

'I shall be sorry to see you go, sir,' said Sam obediently.

'Don't give me that. You're not the type to fawn, Sam –' Tyrconnel broke off suddenly.

Holly had seen the flash of light; now she heard the voices. 'Who's there?' she called. She had not expected to find anyone except perhaps Tyrconnel.

She heard a rustle, and clicked on her torch. 'Who is it?' She swept the beach and its bank of palm trees with light. She saw Sam first: his gaze frozen like a deer's in the sudden light, before he got up, clutching a cloth to his groin, and ran into the trees.

Then her light flicked across to Tyrconnel. He said nothing. He was sitting on a blanket, his hair tousled. Naked.

'Turn that goddamned thing off.'

Holly's hand, with the torch in it, shook.

'I said turn it off.'

Eventually she did.

'I don't – understand,' she said.

'No. I don't suppose you do.' Tyrconnel's voice was soft.

'What do you mean?'

For a second he said nothing; then, 'Let's go back inside.'

'No.' Holly's voice felt thick. 'Tell me. Tell me, first. What were you doing?'

Tyrconnel let out a low laugh. 'What do you think we were doing? We were fucking.'

Holly's chest seized up.

'Surely you've heard the word before.'

'I don't – I don't believe you.' Holly's fingers felt numb as she ran them up and down over the switch of the torch. 'You're just saying that to shock me.'

'Listen, Holly.' Tyrconnel crawled closer to her. She could see his dark shape approaching; now she felt his warm breath on her face, and she jerked back. 'I was going to protect you. But now you may as well know. Some men, you know, like women a great deal. My brother Jamie, for instance – '

'I don't give a damn about your brother Jamie!' Holly heard her own voice ring out.

'Shut up, Holly. You'll wake people.'

'I don't care!'

'Then listen.' He grabbed hold of her shoulders. 'It's for your own good. I'll explain – '

'I don't want to know.' Holly twisted free, running back towards the wooden walk that led up to the house. She heard Tyrconnel's footsteps behind her; he caught at her arm.

'No!' she said. 'Don't walk near me.'

The rest of the way back to the palace was eerily silent.

Tyrconnel caught hold of her in the hallway before she could open their bedroom door. 'Don't,' he said, 'even think of locking me out, Holly.'

She trembled. 'Let go of me. I wasn't.' She sat shaking on the edge of the bed while he lit a cigarette. The flame cast his face in red light as it had a few minutes ago.

'How can you do those things?' she said. 'How can you even think of it?'

'I think of it – ' and she heard a laugh at the back of his throat – 'nearly all the time.'

She wondered if he were smiling. Strangely, she thought so.

'It's like that,' he said. 'I can't say I repent it. I can't imagine being any other way.'

'It's disgusting.'

'Don't – ' He loomed nearer, and his voice took on a warning tone – 'talk to me like that.'

'Well, it is. It's disgusting and wrong – '

He slapped her. Her face stinging, she backed away across the bed and ran towards the door. He blocked her way. She edged back inside, towards the balcony.

'Now. That's better.' Tyrconnel puffed on his cigarette as he approached. 'I shouldn't like you to make a spectacle of us.'

Holly opened the window wider for air; the room was growing oppressive. Then she took a deep breath and said, 'Why did you marry me?'

'Well, I thought it might work. I'm fond of you, Holly – '

'Don't lie.'

'All right, then.' Tyrconnel threw the end of his cigarette

out past the railing. 'Many reasons. A wife is useful, in my line of work. What I . . . prefer, you know, is against the law. Naturally, I don't wish to be suspected, or . . . entrapped. To go to jail. But it's not only that. Other men are prejudiced. They would avoid having dealings with me if they thought I wasn't like them.'

'Does anyone else know? Does your mother? Does Jamie?'

'Perhaps they guess.'

'Then shouldn't someone have told me?' Holly's voice was bitter. 'Didn't *someone* owe it to me to warn me, since you didn't see fit yourself, that I was marrying a queer?'

'I don't like that word.'

'Well, it's what they're called. It's what people think!' She was shouting again. 'So what do you prefer?'

'I never knew you had such a temper, Holly.' Tyrconnel spoke mildly.

'No. I didn't either.'

Tyrconnel was silent. And suddenly Holly didn't want to speak any more, but only to fall back in the bed and sleep. And then she would wake up, and perhaps this would all turn out to have been some terrible dream. Like some of the times before, the actions that didn't fit, the times Tyrconnel was cruel or strange. Like their wedding night.

'Well,' she said, 'you got what you wanted. A wife who was too ignorant to know what to expect. . . .' She fought the tightness in her voice. 'Tell me, did you plan it all along?'

'More or less as soon as I'd met you.' Tyrconnel shrugged. 'I knew it would help that you were young, and – well – I needed the money.'

'What money?' said Holly sharply.

'I knew your father would be capable of . . . investing. And he did. He gave me a cheque at the wedding. Seed-money, you might call it, towards the enterprise I set in motion today. All that cash was a great help in convincing my bankers. Money attracts more money, I find. Your father gave it to me to buy central heating, I believe he said. But I'm sure he'd understand.'

'Would he?' said Holly; and she heard her voice growing louder, almost beyond herself. 'Would he? He tried to warn me, you know. I should have listened. He said I should wait, that I shouldn't get married so young. . . .'

And then, unaccountably, she was sobbing. She felt her body cramping, curling inwards. She hid her head against her knees, and when Tyrconnel touched her, she jumped at first, then let him stroke her back. 'I can't stand it,' she mumbled. 'We can't go on like this, we'll end it. It was a big mistake. I'll just leave and go home.'

'Oh, no.' Tyrconnel's voice was threatening. 'I don't think you'll do any such thing.'

'What do you mean? We can get a divorce.'

'Not in England.' Tyrconnel drew closer. 'It's not so easy as that. Calm down, darling.'

'Don't call me "darling". Don't you dare call me that – '

'You're making a noise.'

And now he held her tight, pinning her arms down, his embrace like a cage.

'Let me go!' she screamed, but he was stronger than she thought. In a flash he had pulled a pillow from the bed and pressed it to her face. She drew in gasping sobs. His hands were hard, pushing down until she thought her head would split in two. Instinctively, she kicked out, but her feet struck against nothing. 'Let me go. . . .' Her voice drowned against the impregnable wet cloth. *Let me go. . . .*

'Are you better now?' said Tyrconnel's voice. 'Calmed down?' His grip on her loosened slightly. But still she had to struggle for each breath.

'There,' Tyrconnel said. 'That's better. Now listen to me. And remember. We made vows, Holly, sacred vows. And I intend us to keep them.' He paused. 'I don't want to be your jailer, Holly. I see no reason you shouldn't be . . . perfectly happy. You'll have a very comfortable life. Whatever you want – money, clothes. . . .'

If there was more, Holly didn't hear it. Her nose ached

from where the pillow had pressed against it, and suddenly her eyes were full of a starry tingling. She blacked out.

She woke in the midst of a dream, fighting for air again, her head aching. And she was surprised to see the bright sun streaming in through the shutters. Tyrconnel was gone. There was a note for her on his pillow, in his large, thin black writing. *Back here at noon*, it said.

She wondered briefly if he was going to see Sam. *Sam.* The whole horror of it came back to her then, and when the maid came to the room, asking, 'You leave today, your husband says?' Holly answered dully, 'Yes.'

If they were leaving, she was glad. At least, once back at Esmé and Hywel's, she would not have to be alone with him. And he would be away from Sam. Whatever horrible temptation, whatever vice, had overtaken him here, would disappear. . . . She still did not believe he really was what he had said. *Homo*, the girls used to call the effeminate music teacher at her school: *faggot, queer.*

She had always associated the words vaguely with music teachers, artists: men in a sphere of their own, perfectly likeable, but men no girl like her would ever consider marrying. According to the more knowledgeable girls, a homo's looks, his fey and girlish manner, would single him out right away. However she tried, she could not match that despised condition – those insult-words – with Tyrconnel. He was strong and masculine. He was probably wrong about himself. He could overcome it.

She was not ready to leave him, whatever he had said. *Even if*, she reminded herself bitterly, *he did marry me for my money.* The shame of having to run back home would be unbearable. And besides – despite everything – she couldn't honestly say that she didn't still love him.

He entered without knocking, startling her. His eyes were red, but he looked otherwise unmarked by the last night. 'You'd better hurry up and get ready,' he said. 'I called Esmé. She's sending a car at noon.'

Holly was still in her nightgown. She struggled to speak

normally. 'Have you – I mean – do we need to say goodbye to the President?'

'I'll take care of that. I'm staying on a few days longer.'

'You are?' Holly's eyes were wide and her face, she knew, betrayed astonishment.

'Yes.' Tyrconnel turned back towards the door. 'I'll join you up at Esmé's the night before we fly.' He paused for a second. 'Are you all right, Holly?'

'Yes.' What else could she say?

A few minutes later the porters came for her suitcases.

'Do you think she's feeling well?' Hywel nodded down at the reclining figure of Holly by the pool. *Sense and Sensibility* lay half finished beside her, face down on the tiles.

'She's just tired, I imagine,' said Esmé. 'Probably the climate. Or do you think . . . ?' Her brows raised, hopeful.

A few minutes later, she bustled down to the poolside with a tray of drinks and sandwiches.

'Must try to eat, dear,' she said. 'Keep up your strength. I know you may not be feeling well. . . .'

Holly raised her head. 'No. Really. I'm fine.' Her voice sounded dull and thick, as it had, on the rare occasions that she spoke, for most of the last few days.

'Well, you never know,' said Esmé brightly. 'A girl's often the last to guess. But I've more experience than you, remember. Four times, after all!'

'What are you talking about?' said Holly, bewildered. She reached up to take a sandwich because Esmé would make even more of a fuss if she didn't. But really, she wished she could be left alone. Not to think; she had largely stopped thinking. But just to be. Warm in the sun, and blank, and numb.

'Well,' said Esmé confidingly, 'is there any possibility, dear, that you're having a baby?'

'No,' said Holly. 'No. Definitely not.'

'Can you be sure?'

Esmé's voice was so warm, so infuriatingly bright, that Holly wanted to scream.

No! No, I can't have a baby. I'll never have a baby, I'll never be normal, like you. Don't you know? Nothing, nothing will ever be normal again.

X

But it was. Astonishingly so. In fact, once she and Tyrconnel got back to London, Holly found it harder and harder to believe in that night scene, that dream sequence on the beach in Manangwe.

Even if it did explain everything.

Tyrconnel was busier than ever now, if also scrupulously courteous with her. He handled her like a piece of fragile china, whose deeper structure he knew he might have damaged though external appearances remained the same. He asked after her health: was she sleeping well? Did she have everything she liked to eat?

For a few days Holly even wondered if Esmé had managed to convince him, despite Holly's denials, that she was pregnant. She thought she had better put him straight. One night when he knocked on her door, she mentioned Esmé's suspicion.

'But you know,' she added, 'and I know that that is impossible.'

'Perhaps not for ever.' Tyrconnel's cheeks cracked into a smile.

If that was an invitation, Holly chose to ignore it. She pulled the sheets up protectively around herself. 'Not now,' she said. 'I think not now. Not after all this – '

'You know,' Tyrconnel broke in, 'I may have spoken too soon. Overstated my case.'

'Never *mind*,' Holly answered in a tight voice. Her eyes were wide, fearful. 'Good-night, Ty.'

She still had not decided what to do. And it only made

things worse when a letter came from her father, announcing that he had decided to take United Alloys public, sell most of his stake in it and retire.

A year ago, Holly realised, she would have congratulated him on his decision. But now she wasn't so sure. She frowned over the pages of her father's sprawling handwriting.

> I have to admit, chickadee, your husband has played a big part in convincing me to take this step. The US is a mature market, and – well, I won't bore you with the details except to say that your husband is creating some exciting investment opportunities over in Africa, and I intend to involve myself as much as possible. Not to mention bagging some big fish down in the Keys in my retirement!
> Tyrconnel may not have mentioned it, but I helped him out with his Manangwe project, and I'm convinced

Holly looked up sharply, oblivious of Reeve's assiduous motions around the breakfast table. 'Did you tell my father,' she said, 'that you used the central heating money for Manangwe?'

Tyrconnel, *Financial Times* balanced in one hand, coffee cup in the other, waited for the butler to go out. 'I don't think he needs to know about that,' he said. 'Do you? In a couple of years' time we'll be able to afford all the heating we want.'

'So he doesn't know. What's he writing about here?' Her fingers batted at the letter.

'Well.' Tyrconnel swallowed calmly. 'When I told him what was arranged, he told me he was interested in investing. All perfectly above board.'

'How much did he give you?'

'About a million.'

'Dollars?' Holly shot back.

'I never knew you were so interested in money.'

133

Holly's face flushed. 'Maybe I should be, now that my father seems to be giving it away.' She was glad that, for once, Imogen was up in the country rather than here. It made it easier to speak her mind.

'I should have thought you'd be glad he's retiring. After all, there's his health to consider.'

'Of course I'm glad!' Holly snapped. 'But I just don't think it's a good idea for him to be getting involved, now – with you.'

'Evidently *he* thinks you'll be delighted.'

'Well, he doesn't know.'

'What?' Tyrconnel's eyes were steely; Holly could see their pupils diminishing in the light.

'You know what I mean.'

'I don't see that it should make any difference.'

'You don't?' Surprise made Holly blurt out the words; and then go on, oblivious of Reeve or whoever else might be listening. 'Well, I do. In the first place I don't even know if – '

'Yes?' Tyrconnel's fingers clenched around his napkin.

'If we'll be staying married.'

'There can be no question about that.' Tyrconnel was standing, slotting his newspaper into his briefcase. 'We are.'

'How can you just say that?'

With a hiss of a sigh, Tyrconnel closed the dining room door in the face of Reeve, who was about to enter. 'Look,' he said in a low voice, leaning over Holly, 'I thought you understood one thing. We are going to be staying together.'

'I don't feel like making any promises just now.' Holly turned in her chair to get up and leave.

Tyrconnel took hold of her, forced her back down again, pinning her shoulders against the chair's wooden frame. 'There's no need for promises. You've already made them. Before me, before God.'

'How can you talk about God? You don't know the first thing about – '

'Nor do you.'

'I wouldn't even call this a marriage. Since you don't love me – '

'I never said that.' Tyrconnel cocked his head. For a moment he looked puzzled, vulnerable, tender.

She weakened, enough to relax against his hold. 'Well, I don't think it's enough. That you should care just a little. What about me? What about – my happiness?'

'But I will do everything to make you happy,' Tyrconnel smiled, 'because you are my wife. I don't intend to be . . . unfaithful to you.'

Holly turned her head away; she found that she could not trust her judgement when she looked at his face. 'Do you mean it?' she said. 'Do you mean to try . . . to be properly married?'

'Yes, Holly. I do.'

She felt his grasp on her lift away, and when she turned to look after him, she saw only his long, narrow silhouette retreating down the hallway. A minute later she heard the Daimler's engine growl and move away. She did not see Tyrconnel leave the house, but she would always wonder, after that day, how he looked when he did so: resolved, brisk, hopeful – or resigned.

She would never know.

It was that morning's conversation which kept her silent when she saw Helen a few days later.

'You seem preoccupied, Hol.' Helen English leaned over to dunk her bread in Holly's bowl of oxtail soup. 'Hope you don't mind. You don't seem to be eating it. I thought you'd find this an improvement over a Lyons Corner House.'

'Oh, it is.' Holly nodded absently at the bright interior of the Soup Kitchen – a new venture started up by a friend of Helen and Nige's, Terence Conran, offering cheap and tasty lunches just off the Strand.

'If you do want yours,' Helen persevered, 'I'll order another. Nige likes me Rubenesque.' Her warm smile invited Holly's in return. Helen, in a city seized by the vogue for diets, pencil-legs and Ryvita, held out for her own roundness, indeed did what she could to maintain it, though her exact size was hard to ascertain beneath the bulky sweaters, trousers and men's coats she habitually wore. 'Now if *you* start dieting, Holly,' said Helen, 'I'll throw up my hands in despair. It's bad enough that I should have such a skinny friend.'

'I'm not that skinny,' Holly protested, anchored at last by Helen's insistent conversation.

'Well, you're just right, anyway.' Helen wiped the last traces of soup from Holly's bowl. 'But, if you'll forgive my saying so, you look pale. Have you been hiding out in the Underground?'

Holly smiled but did not answer. 'How's Nige's book going?'

'Terrific. When it's done we're going to have the whole staff of the *New Review* round to celebrate. This time maybe you can get that husband of yours to come. Twist his arm.'

'I'll try. But Ty doesn't do much these days besides go to work.'

'Well, maybe all that dosh he's making can buy you a fancy man. . . . Sorry, Hol.'

Holly tried to relax; to remove the prim and scandalised look that she knew must have come over her face. 'Your Yankee face,' Helen sometimes called it.

Holly knew that her marriage mystified Helen, and that she would brim over with questions if Holly gave her the least encouragement: about Ty, about his businesses, Jamie and Daphne – 'the whole Carr set-up', as she called it. When Holly came back from Manangwe, unhappiness had nearly pushed her over the verge – made her tell Helen everything. Shame, and the illicit horror of the truth, had held her back then. Now, something else did. Hope. Although she did not dare to trust it too much. Not yet.

'What,' she said now, smiling coyly as she looked down into her tea, 'do you mean by a fancy man? My husband's plenty fancy enough for me.'

She went into the British Library and called up books on sex; searched the subject catalogues for words she dared not even pronounce aloud, and braved the stares of the librarians as she handed in her request slips. *Sexual Behaviour in the Human Male, Sexual Adjustments of Young Men, Sexual Anomalies and Perversions.* For a moment she wondered if they would say *no*: we do not give out such volumes to young ladies.

But the creaking machinery of the library, over the next four afternoons, disgorged its secrets.

She sat transfixed in the cavernous domed hall, reading first the Kinsey Report, whose name had been whispered and giggled over at Spence, though none of the girls had ever seen it. *A considerable portion of the population, perhaps the major part of the male population, has at least some homosexual experience.* . . .

She found the names of further works and called them up, discovering words she had never known before, like *orgasm*, and whole realms of human experience that she had never encountered. She learnt that there were men who dwelt on women's hair, shoes, underclothes – who came to that peculiar peak, *orgasm*, just by touching these things, by being near them.

That there were men who were excited by having women walk over their backs, or whip them. Men and women both who liked to dominate or be punished; who sought a return to their childhood in all their sexual relations.

Every afternoon, she came out of the library reeling. She thought of all the people in the street, drab in their hats and raincoats, harbouring such secrets; and it seemed to her that just beneath the surface of what she saw there lurked a teeming, hitherto invisible underworld.

But when she returned to the library she was calm. She understood things she had not, before. She had a mission. *Homosexual*: she traced the word in every index. The books disagreed. Some ranked homosexuals in various categories: misogynists, mother-lovers, aesthetes. None of these seemed quite to fit Tyrconnel. It gave her hope. *Perhaps he is not a real one. Perhaps he can change.*

For hadn't he nearly said so, that morning when he prevailed upon her to stay? Hadn't he visited her bedroom several times in the last few weeks – attempted gentler caresses than before? And understood, when she said she didn't want him inside her – that she didn't want to risk a baby now, when things were so mixed up?

Some of the books said even *complete* homosexuals could be changed, through hypnotism, through therapy, through suppressing their bad thoughts. Through marriage. She wanted to believe them. Sometimes she ached for Tyrconnel: she wanted to help him. Perhaps he had had a troubled childhood, as the books said. Though, when she had tentatively asked him about it, he laughed and denied it.

'No, darling. I just always rather fancied young men.'

Holly had flinched at that, and Tyrconnel looked straight at her, from beneath his hanging lock of hair, significantly.

'Maybe it's better,' he said, 'not to dig too deep after all, darling. You may not like what you find.'

When summer came, Tyrconnel encouraged her to move up to Stadhampton, to enjoy the sun and the gardens. He would visit at weekends.

Little Laura was already confident on the back of a pony, so long as her mother held her hand. She had learnt to recognise Holly now, for her red hair and 'nice smell'; she was Holly's friend. Daphne, preoccupied with getting back her figure and what she called her 'form' after Davina's birth, was less so. Not unfriendly, thought Holly; merely absent.

She ended up resorting to her old walks around the gardens with Nanny Walters.

'Haven't you got a little one yet?' Nanny would cry, familiar as ever. 'Well, shame on you. Letting down the side. Now, don't mind me, Lady Carr, I always did speak my mind and I've always had the highest regard for you.

I said to myself when I first saw you, "Now wouldn't she make a fine wife for Master Tyrconnel?" '

Holly could only smile patiently at Nanny's reminiscences, of which she realised she had now become a part. An invented part, like all the rest; and yet for a moment or two she was able to recall the world through its old, rosy haze of romance and dreams.

'So,' said Nanny, 'didn't it all happen exactly like I said? When we heard the news, downstairs, we was all so happy. The little American girl and his lordship. Like a fairy tale.'

Now, Holly thought, as the summer of 1959 chilled into autumn, the tale had changed. But it was not yet over. She would win Ty's real love yet, and, what was more, his desire. Some of the books said she could.

She would just have to become what he wanted.

XI

The disc jockey's voice purred over the crackle, '*This* is Radio Luxembourg, your station of the stars, bringing you all the hits of a new decade. And now for the Drifters, with "There Goes my Baby"....'

As usual the music wove and reeled, the reception poor. But still Holly pressed her ear close to the radio, her eyes closed, swaying with the sound, crooning.

Ever since she had stumbled upon Radio Luxembourg, she listened to it every day. It was her connection to a real world – the world of teenagers, young people, America – from which she felt herself growing ever more distant. Cocooned within rooms full of damask and mahogany, her sole rebellion an Elvis poster here in her dressing room, which Imogen had immediately insisted she remove, she clung more and more to the rebel rock-and-roll station and its fading sounds.

Perhaps homesickness had set in late. There had been so much to stave it off at first: the wedding, the novelty of Chester Square, then the trip to Manangwe. Only in the following summer, about a year ago now, had it begun to sink in that she was here, for good. The grey weather, the war-dilapidated streets, the cold houses: she had chosen them. Like her marriage, England had lost its aura of perfection. It was what she made of it.

As Helen and Nige had celebrated their second wedding anniversary and Tyrconnel had announced the *Courant*'s first annual profit – as the Conservatives won the general election last October, doubling their majority and returning Jamie safely to his seat – Holly had sunk into a mild depression. Perhaps it had never quite lifted. The one thought she clung to now was that her parents would be visiting, soon. In August. She had only a little more than a month to wait.

The tray the cook had sent up still lay on a table beside her: lettuce and tomatoes, a dry roll. She had eaten the apple, the only part of it which appealed to her. 'Please, please,' Eduardo had begged her, 'let me cook something, my lady, a little *fettucine*, a little *cotoletta*. Something nice. It is no good to eat like a rabbit. It is not 'ealthy.'

All the same, it was working. Holly rose for a moment to examine the result in the mirror: her reflection, gaunt, knobbly-kneed.

Imogen had noticed. 'Don't you think you're overdoing it a bit?' was all she said.

Helen disapproved. 'I should have thought you'd have more sense,' she had snorted, when Holly told her she had gone on a diet. 'Not on account of that husband of yours, is it? Oh, well. I suppose you'll grow out of it.'

Holly had not answered that accusation; but it was indeed on account of that husband of hers. And it was working. Or at least she thought so. Perhaps.

Oh well, she thought to herself now, turning sideways. *We're nearly there.*

The truth of it was that however many pounds she lost – it was nearly twenty now – the flesh refused to disappear from her bosom, her hips. Her arms, her legs, her face were thin: but the rest. . . .

She had developed her own secret wardrobe, for Tyrconnel; though sometimes, because it was more comfortable than dresses, it spilled over into her everyday life: narrow trousers, like Helen's, worn with loafers and tailored, mannish shirts. She rather liked the androgynous Holly who shot a challenging look back from the mirror, now – her face bare of all makeup except for a thin dusting of powder, her cheeks visible dents between cheekbones and jaw.

Only the hair was a disaster.

She had gone yesterday to André, to have him put the finishing touch to her new look. 'I want hair like my mother-in-law's. Lady Carr's,' she had told him.

He had tried to dissuade her. 'Ah, no! Such pretty curls.' He had patted the pageboy-bobbed red locks. 'You want it all – ' he snapped his fingers – 'to go?'

Holly had insisted, and he had done what she wanted. As she realised afterwards, she really couldn't blame him if her hair did not settle into the sleek cap she had envisaged. Nor had it wound into tiny curls, like Ingrid Bergman's in *For Whom the Bell Tolls*. No one could have guessed that once her hair was cut as short as a man's it would stand up on end.

But there it was. She had tried to pin it flat, to smooth it with hairspray. It only bounced up again. Finally she knew the only thing to do was cut it even shorter. She took her own scissors to it. Now it was spiky and ragged. She had hidden in her room last night until Tyrconnel had come home; then knocked tentatively on his door.

'My God,' he said. 'What the hell have you done?'

She had fled, jamming the door connecting their rooms shut behind her.

A few minutes later, she heard a gentle tap.

'Holly.' The voice was neither a command nor a plea,

just that perfectly neutral yet authoritative tone peculiar to Tyrconnel. 'Let me in.'

She backed away out of the light as he entered.

'Did André do this? It's hardly his usual style.' Tyrconnel ran a hand up the nape of her neck; considering, almost appreciative. The hand rested on her shoulder.

He approached her from behind. Holly felt the familiar quickening, a warm stab of desire. These days it did not take much to arouse her. She had adjusted herself to Tyrconnel's abrupt pace of lovemaking – to his infrequent demands – and, perhaps in response to this, her body had learnt to interpret the slightest touch as potentially arousing. His scent alone, a mixture of tobacco and cologne, could shoot down through her veins, sending even more unsettling messages.

What followed had taken on a familiar pattern. He would ask her to kneel, and climb above her. He took his member in his hands, or forced himself between her buttocks: that did not hurt any more, though it had for a long time. Now she felt only numbness.

Sometimes Holly longed to touch herself in places Tyrconnel never did – but she was not brave enough. The act, for Tyrconnel, was quickly finished, leaving her on a high plateau of desire from which it took hours to descend.

And last night it had been different only in one way. Tyrconnel had caressed her shorn head, clenched his fingers in the short strands of hair. And so she had counted the change, however ugly it made her, a small victory.

Until, falling back beside her, he said, 'It's not the same as the real thing, you know.'

Then he left her.

Not the same as the real thing, she thought now, turning from the mirror. She had thought she was changing him – yet still he talked of men. She had gone to so much trouble, and yet – *not the same as the real thing*.

But she would not admit defeat. She had succeeded, in small ways, in her efforts to reach him. He talked to her now about his days, his work. He rang her from the office sometimes, and took her out to lunch. He had met Nige and Helen, and they had spent several very normal, casual evenings together, during which Tyrconnel took on, and tried to charm away, Helen's veiled suspicion.

All last summer, he had made the effort to spend weekends with her at Stadhampton. Now business started taking him abroad again: to Switzerland, Taiwan, West Africa, Manangwe. He had offered to take her back to Manangwe; she refused. She wondered, but stopped herself from asking, if he would see Sam again there.

For them both, the subject was unmentionable. Holly's slightest hints were countered by Tyrconnel's, 'Don't you trust me?' After all, he had said he would be faithful.

Last spring, he had taken to spending the odd night in his office flat, above the *Courant*'s newsroom. The two rooms were bare and functional, just a bedroom and bath. He only used them, he said, when he was too exhausted to come home. Once a week – twice, at most.

On the surface, theirs was a normal marriage. *If there is such a thing as normal*, Holly thought now. She was beginning to wonder.

She heard the front door bang shut downstairs.

'Ty?' She opened her door and called down. He seemed not to hear her. From the top of the stairs she caught a glimpse of him shedding his jacket on to a chair, discarding his briefcase and wallet – then going out again.

She ran down the stairs after him. 'Ty?'

But he was gone.

She fingered the discarded wallet curiously. Italian leather, smooth, sleek, black; all the usual cards – club memberships, notes of bank accounts and addresses – in all the usual places. Plus a thick wad of cash. The briefcase was heavy, the jacket crumpled where he had dropped it. That was unlike him, Holly thought, and carried the jacket upstairs to his room.

The whole sequence – running in, running out – was unlike him. But no doubt there was an explanation.

The next day Imogen flew back to London from Capri, where she had spent the last two weeks with a childhood friend. Her jaw dropped in dismay when she saw Holly's hair.

'My God! Did André do that? I shall call on him personally and wring his neck.'

'No, really, Imogen. It's OK. I asked André to do it.'

Imogen only stared. The stare encompassed Holly's button-down shirt, grey flannels and brogues. 'Perhaps we should go shopping,' she said, 'and get you something more . . . feminine.'

Meekly Holly assented, thinking again of Tyrconnel's words. *Not the real thing.* Maybe she had gone too far. She would let her hair grow out again, and stop lounging around in men's clothes just because it was comfortable.

That night she and Imogen were in the middle of dinner when Tyrconnel ducked in the front door and ran upstairs.

'Hello Mother, hello darling. Meeting. Must rush.'

Sure enough, when Holly looked into his room later, there they lay. Those same three items: wallet, briefcase, jacket. Shoes this time, too: new hand-stitched ones from his cobbler in St James's.

It developed into a pattern. Three or four nights a week, Tyrconnel would drop into the house and disappear again. He was almost never home for dinner.

'We're getting the first year's results in from Manangwe,' he explained. 'Surprisingly good. The accountants down there have made a hash of things, though. We'll probably have to redo all their numbers.'

Sometimes he changed before going out again, into older suits and shoes. 'Grubby work, darling,' he said. 'More comfortable this way.'

'Do you want Eduardo to save you dinner?'

'No, I'll manage something at the office.'

He streaked past her down the stairs, and was off.

The fifth or sixth time it happened, Holly was downstairs and had time to go to the window and catch sight of him riding away in a cab.

That was odd, taking a cab instead of getting Withers to drive him. When she questioned the old chauffeur about it, Withers said only, 'His lordship said he didn't want to be keeping me up late.'

And, Holly noted, it was two in the morning before Tyrconnel returned.

She began to clock his comings and goings. There was a pattern to these night excursions. They usually lasted two hours – somewhere between nine and midnight. Occasionally later. Imogen, she thought, if she were home enough, would notice them too.

But Imogen was busy these days; she dined out often, several times a week venturing out in evening clothes and diamonds. When Holly asked her, one night, where she was going, Imogen said only, 'I'm visiting an old friend', and gave a mysterious smile.

So there was nothing to stop Holly listening for Tyrconnel's entrances and exits; until finally, she no longer listened casually, but waited. One night she ran to the door in time to see his cab snake southwards out of the square.

A gleam of light caught her eye – another taxi, depositing an old lady two houses down. Before she knew what she was doing she had run out and flagged it.

'Can you follow that cab?' she said, pointing.

The driver gave her an exasperated look. 'I'm not no detective, miss.'

But they were in luck. A traffic light had halted Tyrconnel's cab – she knew it was his, she could see his tall silhouette through the back window.

'*There*,' she said. 'Up ahead. Do you see?' For a moment triumph overcame her nervousness. If Tyrconnel found out she had followed him. . . .

She hunched low against the seat, only looking up from time to time to check that Tyrconnel was still ahead of them.

'Follow that cab,' the driver grumbled. But then he

chuckled. 'Just like in the cinema. Well, I'll tell you this, young lady, I'm not breaking any laws.'

'That's OK,' said Holly quickly. A few minutes later she asked, 'Which way are we going?'

'South bank, I should think. We're on the Vauxhall Bridge Road.'

South bank? thought Holly. What could Tyrconnel be doing in south London?

It was an awfully long way. Traffic was thin once they crossed the bridge. Holly straightened up in the back seat to look around. She saw a few streets of terraced houses mingled with the odd warehouse or office block; then dingier buildings, waste ground. They seemed to be driving on and on.

At last they pulled up. The street, lined with pinched houses facing a long row of locked garages, was eerily quiet.

'You want to get out here?'

'No. No, I'll wait.'

'I kept some distance between us, like. That all right?' The cabby grinned. Amusement with Holly and her escapade had taken over from annoyance.

'Could you stop the engine,' said Holly, 'and put out your lights? Just for a minute.'

Tyrconnel, as he climbed out, didn't seem to notice the other taxi halted some twenty yards behind his. He paid off the driver, climbed a flight of stairs, knocked.

Holly saw the door open to admit him. 'Wait for me, please,' she told her driver, and got out to examine the house.

It was of brick, painted an ugly shade of blue that glowed too bright even by night, under the streetlamps. It had two narrow windows on each floor; the top ones were boarded up, and all the rest were dark.

She couldn't imagine what Tyrconnel could be doing here.

A gang of men rounded the corner. One of them laughed and called out, 'Got a light, miss?'

She turned, alarmed. Her cab was still in sight. The men – Teddy boys, with slick long hair – stared at her as they passed. When they had gone, she ran back to the cab. Suddenly she felt far too conspicuous; she was still wearing the new expensive linen suit she had bought with Imogen that afternoon.

But she had noted the house number, and as they rounded the corner, she spotted the street sign: *Jermaine Street, SE5*.

When, two nights later, she heard Tyrconnel's key in the door at nine o'clock – heard the familiar thud of briefcase and wallet – she went to an upstairs front window to watch him depart, then dressed.

She slid into dark trousers, an old white shirt of Tyrconnel's – a discard, begged one day from Reeve – and then, daring what she had not before, she stole into Tyrconnel's room and searched through his wardrobe. She found a slouchy hat and a dark coat, big enough to conceal her, so long it nearly scraped the ground.

When she walked out to Eaton Square in search of a cab, the driver who drew up said, 'Evening, sir.' Then stared at her reflection in his mirror, with an expression somewhere between perturbation and disgust.

Holly ignored him. She gave him the address: 53 Jermaine Street.

When they arrived she asked him to stop at the end of the block and wait until she came back.

'I don't know if I like the look of this – '

'If you wait, I'll pay you double your meter.' Holly spoke in the coolest voice she could muster.

'You're a lady,' the driver said accusingly.

Holly only nodded.

'Pay me what's on the meter now, and we'll see.' The driver stopped his engine and switched his lights off.

Holly tried to damp down the panic that rose in her as she got out and saw the blue building ahead. 'Please,' she said. 'Try to wait. I won't be long.'

She didn't know what she would do next. She would have to improvise: feel out the lay of things. The cab driver had taken her for a man at first – that gave her confidence.

She climbed the steps of number 53 and tried the door. Miraculously, it was open. No one confronted her as she made her way into the hall, lit by a hanging bulb: linoleum floors and ugly brown wainscoting.

She started up the stairs. At the top, suddenly, a man barred her way. She tried to push past him.

'Who you looking for?' he said accusingly. He sounded young; he was heavy-set, muscular, but she could not see his face. The hall was dim, and it seemed to her, bathed in a curious red light.

She tried to duck around him.

'I said, who're you looking for?'

'Carr,' she said nervously, in as low a voice as she could manage. 'Tyrconnel Carr.'

The man stared unnervingly at her. She bent her head.

'Or – *John*.'

'He expecting you?'

She nodded.

'All right. Here.' The man worked a key loose from a ring that hung on his belt. It had a number on it; Holly peered at it in the dark. Five.

The man passed her on his way downstairs and she was left alone. She moved on, and the hall seemed to grow darker and darker, extending into a sort of black tunnel ahead of her, as if it connected two or three of these narrow houses.

As she walked, it seemed to her that she heard voices behind the walls. Talking, arguing, grunting, playing music. As her eyes grew accustomed to the red light – she saw now that it came from a red bulb in a glass cage overhead – she could see painted figures on the walls surrounding her. Figures of men, some of them familiar, as if copied from photographs: Michelangelo's David, larger than life. And other men, some thin and lithe, mere

148

boys, some older, broader, the outlines of their muscles brutally rendered.

They peopled the walls; they towered over her. Her heart pounding, she searched for numbers on the doors, but there were none. She tried the first door to her left, and it opened without the key. But inside the room was empty, except for a lone figure on a bed, crying.

She withdrew. What was this place? She moved further down the corridor, listening for the sound of Tyrconnel's voice, but she could not distinguish it. A door lay half-open ahead of her. She peered in, only long enough to see the walls: painted blood-red, hung with knives and chains. On the floor she saw a tangle of men. She could not tell how many – how many limbs in the air, how many bodies wrangling, how old and young. She drew back against the wall, her heart pounding.

She wanted to close her eyes and run away. It was real. All that Tyrconnel talked about, all that she had resisted believing. So many men, with other men. Strangers.

But she walked on, and tried each door in turn. None opened. The corridor grew darker, until she could barely see the painted giants on the walls. At the very end of the hall, a door gave way.

The room was vast: a sort of attic, with a curtained window at the far end. A bed, and a ladder propped up against one wall, three men standing beside it. They did not seem to hear the door open; they were arguing.

'You said,' a voice accused, 'you'd take care of him.'

She recognised the voice: Tyrconnel's. His tall figure, his hair tousled, in an out-of-date suit, pointing to a lump on the bedclothes. A boy. Holly couldn't see him clearly; he seemed thin, his chest naked, and mouse-coloured hair hung in his eyes.

'Joey,' said one of the men who stood with Tyrconnel: a heavy young man in shirtsleeves like the one who had barred Holly's way. 'Now your friend John's here, you're going to be nice to him, like we told you.'

'He in't no John,' the boy spat out resentfully. 'I seen him –'

Before he could finish, the other heavy young man stepped over and cuffed him on the head. 'A'right, sir?' he said to Tyrconnel. He held the boy's head up by the hair.

'I'm afraid he's going to have to be punished,' said Tyrconnel, and Holly thought she saw him smile.

She drew back, because for a moment it seemed that he was looking at her; that those narrow, direct eyes had fixed on her through the open crack of the door. But his gaze swept on.

'Here?' she heard one of the young men saying, and before she knew what was happening, or how, the men had wrestled the boy up on to the ladder. One held him fast and the other wrapped rope around his arms, tying them to the frame. His head twisted, writhed as they tied his ankles; his toes scraped at the bare floor.

She watched, wanting to move, to flee, but she could not do it. Tyrconnel shucked off his trousers and moved forward.

And then he hesitated, murmured an endearment, toyed with the boy's long hair. 'I thought,' he said, 'we weren't going to have to do this.'

The boy jerked his head away and clenched his fists. Tyrconnel put his hands around his neck: tightened them. Jammed himself up against him, heaving, thrusting.

For a sickening moment Holly felt herself within that body. She thought, *I have been there.* She wanted to run forward, but felt paralysed, not knowing what the men in that room would do to her if they found her; and then it was all over very quickly.

'Go on,' said Tyrconnel, with a twitch of his head at the other men.

They followed him: did the same as he had.

The boy let out a broken moan. 'I know who you are!' he shouted out, as the second man pulled back. He turned his head to look at Tyrconnel. 'I know who you are, I seen your face in a magazine. It's Lord something. Lord Ca –'

The boy's voice fell silent. Tyrconnel's hands muffled his mouth.

'I thought,' Tyrconnel said, 'we were friends. It would be a pity for that to end.'

The boy spat through his fingers, 'Friends? Don't make me laugh. I hate you.'

'Don't be a bad boy, Joey.'

'How much is it worth to you? I could go to the police – '

'So that's how grateful you are. I found you on the streets, Joey. I gave you money. I rescued you – '

'You're just a fucking pervert, that's what you are.'

Tyrconnel's face contorted. 'So that's what you really think, is it? You little tart.'

'Fucking pervert. I hate you.'

Tyrconnel's face went still. 'How long,' he said, walking to the wall, 'do you think it takes to bleed to death, Joey?'

Joey cursed again.

'You know, I'm quite serious.'

Holly saw Tyrconnel walking forward, as if straight at her. She backed away from the door; she had seen the knife in his hand.

'When they find you,' said Tyrconnel, 'they'll think you did yourself in. Suicide, after all, is common enough among runaway runts like you.'

'You're fucking sick. I'll go to the police this time, I will. I'll go to the papers.'

Still, the boy looked defiant, as if he knew Tyrconnel was bluffing. But then as Tyrconnel took hold of one of his hands and jerked it away from the rope and the ladder, laying the blade against the inside of his wrist, he screamed.

'I don't think you love me, Joey,' said Tyrconnel.

For a second Holly could see clearly: the boy's wrist, above the rope that bound it. The flick of the knife. Slashing twice, three times, thudding against wood. The ladder.

She could see the blood spurt. A scream stopped in her throat.

She heard Joey's shouts, still, and then Tyrconnel:

'What's a life like yours really worth to anyone, Joey? What would you have made of it anyway?'

Now there was only silence, interspersed with the boy's diminishing curses.

Something unfroze in Holly, told her she could move, get away. She walked quickly, silently, back through the door and down the stairs.

The yellow light in the foyer came as a shock. She almost dropped the key on the floor there, but, on second thoughts, clung to it as she ran out the door.

The rest of the night became a haze.

She searched for the cab, which had gone; then a telephone. Until the ambulance came, she hid in the shadows of Jermaine Street. She saw Tyrconnel run out the door of the blue house and disappear round a corner. She saw the ambulancemen knock at the door, heard the arguments; saw the humped figure borne away at last on a stretcher. And she was relieved. She had not been sure that they would come. When she had refused to give her name, she had not been sure they would believe her.

When she tried, later, to think how she reached home, her mind was a blank. She could guess only that instinct had led her towards a main road; that she had followed the lights and traffic and eventually found a cab. Luckily, she reflected later, London was a safe city at night. At least for some.

She found Tyrconnel undressing in his room. And it was then, when she first saw his face, that the nightmare vision overwhelmed her. The darkness, the bodies, the blood. And yet he looked as clean as if water and his memory had washed it all away.

She blinked and walked towards him. Her eyes, her throat felt dry. 'I know where you were tonight.'

'Oh?' His voice, cool and flippant, hit her like a slap. 'I didn't know they let women into the Reform Club. But then, perhaps, to judge by your costume, they couldn't tell.'

'I know where you were,' Holly said again, reaching into her pocket and drawing out the key. Number five.

Tyrconnel blinked, and for a fraction of a second his face froze. 'I've no idea what you're trying to tell me.'

'53 Jermaine Street,' said Holly levelly. 'You tried to kill someone.'

Tyrconnel reached into her hand, examined the key, and, before she could think, went to the window and hurled it out. She did not even hear it fall.

'They'll find out anyway,' she said defensively. 'I'll tell people what I saw. His name was Joey. How old was he? Thirteen, fourteen?'

Suddenly Tyrconnel was on top of her, forcing her on to the floor. He was shaking her, shaking her so her teeth jarred. Then his fist slammed into the side of her head.

For a second or two, not very long, she lost track of where she was; when she came to, he was carrying her into her room. He dumped her on her bed, locked the door to the corridor and pocketed the key.

'I've had about enough,' he said, standing over her. 'You're going to sleep, and when you wake up you're going to forget you ever thought you saw anything.'

Holly shook her head, but it was sore and she could not seem to form words.

That night she lay on the line between dreaming and waking, haunted by visions. Often she seemed to be awake; she could see the room around her, yet it was not her room any more. The walls were red. Men were in it: boys. They crawled over each other like ugly satyrs. They bore down on her, brandishing knives.

When morning came, her eyes were itchy; she found she could escape through the connecting door and Tyrconnel's room, for he had already gone. She dressed and went out into the Square to look for her key. Number five, her proof. But she had no luck. She searched the morning papers, then the evening ones, for news of Joey's rescue. Or his death.

153

'Is this what you're looking for?' Tyrconnel stood in her dressing room doorway that night. Turning away, he tossed a folded copy of the *Courant* on to the floor.

KNIFE WOUNDS

An unidentified male was taken to King's College Hospital last night after suffering knife wounds. Police said the premises where he was found had been declared unfit for habitation and would be closed.

'That's all you'll find,' said Tyrconnel, 'in any of the papers.'

'The police must have . . . known, what that place was.' Holly was aghast.

'There are things the police don't want to know.'

Before Tyrconnel could turn away again, Holly said, 'I could talk to them. Tell them everything.'

'And what would they see? An hysterical girl. Making up stories.'

'But you know I'm not.' Holly's voice was low.

'Yes,' said Tyrconnel. 'You are. If you're a little frightened, Holly, maybe it will teach you not to meddle in my affairs. They're too big for you.'

'But I saw what you did. It won't go away.'

Tyrconnel strode towards her now, with a purpose. He pushed her back in the chaise-longue where she was sitting, his hand arched against the base of her throat. 'You never seem to believe me, Holly, when I tell you you'll have to do as I say.'

'I don't see how – '

He went on, overriding her. 'Now, you must realise I can make your life very . . . uncomfortable. And for what good? The best thing you can do, Holly, is put all these imaginings out of your mind.'

'You know they're not imaginings. You could go to jail. You said so.'

'But I won't.' Tyrconnel paused. 'I think you'll find that

I cover my tracks well. That house you think you saw? It will be closed. Boarded up. Your witnesses? They'll be all over London. If they would ever have talked to you in the first place.'

Holly fell silent. She knew what he said was true. There would be other runaways – other houses, springing up like weeds when one was destroyed. She could not know where they all were. She could not stop them from existing.

That night and the next, she dreamed of them. At first she thought the nightmares would leave her, if by day she could put the horrors from her mind. But her dreams only grew more intense, more vivid. Gigantic red figures towering above her; Tyrconnel, with a knife in his hand, poised to murder her.

During the days, she was preoccupied, frightened, obsessed with the thought, *How can I get out?* Her parents were coming in a week's time. She would have to tell them what had happened. She knew from the mirror that she did not look well, yet could not seem to rouse herself to do the things she knew she ought to: buy some new clothes, trim her nails, repair her hair. The inside of her mind was an uncomfortable place to be.

In desperation she turned to Imogen.

'What?' said Imogen, when she had barely begun. 'You did what? Followed your husband?'

'I had to. I needed to know where he was going. He went to this – house, in south London, and it was horrible. There were these boys, runaways – '

'I don't want to hear any more.'

'But, Imogen – '

'I have no desire to be privy to your obscene inventions.'

'But I'm not inventing anything!'

'Of course you are! You do nothing all day but sit around and listen to that appalling music. . . . It's no wonder if your imagination's running away with you. You need to get out of the house. Find a distraction – I don't care what it is.'

With a look of distaste Imogen turned her back on Holly and lit a cigarette. Holly knew she had to give up.

A few hours later, dressed for lunch, Imogen took a cab to Derry Street.

Her gaze swept neatly over Tyrconnel's new office, starkly modernist in style, nearly empty except for the many-compartmented, black lacquered cube of a desk and the two uncomfortably low leather chairs where Tyrconnel interviewed – or interrogated – his employees. The plate-glass window looked out over the Thames.

'Just what,' Imogen said, 'do you think you've been up to?'

'Mother!' Tyrconnel stood up with an unperturbed smile. 'Sweet of you to drop in. I'd have offered you lunch here long ago. Only you seem to be so busy with Monty of late.'

'That's nothing to do with you.' Imogen's words blasted across the room; her son, without intending to, stepped back as if to swerve out of their path. 'Have you any idea,' Imogen went on, in a marginally softer tone, 'of the story your wife told me this morning? Or attempted to tell me. As, naturally, I would have nothing to do with it.' Resting her polished fingertips on his desk, she leaned forward and spat out the next words in a whisper. 'Faggots. Scabby little runaways. She said she'd followed you to some place in south London and seen you – '

'That's absurd. She's making things up. You know as well as I do – '

'Don't lie to me, Tyrconnel.'

'Mother, I – '

'I know the world as well as the next woman. Naturally – ' Imogen paused to choose her words – 'I had hoped that whatever inclinations you thought you possessed, once you married – '

'Your idea, let me remind you.'

'When you married someone so ridiculously young, I

156

thought you were at least going to make an effort! At least to make your wife happy and keep up appearances. You are a grave disappointment.'

'Oh? And what about Jamie? The perfect husband. . . .'

'*Jamie* has a proper marriage, with a wife who adores him and two lovely girls. I really don't care to hear about anything else.'

'Well.' Tyrconnel took two conscious steps back, until he was framed by the window, the innocent blue sky. 'I don't know what you intend me to do, Mother.'

'Your wife is a loose cannon. Now she *knows*, and now you're going to have to do whatever it takes to shut her up. Your timing could hardly be worse, you know. Her parents are coming in a week.'

Tyrconnel registered shock. 'Christ. I forgot. What'll they think when they see her? All that weight she's lost, and the hair. Let alone – '

'One has to wonder,' said Imogen, 'whether she's entirely all right in the head.'

'I'm afraid she is, more's the pity. If she weren't, it might explain a hell of a lot.'

For a moment Tyrconnel and Imogen looked at each other; not speaking, but measuring each other's thoughts.

A few hours later, Imogen consulted her medicine cabinet. Everything was still there, of course: uppers, downers. Her doctor had prescribed them liberally after John died, but she had only taken a few, finding them too unsettling.

She wondered if they were still any good.

And if so, how? How much, and when?

To slip them into food or drink – a mere sleight of hand. No doubt she could manage it. Anyway, it wouldn't take much. A few sharp doses should be enough to upset the system.

XII

This time the Claytons flew across the Atlantic. It was Holly's mother's first experience of air travel.

'Never again,' she pronounced, in the Daimler on the way into London. 'I would sail rather than go through that, any day. I've never felt so *mauled* in my life.'

Joe Clayton overrode her. 'Don't listen to your mother. Back in the States these days I fly all the time. The sky's the way to go, Hollis.'

Holly smiled at her father. It felt comforting to be called by her old, awkward name. Sandwiched between her parents in the broad back seat, she felt a calm reassurance begin to warm her: as if she had been out in the cold, her extremities nearly frozen.

But she would be all right now.

She tried to concentrate on what her father was saying: something about the house in Florida. But again, for a moment her eyelids drooped. She could not think why she felt so sleepy.

She tried to cover it up. 'That's good, Daddy,' she said. 'You must be going down there a lot.'

'To Cincinnati?' Clayton looked surprised. 'Not these days, honey. That's why I retired.'

'Oh. Sorry. I thought you were talking about Key Isotro.'

'The Keys! Well, that's another kettle of fish. Do you know, I bagged three dolphin just two weeks ago?'

'I think it's appalling,' broke in Holly's mother. 'Killing those poor dear harmless creatures.' Holly couldn't help noticing, looking at her, that she had aged in the last two years. Tiny broken capillaries lined her cheeks, and the yellow tone of her stiffly curled hair had grown more artificial.

'Dolphin the *fish*,' said Joe Clayton, exasperated, 'not

the mammal. I've told your mother a hundred times. Dolphin the fish is just mighty good eating. Oh, well.' He curled an arm around his daughter's shoulder. 'Good to see you, chickadee. It's been a long time.'

'It's good – ' Holly's voice stuck in her throat – 'to see you too, Daddy.'

Her parents talked on, but her head felt heavy and it was all she could do just to keep awake. Even though for days she had worried, and she wondered again now: when will I tell them? How can I tell them? I have to tell them. How can I say it?

When they passed a familiar complex of factories, she said suddenly, unwittingly interrupting them: 'You know, the Carrs used to own this land. They sold it before the war, and, boy, do they regret it now! You know, I keep finding out they own this or that piece of land. . . . Sometimes I think I'll find out they own all of London!' She giggled.

Her father blinked at her, puzzled, then patted her shoulder.

Her mother looked at her strangely. 'Didn't you hear what I was saying, dear? I thought you'd be dying to know Beth Stillman was getting married.'

'Beth?' Holly's voice was small.

'I thought she used to be your best friend.'

'She was. I mean, is.' Holly frowned; she couldn't seem to piece Beth's features together in her head. So she tried harder. If only she didn't feel so sleepy. What could it be? She'd slept for nine hours last night; even the dreams were abating.

For the rest of the journey, despite her parents' sporadic conversation, she was silent.

She made a special effort for dinner that night. But somehow all of her dresses looked wrong. They hung too loosely; the bright-coloured ones showed up her pallor. In the end she wore her new linen suit, although she knew her mother and Imogen would be dressed more formally.

She tried to decorate the suit with Imogen's pearls, a scarf and a pair of ornate pearl clip earrings; the scarf did not quite match and the jewellery was too elaborate for the outfit, but she did not know what else to do. Her hair had not grown out much, but her parents had been too polite to mention it.

Dinner, she thought, went well, normally. Thank goodness she felt more awake. Jamie came, although Daphne was in the country; and it was he who, in the end, kept the conversation going with his tales of drunken journalists and Tory skulduggery. Tyrconnel said little, and Holly, deliberately, wasn't speaking either to him or his mother. Imogen, who once had been her friend. Who now wouldn't even believe her.

Tired from their flight, the Claytons went upstairs to bed early. With Imogen, they had discussed plans: at the end of the week, everyone was going to Stadhampton.

'In the meantime,' said Holly's mother, 'if you're planning any little lunches or tea parties, Imogen, don't let me get in your way.'

'I'll let you know,' said Imogen sweetly, coolly.

As if she were watching from high up on a mountain, Holly observed the little manoeuvres and smiled.

Once his wife was in bed, Joe Clayton found Tyrconnel in the library.

'Ah. Tyrconnel.' He smiled nervously, and took the tumbler of whisky he was offered.

'Cheers.' Tyrconnel lifted his glass.

'Cheers.' Clayton's face dropped. 'Ah, say, Tyrconnel, I don't know quite how to ask you this.'

Tyrconnel looked innocent. 'Ask ahead.'

'I don't know if I'm exaggerating things. Just being a silly old worried father. . . .'

'What do you mean?'

'Hollis doesn't look well to me. She's too thin. And she doesn't sound quite right either. In the car, she kept losing track of what we were saying . . . I thought she'd be excited to see us, but it was like she kept drifting away.'

Tyrconnel's brow wrinkled.

'I just wondered . . . if you thought she was OK. I mean, she might have picked up something. One of those Asian flus. . . .'

'I'd been wondering that myself.' Tyrconnel studied the reflections of light in his glass. 'Not that I like to jump to conclusions. But there has been some – well, to be honest, some peculiar behaviour.'

Clayton answered instantly. 'What kind of behaviour?'

Tyrconnel met the other man's eyes briefly, then looked down again, distracted. 'Well, you see what she's done to her hair.'

'I know. It looks awful. Why'd she do that?'

Tyrconnel shrugged. 'I don't know. And – well, you won't have seen it today, but she's taken to dressing rather strangely too. Putting on bits of my old clothes, just thrown together. And – sometimes she goes out at night and won't say where she's been.'

Clayton looked alarmed.

'Oh, not often, Clay. Only once or twice. But there are odd incidents . . . well, probably I shouldn't tell you. I don't know if it's anything.'

'What? What do you mean you shouldn't tell me?'

Tyrconnel swallowed. 'There are times when she has clearly been – making things up. Not often.'

'What kind of things?'

'Stories. Of a nasty, or even a – scandalous nature. Concerning me. I don't really like to think about it.'

Clayton was silent. After a moment, he said, 'I just don't get it.'

Tyrconnel nodded. 'It's very distressing. I suppose it's as well I should warn you. In case she says anything. You know.'

'What do you mean? What would she say?' Clayton's eyes widened.

Tyrconnel twitched his head. 'Accusations, I'm afraid,

of a rather – nasty nature, to do with my . . . conduct. It doesn't happen often, fortunately, and lately she seems to have stopped. I must say I'm relieved. Of course there's nothing in what she says, but it has all been rather – hurtful to me.' Tyrconnel paused, looking down. 'I'm no professional, but, I'm afraid sometimes . . . One might almost say that some of Holly's behaviour resembled the classic schizophrenic type.'

Clayton straightened, startled. 'No. No. I don't think it can be. I mean – we don't have any of that in the family.'

Tyrconnel gave a faint smile: an attempt at reassurance. 'Of course I don't mean that it *is*. As I say, I'm no professional. I've probably overstated the case. As you can imagine, we didn't wish to alarm you. That's why I didn't mention any of this by letter or over the phone. Frankly, we hoped that by the time you came it would just go away.'

Clayton shook his head. 'My God.'

'I'm sorry.' Tyrconnel studied his father-in-law. 'Of course, we'll all do what we can. What can I say?'

During the next week, mystified and weighed down by an obscure guilt, Joe Clayton attempted to raise his daughter's spirits. To coax the old, contented Hollis out of the alternately nervy and lethargic girl he saw before him.

He did not know much about psychology, and had only his common sense to fall back on. And that common sense told him Hollis was probably just thinking too much. What she needed was entertainment, shopping, seeing new sights. To that end Clayton rented a car and planned trips: Canterbury, Salisbury, Stonehenge. His daughter was mutely compliant.

At other times, unpredictable times, she talked a blue streak about anything in sight – anything that seemed to come into her head.

Something, thought Joe Clayton, was definitely wrong.

A notion occurred to him, and he tried to get his wife to test it. Perhaps Hollis was having some – female trouble.

Perhaps she was trying to have a baby, and not getting one. The Claytons had known that desperate kind of waiting well enough themselves.

His wife, who didn't know what all the fuss was about – all the girls in New York dieted, she said, and why was he making such a to-do about a minor disaster at the hairdresser's? – finally agreed to sound Hollis out on the subject.

Nothing doing. At least nothing that Hollis would tell her mother.

At the end of the week they all went to Stadhampton, and there Joe began to think he was seeing some improvement. Hollis had begun to learn to ride, and he encouraged her to go out and practise.

The second time he suggested it, she was reluctant. 'Maybe some other time,' she said, and looked up at him longingly. 'I was hoping we'd get the chance to talk, Daddy.'

Something in the look on her face alarmed him. 'Oh, no,' he said. 'I mean, there's plenty of time for that, chickadee, but right now the weather's fine and it'd do me a power of good to see you ride.'

Obedient, Hollis changed clothes and went out; when she returned there was even a little colour in her cheeks and she seemed to have abandoned the notion of a one-to-one talk. Fresh air, Clayton decided, and lots of it. That was what she needed.

As for conversation, he was not short of that, because Tyrconnel was looking forward to expanding his mining operations into other African countries, and acquiring a transport network to cut export costs. The two men spent many hours in the library examining and refining his plans.

When the Claytons had a little less than a week left in England, Joe suggested that they take their daughter out to Somerset. He liked the notion of the West Country; something hearty and healthy-sounding about it. He looked it up in his guide. 'See – ' He showed his daughter. 'We could try this place. The Overton House Hotel. Tennis courts, outdoor swimming pool – baths in every room, your mother'll like that. How 'bout if we go out there for a couple of days? That is, if your husband'll let you come with us.' He winked at Tyrconnel, who was sitting across from them in the hunt room at Stadhampton.

'Fine by me.' Tyrconnel smiled. And so it was all set.

The hotel was like an inferior version of Stadhampton – smaller, mustier and serving up a stodgier cuisine. The Claytons tried to pretend they did not notice this. Except for Holly. Her enthusiasm was real. She had not guessed at the relief she would feel at being away from the Carrs.

How easy she felt with her father near. How comfortable. The curious mood swings she had experienced in the last weeks – the jolts of energy out of nowhere, the sleepiness – seemed to have vanished when she left Stadhampton. She was on an even keel. Tomorrow, she decided, or the next day, she would talk to her father.

On her first night at Overton House, she enjoyed an uninterrupted sleep, and, for once, did not wake up feeling groggy. The next morning they drove out to the Quantock hills, and in the afternoon she played tennis with her mother. Tired out that night, she hoped she would sleep so well again.

But it was not to be. The dreams – whose torments had been erratic in the last few weeks, worse when she felt nervous and wakeful, nearly absent when she was sleepy – came back on the second night, more frightening and vivid than ever. Again she saw it all: the flailing bodies, the blood-red walls.

Her screams woke her parents.

Her father ran in to her first, and shook her awake. 'Honey. It's OK. You're dreaming.'

Holly stared, then gradually readjusted to the room around her. At her bedside her father flicked on a light.

'No,' she said, confused. 'It's OK. I can see.'

'What were you dreaming about, chickadee?'

'Oh, Daddy.' Holly was panting, and her sheets were drenched. 'I don't want to remember. It was awful. . . .'

'Shh.' Her father stroked her back, soothed her. 'It's all better now. Let it out. You've got all the time in the world.'

Holly's mother, who had followed Joe out of bed, stood in the doorway.

Holly told them about the dream – this dream blending with all the other ones. It was a relief to speak of it, to conjure it in the light. When she was done, she trembled in her father's arms.

'There,' he said soothingly, as he used to when she was a small girl, 'you've let out the nightmare. Now it won't bother you any more.'

'No,' said Holly. She clung to him tighter. 'That's just it. It wasn't – a dream. It was real.'

'Of course it was a dream,' interjected her mother, her tone not entirely sympathetic. 'It was a nightmare, just like we all have, and now we can all go back to bed.'

'It wasn't a dream,' Holly mumbled, and shook her head.

'What do you mean?' said her father.

She began to tell him.

When she had finished, her father still looked on blankly, understandingly – as if that look of noncommittal acceptance conveyed understanding. Holly was not sure.

She began to be alarmed. 'What's the matter? Don't you believe me?'

Joe Clayton looked troubled. 'I – I don't know, honey. That doesn't matter, really, I guess.'

'Of course it matters!' his wife snapped. She had moved to a chair by the window, where she sat agitatedly smoking. 'Of course it matters where Hollis gets these ideas. It sounds to me like she's been reading dirty books. Where else would she fill her head up with this kind of – filth?'

'I'm not!' Holly shouted back. 'I'm not making it up! You think Tyrconnel's such a perfect husband, I know it seems impossible. But it's true!'

'Now, honey,' said Joe Clayton. 'Be reasonable. Tyrconnel is a perfectly decent, upright man – '

165

'Oh. So I suppose you believe him, too.'

'It's not a question of believing – '

'Yes, it is, Daddy.' The rims of her eyes red, her jaw set in a waiflike face below her cropped, matted hair, Holly was adamant. 'It's just that. You have to believe me.'

'Hollis,' snapped her mother, 'you may have been having bad dreams lately, but that's no reason to take us all on this merry-go-round at four in the morning. You always were a spoilt child – '

'You let her alone!' Joe Clayton's voice boomed at his wife in reprimand.

'Stop it!' screamed Holly. 'If you're not going to believe me, forget it. I never should have trusted you anyway.'

Joe looked down at her, worried. 'We never said we didn't believe you.'

'Well, I don't,' interrupted Holly's mother.

'Fine!' shouted Holly, her eyes beginning to run with tears. 'Have it that way, then! Tyrconnel's your perfect son – the son you always wanted.'

'Now, Hollis.' Clayton tried to stroke his daughter's back, but, sobbing, she struck his hand away.

'Why don't you just adopt him and get rid of me and have what you want?'

'Honey.' Clayton reached out, despairing. 'No one could replace you. You're our only daughter. Now, I might have said some time that Tyrconnel was like a son to me. But I wouldn't have said it if I didn't think it'd make you happy.'

'Don't you see?' Holly cowered, meeting his look with wild eyes. 'He's fooled you well and good. Just like he fooled me.'

This time Clayton held back the soothing words, did not answer. For a moment he wondered, doubted. Surely, he thought, my daughter would not make all this up.

For one thing, where would she have begun to learn it all?

But now, as Holly persisted, the tears, the insistence, the shouting, only seemed to confirm the truth of Tyrconnel's analysis. *Invention. Schizophrenia.* After all, the notion of

Tyrconnel being one of those. . . . It was ludicrous. He was a regular fellow: perfectly straight and normal and decent. You could see that just to look at him.

Joe Clayton laid a soothing hand on his daughter's head. 'I think what you need most, honey, is some sleep.'

'I don't want to sleep. I want you to believe me.'

A few minutes later, Joe beckoned his wife from the room. Sleeping tablets were one thing with which she was always well supplied. He returned to Holly's room with a glass of water and two tranquillisers. He hoped the dosage wasn't too strong. He just wanted her to sleep until the morning. Then they could take her back to Stadhampton. All as planned.

Holly looked up at him, suspicious.

'We believe you,' said Joe. 'Now, will you take these to put you back to sleep? I'm sure we'll all feel better in the morning.'

Reluctantly, with him still watching her, she took them.

Joe looked in on her later as she slept. Hollis would need protecting, he realised now. From herself – from the weakness in her mind. Thank God for Tyrconnel.

Joe Clayton and his son-in-law had one last interview before the Claytons left for France. They agreed it was best that the Claytons should continue on, as planned, to Paris and the Riviera. For them to change arrangements would only alarm Holly; she already seemed worried and overly suspicious.

'Of course,' said Joe, 'we could take her back to the States if you thought that was the best answer. There are very good doctors – '

'Still, it might not be wise to uproot her.' Tyrconnel's steps traced a repeating pattern on the worn Oriental carpet of the front parlour. Both men knew they had only a short time to talk; Imogen, Holly and her mother were due back from shopping at noon, and soon after that the Claytons would be setting off for Dover.

'So – ' Clayton spoke heavily – 'do you know of any-place she could go to – recuperate?'

Neither of them spoke the dread words: *hospital, mad-house, asylum.*

'Mm,' said Tyrconnel. 'A sort of rest home. There are plenty about. I'm sure my mother will know of a few, where perhaps one of her friends has been. Somewhere with nice grounds.'

'Yes.' Clayton nodded. 'Of course,' he said gruffly, 'if there's any trouble about . . . I mean, I know these places' fees can go sky-high.'

'Thank you, Clay. I'm sure we can manage. I'll let you know.'

And now, as a heavy silence fell, Clayton shook his head. 'I just wish I knew where it came from.'

Tyrconnel looked at him warily. 'No one can ever guess the roots of these things.' His brown eyes – hooded, almost gentle – studied his father-in-law. 'I'm sure she'll get better, you know. She's young. It may not even recur. If we're lucky.'

Joe bit his lip. 'I know.' He paused, then shook his head. 'Those crazy things she was saying – '

'You mustn't think too much of it. I suppose . . . Holly was a very sheltered girl. Some aspects – of marriage seemed to shock her.' Tyrconnel swallowed, then spoke again with difficulty. 'Of course one tries to be gentle. . . .'

'Now, I won't have you blaming yourself.'

Tyrconnel looked down; for a moment he hid his face in his hands. 'Of course I try not to,' he said, his composure regained. 'And I try to tell myself – well, there may be other sources for those – fantasies. Holly's been seeing a lot of a rather dissolute couple. . . .'

'She never mentioned any friends.'

'Bohemian types. Chap runs an art magazine. Naturally I try to discourage it. One never knows what sorts of books, or films – '

Joe Clayton cleared his throat. 'Well, there you go. That

may help explain it. And I don't suppose – well, it'll do no harm if she's away from people like that for a while.'

There seemed nothing more to be said. In silence, each with a newspaper in hand, the two men settled down to await the return of the Daimler.

Late at night, two days after the Claytons left for France, the doorbell rang at Chester Square.

Holly ignored it at first. It was almost midnight, and she was in bed. If it was important, the servants would answer it.

But it rang again, insistently. And again.

She went downstairs.

Before she opened the door all the way, they forced it in. It banged against her elbow and she cried out in startled pain.

Four men in boiler suits pushed into the hall and surrounded her.

'If you'll just come quietly, Lady Carr. . . .'

'What?' Holly tried to run back, but they took hold of her. Two held her arms and two held her legs; they were wrapping something like tape around her ankles.

'Just be quiet, Lady Carr. We won't hurt you.'

She registered the flat northern accent, and had time only for the beginning of a scream.

She was being kidnapped.

She did not know when or if the scream ended. Something jabbed her arm. As they carried her out into the waiting van, she felt herself falling into blackness.

XIII

Outside the tall, narrow window, a single cherry tree was beginning to flower; when Holly saw it, she knew it must be spring.

It hardly seemed as if she had been here so long; and

then at times, it seemed an eternity. The same single bed, the same white-walled room with its view of a strip of garden, the same featureless institutional halls.

The objective facts she knew, even now, were distressingly few. She knew that this house – this hospital – was somewhere in Norfolk. She knew that whatever she said, the doctors would greet with the same air of patronising, pretended belief; that they did not really believe anything she told them. She knew that she was not going home any time soon. Maybe, when Tyrconnel said so.

You love your husband, don't you? they said.

I don't know.

She had learnt to move carefully when she woke, because the injections they gave her, and later the pills, slowed her reflexes. She had forgotten the feel of agility, and could still feel surprise to hear herself speak now and realise that the drugs no longer furred her tongue.

But then, she had little occasion to speak. Only her mind, in its numbed state, continued to count out the days like beads on a string.

September, October, November, December. January, February, March. How long?

Until you are better, Mrs Carr. We've told you.

If only she could remember: fill in the empty spaces.

All the first weeks had become a distant blur. She sensed, though she could not remember, that she had struggled; though how she had ever even tried to fight them, what means she could have used, what strength she could have drawn on, were now a mystery to her.

She remembered long isolated days behind the locked door of this same room; visits from Tyrconnel and Imogen, then from Helen. Helen was the only one she would talk to.

Get me out, she said.

She wrote to her parents – *Please, Daddy, take me out of here, take me home* – but the letters they wrote back to her never seemed even to acknowledge the ones she had sent.

Co-operate, Helen had said, sensibly. *That way they'll let you out.*

And so, gradually, Holly had. They had let her out of her room – into the dining room, into the garden. The daily injections changed to pills. Christmas came. And then the news which sent her right back to where she had begun.

Her father was dead. His boat had overturned in a storm off Key Isotro, just after Christmas.

Her memory of that one moment – when she heard the news – was crystal clear. A dull grey Saturday; the Christmas tree still standing in the visitors' hall. Tyrconnel's and Imogen's faces: long, pale, sombre, mouths searching for words.

'Darling.' It was Imogen who reached out to her: who spoke first. 'I'm so very sorry. You will have to be brave. . . .' But she hadn't felt brave; she had felt terrified, then angry.

The world was falling from under her.

She screamed and shouted. She could still remember some of the words. 'It's not true! You're lying. I know you're lying. You killed him!'

'*Holly.*'

With that, Tyrconnel's fist crashed against her cheek.

And then, again, her mind went blank.

She made a recovery. It had taken a long time. Tyrconnel and Imogen no longer came to the hospital, and in a way she was glad. She could almost forget Tyrconnel's face; forget that when she returned from here it must be to him. The doctors all said so.

You are a married woman, Mrs Carr.

She wondered sometimes whether they did not know she possessed a title, or whether they had dropped it intentionally, with all its implied dignity.

They said now that she was improving. Slowly she had moved up again in the hospital's hierarchy. She wandered

171

freely in the corridors; talked to the nurses about the weather.

Today, as usual, she was dressed by the time her pills and breakfast came. The nurses liked that. The pills – only two now – came in a small paper cup. Holly filled her water glass and gulped them down, while the nurse watched her. Then, while the nurse – a middle-aged one, horse-faced and buxom – bustled around her tray, Holly waited for her cue to mention the weather.

But it never came.

'Well,' said the nurse. 'I hear you're leaving us.'

'What?'

'Don't look so shocked. Aren't you glad, dear? Everyone knows you've made good progress. Dr Minard says we're to pack your bags. There'll be a car coming for you this afternoon.'

XIV

Home. She was not sure she knew what it meant any more; only that it was a magic word, the key to her freedom.

She hovered by the narrow window of the hospital's front entrance, waiting for the Daimler to turn past the ill-tended hedge into the drive.

Home. Stadhampton – London. She didn't dare dream of New York. Some thoughts, which cut too close to her heart, she still forbade herself.

And so she would go where they took her. Make the best of it.

You love your husband, don't you, Mrs Carr?

Yes, she had learnt to answer, at last. *I do.*

A car pulled up, but it was not the Daimler she expected: Instead, it was jazzy, dark red and low-slung. The engine purred to a standstill, and Jamie climbed out.

Jamie?

The attendant on duty moved, ever so slowly, to open the door. Holly stood, clutching her suitcase, unnaturally still. She smiled up shyly; she wanted to run right out, but politeness, and a mistrust of her own legs, feet, voice, restrained her.

'Why you?' she said, offering her cheek.

Kissing her, Jamie gave a quirky smile. 'Why me? Is that the welcome I get? I'll go straight back.'

'No!' Holly almost leapt after him.

From outside in the drive, she looked back warily at the sprawling mansion, whose red-brick Victorian exterior concealed so much antiseptic misery.

It felt odd, standing here like this: no shouts, no one running after her. She must really be free.

Jamie, waiting in the car, revved the engine and grinned up at her. His teeth were whiter, his face more tanned than Holly remembered, framed by a strong jaw and high cheekbones. In the sunlight his eyes looked a dark, bright green, almost emerald.

Of all the Carrs, Holly realised, she had the least to fear from Jamie. She was glad he had been the one to come for her.

As he drove away, Jamie explained, 'Ty got called away down to Africa, and Mother . . . well, Mother's busy getting things ready at Chester Square. She has a surprise for you.'

'What is it?'

'I'm not allowed to tell.'

'But – how could you get free?' Holly's tongue stumbled, for she was unused to even so much talk as this.

Jamie laughed. 'Discretionary time. No one'll notice at the House if I miss a Friday.'

Friday. Momentarily floored by the realisation that she hadn't the faintest idea what day of the week it was, Holly nodded. 'You know,' she called, her words losing themselves in the wind and the noise of the engine, 'I don't even really know where we are. Is it Norfolk?'

Jamie reached to open the glove compartment. 'Here. Try and find us.'

Norfolk. 'Are we near the sea?' Holly called.

'Do you want to go to the sea?' Jamie swerved and, looking up, Holly saw the hump of red tractor they had left far behind. Jamie had turned suddenly into a side road. He was driving very fast. The wind tore at her hair, swirled around her throat. She glanced down at the speedometer. Eighty-five.

But somehow she did not want to stop him.

They reached the end of the road a few minutes later. Mud had turned into sand; a path ahead led between low dunes covered with sparse grass, to the water.

Jamie switched off the engine, and in the quiet they could hear the sound of the surf. 'Let's go.'

'You're crazy, Jamie. Are you sure. . . .' Holly was looking down at her brother-in-law's grey trouser-legs, his polished black shoes, when she giggled suddenly. 'I should talk. I was the one in the loony bin.'

Jamie stared at her for a moment in consternation, as if he did not know whether he was allowed to laugh.

'It's all right,' Holly said. 'It's over now. I don't mean to think about it any more. Not if I can help it.'

'Good. Then let's celebrate your freedom.'

Jamie got out, and Holly took off her shoes. 'Wait!' she shouted, fumbling underneath her skirt to unclasp her suspenders. Jamie grinned and turned his back, but still Holly felt her face reddening. Quickly, hunched low in the car, she rolled the stockings down both legs and stuffed them into her shoes. Then she hopped out of the car and ran ahead up the dune, hoping Jamie wouldn't see how flushed she was.

'Aren't you going to take off your shoes?' she called.

'I don't like bare feet.'

'The beach isn't much good without them.'

It made Holly laugh to see Jamie wading through the sand behind her, fully dressed for the House of Commons.

'Wait!' he called, as, seeing the wet sand and the water ahead, she began to run.

'Why should I?' An inexplicable, joyful laughter welled up inside Holly. 'You're not my keeper!'

'For today I am.' Jamie had given up at last – taken off his shoes and socks and left them back in the sand. He scrambled after her. 'Mother'll have my head if I don't get you home in one piece.'

'So. Are you always afraid of Mother?' Holly allowed herself to mock, looking back. It astonished her how easily talk was coming to her now – so quickly.

Jamie answered her in kind, with a cockeyed smile. 'Only when she threatens to belt me.'

'And you a grown man!'

'Ah, but you know us Englishmen. The rules of the nursery never really let go of us.' Jamie had caught up and now stood beside her, the waves splashing his trousers.

'I can't tell when you're serious and when you're not.'

Jamie gave his queer, lopsided smile again, green flashing from his narrowed eyes. 'You're not meant to.'

Holly was silent for a moment. 'You don't know what it's like,' she said. 'Freedom. You know, for months I knew the sea was outside my window – somewhere past the hedges. I could feel it – I heard the seagulls – but I could never be sure.'

'Well, now you know.' Jamie smiled awkwardly. His teeth, Holly noticed, bent slightly inwards in a pleasing way. A deep line, like a long dimple, scored each of his cheeks; the lines made him look especially young when he smiled. But they aged him when his face was serious, as now.

'I meant to say,' he said, 'I'm sorry about your father.'

'That's all right.' Holly tossed her head and forced a smile.

He backed off. 'Bloody freezing out here! Had enough?'

'No.' Holly shook her head mischievously. 'No. Not yet. This is nothing! Have you ever been in Maine?'

'I don't think I've had the privilege.'

'I swam there once,' Holly boasted, 'in the ocean, in October.'

'Well, go on then, if you're so brave. Swim now.'

'What? Take off my clothes?'

'I won't look.' But Jamie studied her, with a wry, flickering smile, as he said so.

'Is that a dare?'

He didn't answer her.

Abashed, Holly turned her back on him and walked out further. The icy water swirled and frothed around her knees, and when a big wave came, she had to run back. She screamed, because the water was chasing her, because she was not fast enough – it had wet her skirt – and, looking back, she stumbled against Jamie.

He took hold of her. His hands on her arms were firm and warm. 'You all right?'

A second wave thundered around them. Holly screamed again, and laughed. Her dress was soaked, and Jamie's trousers too. He held her steady, and she could feel him looking at her. Half of her wanted to cling on; he radiated warmth.

As soon as the sea was quiet he let her go, and she fled up on to the sand.

It was strange, how she was afraid to look him in the eye now. 'I'm sorry,' she said as they made their way back towards the car. 'Your trousers are soaked and it's all my fault.'

'Nonsense.' He sprinted ahead of her to open her door with a smiling, servantlike bow. Holly laughed – tall as his brother, and broader-shouldered, Jamie hardly suited the part of a mincing footman.

She climbed in, her bare feet scattering sand.

'Anyway,' said Jamie, 'I know just where we can go to get warm and fill up.'

He drove them a few miles to a pub in a windswept village, where they took two seats in front of the fireplace, propping their feet up on the hearth to dry their clothes.

'Oh dear,' said Holly, combing her fingers through her

windblown and hopelessly matted hair. At the hospital there had been few mirrors, but she had managed to catch the occasional glimpse of herself in one of the bathrooms: enough to see that, with indolence and hospital food, she had lost the gauntness of last summer, and that her hair had grown out to a bushy chin-length. 'I'll have to do something about this mop,' she said ruefully. 'Get it cut off.'

'No! Don't.' Jamie glanced at her sharply.

'Don't?'

'If I were you I'd keep it.' His eyes rested on her, and he smiled. 'Let it grow really long.'

'If you were me,' said Holly nervously, wanting to shift Jamie's attention from herself, 'you'd make a pretty silly-looking MP.'

'Who says?' Jamie smiled, still watching her. 'There are women MPs after all. And do you think you're silly-looking?'

Holly shrugged awkwardly. 'I don't know. I guess so. I'm too tall.'

'Compared to what? To whom?'

'I don't know.' Holly shrugged, embarrassed. She could feel her face going pink and she wished like anything that she could end this conversation. Luckily the landlord brought their meal then, enormous plates of eggs and chips, hot tea for her and a pint of ale for Jamie. Holly was grateful for the real food and the diversion. She wondered for a moment how much Jamie knew: about her, about Tyrconnel, about how she had ended up in . . . *that place.* Her mind shrank from the real word for it: *hospital. Asylum.*

She decided she did not want to spoil such a wonderful day by asking.

They dawdled over tea, exchanging small talk of far-flung things – Esmé and Hywel's new posting in Guatemala, Jamie's work at the whips' office – and by the time Jamie pulled his Jaguar into Chester Square it was nearly six.

The house looked immediately different from the one

Holly remembered: newer, whiter, its front railings blackened and polished. Imogen waited for them in the front hall, which was itself transformed, new white paint on the walls and pale green carpet covering the stairs. The front parlour, which Holly remembered as gloomy, had been done up in sea shades, with a new, clean-lined sofa of green watered silk and pale marbled wallpaper. The old worn Oriental rugs and brocade curtains were gone, and the real antiques that remained – the Chippendale Gothic clock on the mantel, the Guardi opposite – shone in their new positions of prominence.

'Oh, yes,' said Imogen, in an offhand answer to Holly's questions, 'we've done a bit of work. But wait, come this way.' Like an impatient schoolmistress she beckoned Holly and Jamie up the stairs, past Holly's old bedroom. 'No, further – '

Up under the eaves of the house, in the old servants' quarters, the stair carpeting came abruptly to an end. The four rooms off the hallway seemed recently to have been vacated by workmen.

Imogen took Holly's hand and led her into a broad, low-ceilinged, gabled chamber. At the front, two windows looked out over Chester Square; at the back, a cooker, cupboards and table formed a small kitchen area. Otherwise, the room, like the two smaller ones behind, was quite empty.

'What's all this for?' said Holly.

'Why, darling!' Imogen beamed. 'This is *your flat*. We've left it to you to decorate. It'll give you something to do. Keep you busy. I thought you always wanted a place of your own.'

Jamie's smile twinkled at them both. 'Mother's surprise,' he said to Holly. Then he laid a hand on his mother's arm. 'Mother, darling – I have to go. Holly – hope you're very happy here.'

He gave them both a peck on the cheek and wheeled away down the stairs. Imogen immediately filled the ensuing silence.

178

'Poor Withers. His bad leg just couldn't hold out any longer. So you see, he and Mrs Withers have retired. Which is how their rooms came to be free for you, Holly!' She beamed. 'Jason is our new boy. Waits at table *and* drives. Ty's got a new car, you know. Jason's the chauffeur.'

She led the way down the stairs. So much, she said, seemed to be happening. Jamie and Daphne's latest baby, Elinor, had been christened in March – had Holly seen the pictures?

'No.' Holly wasn't sure, now, if anyone had even told her about a baby.

'*Another* girl.' Imogen sighed. 'But they're making the best of it.' She went on: the youngest Bullenden girl was getting married; the insurance people were going to pay up, after all, for the fire. . . .

'The fire?' said Holly.

'That wretched wing at Stadhampton, darling! I'm sure I told you. One of those times – ' Imogen waved her hand to indicate her many visits to Norfolk the last autumn.

'Oh, yes . . .' Holly did remember now. She fell silent for a moment, in belated mourning for the ugly old Victorian extension: for Grandfather's laboratory.

'One less burden,' said Imogen briskly as she poured drinks in the parlour. 'Well, now. I do hope you like your new flat.'

'Oh, yes, I do.' Holly accepted her glass of tonic, bewildered. Imogen, whom her mind had turned, at times, into almost a monster – she was being kind again. Holly had no idea why. She wondered, momentarily, what Tyrconnel was supposed to do: move up to the new rooms – the 'flat' – with her?

Or was she to be allowed a discreet separation?

Imogen, of course, didn't say.

'Well.' She smiled and lifted her glass. 'Welcome home.'

Holly nodded. She felt tired and slightly lost.

'Of course,' said Imogen, 'no one knows where you've been. We've told them you were in America. Quite understandable, of course, with your father and all that. . . .'

Holly felt a sudden pang, an echo of the old loss, just as she had on the beach when Jamie mentioned it. She smiled mechanically to smooth it over.

'After all,' said Imogen, 'it's likely enough that you would have gone home to look after your mother, in normal circumstances. . . . We thought you would want us to preserve what we could of your reputation.'

Holly wondered what she was supposed to say to that. And then – as Imogen sat, beaming, waiting – she knew.

She swallowed; then made the words come. 'Thank you.'

Tyrconnel returned from his trip three days later, suntanned, his hair a little longer than Holly remembered. He told her he thought he would keep his bedroom on the first floor. 'If you don't mind, Holly.'

'No, no,' Holly said. They sat together in the parlour, waiting for dinner. 'Do what you like.'

She still felt she was a pawn in some elaborate plan of the Carrs'. All this politeness to her. Servility, even. She did not know what it meant.

She understood a little better when Tyrconnel knocked on her bedroom door that night. She was sleeping in her old room, adjacent to his, until her flat was ready.

Clothed only in his dressing-gown, he sat down on her bed.

'What do you want?' she said.

'How do you feel these days, about . . . conjugal duties?' He smiled and reached towards her hand.

She withdrew it. 'I don't see the point. You don't really want to have anything to do with me. Nor do I, with you. I'm here. I'm back. You have what you want. Don't you?'

He shrugged. 'You *are* my wife.'

She edged away under the covers. 'In name. Yes.'

'I thought they were going to teach you, at that place, about marital responsibilities.'

Holly looked back, as blankly as she could. 'Maybe. But

why carry on with a charade? Coming in here to see me. That's what it is.'

Tyrconnel placed one hand on her cheek, experimentally. 'It sounds rather an empty life for you, without a husband.'

She pushed his hand aside. 'You weren't much of one anyway.'

Jermaine Street, the boys, the man that night – she had learnt to forget them. Or at least suppress them. But she could not bear Tyrconnel's closeness now: his clammy touch on her skin. She thought she could do without any man's touch, rather than bear his: exploratory, finicky, disdainful. Perhaps the part of her that desired and craved comfort had died: for she could not imagine exposing herself, giving herself again to anyone. 'Don't worry about me,' she said now, harshly. 'I'll keep busy somehow.'

'How's that? What do you mean? I don't want gossip.'

'There'll be no gossip.'

'Including the fact that we live separately?'

Holly felt strangely calm. 'Including that.'

Tyrconnel stood. He smiled. His eyes surveyed her for a moment. 'I am glad we've been able to come to a civilised agreement.'

Holly nodded. There was nothing else to say.

That week Holly began to decorate her new flat. Helen came by, and they measured walls and windows and made their first expedition to Harrods and Woollands. Holly had a vision of what she wanted already: sleek, bare, modern, in contrast to everything in the rest of the house – Imogen's watered silks and pastels. If there could be no great rebellion, there could be a hundred little ones. They had offered her freedom, within their boundaries? Fine. Then she would take it.

Jamie dropped by, unexpectedly. Holly was on the bare floor of her new sitting room, reading one of a stack of decoration magazines she had borrowed from Nige English.

'Mother's out, I see,' said Jamie.

'Do you want a cup of tea?' The only part of her new kitchen Holly had tried out yet was the kettle.

'Thanks.' Jamie smiled. 'How's it coming along?'

'Oh, you can't see much yet. But it is.' Holly stood and waited for the water to boil. 'By the way,' she said, feeling awkward, 'thanks for the other day. The beach and everything.'

'My pleasure.' Jamie wandered to the window. 'You've got quite a view.'

'By the time I'm finished, you'll be convinced you're in a skyscraper in Manhattan.'

'Hardly what one expects here.'

'Exactly.' Holly rooted in the fridge. 'Milk? Sorry, I don't have any sugar.'

She poured Jamie's tea and a silence fell. They both stood, since there was no place to sit.

'So,' Jamie said. 'How are you?'

His eyes disconcerted her. He seemed too big for the room; it felt odd to have a man here. 'I'm all right.' She shrugged. 'Everything's different. It's strange. It's as if . . . I've been taken out of the world, and everything's changed while I was gone. London's different. The restaurants, the stores, people's clothes. . . .' She shrugged and laughed, looking down at her paint-specked flannel trousers. 'Not that you'd think I'd notice, to look at me.'

'I don't know.' Jamie smiled. 'I've always thought you had great style.'

Holly felt the blood rush to her face, and turned her head away to hide it.

'Sorry. I meant well. You're not much good at taking compliments, are you, Holly?'

'No.' Holly shook her head, glad, for once, that her hair fell in an untrimmed mop around her face. 'No,' she said again, 'so you'd better just not give me any.' She looked at Jamie suddenly, intently. 'I want to know something. Tell me the truth. Do you think there's something wrong with me, because I was in that place?'

'No.' Jamie shook his head; his face was open, honest.

'Do you know how I got there?'

'Mother said . . . you had something of a nervous breakdown.'

Holly nodded. 'I see. Well – for a while, I thought I did, too. I'm not so sure now. That place – it was all so confusing. Before I went in there I can remember feeling . . . funny. Sleepy sometimes, and jumpy others. I don't know.' Suddenly she wanted to tell Jamie the truth. Even though he was a Carr – perhaps because he was. He might understand. 'How much,' she said, 'do you know about Tyrconnel?'

Jamie looked at her steadily. 'I think . . . just about everything.'

'What did you think, when you found out he was getting married?'

'I thought he'd – changed.'

'He hadn't,' said Holly bluntly. The words almost came to an end there. But Jamie coaxed them out of her. He listened. He didn't recoil, even when she came to the horrible parts. He didn't judge her.

Holly talked, and for the first time she began to believe that Norfolk was behind her. She was never going back.

XV

In the crisp darkness of a July night, they all crowded into the Daimler, homewards from Cliveden: Jason the chauffeur, Daphne, Daphne's two girlfriends, Jamie and Holly.

'I'm glad you came,' a voice whispered to Holly, and she turned her head.

'Jamie! I thought you were asleep.'

Between them, Daphne and one of her friends dozed, their heads lolling back against the seat.

It had been an odd expedition. Tyrconnel, who despised

pointless parties, had refused to come; Imogen had come but decided to spend the night with her old friends, the Astors. After dinner, most of the visitors had strolled out towards the pool.

'That girl . . .' Jamie grinned now.

'*You* should have closed your eyes,' Holly retorted. The dark, totally naked nymph – who had run out of the water and been forced, by one of her friends, an older man, to chase after her swimsuit – had been only one of the night's provocations. Beautiful women seemed to fill Cliveden to the brim, many of them friends of Bronwen, the third Lady Astor, an ex-model. And as dinner gave way to a peculiar buzz of insinuation and indiscretion, Imogen, despite her more advanced age, had been in her element. She and the fiftyish Lord Astor had seemed particularly chummy. Were they, Holly wondered now – despite their difference in age – ex-lovers?

Unconsciously she sighed. Thinking back to the evening, she couldn't help feeling plain and naive, conscious of the months she had missed in the world, and the fact that news, fashions, London itself had all moved on, unbeknownst to her. In the King's Road, Chelsea, a new shop, Bazaar, was selling outrageous clothes girls queued up to buy: plastic collars, white lacy tights, short 1920s flapper frocks. Holly hadn't worked up the nerve to go in there yet. The cocktail dress she wore tonight fell safely – somewhat staidly, she sensed – below the knee.

She glanced down at it. Jamie must have noticed, because he whispered across, 'Pink suits you.'

Holly shrugged self-consciously.

'How's the flat coming along?'

She smiled, thinking he was kind to remember. 'Almost done.'

She and Helen had spent days leafing through Nige's magazines and trawling department stores, and finally, in desperation, junk and used-furniture shops in search of the ultramodern. According to some of the salesmen, anyway, 'modern' had last been seen in the 1930s.

Holly didn't believe them. And she knew what she wanted. She had almost laughed, watching Imogen's face as lorry after lorry rolled into Chester Square, displaying their signs: 'Pickle's Used Furniture', 'J. S. Auction Rooms', 'Antiques – Old Furniture – Houses Cleared'. She supposed the overall effect of the upstairs rooms by now was minimalist-modern with a touch of whimsy: white walls, white carpets and sofas, tubular steel, the fireplace filled by a garden sculpture of a naked cherub she and Helen had found in a skip on Moore Street. All that was missing, Holly reflected now, of the Manhattan effect she had once promised Jamie, was a view of skyscrapers. And London itself was even beginning to provide those.

The hush in the car prevented Holly from telling Jamie all of this. She wished she could.

At the other end of the back seat, he sighed.

'I know,' said Holly ruefully. 'Thinking of that girl again.'

'Not my type. Too small.'

Something in Holly's chest gave an unexpected lurch.

'Would you like to come into the Commons some time?' said Jamie suddenly. 'I could show you round.'

Holly glanced forwards towards the chauffeur, whose head twitched automatically as he drove. Everyone else in the car still dozed.

'Thanks,' she whispered quickly. 'I'd like that.'

Three days before her visit to Westminster, Holly acquired a dog. The dog, in fact, found her one day as she lay sunbathing in Hyde Park with Helen. An oversized mongrel with sparse reddish-grey fur and pointed ears which flopped dejectedly down on either side of its head, it nosed around their blanket, licking Holly's hand when she offered it.

'I wouldn't if I were you,' said Helen. 'You don't know where it's been.'

When they got up to leave, the mongrel followed them

all the way out of the park past the Albert Hall and down Exhibition Road.

'Either he's got a taste for culture,' Helen commented, 'or he's spotted a sucker.'

'Maybe he's got no place to go.' Holly glanced back. The mongrel's tail batted and his ears, like his worried brow, furled forward. 'Silly,' said Holly, half to herself. 'I can't keep a dog.'

'Imogen would have kittens,' said Helen.

Suddenly Holly smiled. The stray bounded forward. What was he? she wondered. He looked like a mixture of Irish setter and Irish wolfhound – at least, he was absolutely huge. His head came nearly up to her waist. She'd give him an Irish name. O'Neill, O'Hara, Fitzgerald. . . .

'Fitzgerald,' she said.

'What on earth are you talking about?'

Holly knelt, grinning, to stroke Fitzgerald's odd, floppy ears and bony head. He panted eagerly, tongue flailing. She knew he must be smiling.

'He's probably got fleas,' said Helen.

'Who cares? I'll take him to a vet. Tomorrow.'

That was not such an easy proposition as it sounded. Nor was getting him into the house in the first place, past Imogen. Luckily, when Holly first brought Fitzgerald in, Imogen was out, but when she saw the two of them coming down the stairs later in the afternoon, she exploded.

'This is utterly out of the question. I am *not* having that in my house. We shall call the RSPCA, Holly, and in the meantime – '

'No.' Holly answered quite coolly.

'What do you mean, "no"?'

'He's mine. I've adopted him. I want him to live here. And if, as I gather, this is supposed to be my house. . . .'

'This is ridiculous. Tyrconnel will never stand for it,' Imogen huffed.

Huffed and puffed, thought Holly later – but could not blow the house down. 'I imagine,' she said, 'Tyrconnel just wants to keep me here. Don't you? One little dog should hardly make a difference.' She gave Imogen a wide, innocent smile.

The next few days Holly spent in delighted rediscovery of Belgravia and Chelsea, through a dog's eyes and nose and ears: the pavement cracks, the gaps in fences, the greengrocers' rubbish, the birds. If dogs usually resembled their owners, then Fitzgerald, once shampooed and brushed, was a rangy redhead. Together, the two of them attracted smiles, curious glances and good-mornings. Fitzgerald made London a friendlier place.

The vet she found estimated Fitzgerald's age at seven or eight, which she could hardly believe, because the dog had more energy than she did. He ate three substantial meals a day, and required enormous walks. The only way to pacify him was to take him everywhere, and so she did, in those first days. Everywhere except to her appointment with Jamie.

'You've got a dog!' Jamie's grin cracked his cheeks when she told him. 'Mother'll have a fit. She hates dogs. What kind is it?'

'Very Irish. And not very house-trained.'

Jamie laughed. 'This gets better and better.'

They met in the ornate Central Lobby, relatively empty at this time of day – mid-morning – though, Jamie said, later on it would be crowded with MPs and journalists. He led her on into the Commons chamber itself – surprisingly plain, thought Holly, and small.

'Blast,' he said. 'I meant to tell you, I can't take you to lunch. Or at least only for a quick one across the road. I'm stuck in the House this afternoon. Whip duty.'

Holly crinkled her nose as she smiled. It sounded faintly obscene. She didn't know much about Jamie's job, but she remembered that three years ago his promotion from the back benches to the whips' office had been cause for family celebration – the first rung of the parliamentary ladder, as

Tyrconnel and Imogen saw it. 'You don't have to take me to lunch,' she said now. 'I know you're busy.'

'No, I want to.' Jamie's hand rested lightly on her arm as they walked. 'I don't see much of you these days.'

'More than you used to, I think.'

Jamie only smiled, and beckoned her through to the Star Chamber. Thanks to his position, they could go every-where – the House of Lords, the libraries, the riverfront terrace. When they had wound their way along seemingly interminable upstairs corridors to his office, she found it not to be the dismal overstuffed garret he had described. It had space for two chairs – one, Jamie explained, for him, and one for whatever wayward Member he might be interrogating. A wall lined with shelves held leatherbound legal texts, and a tiny, high window overlooked the Thames.

Holly met Gillian Lawrence, Jamie's secretary, a businesslike, smiling, nearly middle-aged woman who occupied a small outer office of her own.

'We manage,' said Jamie, 'just about – don't we, Gill? At the end of the day we have to bin half the stuff that comes in here. But I'm lucky, really. At least I have a secretary. Some of my colleagues have to share one, or use their wives.'

'But wouldn't Daphne like to work here?'

Jamie laughed, inexplicably.

'What? Is that so impossible?'

'Let's just say,' he said evasively, 'that Daphne's heart is in the country. Let's get some lunch.' He guided her down the stairs, after apologising to Gillian, who was being left behind with her typing, and asking if he could fetch her anything to eat.

And it struck Holly then what was missing: she had been expecting Jamie to have a glamorous secretary, or even two or three, at his beck and call. She was not sure why. Was it something Tyrconnel had said? Hints, half-jealous comments: Jamie's 'famous charm', Jamie and women, how Jamie was far from the perfect husband he appeared. . . .

Jamie, she decided, simply knew how to treat women with courtesy and respect. If Tyrconnel was unable to 'charm' them equally – well, she could guess the reasons.

Lunch was brief, as Jamie had promised. They ate at a bustling, crowded restaurant across from the Commons, practically an extension of the House itself. The single course they'd ordered came so late that they had to stuff it in, shouting at each other to be heard above the noise. There was no chance of intimacy here. But for that, Holly was just as glad. There was something exhilarating in this place: so many busy men, facts and opinions and power all within their reach. She almost coveted Jamie's life.

She would certainly, she realised – though she could not tell him this – like to share it.

He'd been lucky, of course. The Stadhampton seat came his way not long after he qualified as a barrister. 'Never really got to practise,' he told her. 'I wish I had. It would have been good experience. You can always tell the barristers in the Commons by the way they twist the facts round their little fingers. You see them at work. They can argue *anything*.'

'But is that really so good?' Holly smiled. 'Being able to twist the facts.'

'Of course.' Jamie's gaze was frank, direct. With his fine red-gold hair, slightly windblown from their walk across the road – his inward-leaning teeth revealing themselves in an irrepressible grin – he looked, despite his thirty years, more than ever like the malicious cherub in a painting: the kind who, everyone knew, would grow up into more of a devil than an angel. 'No one in the House can tell if you're telling the *truth*,' he went on disparagingly. 'In any case, the members vote the way we whips tell them. Facts don't make any odds. It's all party.'

'It sounds so – corrupt.'

Jamie grinned again. 'Wonderfully. That's democracy.'

'And what gives people like you the right to run it?'

'People like me?'

'James Carr of Stadhampton? The brother of an earl. . . .'

Jamie shrugged, not offended. 'Well, then, who would you rather put in charge? We all have our special interests. Would you prefer trade union leaders? Businessmen?'

'What about – ' the words came suddenly, unexpectedly to Holly – 'women?'

'We've had women MPs.'

'Not very many.'

'Why don't you run, then?'

'I can't. I'm not a citizen.'

'Nancy Astor wasn't, but she became one, and then became an MP.'

Holly shook her head. 'Well, I wouldn't do that. Change my citizenship.'

'Fair enough.' Jamie looked amused. 'You could run for Congress, then.'

'You know I couldn't do that either. I don't think there are any women in Congress at all. And besides. . . .'

'Well? You could be the first.'

'I just . . . couldn't.' The thought seemed about as likely to Holly as that she should, say, go up in a rocket like that Soviet astronaut, Gagarin, who'd just become the first man in space. *The first woman in space.* She giggled.

'What are you laughing at?'

'You,' she said, though she wasn't. 'For a Conservative politician, you have pretty radical ideas.'

'That's the barrister in me – arguing any position to the point of insensibility. Ignore me.'

When Jamie checked his watch again a minute later, Holly felt vaguely injured. Maybe she was boring him, after all.

'Sorry.' He glanced up. 'Rude of me, but we've got the debate on Europe coming up later this afternoon – the boss wants us to join the Common Market, you know – and there might be a few rebels. We need to clamp down on any in-party opposition.'

'Boy, the House of Commons sounds more democratic all the time.'

He gave her a teasing look, half annoyed, half flirtatious. 'Anyway. This hardly counts as lunch. I'd like to see you again. Properly.'

Holly's heart thumped unexpectedly. She wondered what he meant.

As Jamie paid the bill and led her out to where he said she could pick up a cab, none of this happening exactly of Holly's own volition, she reflected that Jamie was like his brother in at least one way. He rarely issued invitations, or asked questions.

He simply stated what he wanted. And got it.

As she rode home, Holly thought about all the ways Jamie was like his brother. And unlike him: in his light-hearted, impish streak, his seeming unconcern for his own achievements, his utter determination to charm.

Charm, she reminded herself, could be deceiving. No doubt Jamie thought nothing of the compliments he bestowed: generous words, sparked by impulse and little else. She would do well not to place too much faith in them.

The problem was, he reminded her too much of Tyrconnel: the Tyrconnel with whom she had fallen in love. She had time on her hands, and she was lonely – she had to face that. She knew exactly what was going on in her mind. And because she knew, she made the mistake of imagining that she could control it.

'Your wife,' Imogen remarked, studying the fashionably abstract framed spider's web of black lines that adorned Tyrconnel's office wall, 'went to the House of Commons today.'

'And so?' Tyrconnel tilted back in his chair.

'To see Jamie.'

Tyrconnel shrugged. Then, when it seemed that some remark was expected, he offered: 'You *know* I couldn't care less, Mother.'

'You know,' Imogen ventured, 'about Daphne, I suppose.'

'No.' Tyrconnel looked puzzled now.

'Her silly fool of a doctor has told her she shouldn't have any more babies. Well, there were complications the last time. But still.' Imogen blew out an impatient puff of smoke. 'She's as strong as those horses she worships. I don't think Jamie should give up so easily.'

'Maybe three daughters are enough for him.' Tyrconnel frowned. 'Mother, are you getting at something?'

'Perhaps . . .' Imogen studied him. 'Later, Ty. I'm on my way to dinner.'

'With Monty?'

She shook her head. 'Bill Astor.'

Tyrconnel chuckled. 'I thought that was all over years ago.'

'It was.'

'I'm not sure I believe you. Baby-snatcher.'

Like the kitchen in Holly's new flat, the phone she had installed had so far been more for show than for use; only her mother and Helen ever called. And so it surprised her when it rang at the end of the week, and the voice at the other end was Jamie's.

'How did you get my number?' she asked him.

'It's in the book. Under "Carr, H., 6 Chester Square", I believe.'

'Sorry. I know that was rude of me. I was startled.'

'What, does your phone never ring?'

'Not much.'

'I'll have to make up for that.'

Holly shifted uncomfortably, holding the phone, feeling her face go red even though no one could see her.

'What about lunch?' said Jamie, into the silence.

'OK.'

'Any particular time. Any place?'

'Wherever – ' Tongue-tied, Holly wondered why he was

inviting her. He had other things to do – not to mention a wife he could be taking out. He didn't have to bother.

'Good. Then how about Vignola's, in Wardour Street? It's a quiet place, a little out of the way.'

'OK.'

'You're not much of a phone talker, are you?'

'I guess not, really.' Why, Holly wondered, did she feel so self-conscious? As if there were anything to be ashamed of in what they were saying. She ought to try to sound friendlier. 'When shall we meet?'

'How about Thursday? One o'clock.'

XVI

Holly spent all morning getting ready for lunch. Her hair had grown past her chin now; when she straightened out the waves on big curlers and flattened it with hairspray, it looked almost long. She wondered if Jamie would notice, or if, searching longingly in the mirror, she was flattering herself. Surely her face had at least begun to grow into her features in the last couple of years. Her eyes were still large and wide-spaced, but her nose now seemed less pronounced, and her cheekbones stood out more. Her mouth would always be a little too wide, her teeth and smile too big, but maybe long hair, once she had it, would draw the attention away from those flaws.

She put on mascara, at which she was gradually getting more adept, and a new pale pink lipstick which flattered her slightly tanned skin. Out of her closet she chose a pink linen shift, Nina Ricci, with a white collar and huge decorative buttons.

When she walked into the restaurant, she could see Jamie right away, looking her up and down in the dim light.

'You look smashing.'

'This is so old-fashioned,' she shrugged, gesturing at her dress. 'I didn't exactly get it at Bazaar.'

'What's Bazaar?'

'The new "in" place to shop. At least Helen says so. I haven't gotten up the nerve.' She glanced around skittishly at the walls: smoky mirrors and Piranesi prints.

'Your hair's grown.' Jamie's gaze slid from her hair to her shoulders: downwards, then up again, so quickly that she could not be sure he hadn't been looking into her eyes all the time.

'I guess it has. Hope so.' Abashed, Holly looked down at the menu. For a while, to her relief, the business of ordering occupied Jamie. He was friends, evidently, with the proprietor, Giuseppe Vignola, and they discussed the ups and downs of the restaurant business, while covertly Holly watched Jamie's face, his hands in motion. He gestured as he talked, in, she supposed, unconscious imitation of Vignola.

'Don't you ever stop?' she said, when they were alone again.

'Stop what?' Jamie smiled.

'Trying to charm people.'

'Me?' Jamie raised his brows.

'You know exactly what I mean.'

'I don't *try*,' he said, in almost, she thought, a note of reproof. 'I can't control my every word. Now, just the other day –'

And he was away, evading her point, launched on the tale of his run-in with a reporter from one of the dailies, which made her laugh at the same time as she realised that he had slipped quite deftly through the net of her accusation.

'At least,' Jamie went on, 'the man wasn't one of my brother's trained attack dogs.'

'What?'

'You know, from the *Current*.'

A few months ago, Tyrconnel had changed the spelling of the name of his paper. Most people these days, he maintained, had no idea what the old name, *Courant*, was supposed to mean. A glaring new logo and more and flashier pictures of actresses amid the newsprint had accompanied the name-change.

Jamie made a face now. 'Of course I told Ty he was making a big mistake. He wants a name people can understand – why not just call it the *Currant*, with an "a"? The *Currant Bun*? Or how about the *Daily Sultana*?'

'Please.' Holly giggled.

'I reserve my right to make bad puns. Anyway, these reporters – I don't know where Ty digs them up. Have you met any of them?'

'No. I've never been inside the *Current*. Only to Ty's offices.'

'Don't you want to?'

'He's never invited me.' Holly shrugged. 'You must know. We don't actually . . . see very much of each other.'

Jamie watched her as she dug a knife into her slice of melon. 'Don't you get bored on your own?'

'No –' Holly shrugged. 'No, there's a lot to do. Helen and I have started going to museums. We're going to start going to lectures in the fall. And then there's Fitz. And besides. . . .' She felt defensive. 'I suppose you're on your own a lot, too, with Daphne living in the country. So you know what it's like.'

'True.' Jamie studied her for a moment; his eyes seemed darker than usual, less green, in the dimness of the restaurant. 'Daph is . . .' He paused. 'Daph is different. She's hard to fathom, really.'

To Holly's relief, their main course arrived. She hadn't wanted the conversation to move on to such personal ground, and now she tried to redirect it by saying how much she liked the *vitello tonnato*.

Jamie seemed not to hear her. 'Do you know what I like about being with you, Holly?' he said suddenly. 'You *listen*.'

'Well, I hope so.' Holly laughed nervously.

'Daphne doesn't listen. She doesn't even take in what you say.'

'Well – maybe she can't help it. She has . . . the children, and the house to think about. She must have a lot on her mind.' Holly felt odd defending Daphne.

'That's the strangest thing,' said Jamie. 'She's actually very good with the children in her absent way. She doesn't fuss, she doesn't worry what they get up to. She always acts as if she's lost in thought – and I'm damned if I know what she's thinking about. Sometimes I think she'd just as soon leave us all behind, and go and live among the Houyhnhnms.'

'The what?'

'I should have thought you'd know,' Jamie teased, 'with your interest in books! The horse-people, in *Gulliver's Travels*.'

'I've never read it,' Holly admitted.

'They're cultured, intelligent, mild-mannered . . . no feelings.'

'Oh.' Holly was taken aback. 'But. . . .'

'I suppose you're surprised I should mention Swift.'

'Not really,' said Holly. Though she was; somehow she had never thought Jamie much interested in books.

'I suppose,' Jamie smiled, 'you think Tyrconnel's the clever one. That's all right. Most people do.'

'No,' Holly protested again.

'I don't mind. I wasn't cast for that role. One clever son was enough, in our family. I was the spare.'

'You shouldn't say that.'

He looked up suddenly. 'I kept on trying to catch up, you know. I had to go to Magdalen and get a first because Ty did. And be president of the Union too, to go one better.'

'So were you?'

Jamie nodded. 'Didn't get me much credit at home! I remember what Mother said: "The Union's all well and good, Jamie, but it's not *real* politics." '

'But she can't complain now. You're *in* real politics. You've proved yourself.'

'Have I?' Jamie laughed. 'Well, if I have, it's never enough.' His gaze fixed itself on Holly. 'I'll always be second, you know. Whatever I do. The House of Commons – it's all well and good, as Mother would say. But it's a sideline. Ty's making the money. He's the one the family really needs.'

'The family,' Holly repeated. 'Meaning your mother and Tyrconnel. But what about you? What do *you* want?'

Jamie shrugged. 'God knows. Here I am. That's all I know.'

'You can't mean that.'

'Oh, I like the House. Sometimes I get a real kick out of it.'

'But you could be anything. You could be Prime Minister.'

'Don't want that. Foreign Secretary, maybe. See? I'm a wastrel, Holly. No ambition.'

'You just say that,' said Holly with a sudden flash of insight, 'because you don't want to compete with your brother. But I don't think it's true. I think you're every bit as clever as he is. And nicer.' She gave a tentative smile.

Jamie returned the smile, but his eyes were clouded. 'Don't,' he said, 'make the mistake of thinking I'm any better than I am. After all – ' he gave a thin smile – 'you've got to remember the family I come from.'

Holly let the remark pass for the whimsy it seemed to be. They lingered over their coffee, until finally, catching sight of Jamie's watch, she gave a start. She was supposed to be meeting Helen at Harrods at 3.30, and it was already four.

'Shopping?' said Jamie, when she told him. 'What for?'

'It's no use. She'll have given up on me by now. She never waits.' Then Holly answered his question. 'It's this ghastly-sounding dinner in the City. I need a dress.'

'Good. I'll help you find one.' There was a gleam in Jamie's eye.

Holly laughed. 'You couldn't possibly.'

'Try me.' Jamie was already motioning for the bill.

A few minutes later they were both in his Jaguar, heading down Shaftesbury Avenue at his customary breakneck speed.

'What was that place you mentioned? Bazaar? The King's Road?'

'Honestly, Jamie, I don't think this is such a good idea. . . .'

Jamie parked the car haphazardly a few steps from Mary Quant's Bazaar. 'I can smell the place. A sort of ghastly incense smell. Patchouli. Beatnik girls in white lipstick.'

'Come on,' Holly laughed. But he wasn't far off the mark. She walked in cautiously ahead of him, taking in all the waiflike females – and sturdy girls attempting to look like waifs, who were far more common – all wearing fringed straight hair, white stockings and pale lipstick. They were about her own age, she supposed, though she had got unused to thinking of herself as so young. *Twenty-one. . . .*

She browsed, all too conscious of Jamie's presence, and soon a glittery dress caught her eye. She reached for it, then retreated. 'No. I couldn't, really. There's hardly any of it.' It claimed to be her size, but would probably barely stretch round her.

'Try it.' Jamie smiled. His hand lay disconcertingly close to hers.

They moved together towards the dressing rooms. Inside, Holly slipped into the dress. Whenever she moved, straps showed, so she had no choice but to remove her bra. The fabric, a stiff and shiny emerald brocade, clung to her from the round, plunging neckline to just above her knees, revealing an outline in the mirror that seemed to her unexpectedly sylphlike. Somehow the dress subtracted from her awkward angles, gave her curves. She went red at the very thought of venturing outside the cubicle in it.

Jamie stood in the doorway of the dressing rooms, waiting. *Damn*, she thought. She would have to show him.

She steeled herself and ran out, her arms folded in front of her chest.

Jamie smiled. 'Turn around. I can hardly see you.'

She obeyed, as quickly as she could, and shrugged. Then, before she could run away again, he reached forward and prised her arms away from her body. His eyes roved, unashamed, from her shoulders to her knees and up again. She backed away, and his hands slipped down to her waist, holding her still.

'Yes,' he said.

She felt her nipples go hard. It must be the cold. And then an unexpected surge. . . .

At once she wanted to melt under the touch of his hands, and to run away and hide. Something strange had happened inside her.

He smiled, waiting for her to meet his gaze, and finally, once she did, let her go. 'If you don't buy it, I'll buy it for you.'

Holly had folded her arms again. Now she shivered. 'It's too tight. And my legs – ' She gestured down helplessly.

'You have incredible legs.' Jamie's gaze flicked over her again. She felt the ebb of what had gone before, like an aftershock.

'You really don't believe it,' said Jamie, 'do you? When I tell you you're a beautiful woman.' He paused. 'When I think of what my brother has done. . . .' For a second his face contorted in anger. 'Never mind.' He smiled. 'What else are you trying on?'

After that, feeling relieved and strangely exhilarated, Holly tried on one outfit after another. She bought two more dresses, and a sort of winter suit – an A-line coat and a skirt that just skimmed her knees, in an enormous black-and-white tartan. She had never worn black and white before. The stark colours made her hair look wildly bright, and she knew even before she wore it outside that people would stare.

'There you are,' Jamie said when they were done. 'A sixties girl.'

Whatever that meant, Holly thought. The sixties had barely begun, and to her they didn't seem to stand for anything.

Leaving her outside the house at Chester Square, Jamie skimmed her cheek with a kiss. For a moment she felt almost angry at the brotherly casualness of it: the way Jamie could act one second as if he owned her, another as if he cared what she thought, how she felt – and yet he was only her brother-in-law. And married. And *he* would never belong to her, even a little bit.

'I'll ring you soon,' he said.

'Jamie – ' Her voice was troubled. 'I don't think you should.'

But he did not seem to hear her. With a grin and a quick wave, he was off.

Maybe he wouldn't call, she thought as she ran up the stairs to Fitzgerald. After all, how many more excuses could there be for them to meet alone? She simply must stop thinking about him, she decided as she clipped Fitzgerald's leash to his collar, nearly losing her footing as the dog yanked her down the stairs.

If Jamie did try to call as he had promised, she was unaware of it, because Helen, having listened with one ear to Holly's explanations for her non-appearance, used her apologies to coerce her into going down with her to Sussex, to visit her mother. 'Come on,' she said. 'Please, darling. Mother'll adore you. And it'll ease the strain on me.'

After two days by the sea, Holly returned to a lunch appointment with Tyrconnel.

He had established a small dining room on the eighteenth floor of the *Courant* – now *Current* – building, where politicians and industrialists could meet the paper's editors, and where he could convey his own guests with a minimum of fuss.

'Saves time,' he explained as he and Holly took a seat by the window. The view – like that from his office – was a panorama of the Thames and south London; Holly could not decide whether the minimalist décor – grey walls, flat carpets, folding chairs – was designed to be fashionable or to prevent diners from wasting too many working hours on lunch.

The food, however, had no such spartan pretensions. They both sipped a velvety lobster bisque as Tyrconnel explained that he had a few business matters to discuss, or rather, sum up, with her. 'Not,' he said, 'that I would wish you to trouble yourself with financial matters. I know you have other interests. . . . By the way, what an unusual dress that is you're wearing.'

'Thank you,' said Holly warily. She had decided to ignore Tyrconnel's comments. She remembered his quizzical look when she had appeared, dressed for the City dinner last week in her glittery green frock. '*Rather bare, darling. . . .* '

'Of course we've never properly sat down,' Tyrconnel said, 'to a discussion of your father's will. I've been aware that the subject might upset you.'

Holly focused suddenly, sharply, upon her husband's face. 'No.' Having assumed that her father had simply left everything to her mother, she hadn't been aware that there was anything to discuss.

Tyrconnel recapitulated her thoughts. 'But,' he said, 'the fact of it is, Holly, your father was rather more far-sighted than that. He divided his estate – I needn't go into too much detail. Your mother, of course, is well provided for; and what could be spared, your father left to me.'

'To you?' Holly stared.

'Yes. Don't look so shocked. We discussed it, darling. Your father was concerned that you should be looked after properly, and so, naturally enough, he turned to me.'

'I don't . . . remember. I'm sure he never told me.' Holly's tongue seemed to have frozen.

'And so – this is all very tedious, but I'll try to sum it up – I've been left with a controlling share in United Alloys. And there are a few important decisions to make.'

'You mean . . .' Everything seemed to Holly to be coming very quickly. 'You *own* UA now. Sort of in my name.'

'Yes. And, well, frankly, I've been looking over the books, and – not to diminish your father's achievements – the margins are quite slim.'

'I don't know what you mean.'

'I mean – ' Tyrconnel took a sip of mineral water – 'I don't believe your father or the other directors took every factor into consideration. The location of the works, for instance. They're surprisingly near central Cincinnati, in an area quite suitable for the sort of suburban tract development favoured by you Americans.'

Holly felt a raw lump in her throat. 'What are you saying? You want to build something else, where the factory is?'

'Exactly. Demolish and redevelop.'

The waiter brought their second course, but Holly ignored it, her gaze fixed on Tyrconnel. 'Demolish – everything? What about the workers?'

Tyrconnel's voice was crisp. 'American labour's just not competitive these days.'

Holly's mind churned. 'I thought – I remember – my father negotiated with them just five years ago, to keep their wages down. They weren't happy, but – '

'It wasn't enough.'

'Then what is?' Holly could hear her own voice, strung-out and high.

'We must be realistic. In a world market. . . .'

Holly heard other words. *Unviable. Predatory prices. Overseas competition.* She stared at her plate, and felt the lump in her throat sinking down to her stomach.

'You can't,' she said as calmly as she could, when he had finished. 'If you've asked me here because you need my consent to close the factory, I won't let you. I know some of those employees. I feel a responsibility.'

'But you're wrong,' Tyrconnel said.

She started to answer, but he gave her no time.

'I asked you here merely to inform you, not to ask your permission for anything. I don't need it. I thought you might like to know my plans. Not that I expect you to take an interest in the corporate side – '

'What do you mean?' Holly felt something burning in her chest. 'You don't need my permission. . . .'

'No.' Tyrconnel smiled thinly. 'I don't. I'm not a trustee. I'm the majority shareholder.'

Holly's head reeled.

'Might I suggest that we leave the matter aside for the present? There was something else I wished to discuss with you. I've planned a trip to Manangwe for the beginning of next month, and I was wondering, as Willem de Vriet did so take to you . . . You might enjoy the sun.'

Holly could only stare. 'You must be out of your mind.' Without quite planning it, suddenly she found herself standing. 'I don't want to go anywhere with you. I hope you're wrong about UA. I hope someone can stop you.'

Already, she knew, no one could. What Tyrconnel had said rang too true. Her father had never liked divided ownership. He had controlled United Alloys; and then, when the chance came along to pass on the company to someone he thought was just like a son. . . . 'Excuse me,' she said. She felt queasy.

'Aren't you going to finish your lunch, Holly?'

She ran out.

Back home, she hugged Fitzgerald tightly. 'I'm sorry,' she whispered into his ear, watching his worried eyes. 'It's not your fault.' She could not stop thinking about United Alloys. She had spent a whole month out in Cincinnati with her father, while he negotiated about wages, that time five years ago. She could still remember some of the men: names, faces, worries.

It had been, she supposed, the first time it had come home to her how different she and her parents were from most people. Eventually she had forgotten that knowledge, submerged it, because there was not much she could do with it.

Nor was there anything she could do now, other than talk to Tyrconnel again. He would not be convinced. And it was her fault. For not talking to her father – not knowing about his will. For being . . . *away* when he died.

She felt utterly powerless.

Jamie's call, when it eventually came, did not cheer her.

'I'm sorry,' he said breathlessly. 'Listen, I'm calling from Stadhampton. I just wanted to apologise – '

'Apologise?' said Holly.

'I don't think I'll be able to see you again before the end of the August recess. We'll be away for about three weeks. Daphne's father's got something fixed up – some sort of lodge, for the shooting in Scotland.'

'That's all right,' said Holly, trying to sound cheerful as she felt her spirits sink. *What does he owe me, anyway?* 'You don't have to apologise. I mean . . .' she laughed nervously, 'you have a lot of other things to do besides keep me entertained.'

'You really think – ' Jamie's voice was low – 'I only see you out of some God-awful sense of duty? To keep you entertained?'

'I don't know,' said Holly simply. 'But it's all right – '

'I want to see you because of *you*.' For a moment Jamie fell silent. 'Damn it, Holly. I can't talk here. I only wish I could. Will I see you when I'm back in London?'

'Jamie – ' Perhaps this was the time to say it. Now that she wasn't going to see him for a while. 'I don't know if it's such a good idea – that we should see so much of each other.'

'You don't understand, do you, Holly?' Jamie's voice was raw. 'I need you. The days when I see you are so much better, brighter, than any other days.'

'Jamie – '

'I can't help it. I've told you . . . how things are. Do you think you're the only one who lives in a burnt-out shell of a marriage?'

The phone line crackled and Holly felt a strange, simultaneous urge to pull away – to freeze Jamie out with his confessions, his needs – and to run the distance of the phone line, all the way to Stadhampton.

'Please,' he said, 'say you'll be there when I get back.'

'I don't know.' Holly gave a feeble laugh, in an attempt to lighten the tension. 'I don't think I have anywhere else to go.'

She had thought of going to Stadhampton that weekend. Now she decided to wait a few more days, until she knew Jamie and his family would be safely away in Scotland.

It was absurd, she thought. She had no reason to feel guilty. So why did she feel that just to see Jamie, in the open, in front of Daphne and the others, was to risk revealing something – a word, a joke, a glance of under-standing – that would betray them?

Perhaps because of this fear, once she got to Stad-hampton she stayed there even after she knew Jamie would be back in London; even after Tyrconnel flew to Africa in the first week of September.

And so she was still in the country when she heard about the attempted coup in Manangwe.

Imogen heard the news first on the radio. When she came pounding on Holly's bedroom door, she was able to repeat it almost verbatim.

'They're not calling it a revolution yet – only an uprising. That's better, don't you think? The blacks – they call them-selves the United Front – have got control of most of Manang, and they've blown up two mines in the north. They've issued a statement – some sort of protest – about "capitalist exploitation". Do you . . . think Ty's all right?' Only on those last words did Imogen's voice waver.

Holly stood back, shivering. It was the cold, perhaps; or was it something almost like hope? A glimpse of free-dom? She dared not think that way. She must not. 'You'd better come in,' she said.

Again they went over the news, what little they knew. And then Imogen, returning to the library to wait for the late broadcast, began to telephone. Arthur Jarrell, Tyrconnel's closest assistant, who nonetheless knew little about his boss's plans or destinations in Manangwe. Charlie Moncrieffe – to see if he had heard anything more. Jamie. Too flustered to locate the numbers in her book, too nervous even to dial, Imogen asked Holly to do it for her. Then she talked. But there was little to be found out. Not even Esmé and Hywel were any use, although near midnight Imogen managed to get through to them, too, in Guatemala City. 'To think,' Imogen fumed, pacing, smoking, 'we thought it was a promotion for Hyw! We thought he could help Ty to get started in central America. Now it could all blow up in our faces, and where is Hyw? Halfway round the world! He knows nothing!'

Holly tried to placate her. 'It's not his fault.'

'What, are you not the least bit worried?' Imogen turned, staring. 'Well, Ty is only your husband. I should think it would show good form just to be a little concerned.'

'Stop it, Imogen,' Holly snapped back. 'Do you really think this is a time to be arguing? We need to know what's happening before we worry about things that . . . may not even be happening at all. Ty might be safe.'

A few hours after midnight Jamie rang. He had found out that the rebellion in Manangwe was confined to the capital, and that Willem de Vriet's Nationalist army was gathering strength.

Holly watched Imogen listening to the phone, pacing, nodding.

'Then where *is* Ty? What do you mean you don't know, Jamie? We need to get him *out*.'

Imogen passed the phone on to Holly. Jamie's voice at the other end was formal, strained. 'Are you all right, Holly?'

'Yes.'

'I'll try to get through to the PM, of course, but you know I probably won't manage it until the morning. In any case it's going to be difficult. Our colonial policy is dissolving, the Commonwealth seems to change shape every few months – and Manangwe really doesn't fit in anywhere. The PM and Willem de Vriet aren't even on speaking terms.'

Holly listened, aware that Imogen was watching her, aware of keeping up appearances. And Jamie continued talking stiffly, carefully, as if he knew the predicament she was in.

She managed a few hours' sleep. When she woke she found Imogen already gone; Reeve informed her that she had taken the car back to London. 'My lady said,' he enunciated further, 'that there is a ten o'clock train, should you wish to join her.'

Holly packed, and let the housekeeper's husband drive her and Fitzgerald to Stadhampton station. Back at Chester Square, she found Imogen's room awash with papers, the radio blaring, Miss Squires taking dictation at a ferocious rate. Imogen wore one of her immaculate Chanel suits; she looked much calmer than she had the night before. 'I think,' she said, 'we are making some progress through what might be known as the back channels.'

Just then the phone rang upstairs, in Holly's flat. She ran up to answer it, Fitzgerald bounding ahead of her.

'Holly.' The voice was low, as if, once again, Jamie did not wish to be overheard. 'How are you? Are you all right?'

'Yes, I'm fine. What's happening?'

'It's a God-awful mess. I'm seeing the PM and the Foreign Secretary at three. Trust Tyrconnel to land himself in the middle of a war six thousand miles away. I'm really going to have to stick my neck out.'

'Surely you can ask . . . well, after all, what can Britain do anyway? We're not going to send in troops.'

'No,' Jamie agreed, 'all we can do is *sound* as if we will. And everyone I managed to get hold of this morning agreed that Macmillan won't want to get involved. He believes in *de*colonisation. And Manangwe, at least under Willem de Vriet, is the world's most backward-looking white colonial state.'

'Well – ' Holly was silent for a moment. 'You don't have to get involved – do you? You could say . . . it's Tyrconnel's problem. Leave him to sort it out.' Her heart pounded at the treachery she was voicing.

Jamie gave a thin laugh. 'You seem to think I've a choice, Holly. Why am I here, if not to deal with such situations? By whatever means.'

A few minutes later, when she had thanked him, numbly, for helping Tyrconnel, more aware than ever of the hypocrisy on her lips, Jamie's voice vanished into the telephone's silence.

That night, Manangwe featured on the news again; but there was a virtual blackout surrounding the city of Manang. No one knew the fate of Willem de Vriet or the other members of his government.

After another tense night, and another day of waiting, the Foreign Secretary, Lord Home, made an announcement. Imogen and Holly, warned by Jamie, saw it on the nine o'clock news. The British government, Home said, condemned the violence witnessed these last days in Manangwe, and confirmed its commitment to the lawful rule of Willem de Vriet and the Nationalist parliament. The British ambassador to the United Nations would be consulting with other members of the Security Council. . . .

The next morning, the first planes were allowed out of Manang Airport and Tyrconnel was on one of them.

Back at Chester Square, uncharacteristically dishevelled in a crumpled suit, he told of the events of the last three long days. He had been relatively safe inside the presidential offices in Manang, although the building had been under constant fire from the United Front.

'What about the mines?' said Imogen, alert as ever even though it was three in the morning.

'Most of them are in safe hands. De Vriet's sending troops up into the hills, against the guerrillas.'

That night, unlike his usual self, Tyrconnel slept for ten hours. When he woke up he made immediately for the office.

Two days later, the newspapers reported that the United Front was retreating from the capital, under assault from imported weaponry.

'We arranged that,' said Tyrconnel, tapping at the morning's *Times*.

'We?' said Imogen. Then a smile dawned on her face. 'Oh. I see.'

'We helped De Vriet out with men, too, from the mines. They'd rather be with the Reds of course, but they're bloody afraid of my foremen.'

Imogen smiled. 'Even I underestimated you, Ty. When the bad news broke, I must admit I imagined that you stood only to lose.'

Holly spoke for the first time. 'How much do you pay the men in the mines?'

Tyrconnel smiled tolerantly. 'Four hundred ronda an hour, darling.'

'Which is?'

'About half a shilling.'

'That's not very much.'

Tyrconnel sighed. 'This is Africa, Holly. Do you have any idea of the cost of living down there? Right. Well, don't start telling me how to run my business.'

'Maybe,' said Holly carefully, 'they wouldn't have started a revolution if you paid them more.'

'Or maybe they would have anyway, Holly. Maybe they would have been strong enough to win it.' Tyrconnel glared at her.

So did Imogen, with eyes almost identical in shape and expression to her son's.

Holly tried to argue, but she knew she was predestined to failure. On moral grounds, she knew she was right. But what sway had moral grounds ever held over Tyrconnel?

She left them and went up to her flat, suddenly overcome by the desire to phone Jamie. She knew the numbers – both his office and his Westminster flat – from having dialled them so often for Imogen. She stroked Fitzgerald for reassurance as she heard the first rings.

To her surprise, the office number answered.

'You're there,' she said, startled.

'Holly.' His voice was neutral.

'I'm alone now. Tyrconnel's downstairs with your mother.'

'God,' said Jamie bleakly. 'What a mess it's all been. I've a feeling the sod's already forgotten he owes his safe homecoming to me.' He sighed. 'Oh, well. Water under the bridge. How are you?'

He said it, Holly thought, in a different way from other people. He said it as if he really cared. She curled up on the floor, cradling the phone under her, glad of a voice that was real, warm, understanding, to talk to.

In the next three weeks, she fell almost imperceptibly into the habit of talking to Jamie late at night. Sometimes she phoned him; more often he rang her first, from his flat or his office, when he was alone. Holly waited – sometimes she thought she lived – for those talks in the dark hours.

He asked her to lunch, and they met once again at Vignola's, but she was surprised how jumpy it made her feel now, seeing Jamie in the flesh. Having to cope with his glances, his gestures, his hands guiding her through the door. When they talked on the phone, she did not fear for her own reactions. Seeing him, the attraction became startling and strong.

'It seems,' he told her one night, 'I've converted you to the telephone.'

'I'm sorry, I keep you up too late. Do you ever get any sleep?'

'I sleep late and unplug the phone. Then, as soon as I'm back at the House, I seem to be on it again.' He laughed. 'I imagine one day I'll find I've grown permanently attached to the instrument.'

'Oh,' said Holly lightly. 'So I'm only one of many voices on the end of it.'

'You're the one I most want to hear.'

The weeks went on: lunches with Helen, lectures at

the British Museum and London University, walks with Fitzgerald, talks with Jamie. The hours on the phone made up for her lack of anyone to talk to at home; Imogen was out more than ever, and had ceased to include Holly in her social life, and Tyrconnel, on the rare occasions when he was in the house, came and went from his own rooms, avoiding hers.

She had grown so accustomed to her talks with Jamie – so dependent on them, perhaps – that she felt at a loose end when for almost a week at the end of October he did not call, and she was unable to reach him. She even summoned up her courage and rang his secretary, Gillian, during office hours.

'Oh,' said Gillian, surprised, 'he's been up for some party meetings at Stadhampton. Here, I'll give you the number.' Then she laughed. 'Silly of me, Lady Carr. Of course you have it.'

Stadhampton. Holly sat, agitated, on her floor, holding her too-hot cup of tea. She couldn't call Jamie at Stadhampton. What was he doing there, for a whole week?

He would be seeing Daphne. Of course. He saw so little of her during the weeks he stayed in London. He would be spending the days with her, with the children. Sharing her bedroom, perhaps.

The thought stabbed her with an unexpected jealousy.

Though she tried not to think about him, about Daphne, she was overwhelmed by an almost shameful relief when he rang the next night.

'Where are you?' she asked; but she knew the answer already. His voice was low, as if he did not want to be overheard. *In the country.*

'I miss you,' he said.

She was too afraid to say the same words exactly. 'I've missed . . . talking to you, too.'

'Can you come out?' he said.

'What? To Stadhampton?'

'Please. I'd love to see you. And next week's hellish. Full of debates, and the '22 Committee and everything.' He paused. 'If you came out, we could – meet in the garden. I'd try to get away.'

Holly answered slowly, and even as she spoke she wondered what she was letting herself in for. 'All right.'

'Will you come tomorrow?'

'Maybe the next day. Saturday.' If she came then, she could see him once, and then he would be leaving. On Monday.

'I'll tell you what.' Jamie paused. 'When you get there, if we don't get a chance to speak – come out to the terrace at midnight, and I'll wait for you.'

This time, there was no denying what she was answering: accepting. 'I'll be there – if I can.'

'See you soon, darling.' Jamie's voice had lightened.

'Bye, Jamie.'

The phone clicked.

She would not go, she decided almost immediately. Not to the terrace. She didn't have to.

And yet by the end of Saturday – the three-hour drive up to Stadhampton, the vast family dinner with Lord Farnham in attendance, along with Imogen, Daphne and the three little girls – Holly knew she had to see Jamie, if only to remind herself why she had come.

They couldn't meet again. She was certain now that she did not want to wreck what he had. For, much as he might complain of Daphne's lack of interest, she could not see it. It was true, they seemed mainly to talk about, and through, their daughters; but with three of them, all so young, who wouldn't?

And so, as she crept down the main staircase in her coat, through doors and passages that still were not entirely familiar to her in the dark, she was sure of what she was going to tell him. That much as she would miss their conversations – much as she needed them – she was going to give them up. For his sake.

At first the terrace looked empty, its low outer wall a line of shadow against the lawn, newly widened to include the strip of ground where the Victorian wing had once stood. Now only a thinness in the grass revealed that it had ever existed.

She and Jamie would be the same. Who would ever know, one day, that they had met here, or that they had ever had secrets to share?

She waited. The fountain, which she could barely see, was silent, emptied for the winter. The night was cold for October. She walked to the end of the terrace, and then something moved, detached itself from the shadows behind a pillar.

'Shh,' Jamie whispered, taking her hand before she could speak. 'Let's walk.'

Holding hands, they ventured down the steps, across the grass where the Victorian wing used to be. At the edge of the lawn trees converged overhead.

'Was it hard to get away?' Holly whispered. She felt like a conspirator. *Well*, she thought, *I am one.*

Jamie shook his head. 'They all roll into bed at ten and leave me to my own devices.'

'How unwise.' Holly spoke lightly. Jamie pulled her closer, taking her hand in both his own. She could feel, more than see, the dark shadowy height of him beside her; the bulk of his shoulders, inside a black coat.

Now he turned, confronting her, blocking out even the moonlight. He held her hand tighter than ever.

'Listen, Jamie,' she said, 'I came to say – '

'No.' He shook his head, and pressed a finger to her lips. 'Don't say anything.'

He bent down, and now, as she could feel his breath on her lips, she blurted out, 'No. Please.'

He pulled back, stroking her hair with one hand, and though she could not properly see his face, she could guess that it wore a bemused smile.

'I don't understand,' she said, 'what's going on. Are you a womaniser, Jamie?'

He shook his head and laughed. 'What a strange question.' Still holding her hand, he turned and began to walk.

'It isn't – to me. I don't know what to think.' Holly heard her feet, and Jamie's, crunching on the leaves, their steps quickening. For a few minutes they would be in a wood, in the shadows; then in the open again, but out of sight of the house. 'I used to think we were only friends,' she said. 'But I don't think that's true any more. It's too dangerous, Jamie. Tyrconnel and I – we practically hate each other. But you and Daphne – '

Jamie stopped again. 'Listen,' he said in a low, rough voice. 'What Daphne and I have is a façade. Strictly for public consumption. I thought she loved me when we were married – I thought I loved her, but now I don't even know. The truth is – she doesn't want me any more. Not in her bed. Not anywhere.'

'I'm sorry,' Holly almost whispered. 'I think . . . she doesn't know how lucky she is.' She heard the tears in her voice, and tried to stop them. But Jamie's fingers sought her eyes, found the corners where the tears leaked out, and brushed them away. He lifted her face towards him.

'I need you, Holly. I'd go insane without you.'

His lips touched hers, lingering, mixing with the salt taste of tears. He took hold of her, pulling her against him, his mouth searching, devouring, drinking from hers. But then he drew back, held still. He was waiting, Holly knew, and she could not resist, just this once. Unlike the other kisses she had experienced before, this one was shared. Jamie waited, let her explore with her own lips and tongue; their mouths pressed together, then withdrew, coming together again and again in a more feverish desire. She heard her own breath, then his, rising in gasps, like the sobs she had barely suppressed. And when they were momentarily exhausted he wrapped his arms round her and held her close.

'I'm glad,' she said, 'it happened once. I didn't know it could be like that.'

And now, despite his efforts to keep her, she pulled away.

'Holly – ' Jamie did not even whisper now. He spoke aloud. But she was gone.

She had freed herself, and now she ran ahead: through the wood, across the grass, in through the low door of the house beside the walled garden. She was in a dark hallway, lost at first, uncertain which was the way to the stairs.

She looked back and saw the door open again behind her.

'I'm sorry,' she whispered.

'No.' He came towards her, and somehow she could feel him smiling. 'You're wrong.'

He gathered her into his arms again; kissed her forehead and each eyelid and the corners of her mouth.

'You're probably – ' Her mouth quirked into a smile – 'wasting your time, you know. I like this, but – I don't like the rest. There's probably something wrong with me.'

Jamie smiled. 'I'll be the judge of that.' He pulled her closer, reaching below her coat, around her waist, brushing silk. As his fingers clenched around her ribs, his thumbs grazed her nipples.

She felt something quicken.

'Do you see?' he said.

'Sometimes I think,' she said, 'it's because you're like Tyrconnel. And then sometimes I know you're not. . . .'

'Shh. Don't think too much, then.' He kissed her.

'I know it's wrong,' she said, later, her voice shrunk to a whisper. 'You're my brother-in-law. You're married.'

'And I happen to love you.' Jamie pulled her up close to him, and she felt the warm strength and size of his body against hers. She felt sheltered, protected, as she had not in a long, long time. 'We can't help it,' he said. 'These things happen, Holly. We only live once. And I know I'll regret it for ever if you don't give me the chance to make love to you.'

'Do you always talk like this? You are a charmer.' Holly tried to mock, but there were tears in her eyes, blurring Jamie's image; for a second she almost imagined that she could replace it with Tyrconnel's. As if they were two sides of the same face: distorted reflections of each other.

Jamie held her as she trembled. 'It's all right, darling. Come upstairs.'

She nodded, and now he took her hand, leading her on. At the foot of the great staircase, he bent and pressed his lips to hers again. This time, she felt an immediate tautness at the tips of her breasts, and down below: a tingling wakefulness. 'It's – queer,' she breathed. 'You make me afraid sometimes. Like that day – when I tried on the dress. You don't even need to touch me.'

'Good.'

He put his arm round her and they charged to the head of the stairs. The steps gave way to a circular hallway, to the vast space under the rotunda, filled with moonlight.

Even in the dark, it seemed to Holly that the eyes of Jamie's father – old Lord John, in that stern portrait at the head of the stairs – bored into her. 'He gives me the creeps,' she whispered. 'Your father.'

'Then we'll go where he can't see us.' Jamie's arms circled Holly's waist and now he spun her away until she leaned on the stone railing, out into the empty space of the rotunda. He grinned and crushed her against the rail and she fell back; but the centuries of masonry held, as she knew they would; and as he kissed her again, more hungrily than before, she knew the dizziness – the sense of falling, of losing control – was inside, as well as outside her.

She felt Jamie's father watching her still; and, more than that, all the banished spirits of Stadhampton.

'Come on,' she said, for it seemed to her suddenly that the rotunda was too public a place. She walked ahead of Jamie down the corridor and opened the door to her bedroom. A fire still burned in the fireplace, but the room felt cold, and a trembling seized her.

'It'll be all right,' Jamie whispered, and pulled her closer.

Her coat fell to the floor, and his jacket, and slowly, lovingly, he undid the buttons of her thin silk blouse. She wanted to hide as he peeled away the layers of her protection, her caution; but the only place to hide was against him.

'It will be all right,' he said. 'I promise.'

When they were both naked they knelt together on the bed, and at first he did not even touch her, but held her hands fast in his, smiling, looking. She leaned forward for a kiss.

'No,' he said, and drew back. 'Not yet. Not yet.' He licked his fingers and touched the tips of her breasts. She felt the heat building in her, and closed her eyes.

'You're more beautiful than I thought,' he said.

She flinched then, hearing the words – *No*, she thought, *I'm not* – but he prised her arms apart when she tried to cover herself. He wrapped himself around her and she felt the heat of his body, the deftness of his tongue flicking the inside of her ear and her neck and the corners of her mouth; the strength of the square, strong arms that held her.

She fell back against the covers, smiling, and at last dared to open her eyes. He was smiling, too. His fingers traced a path down her belly as he leaned up on one arm above her.

'You don't like this? Any of this?' he said. A finger glided across the wetness it found, while another, inside her, gave an experimental pulse.

'No.' She fought against him, laughing. But already he was poised above her, his erection, long and hard, slipping inside her.

He didn't need to do more. 'No,' she said again, but he began to move, at first slowly, then at a faster and faster pace. She felt a wonderful fullness, like something waiting to burst, as he clung to her and reached harder and deeper, until somehow her legs, as if by themselves, had wrapped round him. And still it went on: an exquisite torture. He reached to kiss her, but she shook her head. She only needed this one sensation: their bodies rocking together. She wanted, when the last moment came, to see his face.

When it was over, she clung on to him. Jamie brushed her hair back with a lazy smile. 'Is that what you were so afraid of?'

'I don't know.' She shook her head, bewildered. And then she smiled up at nothing: at the spirits in the room. Still she had that sense that someone was watching her; but now she was glad. Whoever it was had witnessed her triumph.

XVII

On 2 October 1962 Tyrconnel Carr held his first press conference.

Journalists from *The Times*, the *Telegraph*, the *Financial Times* and the *Manchester Guardian*, as well as from some of the less reputable papers, including the *Current*, thronged the small conference room of the Current Building, the dull murmur of their talk and the whirr of flash-bulbs fading as the first speaker moved up to the microphone: a tall, sallow man with dark hair: Arthur Jarrell, Tyrconnel Carr's deputy.

As Tyrconnel himself had joked a few minutes earlier, to his wife and a group of assembled executives, it would take a miraculously dull news day – what with the recently broken spy scandal at Admiralty House and the threat of revolution in the Congo – to propel him and his company to anywhere near the front page. Perhaps – he had joked again, to polite laughter – all newspapers, except the *Current* of course, were monstrously overstaffed.

In any case, the reporters had come, perhaps drawn by the mystique of the Carr family, the source of whose wealth in these egalitarian times remained somewhat mysterious. Or perhaps they were intrigued by the notion of an earl launching himself – his own name, as it were – in the City.

Listening to the last words of Jarrell's introduction,

Tyrconnel Carr felt perfectly calm. He glanced around the newly furnished room: dark blue carpets, curtained and soundproofed walls. This particular sampling of Fleet Street looked a sedate bunch, not what he had feared: no Mods, longhairs or evident boozers among them. His wife – who had dressed in what was for her, these days, a conservative outfit, an off-white dress and matching coat, only a little too short for his taste – sat, visible but not too prominently on display, at one end of the front row. As he went up to speak he knew that everything was under his control. As he wished it.

'Good evening,' he said, with a smile. 'You may wonder why I've decided to take Carr Investments public at so unpropitious a time.'

There was a polite murmur of laughter or assent. The economy was on a downturn this year, trade figures worsening. Tyrconnel Carr had caught them all by surprise.

'So let me explain,' he said, 'why Carr Investments – TCI – offers a unique opportunity to invest in a global network of companies which will survive, indeed prosper, during these times of economic uncertainty.'

The audience sat silent, the only sounds from below the podium the scribble of pencils and the occasional whirr and click of flashbulbs.

He was holding them, Holly thought as she looked up from the front row for the first time. Perhaps she had underestimated his ability to speak in public; imagined that the nastiness which seemed to her to pervade his every word and expression would make itself equally clear to others. Evidently not.

With a certain detached interest, she could almost admire him. Seeing the dark lizard-eyes flicker, momentarily green – or was it only her imagination? – watching him shift, his limbs loose and easy, from one foot to the other, his smiling, half-mocking gaze fixing on different sections of the audience in turn, she could almost remember what she had seen, once: why she had married him.

Of course now, glimpsed in flashes between Tyrconnel's words, Tyrconnel's motions, she could detect another face, another body in motion. Jamie's.

The two brothers had never lost their similarity, though she had long ago stopped mingling their two sets of features in her mind. But they seemed to her now so different in character that there could be no confusing them: the one face perpetually eager, lusty and smiling, the other hawkish and sinister. She had two selves now: Tyrconnel's wife, Lady Carr, with her wardrobe of sedate suits and expensive jewellery, brittle private manners and impeccable public grace; and then there was Jamie's lover. Holly. Herself.

Jamie had no requirements; he accepted her as she was. 'Wear what you want, Holly, *be* what you want,' he said, and he encouraged her to adopt the shortest skirts, the wildest fashions. Her red hair, carefully straightened, grew longer and longer. When she came into the Commons – for since January she had been helping him with research, reading the books he hadn't time to consult on housing and the Health Service and education – she attracted admiring glances. She still couldn't get used to it. One day a photographer snapped her walking up the King's Road with Fitzgerald; Helen spotted the picture later in a magazine photo-feature, headlined 'The Chelsea Set'. 'What did I tell you?' said Jamie. 'There you are. A woman of the sixties.'

Holly had smiled, her vanity secretly pleased. Perhaps 'the sixties' was beginning to mean something after all. Something liberated, and stylish and free: long legs, long hair, the possibility of being twenty-two and not giving a damn for the tea parties and the opinions of the Imogens and Lady Bullendens of this world; the chance to glory in being young, without kowtowing to anyone. She was beginning to feel it.

She was a different woman than she had been a year ago, because of Jamie. He had freed her. Or maybe, in part, she had freed herself.

They never had enough time, enough hours in the day together. Last winter Jamie had snatched time off work; they stole afternoons in out-of-the-way hotels or in his flat, part of a large and anonymous Westminster mansion block. Holly had been nervous, at first, about going there, but Jamie insisted that Daphne never came into town without ample warning, girls and Nanny Walters in tow.

Victorian, high-ceilinged and dark even by day, the flat was sparsely decorated with cast-offs from Stadhampton and bore few traces of Daphne's or the children's occupation. Sometimes Holly longed to bring in a bunch of flowers or put up a picture, just to make the place look more lived-in, better loved. For after all, it had come to mean something to her.

Though of course, in the end it was not hers.

Because of Jamie's work, because of the servants at Chester Square who would notice Holly's absence, they almost never spent nights together. The telephone connected them when Holly could not sleep, or when Jamie was detained at the Commons: long, low, murmured conversations that sometimes almost convinced her he was in bed beside her as she fell asleep.

Most Friday afternoons, when parliament finished early, they drove out to the country in Jamie's Jaguar. Since they couldn't be seen together in the centre of town, they met near Helen's house in Islington.

Holly had had to tell Helen.

Her friend had been horrified, but also fascinated. 'Jamie?' she repeated. 'Jamie, your brother-in-law? Isn't it – kind of like incest?' Her eyes widened as she puffed on a Gitane; her French cigarettes were a new and foul-smelling affectation. 'Gosh, Holly. He is good-looking. But how do you do it? The others'll find out. Does Ty know?'

'Ty,' said Holly shortly, 'wouldn't care.'

'What about Jamie's wife? Have I seen her? Is she the one with the long neck and the tiny brain?'

Holly giggled. 'Oh, Helen. I shouldn't. I do feel mean about her sometimes. I tell myself she'll never guess – or that she doesn't care anyway. If she did, she'd come to London, wouldn't she? Jamie says she never really liked . . . it, you know. It was practically an arranged marriage.'

Helen raised an eyebrow. 'But he's not going to leave her, is he?'

'He can't. And I can't leave Ty.' Holly sighed. 'So we're in the same bind. That's the part I try not to think about.'

'Some men,' said Helen, 'like the risk. Maybe you do, too.'

'I don't!' Holly protested. 'I wish there weren't all this trouble. I wish . . . we could both be untangled, but that's just dreaming. And I think somehow I deserve some sliver of happiness.'

The cause of her unhappiness – Tyrconnel – went unmentioned, then and now. Perhaps Helen understood. Holly did not ask her.

Nor could Holly confide in her friend the sheer desire, almost an addiction, that drew her again and again to Jamie. Was it mere physical craving, whose satisfaction had been denied by Tyrconnel? It felt like more. Jamie often laughed, in those first long afternoons, when their lovemaking would go on for hours. 'Well,' he said, 'you have years to make up for.'

When Jamie had left her, that first time, in the early hours of dawn at Stadhampton, she had told herself it would not happen again. But it took only a day for her resolve to weaken. When she returned to London two days later and he rang her, they had stayed on the phone for two hours.

The day after that, she had gone to her doctor and asked about birth control.

She did not tell Jamie. They met two days later at a little hotel behind Portman Square; she had disappeared to the bathroom but felt too nervous to explain, and Jamie had drawn the curtain and turned off the lights because she asked him to: she still did not feel ready for him to see her in full daylight. But she realised, as they slid together and she felt the hard curve of his shoulders, the flat muscles of his stomach and back, that she would very much like to see *him*. Perhaps the next time.

Afterwards he said, 'It felt different.'

'I – went to the doctor,' she said nervously. 'I thought it was better to be safe.'

Jamie was silent.

'Well, surely you don't want us to have a baby.' Holly gave an anxious laugh. 'Do you? Can you imagine – as if we weren't doing enough things wrong. . . .'

Jamie smiled then – Holly could just see it in the dark – and pulled her closer. 'I don't know. Worse things have happened. But I suppose you're right to be sensible. It's just that some archaic male instinct seems to rear up in me, warning me I've been unmanned.'

'That's silly.'

'I know.' Jamie smiled. 'Is there something you're supposed to do now before we can make love again?'

Rather against her own will, Holly got up to insert more of the messy jelly. She hadn't always bothered, since then, and these days she kept careful track of her periods, heaving an inner sigh of relief each time one came. She could not, in all conscience, bring a baby into her shell of a marriage. Nor did she know how long this, with Jamie, would last, although she could not imagine its ending. Those first few months, she had been plagued by the sense that they were buying time; that discovery, and all the ensuing disasters, would overtake them.

But it hadn't. As time passed they had grown more enmeshed in each other's lives. Jamie had been bold, introducing her so openly into his work at the Commons; but then their family connection was perhaps the best cover of all. No one would dare question it when he introduced her as he did, to his colleagues – 'My sister-in-law, who's been kind enough to offer me a bit of unpaid slave labour.'

He got her a pass to the House of Commons library; deliberately, they rarely coincided at the office. And Holly had grown genuinely interested in the work she was doing there: the unreported background to current events, the factual debates and political battles behind bills and laws. Jamie seemed impressed at the hard work she put in. He even said once, 'You know, if you'd been a man, Holly, you'd have made a fantastic lawyer.'

And so she and Jamie went on. Inevitably, they had grown less cautious. Last February, they had both created elaborate cover stories to enable them to spend three nights in Rome together. For three days, they had gloried in the spring sun and the freedom to walk hand in hand in the streets without being recognised for anything other than what they were – lovers. They ate in restaurants together and kissed in the gardens of the Villa Borghese; they made love and did not have to part at dawn. They lived in a limbo, a dream-world beyond the compromises of their daily lives, and only fell abruptly to earth when their plane landed back in London.

Even as they walked down the airport concourse, they moved apart, on the off-chance that some wandering reporter should catch sight of Jamie. They rode in separate cabs back to town, where at once he was immersed in work.

That summer, several by-elections turned in bad results for the Tories. In mid-July the Prime Minister had engineered a massive reshuffle of his Cabinet on what was quickly dubbed the 'Night of the Long Knives'. Disastrous for some, it had yielded promotion for Jamie. He was now chief whip.

It made him more visible. The press knew his face now, and so he and Holly had to be ever more careful. During the parliamentary recess in August she could not see him at all. She had told him not to ring her while he was away up in Scotland; she had grown to hate the muffled tone of voice he spoke in, when Daphne was in the same house and might hear him.

'Come to Stadhampton,' he had begged her, once he was back. 'Even if it's just for a night. I've been starved of you.'

So she had relented – and almost as soon as she reached

Stadhampton, regretted it. Jamie was away at his constituency surgery when she arrived. She wandered through an empty house only to be greeted by Nanny Walters. 'Oh, do come out,' said the older woman, whose reddish hair seemed to have brightened with the years. 'That's Mrs Carr just gone now, out in the field with the girls and their new ponies.'

Catching sight of her aunt over the fence by the stables, Laura had galloped up. 'Look!' she demanded. 'Aunt Holly. I can jump.' Having demonstrated – clinging on to her pony's back with admirable tenacity – she slid down and ran to Holly for a hug. 'You smell nice. You always do. Where's Fizz?'

Fitzgerald had ambled away from Holly's side in search of some scent, and Laura ran off to look for him. 'Fizz! Where are you?'

Daphne trotted up to the fence and slid down too, kissing Holly on the cheek. 'Well! What brings you here?'

'I don't know. The weather's so good. . . .'

'Yesterday we had to put Hyacinth down. We're very sad.' Daphne's wide blue eyes were mournful. With her clear skin, her long neck, her short hair blowing in the open air, she looked prettier, and more fragile, than Holly had remembered.

'I'm sorry,' she said. She couldn't even remember which horse Hyacinth was.

Daphne smiled faintly. 'She was old, poor thing. I think only Laura understood . . . Davina! Careful, darling!' She ran to take the reins of her second daughter's pony. 'The girls are doing so well. I only wish Jamie were here to see them more often. He was such a dear about Hyacinth. . . .' Her blue eyes scanned the distance, disconsolate. 'Really! These silly surgeries. I don't see why, when he's only here at weekends, he has to go off and spend his time with all those ghastly people from the town.'

'I know,' said Holly sympathetically.

'He's so grateful, you know, for the help you've been

giving him. I think you're an angel. I can't abide that place . . . you know, the Commons.'

Even after she had waved goodbye to the girls and coaxed Fitzgerald back up to the house, that scene plagued Holly. It would have been easier if Daphne had been jealous or spiteful. Instead, she had showered Holly with gratitude.

That night, Holly pleaded a sudden bad cold and ate dinner in her room.

Jamie found her only the next evening as he was getting ready to drive back to London.

'Where've you been?' He looked angry; bewildered, too.

'Something came over me. I . . . didn't feel right about being here. I *don't* feel right.' Holly spoke in a low voice; they were standing in the front hall, where anyone who chanced to come in might hear them.

'Well, now I've got to go back to London,' said Jamie, annoyed. 'You might at least have let me know you were here.'

Holly turned away.

'Are you going back? I'll drive you.' Jamie's voice lowered as she half turned back towards him. 'Come on, Holly. Let me drive you.'

And so, lying blithely – she was surprised how easy it had grown – she had apologised to Daphne for leaving so early: 'I still don't feel too good. I think I'd better see my doctor in London.'

Daphne and the girls had seen them off, waving.

'I feel rotten,' Holly had said as Jamie sped off down the drive. 'I feel like a complete hypocrite. A liar.'

'So,' said Jamie, 'are we all.'

And why was it that after arguing all the way down the road, when they had made up and made love, quickly, secretly, in the empty house at Chester Square, it had been more explosive and passionate than ever?

Holly shifted uneasily on her seat in the conference room, trying to force her attention back to Tyrconnel's speech. People would be watching her.

'In the financial year 1960–1961 the United Manangwe Mines recorded a profit of almost half a million pounds. The Current Newspaper Group, comprising the *Current*, the *Sunday Current* and *Picture Week*, reached a combined circulation of 400,000. These alone, if I were to extrapolate in terms of profits per share . . . .'

Holly realised with some shock that Tyrconnel was talking now about sugar refineries in Honduras, a cargo shipping line, further mines in central and East Africa, and property developments in Cincinnati, Los Angeles and London. She hadn't even realised he had so many projects off the ground. She hadn't known, until tonight, that he was making so much money, so quickly. He had come farther in four years than anyone, including the financial reporters in the room, could have expected.

He finished his speech and stood poised, ready for questions. A *Financial Times* reporter jumped to his feet.

'What,' he said, 'do you expect your average annual returns to be over the next economic cycle?'

'I believe – ' Tyrconnel was already nodding towards the next waving hand, the next question – 'I've already answered that. Consult your notes, Mr Fyfield.'

Reporters chuckled; Tyrconnel tossed back easy answers to the next few questions. Then he checked his watch and announced, 'I'm afraid that's all I have time for.'

He made his exit as he and Arthur Jarrell had planned it, stepping down from the podium to take Holly's arm and stride out of the hall. Jarrell protected their right flank; Domingo, Tyrconnel's new chauffeur and bodyguard, walked on their left. The reporters still shouted questions after them.

'Are you a millionaire yet, Lord Carr?'

Tyrconnel only smiled.

'How much money do you stand to make from the share offer?'

Walking on, Tyrconnel called back, 'Not as much as our shareholders stand to make in the next few years.'

'Are you planning on going into politics?'

'My brother's in politics. One's enough in the family.'
They had almost reached the door. 'Hurry up, Holly,' he murmured.

'Lady Carr!'

Holly turned, startled.

'When are you planning on having a family, Lady Carr?'

Holly blinked, dazed by the flashbulbs that were going off all around her. 'I don't know,' she said. 'As soon as we can.' She smiled, and now Tyrconnel and Domingo hurried her out through the lobby of the building and into the car.

'By whom, I wonder?' murmured Tyrconnel.

Soon the engine of Tyrconnel's car, a '60 Bentley, purred into action and Domingo sped them away.

Holly decided she would ignore what Tyrconnel had said. Ignoring him was the only way of getting through these disagreeable and fortunately infrequent public occasions.

'So?' said Tyrconnel now. 'When *are* you planning on having babies?'

Holly controlled her breath, her voice. 'You know I won't be.'

'Why? Can't Jamie manage it?'

Stunned, Holly sucked in her breath.

'You didn't think I would remain wilfully ignorant, did you, Holly?'

Her mind was running through the consequences. If Tyrconnel knew, then soon everyone would.

'Don't worry,' he said. 'Do you think I care? I'll keep your secret. It would be no use to anyone for Jamie to be found out.'

Holly forced out a reply at last. 'Whatever I do, it's none of your business. As far as I know you gave up all interest in me two years ago. If not even before that. As soon as you had my father's money. As soon as we married.'

'Well,' he said. 'As I say, I *don't* care. Just be sure you don't get yourselves talked about.'

'I imagine you would know all about that. About secrecy.'

'I do,' Tyrconnel agreed. 'And if you mean to go on as you're doing you'll have to learn.'

Holly's fingers clenched and unclenched in her lap. She was wearing her diamond and sapphire engagement ring, because Tyrconnel liked to display it at parties. It was funny, just now she couldn't even remember what tonight's party was. Only as they pulled up in front of the Foreign Secretary's house did she recall that it was a dinner with the Colombian ambassador, arranged from afar by Hyw Campbell.

Colombia. Another conquest for TCI.

'By the way,' she said as they climbed out, 'where are you living these days? Just in case anyone asks. Still at Chester Square? I don't seem to see you.'

Tyrconnel's hand clenched, hard, on her elbow, but he did not answer. The light from the Foreign Secretary's front hallway was already shining on them.

She was in the library of the Commons when she next saw Jamie.

'He knows,' she said. They stood in a corner, surrounded on three sides by volumes.

'Tyrconnel?'

Holly nodded.

'That's all right. I told him. Or rather, he extracted it from me. Holly, what's wrong?'

She couldn't explain it then, where they might be overheard. Nor could she make him understand, on the phone that night. He shouldn't just have given in, even if Tyrconnel had confronted him. He could have brazened it out, kept their secret.

'What difference,' said Jamie with a sigh, 'does it really make?'

'It was just us, once,' said Holly darkly. 'It won't be any more. I know Tyrconnel. He'll use it against us. Whenever he gets the chance, he'll remind us. It's his little bit of power.'

'Tyrconnel has more power than that. If he chooses to

exercise it. The power of the purse, it's called. Holly . . .' Jamie's voice reached out to stroke her, to soothe her. 'Honestly, it won't matter if we don't let it. Will I see you on Friday?'

Their Friday afternoon. The first in a long time. So what if Tyrconnel knew, after all? Holly nodded, with longing in her eyes. 'When?'

XVIII

One of the hits of the last few months' hammered on the car radio, nasal, insistent, almost irritatingly unforgettable: Holly had fallen for it at once.

'So who are this lot?' said Jamie, jamming down on the accelerator.

'The Beatles. Haven't you heard of them?'

'Don't look at me. I'm just an old fogey. Out of touch.' As he answered, Jamie gave Holly a glance, up and down her black-stockinged legs, that was far from old-fogeyish. He was driving the Jaguar at seventy down a B road somewhere in Oxfordshire: where exactly, Holly didn't know, because she had given up reading the map. A breeze blew in her hair through the windows, and she hugged the black and white checked jacket of her favourite suit – the one she had bought with Jamie more than a year ago now – closer around her, singing along with the radio. *Love, love me do. You know I love you.* If only life were so simple.

'You have all the musical sophistication of a fifteen-year-old,' teased Jamie.

Holly turned the volume up. 'I like it.'

'You even know all the words. Not that there're many to know.' Jamie paused. 'Are you still worried?'

'Not as much as before.' Holly had to admit she had got used to the idea of Tyrconnel's knowing; and, having thought things through, she had realised that any attempts by him to use his knowledge would only backfire against Jamie.

'Ty wouldn't want me to lose my seat,' Jamie said.

'I know. That's exactly what I was thinking.' Holly frowned. 'Are you really so much use to him, though? I mean, after Manangwe.'

'Well, there could always be more trouble.' Jamie's foot eased off the accelerator and he neglected to pass the car ahead, which meant he was thinking. 'More eruptions in Central America or East Africa . . . though I'd rather grease the wheels for a hundred back-room deals than have to pull off another Manangwe.'

'Back-room deals?' said Holly suspiciously.

'The Board of Trade. Industrial policy. Hardly anyone bothers to read the fine print but my brother. After all, who else cares about mineral tariffs or the size of drill bits?' With a brief laugh, Jamie accelerated into a straight stretch of road. 'And then there are the taxes . . . hundreds of minuscule provisions in every Budget. Mac the Knife, as we know, goes for the grand gesture. Hardly notices the rest.'

'I see.'

'You sound censorious.'

'No. . . .'

'Your husband,' Jamie said – as always, with a certain circumspection in his voice – 'knows enough not to ask favours, except when it's essential. He usually has excellent judgement. That's why it beats me why he's taking his company public.'

'Why?' said Holly; but now the car was slowing. 'Is this the place?' she asked.

Jamie had pulled off the main road into a lane. 'Almost there. I told them to have our room ready.'

Holly was glad he always arranged these things. She could never get over a certain awkwardness at hotel front desks, the feeling that the management could see right through her. But Jamie's unruffled courtesy always smoothed the way. He paid in advance; later on, they would drive off as if to dinner, and simply never return. They never went back to the same place twice.

Jamie switched off the engine and they sat for a moment in the courtyard of the Boar Inn, a long sprawling thatched house soaked in the afternoon autumn sun. For a moment they were silent, savouring what was to come.

'At long last.' Jamie's mouth curled and his gaze roved down to Holly's thighs, where she knew her skirt barely concealed the tops of her stockings. He took her hand and raised it to his lips.

As he did, a lock of hair fell, red-gold, over his left eye, and for a second she was reminded of Tyrconnel. She jerked up her hand to brush it back. All the while she held his gaze. She had grown bolder in this last year of having him; loving him.

'Maybe we could stay the night after all,' he murmured.

'No.' She answered abruptly, not letting herself go. 'Better not.' Still Jamie held her hand. 'Come on,' she said cheerfully. 'We're wasting time.' She pulled free and hopped out of the car.

As usual, she let Jamie do the talking at the reception desk; in a few minutes they had unlocked the door to a cosy double bedroom under the eaves. Holly emerged from the bathroom, half undressed. She knew Jamie liked to see her this way first; later, naked. All in good time.

He stood by the window waiting, still in his suit. His waistcoat was buttoned, his red silk tie still tight around his throat. As she came into the light, his eyes followed her.

'You're still dressed,' she said.

He only smiled, for he knew that she liked to move slowly down to the naked outlines of his body, to peel his garments away one at a time.

Once, she remembered, she had been frightened of nakedness, especially her own: afraid she was somehow repulsive, for Tyrconnel found her so. Even though she knew the reason, the curse of his revulsion had remained with her, making her wonder: was it the fullness of her hips? The pronounced inward dent of her waist? The freckles that sprinkled her shoulders, or the paleness of the rest of her?

Jamie had learnt to reassure her: not so much with words, but simply by accepting her, desiring her. And it had surprised her how after only a few months with him, she had lost her self-consciousness, too.

She reached up to loosen Jamie's tie. In turn, he skimmed her body with one hand, smiling lazily; stroking the curve of her hip, where her stocking gave way to bareness, then to the white lace of suspenders and panties: 'good girl's underthings', he had said once, but he liked them. 'Can't I be bad, too?' she had said, half affronted.

He had grinned. 'Whenever you want.' But perhaps this was her real self. The virginal white of a good girl, who was no longer, at least, a virgin. . . .

He cupped her breast, his thumb stroking her nipple: arousing it, waking it as already his lips had awoken her mouth, her neck, readying her body for sensations to come. And she held him close as he kneeled down, still nearly fully dressed. Something about her exposure and his composed, clothed exterior excited her, so that often she did not tear his clothes away until the last minute. He buried his face between her breasts, tugging her panties down.

'You always smell so good,' he said, smiling, breathing in the scent of her skin.

'Perfume,' she said.

'No. You.'

As always, she had doused herself in Chanel: the scented oil in her bath, then powder, then perfume. She craved delicious smells as much as ever. But she loved Jamie's scent, too, even though it was only soap and salt skin and the slight sweetness of his hair.

They edged back from the window, up against the rough plaster wall, as, licking a leisurely path down her stomach, he began to kiss her: there, among the coppery hair, as naturally as if he were kissing her mouth, her lips, her

233

tongue. It had taken her a long time to get used to that. Now it took her almost no time to respond. She held the back of his head, pressed him to her, then cried out, 'No!'

Jamie stopped, lifted his face with sparkling eyes.

'Not yet,' she said, and he gathered her to him, her face buried against his chest, her arms clasped round him. Gently he picked her up and set her down again, on a tall Queen Anne chair covered in red velvet. She arched her back and, kneeling, he plunged inside her. She felt sensitive, swollen, every inch of her wanting him, and his body hurled itself against hers, again and again, his eyes searching hers, gleeful.

At last she could hold out no longer, and the delight, then the familiar exhaustion overcame her. She fell, limp and sweaty, back in the chair. 'Maybe we'd better move,' she breathed.

'But,' he said, 'where are you going? We haven't finished.'

She stared at him, stunned, and then began to laugh. 'You mean *you* haven't. You're holding out on me again.'

'I could come at a better time,' he suggested, falling down on to the floor, and there it was: his erection, big as ever. And she knew then, even before it had happened – before they had crawled up into the bed and made love again, at their leisure – that he could indeed, as he had often boasted, go on longer. It was, he claimed, one of the few advantages of approaching middle age.

Except that he was only thirty-one, which made her rather doubt his reasoning.

Some time later, they lay under the covers, becalmed. 'You never finished telling me,' she said, 'why Ty shouldn't have taken his company public.'

Jamie chuckled. 'Your mind works in the strangest ways.'

'I just wondered.'

Jamie curled his arm around Holly's shoulders. 'Well, you know who owns a third of the shares in TCI just now.'

Holly shook her head.

'Mother, of course. Ty felt he owed it to her. He always used to promise her that once he owned something substantial, she'd have a piece of it for herself.'

'Generous of him,' said Holly drily.

'Well – ' Jamie shrugged. 'Fair enough. There's plenty to go round, and Daph and I, and Esmé and Hywel, put together we've 10 per cent or so. But that's not real selling power. Only Mother has that.'

'But she wouldn't sell.'

'She *couldn't* sell, so long as the company was private. No one to sell to, except Ty. You see, that's what he's bargained away.'

'The right to buy his mother's shares?' said Holly, puzzled.

'More than that. Control. Any time Mother wants to punish him, all she has to do is put her shares on the market. If she did it all at once, the price would drop.'

'The price has gone up 5 per cent in just the last two weeks, though.'

'That's because Ty's likely to get high returns. For anyone who's willing to put in the money without looking too closely at his methods. But he needs control to run TCI the way he does. He doesn't have that without Mother's shares.'

'Well, he must feel pretty sure she'd never sell.'

'It's possible he's just a little too confident of her good will.' Jamie eased himself up to a sitting position; silently Holly admired the contours of his back: the way his shoulders narrowed into his waist. 'Mother,' he went on, 'is a master manipulator. She'll find the occasion to punish Ty for something – somehow – just to show who's in command.'

Suddenly Holly smiled. 'You mean he's put himself . . . under her thumb? More than before?'

'We've never either of us escaped from under it,' said Jamie grimly.

'You can't mean that.'

Jamie leaned back against the bedstead, forcing a smile. 'I've played her little games for so long as I can remember. When we were small, she used to stage contests out in the grounds at Stadhampton. Tree-climbing, shooting, swimming. Tyrconnel versus me. Guess who won the prizes.'

'Prizes?'

'Well, being in her good graces, as opposed to being ignored.'

'But Tyrconnel's three years older.'

'That didn't matter. Finally, I learnt to say, "What a lovely dress, Mother", or "How pretty you look", just to distract her from thinking up yet another competition. But that, in effect, is the way she still operates.'

'How can she?'

Jamie shifted. 'Well, Esmé needs whatever pittance Ty's willing to give her and Hywel for their services – at the rate she goes through nannies. And then, as for me, there are Mother's connections. . . . Amazing, really, that so many men at what one would think a more dignified age still imagine themselves in love with her.'

'Who on earth do you mean?' Holly smiled, puzzled.

'*Everybody.*' Jamie laughed and absently stroked her hand. 'Half the Cabinet.'

'You mean Macmillan?'

'Oh, no, not the big man. But an awful lot of the others have *had* her in their day. Sorry to be so rude. But Mother used to have quite a reputation. With everyone except our father, that is. He never knew. So you see, even these days she has a good number of strings at her fingertips. If she wanted me out of office – '

'But she won't. Of course she won't.'

Jamie shook his head. 'No. I suppose not. I'm too obedient.' He gave a rueful smile. 'Forgive my rambling, darling.' He rose and moved towards the bathroom.

Wondering, Holly listened to the water tumbling into the bath. Jamie was rarely so introspective; and she knew that probably, already, his mind was on other things than the past. Which was just as well. They would have time

for a quick dinner at some secluded place, before he dropped her off at the station in Oxford. They had managed
Fridays before, this way: he heading for Stadhampton, she
by train back to London.

Jamie turned in the doorway. 'Darling,' he said, and
looked worried.

'What?'

He looked at her tenderly for a moment, then shook his
head. 'Nothing.'

'What?'

'No, it's really nothing. Back soon.' Jamie closed the
bathroom door, his chest tightening. He didn't know what
had come over him then – the urge to confess. What
possible good could it do?

He gave a rueful smile as he stepped into the hot water,
thinking of his mother's remark long ago, when he had
been punished at school after admitting he had written the
essay handed in by a more powerful and illiterate older
boy. 'Why on earth did you tell them?' she had scolded
him. 'You're too honest for your own good, Jamie. Just
like your father.'

The water was almost painfully hot, but he sank in,
fairly sure his mother's words were true no longer.

The winter and spring of 1963 brought trouble for Tory
politicians in general, and James Carr in particular. In
January, a month of record cold, electricians' strikes
several times plunged Stadhampton into darkness. By the
end of March, Jamie was enmeshed in party scandal. It
all spiralled out of a seemingly trivial affair between the
Secretary of State for War, Jack Profumo, and a young
girl, Christine Keeler: the same one, it turned out, whom
Jamie and Holly had both glimpsed running naked from
the pool at Cliveden almost two years ago.

'*That* girl?' gasped Holly, when Jamie told her about it
on the phone. 'She didn't even look eighteen.'

'She's nineteen,' Jamie countered, 'or was, when Jack
took up with her.' At first he was inclined to laugh off

the notion that Christine had passed defence secrets from Profumo to her Soviet lover. 'And as for illicit affairs in the House, Profumo's the tip of the iceberg.'

'Oh?' Holly paused, huddled over the phone. 'Then what are we – the bottom of it?'

Jamie only laughed; and finally she did, too. The possibility of their being found out was simply too scary to contemplate.

It was a spring of rumours. First Profumo; then the Commonwealth Secretary, Duncan Sandys, who attempted to resign, apprehensive that he might be cited as a co-respondent in the acrimonious divorce of the Duke and Duchess of Argyll. Holly lived in fear that any day she would open the morning papers to find her name and Jamie's splashed all over the front pages.

In March, Profumo denied all the allegations before the House of Commons; in June he confessed that back in March he had lied. Jamie, who as chief whip should have prevented the disaster, had no choice but to offer his resignation.

For a day, Holly nearly held her breath, afraid for Jamie. But in the end, Macmillan was loyal. 'If you resign,' he told Jamie, 'I shall resign.'

Jamie telephoned late that night, exhausted after a raucous debate in the Commons.

'My God,' he said, 'I wish you were here right now.'

'I know.'

'Sometimes I get so fed up with keeping us secret, I want to blow it all away and tell everyone. To hell with the scandal.'

'Darling.' Holly's heart pounded unaccustomedly fast. 'If you mean – about us, I wish you could. But. . . .' Images flashed through her mind. The headlines. The divorce trial: Daphne on the court steps, tearful, with her children.

'What's the worst that could come of it? I could go back to practising law. Clients have an even shorter memory than politicians.'

But something told Holly that here Jamie was wrong. A prominent politician and his brother's wife? No one would forget. And Jamie might come to rue the day he had given up a whole career. . . . 'If we were just any two people. Even two *married* people.' She sighed.

'I know.'

They both knew they had no choice but to go on as they were.

Summer came, and yet again Jamie was swept up in political concerns. Early in October, Macmillan was forced by unexpected illness to resign. After a frenzied in-party election, he was replaced as prime minister by the unlikely aristocrat Sir Alec Douglas-Home. A few weeks later, Jamie swept Holly off for a weekend in France to celebrate a temporary lull in the House. 'Or,' he remarked, 'a stay of execution. We'll never win the next election.'

They took a room in a château-hotel south of Orleans, where they made love in the four-poster bed, on the gilt chaise-longue, on the carpet in front of the burning logs in their massive carved stone fireplace.

'I love you.' Jamie's hand traced the patterns cast by the flame shadows on Holly's breasts.

'I love you, too.'

'I wish it were always like this.'

'But it can't be.' Holly smiled. Time was too short to be mournful.

It was also too short, she decided, to worry about the fact that in the hurry of packing she had forgotten her diaphragm.

It might, she realised, almost have been deliberate. The round rubber cap with its accompanying jelly could be, frankly speaking, a nuisance. She had enjoyed the spontaneity of lovemaking without it; and anyway, when she got back to London and counted up the days on her calendar she realised that she was probably safe. *Safe.* What a funny word. When she remembered how much she had once wanted a baby.

She still did. But it only struck her a few weeks later, when, in the middle of the Beatles' Royal Variety performance, Helen leaned over and whispered that she was pregnant.

'*What?*' Holly almost shrieked.

Helen nodded, her eyes glowing. 'I was afraid to tell you.'

'Why?' Helen had been reluctant to come along tonight, despite the fact that the concert was the year's hottest event: Jamie had pulled strings to get them tickets. Holly knew that Helen idolised the Beatles rather less than she did; 'I feel *old*,' Helen had complained as they pushed their way in through the ranks of teenage girls in miniskirts.

Maybe, Holly thought now, it was more than that. Maybe she wasn't feeling well. Maybe she needed her rest. . . .

'You look shocked, darling,' said Helen.

'No! Just guilty for dragging you along here, now. Why didn't you tell me?'

Helen shrugged. 'Superstition, maybe. I still don't quite believe it myself. Nige and I've been trying for almost four years.'

'So when's it going to be?'

'End of May – beginning of June.'

'Nige must be happy.'

Helen nodded. Already – or so it seemed to Holly – her face had taken on hints of that round, Madonna-like rapture she associated with new mothers. Her mind clicked through the months. After Christmas Helen might start to show – by the spring she would be really, visibly pregnant. If, by chance, something *had* happened during those few days in France. . . .

She snapped off the thought before she could even finish it. The absurd thought of Helen and her having babies at the same time, strolling their prams in the park.

'Holly.' She felt Helen press her hand. 'You aren't upset, are you? We'll still do things together, you know.'

Holly smiled – at her friend, and her own silly thoughts. 'Of course I'm not upset,' she said. 'It's wonderful.' She reached over and gave Helen a big hug. The Beatles had started singing their latest big hit, 'She Loves You', but suddenly they were the farthest thing from her mind.

In Dallas, President Kennedy had been shot.

Holly heard the news, standing in her bathroom at Chester Square: one minute, 'Please Please Me' had been playing on the radio; the next, came the makeshift announcement. Her chest tightened and loosened in absurd relief. The President was murdered; maybe the world had gone crazy, but she was safe.

At that very same minute she had glanced down at her panties and found a stain. She was not pregnant. Yet at that very minute, too, she felt a twinge of regret at the lost germ, the lost chance of a baby, hers and Jamie's. She hated to think it could never happen.

In the next weeks and months, she began, without quite acknowledging it to herself, to play with chance. The diaphragm was a nuisance; and maybe she didn't really need it after all. Helen had been *trying* to have a child, and still it had taken her four years.

Anyway, it was all so easy and natural without the diaphragm. She was tempted to take small risks at the beginning of a cycle, at the end. Often, these days, Jamie phoned at the last minute, and she had to hurry out to meet him, so it was easy to forget. And as the winter passed, she remained still safely un-pregnant. It was all right.

The new Prime Minister, Alec Douglas-Home, depended on Jamie more than Macmillan had. But Jamie could not return his faith. Sometimes he would fume to Holly on the phone.

'He's hopeless! He refused to do that television talk, yet

again. I tried to tell him how important it was. I told him three-quarters of UK homes have a TV! "Do they re-ally?" he said.' Jamie imitated the new Prime Minister's tight-lipped, aristocratic accent. ' "Do you mean working-class people have televisions? Fancy that." '

'In all honesty,' Jamie told Holly and his secretary, Gillian, in a low voice, over lunch, 'I really don't fancy our chances, come the election.'

Gillian twinkled. 'Disloyalty. Thinking of switching parties, are you?'

'All the best aristocrats are Labour these days,' returned Holly. 'Look at Anthony Wedgwood Benn.' For a second her gaze and Gillian's crossed, and she wondered if the other woman *knew*. It was precisely why Jamie arranged outings like this, of course, from time to time. To allay suspicion.

If Gillian guessed, she was too sensible to show it. 'I just hope Stadhampton stays solid for the Tories,' she said. 'I don't fancy getting a new job. Though I don't know about you, Holly. Perhaps you'd just as soon defect –' she winked – 'to Mr Benn.'

Helen's stomach bulged early, and by February she was swearing she was pregnant with twins. 'My God,' she moaned over the phone. 'I feel as if I've aged thirty years. I've got varicose veins! Do you fancy trading bodies?'

Holly itched to ask Helen what it was *really* like. What else happened to your body? How did it feel?

At the beginning of April she realised that soon she might be able to answer those questions for herself. She was ten days, then two weeks, late.

Finally she made an appointment with her doctor.

XIX

At first her overwhelming feeling was one of relief. It *could* happen. She could have a baby.

It only struck her with full force that what could happen, definitely would – that there was no stopping it now, no turning fact back into safe speculation – when the obstetrician ticked the weeks off on his calendar and said, 'It should come around Christmas, I should guess. Better do your shopping early.' Dr Harvie was a kind, elderly Scot, recommended by Helen, who was using him herself. 'Now I normally work at St Margaret's. Shall I let them know?'

'What? Oh. Yes . . .' Holly shook her head, coming to in a rush. 'You are . . . really sure?'

A few minutes later she walked down Harley Street in a daze and flagged a cab. Suddenly what she had dreamed of was real. Whom would she tell first?

Until a few years ago, she had always imagined telling her husband. Now, since she did not know whom to tell, she carried the news up the stairs to Fitzgerald.

'I'm pregnant.' She dared do no more than whisper it. 'I'm going to have a baby.'

Fitzgerald thumped his tail, his brown eyes, fogged these days by cataracts, shining at her. He smiled – *But can dogs smile?* she thought. *I'm going mad.* Then he leapt over her knees, laddering her tights, and whined at the door for a walk.

'Poor old Fitz,' she said, fetching his leash. He was getting older, even slightly arthritic; there was no denying it. She walked him a long way down the King's Road. There was so much to think about. Suddenly her ordinary life seemed fraught with problems – challenges, anyway. Where would the baby live? In her flat? Or would Imogen insist on having rooms redone in his – or her – honour?

How would Imogen take the news? She knew exactly how things were between Holly and Tyrconnel. What conclusions would she draw – or pretend to draw?

How would she, Holly, ever walk the dog when she was heavily pregnant? Helen said she could barely make it out of bed some mornings. She would need to get someone to look after Fitz. Maybe a nanny.

No, silly. Nannies are for babies. But she wasn't sure she wanted some stranger looking after her baby. She thought of Nanny Walters: her shrill voice and lacquered hair. . . .

When she got back home, late in the afternoon, she knew there was one thing she must do before anything else. She called Jamie and invited him to lunch at Vignola's.

'The old haunt,' he said, with pleasure in his voice. 'Any particular reason?'

'See you at one,' Holly said, and hung up before she could lose her nerve and let everything spill out.

The next day she dressed in her old favourite, the black-and-white suit they had picked out together: it was really too long now, though she had taken the hem up just last year. She examined her reflection: she certainly didn't look pregnant, yet. Nor did she feel ill; though a slight queasiness overtook her at the restaurant when she realised that she had arrived fifteen minutes early and would have to wait.

She could not help smiling at Jamie's approach: his sauntering step, his bright tie – an almost psychedelic mix of reds and pinks that jarred with the necessary sobriety of the rest of his clothing.

As they studied the menu, she sipped her wine. She knew she would not feel any appetite until she told him.

'Jamie,' she began. Something stopped the words in her throat. She looked at him with wide, fearful eyes. *How beautiful he is.* For a second, with absolute certainty, she knew she was going to lose him.

'Yes, darling?' He reached out; stroked her hand under the table.

'I'm pregnant.' The words came out in a whisper.

'Are you really?' Jamie's words were a whisper, too. He looked pale for a moment. He was horrified, she could tell.

And then his face broke into a big grin. 'Are you honestly, darling? You're not just having me on? Because if you are. . . .' He tried, but failed, to take his smile into a look of mock-censure. 'If you are teasing me, I shall have to be very severe with you.' His eyes glittered.

'Yes. I'm pretty sure.'

'Well, this – ' Jamie gulped and drew his napkin to his nose, suddenly. Holly saw the tear that had leaked out of one of his eyes; he was dabbing at the other hastily. 'This,' he said, 'calls for a celebration. Vignola's hardly seems enough. It should be the Ritz. . . . Do you feel well, darling?'

'Never better.' Holly sank back against the banquette, every muscle relaxing from sheer relief. She watched silently as Jamie waved Vignola over and ordered the best wine on the list. Suddenly she felt ravenous.

Telling Tyrconnel was more of a problem. His hours were so erratic that she never knew when she would find him at home. Breakfast, with Imogen present, was not the place. After several days of being unable to locate him, she finally asked Jason to drive her to his office.

His secretary nodded her through.

He was in a meeting with Arthur Jarrell, his black cube of a desk covered in neat stacks of papers.

'Hello, darling.' He looked only mildly surprised. 'Bad timing, I'm afraid. Arthur and I are just about to step out to lunch.'

'Could I speak to you for a minute, before you go?' Holly backed out of the office. 'I'll wait.'

A few minutes later, Arthur Jarrell, with a nod and a sardonic smile, ushered her into the room he had just left.

She closed the door carefully behind her to prevent his eavesdropping. 'I just came in,' she said abruptly, 'because there's something I thought I ought to tell you. I'm pregnant.' To her surprise, the words came out easily.

Tyrconnel stopped in the middle of closing his briefcase. 'Well.' He seemed to be working to compose his face; the narrow lizard-eyes were expressionless. 'What should I say? My congratulations to Uncle Jamie.' He smiled thinly.

'Is that all you have to say?' Holly felt both chilled and relieved. She had feared his anger.

'I've never been exactly obsessed with the matter of heirs, but I should be pleased if the child were a boy.'

'Well.' Holly turned, smiling brightly, her composure on the brink of disintegration. 'I suppose you have a 50 per cent chance.' She preceded him out of the office, but was unable to avoid riding down in the lift with him and Arthur Jarrell. From the lobby she watched the two men slide into Tyrconnel's waiting Bentley; the latest chauffeur, she noticed, was blond, with an angelic little face. If he were anything like the others, he would be twenty rather than the sixteen he looked, and far less of a novice, too. Tyrconnel touched the boy's shoulder as he slid in; Arthur Jarrell eyed him up and down.

Arthur Jarrell, she remembered, was unmarried. For a moment she wondered. . . .

What am I coming to? she thought. For years, now, she had taught herself not to speculate about what Tyrconnel did. She had watched as his behaviour with other men – especially young men, his employees and personal servants, who came and went with lightning speed – became more flagrant. Or perhaps it seemed flagrant only to her.

Gradually, men of Tyrconnel's kind were becoming more visible. In parliament there had been attempts to legalise homosexuality, though Jamie had never supported them, and Holly knew without asking that Tyrconnel had been behind this public silence. For Jamie to take a stand would only attract attention to the family: to himself.

Holly watched the men drive off. Then she smiled at Jason, who had inched the waiting Daimler forward to collect her. The last thing she wanted to think about right now was Tyrconnel.

It was mid-afternoon when Tyrconnel returned to his desk and had his secretary ring the number. He couldn't be bothered to remember it.

The phone rang in his office and he picked it up. 'Jamie? Little brother? Well done.'

By the evening, Tyrconnel had told his mother. Holly knew, because Imogen knocked on her door, all smiles. She wore a short, sequinned indigo dress and an unseasonably warm mink stole; the cloud of Joy surrounding her announced that she was going out.

'I just wanted to say congratulations, Holly, dear. Ty told me the wonderful news.'

'Do you want to sit down?' said Holly reluctantly. Fitzgerald had edged up behind her and was sniffing the air and whimpering.

'I don't think I will. I've never been sure I'm not allergic to dog hair, you know. If you'd like to pop downstairs I can give you the name of a man. . . . Not the same one who delivered Ty and Jamie, of course, but he took over the practice.'

'Thanks. I've already got someone.'

'Well, then.' Imogen smiled again. 'I must be going. I do hope it's a boy. Don't you?'

'I don't know.' Holly's gaze was steady. 'I think I might like a girl.'

Imogen, she noted, only smiled, and didn't venture to argue the point.

For the first few months, Holly wondered why pregnancy was supposed to be an uncomfortable time. She felt terrific. She had no morning sickness; her skin was clear, her hair shone. She felt as if she were floating on her own private cloud. Sometimes she longed to share her secret with the grey Londoners she saw when she was out walking Fitzgerald. They looked so tired, in their raincoats. So unappreciative of life.

Even her visits to an increasingly housebound, fatigued and impatient Helen failed to dampen her enthusiasm. 'I can't wait till it shows. I don't mind if I get big,' she told her friend. 'Then I'll really know it's there.'

'Believe me,' said Helen, lank-haired, reclining below her billowing belly on the sofa. 'There'll come a time when you *always* know it's there. I keep telling myself: two more weeks to go.'

Helen's waters broke on the second of June, and a panicked Nige phoned Holly to tell her his wife had gone into hospital. Together that night they paced the waiting room, until Nige told Holly to go home and get some sleep. Early the next morning he rang again to say that the baby was born: a healthy boy.

Holly moved a little anxiously through the corridors of the maternity hospital in St John's Wood. Behind the antiseptic walls she could hear the groans of women in labour.

But when she opened Helen's door her friend was beaming. Her face was pink and her hair damp, but overnight she seemed to have recovered the vitality the last few months had drained away. Her little boy, Frederic, lay in her arms and her room was lined with flowers.

'So there.' Helen held the baby out for approval. 'It's over. Thank God. I'm beginning to think one's enough.'

'Oh, Helen!' Holly bent to admire Frederic: his perfect nose, his small curled hands. Soon she would have one just like him. Or nearly.

'You should see his toes!' said Helen suddenly. 'They're absolutely tiny, and perfect, Holly. I've never seen anything like them.'

For the next hour, Holly laughed inwardly as her usually forthright friend lapsed into unashamed sentimentality. It would be hard to find a baby more adored than Frederic English.

Holly only ached a little when Nige came in and she remembered: when this happened to her, Jamie wouldn't be able to be there – waiting outside the delivery room, visiting.

Already he had told her he would do everything he possibly could for their baby. He would visit; he would take him or her to the zoo. 'I'll be the most attentive uncle in the world, Holly,' he said. 'You'll see.'

But an uncle could only do so much.

Helen, once recovered from the birth, was eager to go shopping with Holly for baby things; Imogen had already sent for a complete layette from Harrods. Every day – under Imogen's orders, Holly was sure – Eduardo asked after Holly's appetite, and to find out if there were any special delicacies she desired. Tyrconnel bought her a pair of very showy diamond earrings, and Jamie – in the guise of uncle – sent her a fleecy blanket for Fitzgerald, a pram and a case of champagne. Everyone was being so good to Holly that she was able to put most of her apprehensions aside. Imogen and Tyrconnel acted as if no doubt about her child's paternity had ever entered their minds.

If Holly had not felt so permanently elated, so filled to the brim with happiness, she might perhaps have doubted their goodwill. As it was, she moved blithely through the first five months of her pregnancy. She met Jamie more often at his flat these days, since he was wary of taking her on the long drives from London which used to fill Friday afternoons. 'If anything should happen . . .' he would say, his brow drawing up in lines of apprehension. He was absurdly cautious, Holly thought, even for a father-to-be. He had, after all – though she did not like to remind herself of it – been through all this before.

So they continued to meet, and to make love; her slowly changing shape did not seem to deter him.

On the day Holly became, by her count, five and a half months pregnant, she took a cab to the Westminster flat carrying a bottle of cider, a parcel of smoked salmon and a lemon. Sometimes she developed the most enormous cravings.

Because she was a little early, she let herself in and arranged the salmon on a plate – it was all she could do to keep her hands off it – and went into the bathroom to check herself in the mirror. She shopped carefully these days, still staving off the moment when she would have to move into the frumpy Empire-line maternity dresses that seemed to be the only ones on sale; luckily her belly was still small enough to fit into normal clothes, a size or two larger than usual. Today she wore a triangular mini covered in dizzying swirls of black and white.

As she was brushing her hair – carefully, as ever, with her own brush from her own handbag, leaving no traces – the doorbell rang. Thinking it must be Jamie, she went to open it.

The person waiting in the hall was small, blonde and female. She clutched an imitation leopard-skin bag.

'Mrs Carr?' she said.

'Yes?' Holly answered before she could think. 'How can I help you?'

The girl tossed her head; her hair was flaxen-coloured, probably bleached. 'P'raps I'd better come in.' She moved past Holly into the foyer.

'What do you want?' said Holly, suddenly alarmed, thinking, *Reporter? Busybody? Spy?* How could she get rid of her?

'My name's Diane Pritchard,' said the girl. 'And there's something I think you ought to know. Your husband and I are in love.'

The door thudded closed behind Holly, of its own accord.

'You are?' She heard her own voice: cool, with an unearthly echo.

'Are you all right, Mrs Carr? P'raps you'd better sit down.'

Gritting her teeth, telling herself she was not going to be instructed to sit down in her own house – well, at least more her own house than this girl's – Holly straightened her spine until she could look down on Diane Pritchard. 'Who are you?' she said. 'What are you trying to do? Are you from the papers?'

The girl, looking relaxed now, turned her head to scan the contents of the living room. 'No.' She smiled suddenly, and the effect, Holly noted ruefully, was transforming. The bleached hair, the cheap white dress, laddered tights and the round face, with its none too perfect skin, took on a momentarily enchanting girlishness. 'Maybe we'd better sit down after all.'

Reluctantly, Holly agreed.

For the next half-hour she sat immobile while Diane Pritchard talked. She felt almost as if her body sat, while her spirit hovered somewhere above, yet heard it all.

Diane Pritchard came from New Zealand. She had come to England 'on a lark' and ended up working as a temporary secretary. For two weeks she had been placed at an estate agent's office in Stadhampton whose owner was active with the local Tories. He had asked her along to a meeting, where Jamie had spotted her folding chairs, and offered to help, and – Diane gave a coy shrug – 'It went on from there.'

Holly only nodded.

'He keeps on telling me he's going to tell you – sorry, Mrs Carr, no offence, but I thought it was time to clear the air, like. I always told him if he wanted to see me, he had to take it serious. "Jamie," I told him, "you got to bring things out in the open. If you was your wife, wouldn't you want to know?"'

Holly stared at the girl. 'What makes you think he's in love with you?'

For the first time, Diane squirmed. 'I just know.' She smiled. 'He's always been such a gentleman. Never minded about being seen with me. When I moved back to London he took me out – introduced me to some of his friends from parliament. I think it gave him a kind of thrill.'

Holly looked at her. 'Did it,' she said neutrally. All she could think was, *Please let it end. Please make her go.*

'So what are you going to do?' Diane Pritchard demanded.

'Do? I don't know.' Holly blinked; her cheeks felt stiff and dry. 'Anyway, I think you'd better go.'

To her surprise, Diane Pritchard stood up, obediently. 'I

know it's a shock,' she said. 'But I believe in getting things out in the open. Don't you?'

Holly didn't answer. Casting her a curious look, Diane Pritchard picked up her leopard-skin bag and sauntered out.

Holly rose, a minute later, and locked the door behind her. Then she took off her shoes and stretched out on the sofa, closing her eyes. She was thankful that the baby lay quiet in her womb just now. Too many thoughts and feelings churned inside her already. *Betrayal.*

It was tempting, of course, not to believe the girl. But then why would she come here, out of the blue? Why pick on Jamie?

A few minutes later, a key turned in the lock. Holly started to raise herself to her feet.

'Hello, darling. Don't get up.' Jamie came over and kissed her forehead. 'You look tired.'

'I've just had a visitor.'

Jamie had dropped his briefcase on the floor and was shrugging off his jacket. 'A visitor?' He turned, surprised. 'Here?'

'Maybe you know her. Diane Pritchard?' Holly folded her hands over her stomach, attempting to still her rising queasiness.

'Let me see. Diane Pritchard . . . met her in Stadhampton once. Australian girl. What did she want?'

'How can you be so goddamned nonchalant?' Holly's voice burst out before she could think. 'I know you're lying. You're so transparent, Jamie. I know you slept with her.'

'Easy . . .' Jamie's eyes widened as he slid on to the sofa next to Holly, reaching out for her hand. 'You really mustn't get upset, Holly. It isn't good for you.'

'No. I'm sure it's not.' Holly snatched her hand from Jamie's. 'Well, then, if you'd known she was going to come, you should have stopped her. Paid her off, or whatever it is you do with your other mistresses.'

'I don't have any other – mistresses.' Jamie's voice grew

heated. 'I don't like that word to begin with. I think of us as lovers. I don't have any other lovers.'

'Then why on earth should she have come here? Why *did* she? Why did everything she said sound so much like the truth?'

'Holly – I don't know what you mean.' Jamie looked baffled.

Numbly Holly recited the details; repeated, with distaste, everything Diane had told her.

'She's making it up,' he said flatly when she had finished. 'The girl's obviously deranged.'

'Come on. You know it sounds true. It *is* true. All that politeness. The little risks you like to take. . . .'

'Holly.' Jamie reached for her hand, his eyes searching for hers. 'Please. Bear with me. I'll be totally honest. I did – go out once with Diane. It was almost two years ago. I suppose I was a coward, but I was afraid to tell you.'

Holly's mind raced. *Two years ago*. That was when Tyrconnel had taken TCI public. Not long after, she and Jamie had driven up to Oxfordshire . . . 'Once?' she said. 'Only?'

'I'm not sure.' Jamie looked uncomfortable. 'She kept ringing me up. For a long time I wouldn't see her, but she kept on. . . . She's not right in the head, Holly. I broke down, finally. I saw her once last winter, just for a drink . . . I knew, as soon as you told me about the baby, that it had to stop.'

'Stop?' Holly looked up sharply. 'How could anything "stop" when it hadn't happened for almost two years? Or so you say. How could she come in here and make all these demands? Is there more to it? Have you told me the truth, Jamie?'

'I don't know. I . . .' Jamie ran a hand through his hair.

Throwing off his other hand, Holly stood. She stroked a polished desk-top; looked out the window, with its uninspiring northern view of the street, of other mansion blocks, which she and Jamie, standing here, embracing, had pretended to admire through the curtains. It had seemed worth admiring, then; it had meant something.

And she knew even as Jamie followed her, putting his arms around her, searching for her gaze, making excuses, that she had been fooling herself for far too long. Today, when Diane Pritchard came, she had felt like a wife betrayed. But she wasn't.

Helen, she remembered, had warned her once, though she had quickly forgotten it. *A man who can cheat on his wife can cheat on you.*

'Diane meant nothing. Once I knew I loved you, I didn't want anything to do with her or anyone else.' Jamie wrapped his arms around Holly, but she felt she had shrunk to a small core, far away from him.

'Once you *knew* you loved me?' she said. *He told me he did, at the very beginning.*

'Perhaps I've always known. But I didn't always realise how much. I've failed you, but I'll try to change. Honestly. Can you believe me?'

Holly looked up, her vision blurred. 'Oh, I do. I do believe you. But that's not the point.' Her voice grew tight and she tried to wrench herself away. But the harder she struggled, the tighter Jamie held her, until at last she was pounding at his shoulders, blinded by tears. 'Don't you understand?' she cried. 'We broke all the rules – I only did it because I thought it *mattered*.' She shook her head, her fists clenched tight. 'And now, to hear about that girl . . . that you took all the risks for her, and told the lies. . . .'

'I was wrong.' Jamie spoke soberly. 'It was a mistake.'

'Then,' said Holly, 'we must have been a mistake, too.'

She found that now the tears were drying, tightening the skin on her cheeks. She could slip away from Jamie, and he did not try to hold her. She reached for her coat, her handbag. 'Goodbye, Jamie.'

'For now,' he said. 'I'll call you.'

'No, don't bother.'

'Darling – '

She heard his voice from the foyer and hurried out. She

knew he wouldn't follow her; they were always careful, in the public spaces of the mansion block, not to make any kind of show of themselves.

Old habits die hard. Too hard for Jamie to come running after her now. He wouldn't. Once he realised she was gone from his life, he would leave her quite alone.

She was wrong about that. Wrong, too, when, in those first hours she nursed the hurt inside her and imagined that she could never feel the smallest shred of love for him again. Their lives had been too intertwined for that.

Even by that night she was remembering. The day he had picked her up from the hospital in Norfolk, fragile and uncertain and elated. They had gone to the beach – she had felt the attraction even then.

Perhaps that had been the best time of all: before anything dangerous began. There had been no guilt then, only the *frisson* of possibility, of a taboo on the verge of being broken.

But she knew she was fooling herself if she believed that. She would not have given up what she and Jamie had, for all the world. He had been the one who finally took her virginity, who taught her what love really meant.

And then betrayed her.

That night, the phone startled her out of a delirious half-sleep. She leapt up to answer it before she remembered.

'Holly?'

She heard his voice. Half of her wanted to hang up, but she couldn't. Not yet.

'I can't sleep,' he said. 'I've been thinking . . . about the baby. You know, whatever happens, it's still ours.'

'What makes you say that?' Her voice was thick. 'You're its uncle.'

'I can't let it go this way, Holly. Can't let *you* go.'

'You have to. I want you to.'

'You don't know what you're saying.'

'I do know what I'm saying.' Holly paused, suddenly

awake, trying to compose her words. 'Right now I feel . . . as if everything we did was wrong.'

'Don't say that, Holly.'

Because she could think of nothing else to say – because suddenly she felt immensely weary – Holly hung up.

The next days were no easier, though she had hoped they might be. Jamie continued to call, the phone ringing at strange hours – six a.m., noon, four o'clock – until, exhausted by the arguments, she eventually stopped answering it, and disconnected the cord.

She was sure that everything was over. As the hours passed, she felt more and more as if a veil had been lifted from her eyes. She could see clearly now.

What had she and Jamie intended to do? Go on as they were for ever? Would she have remained his mistress at thirty? Forty? She had not thought so far ahead before.

She began now to think of the rest of her life: to wonder what would become of it.

For now, she could do nothing. She was in a strange physical limbo, easily tired, easily tearful. She would have to wait for the baby: three and a half more months. Then she would see.

The phone rang and rang at Jamie's flat. At last he picked it up, because he hoped – unreasonably, he knew – that it would be Holly.

Instead of her American accent, he heard a mix of Antipodean and cockney. He remembered it all too well.

'Got you in, did I?' said Diane Pritchard. 'About time.'

'What do you want?'

'I liked your wife. Nice lady.'

'Diane, that's none of your business. I've tried to tell you again and again. It's over.'

'I think – ' Diane paused, and then giggled. 'I think it's not over unless I want it to be. What's it worth to you?' Suddenly her voice had taken on a harsh edge.

'I won't listen to threats.'

'I'd like £500. I've been thinking about starting up a business.'

Jamie gripped the phone tighter. 'I've nothing to say to you.' His palms were sweating.

'Lots of people'd be interested in my story if you aren't. I'll go to the papers. You know, like that Christine Keeler. I don't think your wife'd fancy that.'

Jamie felt his whole body overheating now. Every time Diane mentioned his 'wife' he broke out in a fresh sweat. It was true, Diane had never laid eyes on Daphne. But how long would it take her to find out that it had not been Daphne she met that afternoon?

He stalled for time. 'I don't have anything to say to you.'

'One little favour. Think how much easier it would make things. Tell you what, I'll call you back tomorrow, give you time to think. All right?' She hung up.

Breathing heavily, trying to calm himself, Jamie paced around the room before dialling a number.

'Good afternoon, Lord Carr's office.'

'Can you put me through, please?' Jamie wiped his brow. His hair felt damp and lank. 'It's his brother.'

A few seconds later Tyrconnel came on. 'Jamie! Well, how are you? This is unexpected.'

Jamie felt his whole body being taken over by a chill. For a moment he was in the garden at Stadhampton, staring up the trunk of a tree he couldn't climb. And then at his brother: ten when he was seven. Or nine when he was six. Which? He couldn't remember. 'Ty,' he said hesitantly, 'I've never asked you this kind of thing before. I'm in trouble. Someone's – making threats. She wants £500.'

'Is that all?' Tyrconnel chuckled.

'What do you mean, is that all? I'm broke. And we could be having an election any day. I can't afford this, in any sense of the word.'

'Does Daphne know?'

'Good Lord, no.'

'Then I'm sure,' said Tyrconnel calmly, 'everything can be fixed. Now, is this person due to be getting in touch again?'

A few minutes later Jamie hung up the phone in disbelief. Tyrconnel had promised to make the arrangements; it would all be taken care of.

Diane Pritchard loitered nervously under the departures board at Paddington Station. She had come out of her way, and it made her uneasy that she was supposed to be meeting Jamie's secretary, rather than Jamie himself.

She clutched her leopard-skin bag. One of her heels was loose. A woman in a dark coat was approaching: small, black-haired with a pronounced streak of grey. For reasons Diane could not quite discern, she looked rich.

'Excuse me.' The woman smiled and extended a thin hand. 'Are you Diane Pritchard?'

Diane nodded.

'I'm Gillian Lawrence. Would you like to come with me? My car's just out front.'

'All right.' But Diane hesitated when the woman beckoned. 'This won't take long, will it?'

The woman gave her a confidential smile. 'No. No time at all. I thought you'd prefer to meet in private.'

Limping a little on her broken heel, Diane followed.

The car was a nondescript, large black Rover. The other woman unlocked the front doors and indicated that Diane should get in beside her.

'I'll drive off a bit, if you don't mind.'

The woman's driving made Diane distinctly nervous. She watched as the small, black-leather-gloved hands lurched the car from gear to gear. They careered out into the middle of a busy thoroughfare, then veered, across several lines of traffic, into a smaller street.

'Where are we going?' asked Diane nervously.

In response, the other woman rammed in the clutch and screeched to a halt. 'This should do.'

She climbed out, but before Diane could follow her,

hands seized her from behind. A thick forearm crushed her neck against the back of the seat.

The other woman studied her. 'I shouldn't bother trying to get out, Miss Pritchard. My friends will take care of that for you.'

A second later, Diane's door flew open and she was wrenched out, feet first, her body bumping on the pavement. She screamed, but realised too late that the street – an alley lined by garages and the backs of warehouses – was quite empty. No one would hear her.

Imogen watched.

Scripps and Keegan were professionals, ex-boxers. It had been tricky finding men who didn't have scruples about hurting a woman.

First they threw Diane Pritchard against a brick wall. Keegan gave her a few cursory jabs in the ribs. The girl held her hands over her face. 'What'd I do?' she whimpered.

Imogen walked closer. 'I hope you understand,' she said, 'you're not to start talking to the papers. Not that they'll be so keen to print your story once they find out you're rather less than photogenic.'

Diane curled back against the wall, and started to struggle to her feet. 'What are you lot,' she hissed, 'cowards? All I want is money.'

'That's not the point,' said Imogen calmly. 'We want you *away*, Miss Pritchard. You're a liability. Scripps?'

Obliging, Scripps kneed Diane Pritchard in the belly.

'Coward!' she shouted up. 'Getting your heavies to do all the work for you . . . I bet you're afraid of blood.'

'On the contrary,' said Imogen. 'I'm not afraid. Keegan?' She held out her hand; the burlier of the two men placed a knife in it. Kneeling down, she rested the blade on Diane's cheek.

The girl squirmed back but Keegan grabbed her and held her still.

'The next time you feel like talking,' said Imogen, 'remember this.' Her eyes glittered, white lights on black, as she slid the blade across a stretch of pale, rouged skin.

Diane Pritchard screamed. The wound gaped and began to pour blood.

'We'll come and get you again,' said Imogen, 'if you talk, and the result the next time will be far less pretty. Here's a ticket – ' She slid an envelope into the front of the girl's dress. 'I suggest you go home. If you stay far enough away from this country, we won't have to trouble you again.'

Then she stood, handing Scripps the keys to the rented car.

'A bit near the eye,' Keegan ventured. 'Think she'll be all right?'

'Nothing a good plastic surgeon couldn't fix,' said Imogen. 'Not, I suppose, that she can afford one.'

She let the men drop her off at Marble Arch and took a cab the rest of the way home. Once she had changed, she went to Jamie's. She knew he would be waiting.

In fact, he had been waiting so long that he had already started on the gin.

'Buck up,' she said, planting a kiss on his damp forehead. 'It's all over.'

'It certainly is.'

'For Christ's sake don't look so glum!' Since Jamie showed no signs of fetching her a drink, Imogen went to pour herself one. 'Diane Pritchard is a two-bit little tart, and I'm sure you won't have to look very hard to find yourself another.'

'I don't give a fuck about Diane Pritchard.'

'If you mean someone else – ' Imogen's voice turned chill – 'you know damn well that had to end. It went on far too long.'

Suddenly Jamie rose. 'Thank you, Mother. I don't think I need a lecture just now.' His hand hovered over the gin bottle; then he shoved it to the side. 'I can run my own life, you know. Goddamn it. For once, why don't you just leave me alone?'

Clutching her handbag, Imogen stood. Her lips were white. 'All right. I'll leave you alone. But let me tell you one thing. Who do you think took care of Diane Pritchard? Who do you think had to find the men – who had to *meet* the girl, because you were such a damn fool you couldn't even give us so much as a week's notice?' Imogen gave a short laugh. 'Do you know, I had to drive? I haven't driven in forty years. I don't even have a licence.'

Jamie was silent.

'So think again,' said Imogen, 'the next time you decide you owe us nothing.'

Jamie was still silent as she walked out the door.

Two days later the Prime Minister, Sir Alec Douglas-Home, called an election.

Labour carried it, much as the pundits had been predicting: perhaps because Harold Wilson looked a more convincing leader than the fuddy-duddy Douglas-Home; perhaps because the Tories were simply burnt out, and the country, no longer so prosperous as it had been in their heyday, wanted a change. Some spoke of Profumo, and the scandals that had dogged the Tory party, even as little as two days before the election, when one of the more downmarket papers ran the story of a New Zealand girl who claimed to have enjoyed a liaison with the Conservative chief whip.

However, there was no photo of the girl, the story looked highly dubious, and none of the other papers gave it any play – least of all the scandal-seeking *Current*, which endorsed Douglas-Home.

The story had little effect in Stadhampton, where the voters returned James Carr, albeit with a reduced majority.

When the shadow Cabinet was appointed, James Carr lost his place as chief whip. But, all things considered, the pundits agreed, he had been lucky. After all, he was only thirty-three; he had a long political life ahead of him.

XX

Corinna Clayton Carr was born on 10 January 1965, at St Margaret's Hospital, St John's Wood.

She was not named after any other Claytons or Carrs, but almost by chance. When Holly felt the first spasms of labour, she had been sitting on a sofa, reading some of her old favourite seventeenth-century poetry. She had clung to the book then, as she breathed in, trying to keep calm:

> Then, while time serves, and we are but decaying,
> Come, my Corinna, come, let's go a-Maying.

All through her labour of fourteen hours, those words had stayed with her: they became a kind of chant. That name, come upon by accident, pulled her through: *Corinna*.

And so, when they told her that she had a baby girl, it seemed the most natural thing in the world to call her Corinna.

In the morning, when the nurse came to open the blinds in Holly's room, smiling and saying, 'I'll just bring your baby now, Lady Carr,' Holly felt emotions flood her at the very words. *My baby*.

She looked in wonder at the small, wrinkled face. Still deep in the anaesthesia last night, she had not seen it. Now, for a fleeting second, it seemed a stranger's face; then at once she knew it, and knew that this face would become dearer and more familiar to her than anyone's.

Helen had told her it was like falling in love. And she was right.

Flowers came: from Holly's mother, from Helen and Nige, from the staff at Chester Square.

Later in the morning, the nurse shook Holly awake. 'Lady Carr? You have a visitor.'

It was Imogen. Wafting Joy, she laid a box from Cartier

on Holly's knees. It proved to contain a chunky gold and diamond necklace.

'From Ty, darling,' said Imogen. 'He's in Paris, of course, but he asked me to pick you up a little something.'

Imogen declined the chance to hold Corinna when the nurse brought her in for inspection. 'Very pretty, dear,' she said to Holly after a cursory glance. 'I'm glad she doesn't have any ghastly birthmarks. Not a boy for Ty, alas, but we won't say anything, will we?'

Later on, that afternoon, the nurse popped her head in again.

'Another visitor, Lady Carr. It's your brother-in-law.'

'No! Nurse – ' Holly called in desperation, for the nurse had already vanished again. 'Tell him I can't see him. I'm sorry. I'm too tired. . . .'

But no one seemed to hear her. A minute later, Jamie stood in the doorway. An enormous bundle of flowers filled his arms, wedged awkwardly against his chest. 'Well,' he said, and smiled. He leaned back to close the door behind him.

He's wearing a new suit, Holly thought absurdly, irrelevantly. She hadn't seen him in four months. He looked more tanned than she remembered, which, perhaps, was the reason why his eyes seemed so intensely green.

She said nothing.

He placed the flowers on her bedside table. 'How are you feeling? I gather . . . the nurses said it went well. As these things go.' He smiled, abashed.

Holly smiled back. 'Yes. As these things go. It's all right. Now that it's over I already seem to be forgetting it.'

'You look wonderful, for – well, you know. For a woman who's just had a baby.' Jamie laughed nervously. Then his face grew serious. He looked into Holly's eyes until she was forced to look back. 'Have you thought about things, Holly? About us?'

'If you mean have I changed my mind, I haven't.'

'I don't want our baby to grow up without a father.' Jamie paused, looking down. 'Can I see her?'

Holly nodded. Her body seemed to be trembling all over.

Jamie went out to speak to the nurse, who brought Corinna. For a few minutes they were silent, all three together. Perhaps, Holly thought, this would be the first and last time.

Jamie didn't say any of the usual things about how tiny the baby was, or how she had her father's eyes, her mother's nose. He said nothing, but only touched Corinna's soft head; it was smaller than his hand.

'Are you sure there's no chance?'

His voice was low; Holly realised her arms were shaking. 'Please, Jamie. Don't bring these things up.'

'Did you get any of my letters? Did you get the flowers?'

'What flowers?'

'At Stadhampton. I sent them – bunches of them. No message. But I thought you'd know.'

'Nothing came.' Holly looked at him, perturbed. She had spent most of her last few months of pregnancy in the country, in part to escape London and its associations. Now that she thought of it, she had a vague memory of flowers being delivered. . . . One day she had found the kitchen full of them, and the housekeeper had explained, 'My gentleman friend. He's after me to marry him. I'm starting to think he's going daft.'

Holly shook her head. 'Well. It doesn't matter now.'

Jamie gave a tight answering smile. 'No. You're right. What matters now is Corinna. She's beautiful, you know. Our daughter.'

Holly gave a shaky smile. 'I think you'd better learn not to say that. "Our daughter." '

'Can I hold her?'

Silently Holly relinquished Corinna, who let out a cry of alarm, then settled quietly into Jamie's arms. 'You have so many daughters,' she said. 'You must – have a gift for creating them.'

Jamie turned suddenly. 'I know I did everything wrong,' he said. 'But I'll change, Holly. I promise.'

'Even if you changed – ' Holly whispered now – 'it would still be all wrong.'

'I can understand why you feel you can't trust me. Why you hate me.'

'No. I don't hate you. You're – a good person at heart, Jamie. I know you can be better, make something better of your life.'

'Then help me.'

Holly looked at him sadly. 'No.'

'You don't understand.' Jamie's face was bleak. 'My life is utterly empty. I feel trapped – trapped in my job, trapped with Daphne. . . . The only way out is you.'

'No.' Holly shook her head and reached up for Corinna. 'It's you.'

Jamie walked out into the street. Bare branches waved in the wind overhead. He pulled up his coat collar, instinctively concealing his face, but all too soon he heard the familiar sound of footsteps behind him, running.

'Mr Carr?'

Piss off, he wanted to say. Piss off and go home. But he couldn't afford to.

'Well, Jenkins,' he said, turning, recognising the small, shaggy figure in a grubby raincoat, with salt-and-pepper hair. A camera snapped at him before he even saw it coming. Jamie's voice was patient, sardonic. 'What possible news value is there in a backbencher's visit to his sister-in-law in hospital?'

'Long visit,' said the reporter. 'You were in there for over an hour.'

Jamie threw up his hands and walked faster. The man was an albatross. He'd been hanging on Jamie for months now. Ever since the Diane Pritchard story came out, after which Diane herself had proved untraceable, Nile Jenkins from the *Express* had dogged Jamie's steps as if he scented something. What, Jamie didn't know; he wasn't even in office any more.

'Jesus Christ,' he turned and hissed. 'Can't you leave me alone, Jenkins? Can't you tell when a man's had enough?'

The staff at St Margaret's believed in allowing mothers a long, undisturbed convalescence; so much so that they balked at allowing Holly to breastfeed, though Dr Harvie, a rebel believer in the practice, prevailed.

Holly was glad he did. Day by day as she fed, Corinna seemed to change and grow, and the long hours they spent together this way allowed Holly to witness it. She had come to realise – though she knew she could hardly be objective about it – that Corinna was an exceptionally beautiful baby: smooth pink skin, large wide-spaced blue eyes, rosebud mouth and straight nose.

She was four days old, and feeding greedily, as usual, when Tyrconnel appeared, unannounced.

'I see I've stumbled upon the suckling of the young.'

Holly looked up warily. 'How are you?' she said.

'Very well, thanks. You look a bit bedraggled. Mother called me in Paris to let me know I hadn't got a son.'

Holly adjusted Corinna in her arms and didn't answer. The baby had stopped feeding, so she started to pat her on the back to bring up air.

'Let me have a look.' Tyrconnel held out his arms to take Corinna.

'Be careful.'

'Babies are very resilient, so I'm told.' He slid Corinna out of Holly's lap and weighed her in his hands, at arm's length. 'I suppose she'll pass for one of us. She has Daddy Jamie's nose.' Slinging Corinna up on to his shoulder, he opened one of the room's sliding doors. Holly had had no reason to use the balcony outside, though the nurses told her that in warmer weather the mothers often liked to sit there with their babies. As a cold breeze blew in, Corinna started to whimper.

'What are you doing?' said Holly, alarmed. She realised too late that she should never have handed Corinna over. Twisting her head to look out through the glass doors, she could see Tyrconnel and Corinna outside; furiously she rattled the railings at the sides of her bed. She did not know how to fold them down.

'Pity she's a girl,' called Tyrconnel. 'So expensive to raise. All those schools, and lessons, and coming-out balls. And then what do they do at the end of it all? Have more babies.'

Holly struggled with the bed-railing. It would not move. Shame and embarrassment kept her from calling out for a nurse.

'So, Holly,' Tyrconnel went on in an amiable voice, 'since you decided to lumber me with my brother's child, why couldn't you at least make sure it was a son?' He leaned out over the balcony railing, extending Corinna in his arms, over the street.

Over nothing.

Holly's breath stopped. Then all of a sudden, it released itself. 'Nurse!' she screamed. She threw her legs over the railing and tried to hurl herself out of bed. But when she landed, her legs crumpled beneath her. She struggled up to her knees. '*Nurse!*'

By the time the nurse came, Tyrconnel was standing inside the balcony door. It was closed again. He smiled. And Holly, standing now, gripping the bed-rail and the edge of a chair for balance, almost wondered if it had all been a dream.

But no. She had seen it. Even if no one would ever believe her.

'Something wrong?' The nurse, a young and pretty one, reached to take Corinna, who was still bawling.

'My daughter doesn't seem to like me,' said Tyrconnel, flashing the nurse a self-deprecating grin.

'Never mind. Happens all the time,' the nurse said.

And Holly knew that if she even began to tell what she had seen her husband do, no one would believe her.

She had been through this all before.

After a week in hospital, Holly was allowed home to

Chester Square. Imogen came for her, accompanied by the new nanny, Miss Sparks.

'We thought,' she said as the car pulled up by the front door, 'that the blue room on the third floor would be best for baby. Nanny will be sleeping next door.'

Holly was startled. 'I thought we agreed. . . .'

She remembered the endless arguments. She had not wanted a nanny in the first place; and though Tyrconnel and Imogen had prevailed, they had conceded that the baby could sleep in Holly's room.

'Yes, well, Nanny and I talked it over. I think there's really no reason you should make her job more difficult.'

'But – '

'Ty agrees with me. Be reasonable.'

Holly was silent. She clung to Corinna as she went indoors, waiting for the sound of Fitzgerald's frenzied barking to greet her.

But she heard nothing.

She ran upstairs, looking for him; then down into the cellars, the kitchen. At last it was Eduardo who, when confronted, gave way and told her. Fitzgerald was gone.

'What do you mean, gone?' Holly demanded.

Imogen stood on the kitchen steps, her expression regretful. 'We wanted to break it to you gently, dear. Your dog was in pain – '

Holly did not for one moment believe it. And gradually, in the course of that afternoon, she found out. The servants didn't want to tell her anything. Fitzgerald's vet, when she phoned him, absolutely denied having put the dog to sleep. Fitzgerald had not been at all seriously ill.

'So who did?' Holly demanded of Imogen. 'Who – got rid of him for you?' Tears stung her eyes.

'A perfectly decent, reputable man.' Imogen took a calm puff of her cigarette. 'You have to admit, we have the baby's health to think of.'

'What do you mean, the baby's health? She's my baby! What would Fitzgerald ever have done to her?'

268

She railed at Imogen, but Fitzgerald was gone – gone for good.

It was then that she began to understand. They were taking over.

Imogen sent out announcements for a christening at Stadhampton, on 14 February. Everyone came: the Farnhams; the Bullendens; Esmé and Hywel and their children, home on leave, this time from Egypt.

Despite the cold, there were photographs outside the church, taken by a photographer from the *Sunday Times* colour supplement who was doing a feature on the christening and on Stadhampton House. Holly, in a short pink dress and bouclé coat, her hair twisted up beneath a broad-brimmed hat, was, for a few minutes, the centre of attention. But Nanny Sparks came to take Corinna as soon as the photographer had finished. 'Must spare your strength, Lady Carr,' she said with her characteristic pleasant firmness, which seemed to Holly to be growing daily more dictatorial.

Tyrconnel, though he walked back to the house beside Holly, carried on a steady conversation all the while with his deputy, Arthur Jarrell. Imogen walked with Charlie Moncrieffe, Jamie with Daphne.

Holly and he had not spoken again since that day in hospital. And yet today, as Corinna was christened, Holly had felt his presence behind her in the church; his gaze on her, despite Daphne, despite everyone, so strong that she knew that if she looked back and met it, it would not waver from hers. But she did not.

Back at the house, there was lunch; then games for the children in the ballroom, arranged by Esmé, while the *Sunday Times* photographer moved his tripod and lights from chamber to chamber, recording the renovations of the last few years: new paint, new parquetry, new gilding.

Corinna had been packed straight off to the nursery with Nanny Sparks, and now Holly sat on a chair in the ballroom beside Esmé, watching the other children run races on the wide, empty floor.

'Go on, Hyw! Go on, Clara!' Esmé shouted. 'You can do better than that!'

Broad-hipped, her hair showing streaks of grey, she had grown more matronly in the last few years. And yet, thought Holly, she resembled her mother. Not in looks, but in character: in her sheer determination that her children would be the best – would know no bounds.

Holly heard the voices from the floor, like distant echoes:

'Grandmama, he cheated. Tell him he cheated – '

'I was in first! I know I was.'

'Mungo's stupid, aren't you, Mungo? He's just *thick*.'

And Imogen's voice, young, uncharacteristically gleeful, in the midst of them all, conciliating, punishing.

'I know your brother's older, Mungo, but you'll just have to try harder. . . .'

Holly watched it all, heard the crowing, the raucous taunts. The superior confidence of children raised by boarding schools and nannies, never told that they were poor or weak or wrong – except, of course, when they lost. In a few years, Corinna would be one of them: a Carr.

No, thought Holly suddenly. And then she knew that, without intending it, she had made her final decision.

XXI

Cold and wet from the rain, Holly rang the buzzer outside the door of the Georgian house, converted to offices, on Marylebone High Street. She had already learnt that two hands could not manage both a baby and an umbrella, but there could be no question of leaving Corinna with someone else. Whom could she trust?

This was their second day on their own. Yesterday she

pushed Corinna, in her pram, all the way from Belgravia to Bloomsbury. She had spent days preparing, but only on that morning, when Nanny Sparks took to her bed ill, had she known that she could escape. She filled the bottom of the pram with Corinna's clothes, and some of her own; over her shoulder she carried a small overnight bag. Reeve and Clare had seen her go out. She waved goodbye.

When she had walked as far as she could – far enough from Chester Square, she hoped, to be safe – she looked for a place to stay. The Carlton Hotel, one of a row of anonymous bed-and-breakfasts off Russell Square, looked plain and clean enough on the outside. Inside, it turned out to be dark and musty. She could not tell if the desk clerk believed the story she told about 'coming to meet her husband'. But he had asked no questions.

That first night, looking up at the single bulb and partitioned ceiling of her room, Holly had almost wanted to run back home.

Now, she told herself, things were better. They couldn't help looking better by day. She had money in her bank account: for the last three months she had let Tyrconnel's contributions to it, what he called her 'clothing allowance', pile up unspent. She had jewellery, too, to which she could turn in an emergency. Her sapphire ring, diamond earrings and necklace, Imogen's pearls. She felt no guilt at taking them away with her. Tyrconnel, after all, had taken her inheritance: United Alloys.

She would need to tell that to the lawyer, too. There was so much to remember.

On Holly's second ring, a secretary opened the door. 'What a beastly wet day! Are you Lady Carr?'

'Yes. I phoned earlier.'

'Is that your baby?' The secretary looked down at Corinna in surprise for a moment. 'She's tiny.'

A few minutes later, Holly was shown into the office of Christopher Wright, the firm's senior solicitor, a grey-haired man whose eyes appeared very large behind his thick spectacles. His reaction, though more paternal, was

271

much the same as his secretary's. 'What a very little girl,' he said. 'How many months, Lady Carr?'

'Just five weeks,' Holly told him, and he shook his head.

'What a pity.' He paused, and after a few more civilities and the offer of tea, turned to business.

The office was long, narrow, sparsely adorned; it might have been half of a Georgian room. Christopher Wright was similarly hard to place: deliberate, soft-spoken, polite Home Counties accent. Nige English had recommended him, and Holly did not even know yet how much his services would cost.

'I suppose,' Wright said, 'it's almost superfluous to ask – but divorce is a serious business. You are quite sure you want to take this step?'

'Yes, I am,' said Holly. She glanced nervously at the broad sofa where she had laid Corinna to sleep. 'I'm afraid there's no way back.'

She emerged an hour later, her head spinning with facts. There were three routes to divorce in England: adultery, cruelty, desertion of three years or more. Adultery: that was the standard method. Had her husband, asked the solicitor gently, been having affairs?

'Yes,' said Holly. 'Yes and no – ' She fell silent, too ashamed to speak.

'Of course anything you tell me will be kept in the strictest confidence.'

'He – had affairs,' Holly blurted out, 'with men.'

She had thought that would settle the case, once and for all. But Christopher Wright looked grave.

'Ah,' he said. 'I see.' And then he told her the bad news. The law made no provision for such cases. Homosexual acts did not count as adultery for the purpose of obtaining a divorce. The usual procedure in such cases, as in most these days, was a subtle form of consent. Both parties being agreed upon divorce, one would take the blame for adultery. Evidence could be arranged. . . .

'I – I don't think my husband would accept that.'

Wright sighed. 'I take it he doesn't want a divorce.'

They agreed upon a course of action. Wright would test Tyrconnel out on the issue of consent, but if he refused it, Holly could try another possible ground: cruelty. They would seek a temporary financial settlement. What, approximately, asked Wright, was Lord Carr's annual income? Had Lady Carr brought funds to the marriage?

Holly could see Wright try to conceal his dismay when she admitted her near-total ignorance. They had agreed, at last, to meet again tomorrow, to try to work out some estimates.

'But you will write to Tyrconnel? Today?' Holly urged him. Only when Tyrconnel got the lawyer's letter would he understand the reason for her disappearance. Until then, the police might be looking for her. Or Tyrconnel and Imogen on their own; or their friends . . .

Big, muscled men in boiler suits. Ready to put her away, this time, where no one would find her.

She focused on Christopher Wright's face, to keep down the fear. He was saying goodbye.

'And good luck, Lady Carr.'

The rain was heavier, now, as she walked back towards Russell Square. She hailed a cab. Corinna started to cry. She must be hungry by now. Holly's breasts leaked and tingled. 'Hush, Corinna.' She held her close. 'We'll be home soon.' *Home.* She tried not to think of the Carlton Hotel. As the cab's meter clicked over she wondered how much it would cost. Could she afford cabs? She had never had to wonder that before.

Once she had Corinna fed and changed, she knew she needed to hear Helen's voice again.

Last night, Helen had applauded her when she told her she had run away. 'You know,' Helen said, 'I hope you don't mind me saying it – but I'm glad you've done it. Really glad.' She had only scolded Holly for not coming to her house. But then, as Holly said, that was the first place the Carrs would look.

Now, when she phoned Helen from the dingy box in

the hotel lobby, her friend told her she was right. Tyrconnel had come to the house in search of her last night.

'What did you tell him?' Holly's heart pounded in panic.

'I said I knew nothing. I don't think he believed me.'

'Did he come on his own?'

'Yeah, he did. Why – '

'Never mind.' Holly tried to banish the thought of men in boiler suits.

'I think,' said Helen suddenly, 'I've found a place for you to stay. I went to see the landlady today. It's in Highgate. I could meet you there tomorrow. . . . Let's get you out of that hotel, all right?'

'OK.' Holly went back to her room and collapsed with relief.

The next day Helen showed her round the flat. It occupied the first floor of a converted terraced house, with a bay window to the front, bare floors and walls of a gloomy shade of green. The landlady, elderly and Italian, was eager to show her the garden. 'It will be nice for the little one,' she said, 'in summer.'

By the summer Holly intended to be away from here. But she did not mention that. She weighed considerations in her mind. True, the flat was dreary, but she was doing well, Helen had told her, to pay only £5 a week. Her £300 might have to last her into spring, though Christopher Wright had assured her that morning that as soon as he and Tyrconnel's solicitor arrived at a separation agreement, she would start to receive an allowance. The legal fees could wait until the divorce settlement.

There was the money to think of; and then, Helen had gone to some trouble to find this place.

'I like it,' Holly said, and put the best face on it she could. Helen, holding Corinna, was testing the threadbare brown plush sofa.

'Good,' said the landlady. 'When you move in? You pay cash?'

Holly paid; she had handfuls of cash, being wary of

going too often to the bank, where Tyrconnel would know to look for her. Helen helped her move in. There was not much to move, given Holly's few possessions, but Helen had had the foresight to pack sheets and blankets in Baby Blue, which was parked outside. They walked to the corner shop and bought instant coffee, milk, bread and ham, as well as sponges and a broom. While Holly nursed Corinna on the sofa Helen busied herself in the kitchen, emerging with coffee and sandwiches.

'I'm sorry,' said Holly. 'I've dragged you away all afternoon. I've made you leave Frederic – '

'Never mind. He's got Solange to look after him.' Solange was the Englishes' surly au pair. 'I've never held with this breastfeeding business, thank God. By now he'd be chewing my nipples off.'

'Oh, Helen.' Holly raised a feeble giggle; if felt like her first laugh in days.

'Cheers.' Helen lifted her coffee cup. 'To the single life.'

Holly lifted hers, too. 'Oh, Helen,' she said. 'I don't *want* the single life. I've never wanted it. I don't even believe in divorce.'

'Pet, once things are settled I'm sure you can marry again. Put all this behind you. Think of yourself – a desirable divorcee, with a nice little place, maybe in Chelsea – '

'But, Helen,' Holly broke in. 'I'm not staying.'

Helen looked startled. She thrust a hank of mouse-gold hair behind her ear, and her long brass earring jangled discordantly. 'But what will you do, then? Go back to the States?'

'Yes. That's all I've really thought about.'

Helen mulled this over for a few moments. 'Oh.' She bit her lip. 'You mean you'll be leaving us? For good?'

Holly shrugged. 'It's the only way I can be far enough from *them*.'

'I know how you feel. But don't you think it'll be hard, putting Corinna on a plane for visits?'

Holly looked blank.

'You know. When she comes to see her father.'

'But she won't.' Holly's gaze was straight. 'She won't be visiting the Carrs. I don't even want her to know they exist.'

Helen, stunned by the vehemence of Holly's words, kept silent.

Those first days alone with Corinna were the hardest. Every morning, waking up at five or six to the baby's cries, Holly had to adjust herself anew to the serviceable, ugly dinginess of her surroundings. She had taken Chester Square for granted, but now she missed its comforts – its reliable heating, its wall-to-wall carpets, Eduardo's cooking. Until now there had always been someone to lend a hand with the baby. When Corinna cried at 3 a.m., Nanny Sparks had given her a bottle and quietened her down. When Holly had needed to go out alone, Nanny Sparks had always been there.

Now Holly had to plan her every excursion around Corinna: would she carry her, or try to manoeuvre the pram? Would there be enough nappies? She had been dimly aware, before, of something called a nappy service; now she had to find one in the yellow pages, and rinse out Corinna's old wet nappies to wait until the lorry came.

Corinna seemed blithely unaware of her change of circumstances. She slept and ate and slept again, wherever she was placed, on a bed or sofa or in her pram, only crying when she sensed Holly's absence. She was too little to crawl or sit or even turn over on her own; Holly had been unaware, until now, of a newborn's absolute dependence.

But Corinna was too young, too, to complain. She looked up into Holly's eyes, trusting and unreproachful for what her mother had done – what she was doing.

Holly hoped it would stay that way.

Their days soon took on a pattern. Corinna would wake Holly, who would feed her, and then wait for the post, in case there was any news from Christopher Wright. She ate toast for breakfast and a sandwich for lunch and tinned soup or baked beans or a couple of boiled eggs for dinner, because beyond lighting the gas ring and boiling water she had not the slightest idea how to cook. The rest she was managing: sweeping up, cleaning the kitchen, sterilising the bottles for when Corinna was still hungry and she had no more milk to give her.

They did not go out often – only to the shops at the end of the block. Holly was afraid of being sighted. She did not say so to Helen, but even Baby Blue's being parked too prominently outside when her friend came to visit made her nervous. Helen, she knew, had never really understood her fear of the Carrs and what they might do. But it was real.

Every morning Holly listened for the clank of the letter-box, and several times in the first two weeks she phoned her solicitors. But still they had received no reply from the Carrs. At last, in the middle of March, she phoned Christopher Wright and he had some concrete news.

'They've answered,' he said. 'It's not good. They want to know your whereabouts.'

'I'm not telling them.' Holly was adamant. 'Did they say anything else?'

They hadn't replied, Wright told her, to his suggestion about negotiating. They were stalling.

Two weeks later, after another exchange of letters, Wright reported that Tyrconnel's lawyers intended to contest any attempt at divorce; also to sue for custody of Corinna.

'No,' said Holly, in shock.

'I shouldn't worry, Lady Carr. Judges nearly always prefer the mother, especially when the child is so small. Now, it seems to me that the only route – if you still want a divorce – is to pursue the charge of cruelty. You'll need to tell me everything you can.'

The next day she went into Wright's office and told him about Norfolk. If there had been doctors there who knew she didn't belong – if, as she had become almost sure,

Tyrconnel had had to bribe someone to keep her there – surely that was cruelty beyond all the usual bounds.

When she told Wright, for a moment there was a worried glint in his spectacled eyes. But he agreed. He would contact the hospital, in search of witnesses.

The month of April dragged on. Holly scheduled another meeting with Wright.

'To be honest,' he said, 'it's not good. The problem's not so much that no one at the hospital will talk – just that the whole staff's changed, except the director. And he maintains that you were admitted showing signs of nervous depression, and that by the end of your stay you fully accepted that you had been . . . disturbed.'

'But I wasn't.' Holly leaned forward, fretful. 'I said that because that was the only way they'd let me out.'

'All the same – ' the solicitor threw up his hands – 'he's a doctor, a reputable man. He's not likely to change his story. And there's another difficulty.'

'Yes?' Holly was apprehensive.

'If we pursue this angle – the hospital – there's a risk that your husband's side will turn it against us. When – ' Wright swallowed, hesitating – 'it comes to custody of your daughter.'

'What? You mean – they'll claim I'm . . . ill, that way? That I can't look after my daughter?'

Wright nodded slowly.

Holly fell back in her chair and closed her eyes. 'They've got me, whatever I do. Haven't they.' She thought for a moment. 'What about . . . other cruelty? There were times Tyrconnel hit me.'

'Do you have witnesses?'

She shook her head. Only servants, perhaps: Carr servants. And, though Tyrconnel might have been frighteningly violent at times, his usual methods of threat had left no marks. 'He held Corinna out in the middle of the air, from a balcony. She could have been killed!' she said.

'Did anyone see it?'

Holly thought of the nurse coming in; her husband smiling by the balcony door at St Margaret's. 'No,' she said miserably.

Christopher Wright sighed. 'I'm sorry. It may not seem fair, but if you want to press a cruelty charge and succeed, you'll need witnesses.'

'What kind of law is this, anyway?' Holly felt her face growing heated. 'Are you trying to tell me there's no way I can get a divorce? None at all?'

'You're not the first,' said Wright patiently, 'to be unhappy with the current laws. There are proposals to reform them. Perhaps in a few years. . . .'

'I can't wait a few years!' Holly sat back, forcing her gaze to the ceiling, close to tears. 'I'm sorry. It just feels as though the law was designed to trap me. To make me its one exception.'

Christopher Wright did not disagree.

'Never mind,' said Helen, when she stopped by with Frederic for tea. 'I'm sure Tyrconnel will give in sooner or later.'

'You don't know Tyrconnel. It's not even that he cares about staying married. If *he* wanted a divorce, it would be different. But since I do. . . . He can't bear to give in. It means he's lost.'

Christopher Wright had agreed to hold a strong line: to write to Tyrconnel's solicitors insisting that a cruelty charge would be brought, and demanding that financial provision be made for Holly immediately.

But Holly felt despondent all the same. The negotiations, let alone the court case, looked like dragging on for months. Half her savings were already gone. She did not have copies of any of her husband's financial statements, or even her father's will; Wright was having to contact Joe Clayton's lawyers in New York for that. More delays. Holly cursed her own lack of foresight, her stupidity.

'Silly,' said Helen. 'How could you know? How could

you have gone snooping around in Tyrconnel's papers? It would have looked a mite suspicious.'

Still, Holly thought, *I should have known*. She was only beginning to realise how unworldly she was.

Towards the end of April she was shopping at her local greengrocer's when she ran into Nanny Walters. She caught sight of a svelte form in black, and recognised the coil of bouffant russet hair too late. Nanny Walters turned and spotted her.

'Lady Carr!'

Her tone was neither hostile nor unduly surprised. The sales assistant gaped up at Holly, whose hand had frozen round her purse.

'Nanny.' Holly stared. 'How are you?'

'All right, my lady. And yourself?'

Nanny was waiting for her at the door, Holly realised. She paid for her vegetables.

'We was all wondering where you'd gone,' said Nanny, as Holly moved past her to where Corinna waited, just outside the shop window, in her pram. 'Lord knows I wouldn't have thought to see *you* here. I was just visiting my sister, she lives up by Archway Road and asked me to fetch her a bag of pickling onions.' She raised them in the air by way of demonstration. 'But like I said, I never thought I'd see *you*.'

'I'm – just visiting the area. I don't live here.'

'So how's the little one?' Nanny bent over the pram, her beaky nose curling as she smiled. 'The precious. I always told Lady Imogen, if only I didn't have Master Jamie's girls to look after, I would have been ever so happy to see to this one. Wouldn't I?' She waggled a finger at Corinna's nose; then turned suddenly to Holly. 'So when are you coming home, my lady? That's what we all want to know.'

Holly gulped. She wondered how much Nanny Walters could be trusted. Yet she sensed that the only way to ensure the woman's secrecy was to get her on her side. 'I'm not – coming back, Nanny. I was just too unhappy. The truth is – Tyrconnel and I are getting a divorce. And until we do, I don't want him to know where I am. Please, Nanny. Don't tell anyone you've seen me.'

'A divorce!' Nanny's brow wrinkled. 'You can't. You can't ever.'

Holly nodded. 'Please, Nanny. Don't tell anyone.'

'All right, my lady, I won't. You'll come back, though.' Nanny looked both puzzled and obstinate. 'I'll bet I know what you need. A good visit home. A trip to America.'

'Yes,' said Holly uneasily, 'I'll probably go there. Eventually.'

'That's it. You have your good visit home, and then you come back to us.'

Holly shook her head, wondering if Nanny understood. 'I have to go now. It's been nice seeing you.' She spoke hastily as she waved and set the pram in motion, in the opposite direction from home.

As soon as Nanny was out of sight she doubled back around the block. Inside her flat, she bolted the door behind her and closed the curtains. She felt visible, pursued. In the last few weeks she had developed what was perhaps a false sense of security. In a strange neighbourhood, surrounded by strangers, she had felt safe from seeing anyone she knew.

She had to think calmly. She could move; break her lease here and start all over again. Another flat, another neighbourhood. But how could she be sure someone attached to the Carrs wouldn't stumble on her again?

Besides which, she could ill afford the penalty for breaking the lease.

In the end, she decided to stay. Maybe Nanny, after all, would keep her word.

At the end of that week Corinna developed a cough and what felt, to Holly's bare hand, like a fever. For a whole night she wailed in misery; Holly paced the flat, rocking the baby in her arms, pressing a damp cloth to her forehead to cool her. She did not know if she was doing the right things; Corinna had never been sick before. What if it were more than a cold? By the morning, she was frantic with worry.

At eight o'clock she took Corinna to the clinic a few blocks away; there was a long queue of sniffling and sneezing patients and Holly felt too exhausted, by the time they reached a doctor, even to be relieved at his verdict that Corinna had an ordinary cold. He prescribed a syrup and Holly wrapped Corinna up warmly again, stopping at the chemist's on the way home.

She backed the pram awkwardly through her door, ready to collapse into bed once she had given Corinna her medicine.

Even before she went any further, she felt another presence. She heard breathing, the gentle sound of something moving in the living room.

She spun. And there on the living-room sofa, stubbing out her cigarette in a saucer, was Imogen.

'And so you see – ' The older woman stubbed out her third cigarette – 'it's the only reasonable solution.' She smoothed the skirt of her neat dark blue suit. One tiny wrist wore a chunky gold cuff which matched her earrings.

Holly, still wearing yesterday's clothes, was aware of her own shabbiness and dispirited fatigue. The panic of first seeing Imogen had left her, once she realised that her mother-in-law had come alone; the landlady, Imogen explained, had let her in.

'I'm not coming back,' Holly said now.

Imogen smiled again. 'Please.' She stressed the word. 'Let's all be frank. I am sure there are – terms, under which you would. You have only to name them. A larger allowance, perhaps? A different flat, away from Chester Square?'

Holly touched the pram beside her, which still held Corinna. 'No.'

Imogen's eyes flashed. 'Leave my son, and I warn you, you will come out with nothing.'

'Oh, no. I have rights. There's my father's money, for one thing. The shares he left to Tyrconnel. Whatever they were worth back then, at least, is rightfully mine. Once we're divorced.'

'But there will be no divorce.'

'You can't speak for Tyrconnel. If he feels so strongly about this, why isn't he here?'

Imogen smiled. 'I'm the only one who knows where you are. And besides, Ty might lose his temper. Not that it would mean anything. He doesn't intend to let you go.'

Holly shook her head; it was beginning to throb with exhaustion. 'I can get a divorce, whether he wants to or not. I can charge him with cruelty, my solicitor says so. Look at this.' With one hand still, protectively, on Corinna's pram, she reached into a drawer of the battered desk, then flourished her copy of Christopher Wright's latest letter to the Carrs. It was full of legalistic detail which she hoped would intimidate Imogen, even if circumstances remained as dauntingly against Holly as ever.

Imogen tossed the letter on the table without a glance. 'Cruelty,' she snorted. 'Well, let me mention a charge or two. Whatever will the judge make of the character of an unstable young woman who spent eight months in a mental hospital? Who emerged, to begin an adulterous affair with her husband's own brother, and, in all probability, bore his child. . . .'

Holly stood stock-still, frozen by Imogen's words. *She knew.* 'You have no proof of that.'

'Maybe not.' Imogen flicked the switch of her lighter. 'But I know everything about you and Jamie. I made it happen.'

Holly forced herself to stay standing. Her knees felt weak. 'That's ridiculous.'

'Is it? Perhaps more ridiculous that Jamie should have turned to you, without some prompting. After all, there are so many girls in his life. So many, many girls.'

Silent, Holly let her legs give way and sat. She stared at Imogen.

'It was easy. There you were – lonely, disappointed in your marriage. It was only a matter of time till you looked elsewhere. Jamie and I agreed that it should be he who picked you up that day from hospital. Do you remember?'

A chill had taken hold of Holly's heart. She didn't answer.

'Because – ' Imogen smiled – 'I knew you'd be happy that day. Sometimes one falls in love, almost without noticing, when one is happy. Very likely with whoever's nearest.'

Holly's heart pounded. 'Did you tell him . . . to phone me? To take me out?'

Imogen shrugged. 'Jamie knows how to do these things. I left the details to him. It didn't really matter how it happened, so long as you gave us a son.'

'A son?' All Holly's world was in confusion: a kaleidoscope, the colours drifting down.

'An *heir*,' said Imogen, drawing on her cigarette, 'of course. It wouldn't have mattered if Jamie and Daphne had managed to have a boy. But they couldn't. And then Daphne was told she wasn't to have any more children.' Imogen puffed again, tilting her head, her black gaze spearing Holly. 'Ty didn't realise how much he needed a son. A male heir. But I did. You see, we all die. Only the *family* goes on. John taught me that.'

Holly was silent.

'It took so long! I suppose you were clever – went to a doctor and got fixed up.' Imogen's voice was mocking.

Holly had gathered strength. 'I didn't want to have a baby. And Jamie never pressured me.' That seemed to her now to be her only defence against what Imogen said. Her only hope that Jamie had cared, that what they did and were together had amounted to something besides the fulfilment of Imogen's plan. He'd said he loved her. They'd been together for almost three years. . . .

'I chose,' she said slowly now, 'to have a baby. Or at least – I let it happen. Jamie never made me. And I'm so very glad it was a girl.' She almost said more – that she

284

was going to take Corinna away, that the Carrs would never lay eyes on her again. But she held her tongue.

Imogen shrugged. 'It was worth a try.' She looked at Holly evenly. 'So you see, I know everything. If you try to divorce Ty you will come out in shreds. We have the evidence.'

'But I do, too.' Holly marched forward. 'Here – look what the lawyers say – ' She thrust the letter again at Imogen.

'I don't need to read that.'

'Yes! Yes, you do. Go on – look at it.'

'I haven't got my glasses.'

Holly was breathing quickly. 'You don't have glasses. You never had glasses.'

For the first time, Imogen looked flustered. 'That has nothing to do with – '

'You can't read. Can you?' As soon as Holly said it, she knew. All those evasions and excuses for the way Imogen picked her way round the simplest tasks. The servants who phoned and typed for her; her sons, who read her the papers. . . .

'Of course I can read. Don't be absurd.' Imogen's mouth quivered.

'Maybe you should go now.'

Imogen looked up, her black eyes shining. 'You think you're very clever, don't you? Well, remember: whatever you try, Holly, we'll win. Take your case to court – I know the judges. We know everyone who matters in this country, and you're only a pitiful little outsider. We have money. We can hold out longer than you, I promise you that. And wherever you go, wherever you take the child, we'll find you. You'll never get away.'

A few seconds later, she picked up her handbag and gloves and walked out.

In the street, a low patter of rain brushed the rooftops. Imogen stood in the open air, trying to breathe, the old panic, the relic of years long before, still clutching at her throat.

I cannot read. It was true. She never could. At first, her mother had understood; said she would pick it up in time. It didn't matter.

But as she grew older, still the words made no sense. Her mother hired a new governess, who made her sit at a desk for hours and rapped her knuckles with a flat wooden ruler whenever she made mistakes.

It only became worse. The letters swam before Imogen's eyes. *Said* turned into *isda* and *dais*. Numbers changed order. The ruler marked red slashes on her knuckles. She couldn't breathe.

She stopped trying; she went blank with fear at the sight of printed pages. Governess succeeded governess, but she soon learnt that most of them could either be charmed or overpowered. She became a wicked girl, a rebel. At sixteen, she couldn't even read the rhymes in a nursery book, but it didn't matter. When she sneaked out to the casino at night, the men there didn't care about what books she read.

When she was eighteen, she had married Errol Rutherford. He never seemed to notice anything wrong with her: her vast, reckless great love – drunkard, card-shark, petty criminal. On the day she left him he was as ignorant of her soul as on the day she found him. And yet, in a way, he had made her.

It was then, back in England, with a small daughter, that Imogen realised for the first time how helpless she was. There was no money – only the little her mother had left her. She needed a job, but, unable to type or even read a column of print, what could she do? She couldn't even be a sales clerk, because every time she tried to add a column of figures the numbers shifted before her eyes.

She must have a husband to support her. And money. With money she would be safe. There would be servants to cook, because she couldn't read a recipe; a chauffeur to drive her, because she couldn't remember directions. There would be butlers and maids to dial the phone, secretaries to read her mail to her and type her letters – which she signed with a varying combination of slashes and dashes.

She got her news from the wireless, from her husband, later from her sons. She had developed a phenomenal memory. For a while she had been afraid her sons would inherit her funny eyes. She made sure that, unlike her, they had a kind young nanny. 'Not too much reading,' she would tell Nanny Walters. . . .

Because even when they were little she knew that one day her sons would protect her. She had it all arranged: one to make money, and one for the law. Her sons and her money would be her fortress. No one would know.

Imogen shuddered, and slowly regained her calm as she made her way round the corner to the Daimler.

After all, perhaps it did not matter. Holly knew her secret, true: but she had other things on her mind. Seeking a divorce she would not get – taking care of the child. *The child*, thought Imogen. And suddenly she knew what Ty's lawyers must do.

Holly held Corinna in her arms and cried.

What use, her petty victory over Imogen? Imogen had won.

Jamie – it had all been a lie. Planned by Imogen from the beginning. She had instructed him: father a son.

Did that mean, Holly wondered, that she could believe nothing Jamie had ever said to her? She wasn't sure.

She remembered, now, how once Jamie had tried to excuse himself: '*Once I knew I loved you. . . .* '

Perhaps, however it had all begun, he had come to love her. It was a small consolation.

But it didn't matter. She only knew, now, that she hated everything she had done and been. More than she hated Imogen or Jamie, she hated herself.

She whispered to Corinna: whispered her love, because it was the only thing that seemed to redeem her. 'My love,' she said. 'My love. I can't lose you. You're the only good thing I've ever done.'

Three days later a letter came from Christopher Wright: short and ominous.

Lord Carr's lawyers had written to inform him that they were preparing to request a court order for Lady Carr to return her daughter, Corinna, to her husband's custody. They would inform the court of Lady Carr's past record of mental instability.

Holly stared numbly at the block of print and thought, *This is the end.*

XXII

It was late when Jamie swung his Jaguar into the space in front of the house in Chester Square.

He rang the bell, and when a weary Reeve answered, let himself be shown into the library. His mother was waiting.

'Such a long time,' she said, lifting her glass, which was already full. 'Help yourself. You know your poison.'

'Where's Ty?'

'Tokyo, I think. Can't keep track of him these days. How's Daphne?'

'Fine.' Jamie's mouth thinned into a line as he poured gin. Daphne was anything but fine these days. She had said nothing, but her every look was remote, reproachful; her every sentence limped away like a wounded foal. Ironic, that she should get this way just when he was doing nothing wrong. 'Any word,' he said, 'on Holly?'

'I've seen her.'

Jamie spun round. He saw a smile playing on his mother's lips. 'Seen her? When? Why didn't you tell anyone?'

'I told Ty. He didn't seem very interested. He thinks his lawyers will be able to starve her out till she comes round.'

'So where is she? Where is she living?'

'You seem all eagerness to know. I'm not sure it would be a good idea to tell you.'

'Goddamn it, Mother – '

The next morning Jamie wound his car through the unfamiliar streets of north London. Unspectacular streets, some prettied up, some genteelly shabby; Holly's building was in one of the latter, a brick house distinguished from its neighbours only by the number on its front door.

He rang the bell for the first-floor flat. Holly's name, he noticed, was not on it. No one answered. He rang again and again. Finally a dumpy lady in black opened the door. 'What you want? You disturb everybody.'

'Does Holly Carr live here?'

'Who?'

'Holly Carr. Young woman with a baby. Red hair – '

'Oh, she. She gone. She leave early this morning. London Airport.'

'Did she say where she was going? What airline she was flying?'

'You talk so fast. What you want?'

Forcing patience on himself, Jamie repeated.

'No,' said the landlady eventually. 'I don't know. She leave without giving me even one day notice. How should I know?'

Jamie was already running down the steps. 'Thank you – '

Panting, he launched himself into his car and took off. She couldn't go. She couldn't just go like that. Disappear. . . .

Maybe he had started to give her up in the last few months – maybe he had started to take her at her word. But somehow he had always counted on seeing her again.

Rounding the corner into a street of shops, he saw a call-box. He pulled up and rang Gillian at the office. 'My sister-in-law's disappeared,' he told her. 'Can you do me a favour, Gill? Urgent. I think she's on a flight to New York. Could you ring all the airlines and see if you can find out what flight she's on? Say whatever you have to. Say it's family – an emergency message. . . .'

He jumped back into his car and screeched out of the small shopping street and out, out whatever way he could go, towards the North Circular. He didn't know whether he had chosen the fastest route; traffic was heavy and again and again it came to a standstill as he pounded at the wheel.

At last he was in the clear. He saw the signs for the airport. International Departures.

He pulled up outside British Airways and, ignoring the protests of a horde of shouting porters and cabbies, abandoned his car outside their doors.

He found a phone just inside the concourse. Gillian's line was clear. *Thank God*, he thought. She picked up.

'You're in the right place,' she said. 'It's BA, flight 103.'

He scanned the boards for its time of departure. Eleven o'clock. It was eleven now, but they might not have taken off yet. He ran towards the gate, past passengers, baggage, porters with trollies.

The departure lounge was suspiciously empty.

'I'm looking for flight 103,' he told the attendant at the gate, breathless.

'I'm sorry, sir. It's already boarded. They've just been cleared for takeoff.'

He stopped – stopped running, stopped looking. Everything stopped. *Already gone.* In the distance he heard a plane's engines roar. He did not know if it was the one. He was too late.

'Mr Carr!'

He heard the rough, friendly voice – there was something unpleasantly familiar about it – and turned. Nile Jenkins, the reporter, grinned at him. 'Whatever brings you here, Mr Carr?'

'None of your business.'

'What a way to treat an old pal! I'm not on your case any more, you know. Management got tired of tracking you. I'm here on account of this pop group – you know? The Even Stevens, Bristol's answer to the Beatles. They're going to America.'

'Are they?' Jamie managed a thin smile. 'Well, Nile. Best of luck, eh? Can't say I've missed you.'

As he walked slowly back towards the concourse, towards his car, Jamie thought for a moment about what would have happened had he found Holly in time; had he stopped her, pleaded with her, made her stay. Nile Jenkins would have witnessed it all. His big story, the scoop on James Carr he'd been waiting for. Headlines, photographs. For Jamie, the end of everything.

Or perhaps the beginning.

He had missed that chance. And who could say, now, that Holly wouldn't have left for New York even if he had found her? He didn't know. He would never know. His life was a compromise with such absolute truths; and so, he sensed now, it always would be.

He walked out through the swinging doors and back towards what he had left.

New York, 1965–1983

I

The door opened, revealing dusty, warped floorboards and walls of a mottled grey. No sunlight; or only a few thin streaks of it, filtered by the buildings across the street, and the dirty windowpanes.

Mr Ortega played with a switch on the wall. 'Sorry,' he said. 'No light.'

'That's OK.' *Lord help me*, thought Holly. If it had come to this, maybe it was better not to see anything too clearly.

She crossed the threshold.

'You'll like Brooklyn,' offered Rosie, behind her. 'Hey, I know this place don't look like much, but it's clean. My father says so. No cockroaches.'

Mr Ortega, Rosie's father, glanced back at her with a half-smile: warning or joking, Holly couldn't tell which. He shrugged. 'Anyway, the rent is cheap. And Rosie said you were looking for something...' He refrained from repeating the word *cheap*. Instead, he merely looked up and down Holly, in her once-expensive dress and shoes, in puzzlement.

Corinna, in her arms, let out a squawk.

'Here,' said Rosie. 'Let me take her.'

Gratefully, Holly handed Corinna over. She didn't know where she would be without Rosie. In fact, it was hard to believe that she had known her for less than three months. When she had first arrived, loaded down with baby and suitcases, at her mother's new, glitzy apartment off Sutton

Place, it had been Rosie who opened the door for her. Rosie was – had been – her mother's maid.

There came a thump, like a basketball landing on the floor above, then another. Holly wondered who lived there, and whether she would get used to such thumps as a regular feature of her life. She didn't suppose she had much choice.

She moved forward into the living room: twelve feet or so square, with a tall, dusty bay window. Behind it, a galley kitchen divided the front of the apartment from the one bedroom and walk-in closet at the back.

Holly opened the closet door. A puff of dust rushed out to meet her. 'Big enough for a bed,' Rosie had said. If Holly made this her bedroom, Corinna could have the other room. Holly had never slept in a room without a window.

She supposed she would get used to that, too.

For the choices that had faced her in the last month were stark: give up the apartment at River Towers, or watch what was left of her mother's estate drain away just paying the rent.

'It's *rented*?' she remembered repeating to the lawyers in astonishment.

The elder of the two – partners in a reputable mid-Manhattan firm – had nodded. He seemed, Holly thought, to be regulating his expression, avoiding any revelation of the distaste he might well feel at the disarray in which Mrs Hollis Heyward Clayton had left her affairs.

But then, Holly could only suppose that her mother had not intended to leave her affairs, not to mention her life, quite so abruptly as she had.

Holly had had to conceal her shock on first seeing her: she looked shrunken, wizened, more than could be expected of a woman of sixty-three. It was the arthritis. In the last few years her joints had grown so stiff that she relied heavily on painkillers, and rarely left the River Towers apartment. Rosie did all her shopping. She had not stopping drinking, either. Holly knew that was not good.

A wave of guilt washed over her as she realised that this was why her mother had never visited her in England. The trip would have been far too much for her. In her letters she had complained of aches and pains, but Holly had never known. . . .

Ill-health did not improve Mrs Clayton's temper. She complained about how little money she had – 'Your father cheated me,' she said – and about the arthritis, and Holly's unexpected, unwanted appearance. The reunion had not been a successful one. In fact, from the first day, they had argued almost nonstop.

Holly tried to put the arguments out of her memory. They did not matter now.

Five weeks after Holly arrived in New York, her mother took an overdose. It was, by all the evidence, an accident: too many painkillers combined with alcohol. Since Mrs Clayton so often slept late, Holly and Rosie did not think of checking on her until well after noon, that morning when she did not get up.

By then it was too late.

Holly had blamed herself, as Rosie did – for not keeping a closer watch on her mother, for not recognising the dangers. They supported each other through the doctors' visits, the police interviews, the inquest.

At the funeral, near the Claytons' old summer house upstate, Rosie had taken Holly's hand, and with the gravity of someone far older than her twenty-two years, had assured her: 'The worst is over. Remember that. You're going to be all right.'

Except that, in its own tangled and nightmarish way, what had followed had almost been worse. Holly had known nothing of her mother's finances. Very likely, the lawyers told her, her mother had been swindled. Though Joe Clayton had left her several million dollars at his death, enough for her to live on comfortably several times over, by the time she died Holly's mother had almost no investments to her name. The stocks she had bought, on the advice of an 'investment adviser' of whom the lawyers had never heard, had dropped catastrophically in value. Two years ago, she had moved from the apartment she owned on Park Avenue to the rented one in River Towers, probably in an attempt to raise some cash. She had enormous debts, including back taxes; Holly's mother had never been particularly good about paying bills.

The lawyers estimated that by the time all the debts were cleared, Holly would net about $20,000. It wouldn't be enough to keep her and Corinna for long; and in the meantime, she had only what the lawyers would advance her.

She no longer dared to look far into the future. She knew that she would have to move, get a job, find a babysitter for Corinna. Everything cost much more than she had ever realised. The River Towers apartment alone cost nearly $1,000 a month. After giving the landlord her notice, she had searched high and low for an apartment she could afford in Manhattan, but found nothing.

Once again, Rosie had come to the rescue. Her father managed a few buildings in Brooklyn Heights, and luckily in one of them – not the cleanest or best repaired – there was a vacancy.

Holly had never set foot in Brooklyn before, or in the subway, until today. Her parents would never have let her. She smiled grimly, now, at the thought.

Rosie, who rode the subway every day, sometimes with a two-year-old and three-year-old in tow – the products of an early marriage which had recently broken up – had sympathised, though in a limited way, with Holly's plight.

'What was the matter with your husband?' she said, when Holly first told her about her marriage. 'Did he beat you up? No? My husband Ramon, he did it bad. I gave him three chances. I said you give me a black eye one more time and that's *it*. So . . .' she shrugged, 'he did. I was out of there.'

Rosie's approach to most problems was strictly practical. Right now she was standing in the kitchen in her orange miniskirt – her non-working clothes were as different as they could be from her maid's uniform – and grinning as she examined the blackened grease inside the oven. 'Boy. You've got your work cut out for you.'

'Well – ' Holly shrugged, resigned to the worst. 'You know I can't cook. So what am I going to do with an oven anyway?'

Suddenly they both laughed. Nothing – not even this place, Holly thought – could be as bad as it looked.

'So,' said Mr Ortega, rattling the keys in one hand. 'You take it?'

'Yes. OK.' Holly nodded. 'I'll take it.'

Rosie had mentioned to Holly that maybe – just maybe – her mother, who already looked after Rosie's own two children while she worked, might also be willing to mind Corinna.

Now, in the Ortegas' basement apartment, over coffee, Rosie put the proposition to her mother.

By the time she had finished, Annamaria Ortega was already won over. She took Corinna in her arms and touched the thin blonde down on her head. '*Guapa*', she said, and again, '*Es guapísima.*'

'She says your daughter's beautiful,' said Rosie.

Mrs Ortega turned to her daughter, saying something else in Spanish.

'She says, are you moving into that apartment so she can see *Carina* sometime again?' Rosie flashed Holly a conspiratorial grin, and Holly knew that that particular battle was already won.

She felt a little sad to leave the Ortegas', with its bright-flowered wallpaper and smell of cooking, for River Towers – cold and empty, with the feel of death still about it. Maybe it would not be so bad, after all, to start again: to make a home for herself and Corinna in a part of town where she had never lived before.

New York had changed anyway. She had seen that within a few days of coming back. Her mother had replaced her old home with River Towers; all her old schoolfriends had moved – some to the suburbs, others to places as far away as Texas and California. So this was not like coming home: it was beginning again.

With Corinna heavy in her arms, she walked back towards Clinton Street for another look at the building where she would be living. Nineteenth-century brownstones lined the pavement, some newly whitewashed, some soot-streaked and more dilapidated. Her building was, unfortunately, of the second kind. But maybe that would change. Trees, anchored by wires and rubber rings, clung to a precarious life at intervals along the pavement. For the oddest of reasons, the street made Holly feel at home. It reminded her of London.

It was not London, of course. Rosie had warned her that it was a mixed neighbourhood: some old habitués, some urban pioneers, a good many still-dilapidated boarding-houses and their occupants. It occurred to Holly now that it had one great advantage. She could make it nearly impossible for Tyrconnel to find her here.

He and his lawyers had not called or written in the two and a half months she had been living at River Towers. But she knew they would, some time. They must.

And by the time anyone came trying to contact her, she would be gone. The doormen at River Towers needn't know where. She would be untraceable: ex-directory. In a big city, it was easy to disappear.

Gone, she thought, hugging Corinna close, *gone for good. And safe.* Sustained by that thought, she did not even think of being nervous as she walked down into the darkness of the Court Street subway.

Her lease on the new apartment began on the first of August, in two weeks' time. Every day Holly carried Corinna down to Brooklyn on the subway and worked all day cleaning the apartment at Clinton Street: sweeping floors, washing windows, sponging walls. She had no time to repaint the place now. When Rosie was free from work, she helped, and on the first of the month she came up to River Towers to keep an eye on the movers who were shifting most of Holly's mother's furniture down to Brooklyn.

'It'll never fit in that place,' she said.

Holly knew that well enough. But she hadn't had time to sell the furniture, and couldn't leave it behind. It came in an eccentric mix of periods and styles, most of it reproduction, none particularly valuable. The good pieces Holly remembered – the antique rugs, the Whistler – had never been in evidence at River Towers, so she could only suppose her mother had sold them.

When Rosie and the movers had gone, Holly looked around at the unlovely, not especially loved, assembly of objects that filled her living room. The afternoon light that shone in through the bay window did not flatter them: the heavy-legged mahogany dining table, the Victorian sofa, the too-numerous lamps. Some of it – half of it, maybe – would have to go.

And the floor was still bare, and the walls were still grey and patchy. Yet, she supposed, this was home. She opened the window and the evening air smelt damp, unexpectedly fresh.

'Well?' she said to Corinna.

Corinna shouted back: not a word, but a noise, a decided sound. Affirmation. Holly wove back through the furniture to pick her up, and smiled.

Two weeks after the move, Holly left Corinna with Rosie's family for a few days and flew down to Florida to clear out her father's house at Key Isotro.

The house, Pelican's Reach, was the only substantial asset in her mother's estate, and had, in fact, only come to the lawyers' attention when they were halfway through sifting Mrs Clayton's papers. Holly had been surprised, at first, to hear that she had not sold it; but then, that was like her mother, too. Never having spent much time at the house, she could easily have forgotten its existence.

Now, assuming it could be sold, it would just about pay the lawyers' bills. Though Holly didn't like to leave Corinna behind, she was the only person who could do this particular job. With any luck, she would be back in New York soon.

At Miami she changed planes for the short hop to Key Isotro. The second plane only seated about twenty-five, and its lurching progress alarmed her. She clung to the arm of her seat and watched the horizon judder up and down outside her window. The businessman in the seat beside her grinned. 'Should have driven it.' A highway and bridges linked Miami and the Keys.

'I can't drive.'

'You're kidding.'

Holly fell silent, reluctant to explain this peculiarity to her neighbour and his raised eyebrows. She closed her eyes for what was left of the flight, and felt enormously relieved when they landed.

She took a cab to the house at Pelican's Reach, and, letting herself in, was overwhelmed by a mouldy stench. At once she went round, opening the wooden slats of all the windows as far as they would go. The house was dark, the air inside suffocatingly damp, though cooler than outdoors. It was no wonder everything from the sofas to the walls to the pictures on them had mildewed.

She inspected the kitchen and found what she took to be a caretaker's number, in her father's handwriting, on a pad by the telephone. But when she picked up the receiver, the line was dead. *Of course*, she thought. Probably no one had paid the bill for years.

That afternoon she located Key Isotro's sole estate agent; she talked to the caretaker and found a gardener to clear out the subtropical jungle nearly swallowing the house. Since the electricity in the house was still cut off, she went to bed when it got dark; and so the next morning she woke up just after five.

She had chosen her father's old bedroom to sleep in, and now, seen in the daylight, it unnerved her. The room, with its fishing rods leaning in the corner, looked – except for the cobwebs everywhere – as if he had just left it. As if there should be sounds: the hum of her father's shaver, the bubble of the percolator, the maids' voices talking together, the smack of her own feet on tile floors. *Come on, chickadee, let's get out there early, before that sun starts to bite. . . .*

Instead, the house was deadly still.

She knew she wouldn't sleep, so she put on her swimsuit and went out to the cove. The path to the sand was still there, barely visible through the mangroves that choked the backyard.

Never, ever swim alone, her father had said. She could hear his voice now. But she disobeyed it. She immersed herself, soaked her hair in the cold water. She heard his voice again. He had taught her to swim, then to sail here. *Hold on, chickadee! That's it! Remember your balance. . . .*

She felt her throat go tight, and turned back from the water. She did not like remembering this way. All of a sudden, she knew it had been a bad idea to come. If there were anyone, anyone else who could do this. . . .

Back indoors, she grew calmer. There simply was no one else. The only answer was not to think of her parents, either of them; not to return to the old haunts.

Except that Key Isotro seemed to contain nothing else.

While the gardeners went to work that afternoon, she walked down again to the harbour. Surprisingly, the long palm-dotted waterfront was still a sleepy place, perhaps because for many Key Isotro was only a stopping-point *en route* to raunchier Key West. The stretch of docks where her father used to keep his boats had expanded into a new long white shelter. A figure was coming out of it towards her, along the walkway, waving.

She squinted to see him, then waved back. 'Chris!'

He came to meet her on the shore, at an easy jog.

301

'I didn't expect to see you,' she said. 'I figured you must have moved on.'

'Nope. Still here.' Chris Deakin was short and lean, his skin darkened and wrinkled by years of sun; he remained, to all appearances, the same indefinable age – late thirties, early forties – as when Holly had last seen him, in her teens. Back then he had been her father's occasional captain and handyman.

'So how are you?' Holly said.

'OK. Still pretty beat up about your dad.'

Holly nodded. 'My mother's dead too, now.'

'You're kidding.' Chris rested a hand on his grey-blond head, sheltering his eyes. 'Wow. You know, I'm sorry. I. . . .'

'It's OK.'

Wanting the company, perhaps even wanting – despite herself – to reminisce, Holly offered Chris Deakin a drink at one of the cafés near the harbour.

'You know,' said Chris, as soon as he sat down, 'I still feel real bad about your father.'

'I know. But – ' Holly's shoulders twitched – 'these things happen. It wasn't your fault.'

'I was there.' Chris's eyes, light blue and bloodshot, looked straight into hers for a moment.

'You were?' Holly swallowed. Her throat felt dry. 'You mean – you were on the boat with him?' She wanted to ask more, but something made her hesitate. 'What . . . what happened that day? Do you mind telling me? No one ever really explained to me.'

Chris looked at her steadily. 'I'd tell you, if I really knew. All I know, Holly, is it was one of those days – perfect one minute, then the next you don't know what the hell's caught you.' He slipped a hand round his glass of beer, which was wet with condensation. 'I remember that boat. That was an amazing boat your father had. The *Mirage*. She should have handled it.'

Holly nodded, afraid to break into Chris's thoughts.

'I try to remember,' he said, 'but, honest to God, I can't. Not much. I worry and worry at it, you know. But . . .'

He shrugged. 'I think . . .' He spoke very slowly now – 'when the storm came, we must have tried the engine. I remember seeing your father slip. He shouted. . . .'

'Go on, Chris. It's OK. I want to know.'

'Later everyone said he probably hit his head. I don't know. Because, I don't know if you know – ' Chris Deakin's gaze flickered over Holly's face – 'They never found the body.'

'I know.' She looked at him steadily. 'So how did you make it through, yourself?'

'The Coast Guard found me. I guess. I don't remember much. They said I was hanging on to a piece of the hull. I'd been out there six hours.'

Holly didn't know what to say.

'You know, he was a great man, your dad.' Chris gulped down the last of his beer, and Holly waved to the waitress for another.

'It was funny, all those business guys coming down here in their business suits and pretending they were, like, the old man and the sea. But I think your father really meant it. He always said he'd spend his life down here if he could.'

'I know. I think he might have.' Holly thought briefly of her mother; of the Park Avenue apartment, of trips to Europe and Balenciaga gowns. Opposing aspirations.

This had been her father's escape: among men, fleeing and seeking similar things. Women had had little to do with this particular dream of his. Pelican's Reach, she supposed, in the end, had even excluded her.

Chris finished his second beer and gave a weak grin. 'Sure you're going to sell? That's some house you've got there. Needs some work.'

'I'll have to sell,' said Holly briefly. 'Too bad. But I don't think I'll have much time to come down here any more.'

A few minutes later they parted.

That evening, Holly started going through the house, throwing out everything that was useless or beyond repair.

The estate agents had the keys; if she could manage to clear the house tonight, she could leave tomorrow. Suddenly she wanted to, desperately: to get back home to Corinna. She would just have to work all night.

One small room, off his bedroom, Joe Clayton had kept as a study; its neat arrangement of desk, phone and filing cabinet looked out of place here, almost ill at ease. But there they were.

Holly poured herself a coffee and started sifting through papers. Most of the documents in the files had to do with United Alloys. Since that company had ceased to exist four years ago, she put them all in boxes to be thrown out. Not until she reached the bottom file drawer did she find anything to catch her attention.

Will, the folder was labelled. She had never read her father's will, though by now she was all too familiar with her mother's.

She opened the folder. Inside were three different sets of papers: three different wills. She had always had a vague notion that her father had changed his will a few times; now she looked through each of the versions. The first, dated 1938, left everything to her mother. The second, made when she was fifteen, left United Alloys – which her father had then still wholly owned – to her, Holly, in trust until she was twenty-five. Everything else – a complicated jumble of stocks, bonds and properties – went to her mother. Then came the third. It was dated 12 October 1960.

I, Joseph Clayton, of New York, New York, declare this to be my will, revoking all my prior wills and codicils . . .

A thick bundle of sheets. Too much to read now. Holly flipped through the pages: bequests to her mother, details concerning the company. And then, 'I devise and bequeath to my son-in-law, Tyrconnel Carr. . . .'

Her heart seizing up strangely, Holly read on. Her father

had given all his shares – a controlling interest – in United Alloys, to Tyrconnel, outright.

She knew that that was what he had done. Years ago, Tyrconnel had told her. So why did it come as such a shock, merely to see it in writing?

She flipped disconsolately through to the end of the will, and a thin carbon copy fluttered out.

> Pelican's Reach, Key Isotro
> 30 October 1960

Dear Tyrconnel,

As promised, a copy of the new will. Good to talk to you the other day – you've eased my mind. As we both said, this may only be temporary – let's hope she gets better. It's a comfort to know you're there to look after her, and also that I can trust you to handle her affairs, should anything happen to me. (Though, God willing, I've got a good few years left to run!) Of course I never expected a girl to run the business, so I'm glad now that there's someone I can 'hand on the reins' to. I'm afraid the way things looked in London, she may always need a watchful eye on her. I know you'll do what's best.

My regards, and my wife sends her love to you all –

> J. C.

And so there it was: the date – October 1960, just a month after she had been taken away to the hospital. Her father thought she was mentally ill, that she might never be quite right in the head again. And besides. . . . *I never expected a girl to run the business.*

No, she thought with a sudden vehemence, which surprised her, he never had, had he? Never even thought about it.

Because she was a girl, she was incapable. That assumption had underlined everything he did for the last twenty years of his life. The special arrangements, the trusts – the final bequeathing of everything to Tyrconnel.

She had never questioned it, perhaps because she had

never thought about it all before. The supposition, never stated, that because she was female she was bound to spend her life in waiting: for a dance partner, for a fiancé, for a husband. That when such a one came along, then her fate would be decided. Nothing to do with her own choosing.

Her father had waited, too. Throughout most of her childhood he had waited for a son who never came. And yet that mythical son had figured in her father's thoughts even when Holly was sixteen, eighteen. '*Now, if you'd had a brother. . . .*'

He had assumed, just as she had, that she would marry: that whatever else she did, before or after, was of little account. Marriage had been the pinnacle of her dreams. A perfect husband, perfect home, perfect babies. . . .

She saw that dream now for the ruse it was. For eighteen years it had dazzled and blinded her; she had stamped down any other dreams, any other ambition she might have had.

Her father had believed her settled, even if she was not happy. What did that matter? She was taken care of.

And within two months of sending his letter from Pelican's Reach, Joe Clayton was dead. Tyrconnel had inherited almost everything. He still had all that money now. She did not know if she would ever see it again; and that was, little as she liked to acknowledge it, her father's fault. Maybe she could have learnt to run the business. *How could Daddy know?*

She stood up, anger heating her face. On the other side of the house the sun was rising, creating a misty light that poured through the screened window from beyond the mangrove trees.

How could he know?

She paced the room. There were so many things she had never been allowed to do, just because she was a woman: handle a boat, ride the subway, manage money. . . . She had accepted those limits, as if they were a privilege: something specially female, like wearing high heels and long hair.

When she could have been anything – a professor, a doctor, a lawyer. . . .

A lawyer.

She still could. There was nothing to stop her. She could go back to college. She might have to go to night school – it might take a long time – but hadn't Jamie said it once? *If you'd been a man, Holly, you'd have made a fantastic lawyer.*

The Carrs had used the law: bent and twisted it. Because, after all, the law was only a set of rules, of procedures. A knowledge.

A knowledge which, she had learnt the hard way, brought power like no other.

It was not too late. She was twenty-five; she had years before her, and no other ambition. She would go to school, she would learn: and then one day, she would be able to face up to the Carrs and get back what was hers.

She shivered. The morning sun dazzled her eyes, and the last of her coffee had gone cold.

She would get even.

II

'Lyall, Kravitz.'

'Hello.' Holly adjusted herself as quickly as she could to the telephonist's brusque response. 'I'm calling about the ad your firm placed in the *New York Times*.'

'Ad?'

'Yes,' Holly persisted. 'For a secretary?'

'You want to speak to Leonard Green.'

A click and a silence followed.

'Leonard Green,' a male voice barked.

What am I going to tell him? thought Holly. *Why am I doing this? What makes me think I have even a hope?*

*

During the last six weeks – aware, with every passing day, of her funds draining away – Holly had taught herself to type. Sometimes she hammered away at the keys of her mother's old Corona for nine or ten hours at a stretch. Through sheer desperate persistence, she had seen her typing speed rise, from twenty to thirty, now forty words a minute.

She knew well enough that she had no qualifications, no formal experience; yet still she hoped that somehow she might get herself a secretarial job. If she couldn't manage to, soon, she would have to take whatever she could get – waitressing, or work in a shop – and that, she knew, would barely pay her rent.

Last month she had sold her jewellery. There had seemed to be no other way. The movers' bill came, she owed Mrs Ortega money for looking after Corinna while she was in Florida, and the lawyers had refused to advance her anything more.

So she had taken her engagement ring, her diamond earrings and necklace and her baroque pearls up to the Jewellers' Exchange on 47th Street. Wandering, feeling increasingly naive and out of place, among the black-coated Hasidic Jews who seemed to run all the hundreds of stalls in the vast indoor market, she had laid her small bundle down at last on one of the glass counters.

The young man behind it, pale and plump-faced, smiled, then examined the jewels dispassionately.

' "To Holly",' he read the engraving inside the ring. 'Is that you?'

Holly nodded, and he smiled apologetically.

'Too bad. Engraving lowers the value.' He offered her $2,000 for everything except the pearls.

'I honestly couldn't give you much for those,' he said. 'They're highly flawed. All covered up by the design, see? . . . I mean, I could give you fifty or so. . . .'

Holly kept the pearls, shoving them into the bottom of a drawer when she got back to Brooklyn. So much, she thought, for Imogen's generosity.

The rest she sold, after shopping around for a few more estimates, to the young man at the first stall, for $2,300. And she found that as she left the great hall, cash in hand, she felt not bereft, but lighthearted. It was the first time, she realised, that those gemstones had been of the slightest use to her.

Now, she felt a little less sanguine. More than half that cash was gone, and she didn't have even a hope of a job. Gradually, she had been forced to lower her sights. The law firms where she had first hoped to work seemed to want only secretaries with legal experience. Where was anyone supposed to get that experience, she wondered, if none of them would let someone *in*experienced in the front door?

She had put in six applications to law firms, in the hope that one might not prove so rigid in its requirements; but she had not had even an interview.

One advertising agency in a dingy part of town had interviewed her; so had a charity. The rejection letters came a few days later. Last week, she had put in an application to sell perfume at Lord & Taylor.

It was not as if, she realised now, Leonard Green, of Lyall, Kravitz & Green, Attorneys, would really want to hire her. She had probably been foolish even to telephone in answer to their ad:

Secretary for growing Park Avenue international law firm. Intelligence, initiative more important than experience. . . .

She wouldn't get it. Of course she wouldn't. On the other end of the phone, Leonard Green was beginning to sound impatient.

'So. Do you have any work experience at all?'

It sounded as if that would be his last question before he politely – or impolitely – dismissed her. Holly thought quickly. 'I've worked – I've been an assistant in the House of Commons,' she said. 'In England. I used to live there.'

She had never mentioned that before – had not intended to now.

But suddenly Leonard Green sounded interested. 'Really? I'll tell you what, why don't you come in? Tomorrow at eleven OK with you?'

'Sure.' Holly's arms and legs were shaking from sheer nerves as she hung up the telephone.

She reached 54th and Park well before eleven. The building, occupying the corner and most of the block, was an uninspired oblong of stone and glass. Holly stood in the lobby waiting for the elevator, her body covered, despite the cool October day, in a thin film of sweat.

She had chosen the wrong thing to wear: she knew it. Her honey-coloured suede suit with a silk blouse and matching boots might have looked right in Soho; but it was probably too far out for a law office. *Damn.* Unfortunately, it was also the only outfit she still possessed that was not yet worn out or baby-stained.

Every one of the men, she noted, who filled the lift after her was wearing a shapeless, American-cut suit of an almost identical grey. Probably Leonard Green would be, too.

She got off on the fourteenth floor and took a seat, as instructed by the receptionist. The space behind the reception desk was piled high with cardboard boxes.

'Miss Clayton?'

She looked up, startled. The first thing she noticed about Leonard Green was that he was not wearing shapeless grey, but well-cut, rather close-fitting charcoal pinstripes.

She shook his hand and tried not to notice that as she stood, he looked her over, too.

Leonard Green was not what she had expected. He looked younger than he had sounded, forty perhaps. And, in some indefinable way, darker: thinning dark hair, dark eyes, dark close-cropped beard. He was handsome, she supposed; but something in the intensity of his look frightened her a little, too.

'Just down here, Miss Clayton.'

Holly wondered, as he ushered her ahead of him into his office, whether there wasn't just a tinge of southern drawl in his voice, now, even though on the phone it had sounded sharp, aggressive and utterly New York.

She handed him her c.v. when he asked for it and sat on the edge of the one free chair. Beyond Leonard Green's shoulders, she could see the broad sweep of Park Avenue: a welcome sight to him, she imagined, after the chaos of this room, whose every available surface was covered with books and papers.

He noticed her looking, and smiled unexpectedly. 'We've just moved in. You see our problem.' Then he glanced down again. 'You don't say anything here about short-hand.'

'The ad didn't mention shorthand.'

'It's a plus.' Leonard Green spoke quickly and his face was unexpressive.

'I can take notes fast, by hand.'

'Hmm.' Leonard Green let out a noise that was some-where between a growl and a throat-clearing. 'Well. This looks pretty straightforward. Spence School. Admitted Smith 1958. Why didn't you go?'

'I got married instead.'

Leonard Green nodded, perching his chin on the tips of his fingers. He seemed to want to hear more.

'I married – an Englishman, when I was eighteen. That was how I happened to work at the House of Commons. My husband and I are – apart now.'

'Divorced?'

Holly nodded. It seemed neater, although it was not true.

'And so what makes you think you're the right person to work with us?'

Relieved that her questioner had moved away from per-sonal ground, Holly almost forgot to think about her answer. 'I need – ' she started. 'I want to work here because I'd like to get legal experience. I plan to start college next year, somewhere in the city. It'll have to be part-time. Once I've got my BA, I want to go to law school.'

She was astonished at the speed with which it had all come out.

'That's a pretty tall order. You're talking eight, nine years of work if you plan on doing it by night school.' Leonard Green smiled calmly, and yet there was something faintly predatory in the way his flat, dark gaze met her own.

Holly felt a strange tremor, deep inside her, as she looked back. 'I know it'll take a while. But I've thought it all through. It's what I want to do.'

'Corporate law? Criminal law?'

'I was thinking of – divorce. Family law.'

'Because you're divorced?'

Holly nodded, abashed. In fact, she hardly knew yet what she would specialise in, so she was relieved when Leonard Green changed tack.

'I've got to warn you,' he said, 'it wouldn't be easy for you here. We're riding on as small a staff as we can. You'd have three associates to work for, as well as me. Mainly me.' Leonard Green grinned, this time amiably. 'You'd be doing all our typing, filing – keeping this whole end of the office under control. And, frankly, it doesn't sound as if your typing's all that – '

'It'll get faster.' Holly looked down, realising she had interrupted. But something in the way he spoke – of 'you', as if she had at least a chance at the job – had made hope leap within her. 'I'm working on my typing,' she said. 'I've been teaching myself. I've only been doing it since August. I'm sure it'll get better.'

Leonard Green eased back in his chair and asked her a few questions about the House of Commons. Holly relaxed then, knowing that what she'd done there had actually been fairly responsible, high-powered. And if the worst came to the worst and he wanted a reference, she supposed she would just have to give him Jamie's name. . . .

To her relief, he didn't ask. Instead, he started to tell her

312

about Lyall, Kravitz & Green. It was a new firm, only six years old, specialising in corporate and international corporate law. 'We're small,' he said, 'and we intend to stay that way. Three partners at the moment, and five associates. One secretary.' He held up a finger for emphasis. 'Oh, and Judy. The receptionist. You can see it's chaotic, and likely to stay that way for a while. There'd be some overtime. Now, I don't know if you could fit that in with night school. . . .'

New York, Holly noticed, seemed to have taken over in his voice, his southern drawl gradually vanishing. 'I'd just have to manage,' she answered him. 'To tell the truth, going to school's my long-term plan. But more than anything, I need to get a job right now – before I can go to school or do anything else.' She smiled, and hoped she did not look apologetic. 'I may not be as experienced as some of the other people you see. But that's why I'm here. I *want* to get experience. I want to learn.'

She wondered, for a moment, if that had sounded over-confident. But Leonard Green smiled as he leaned forward on his desk. 'I seem to remember,' he said, 'our ad mentioned initiative. I guess I've got to grant you that.'

Holly started work at Lyall, Kravitz & Green the next Monday.

III

In March 1968, Holly heard from her husband for the first time in three years.

The Ortegas received the letter, because she had asked for any mail for her to be forwarded to their address when she left River Towers. It was part of her effort at concealment, at burying the past; as had been changing her own name, on all her records and documents, back to Clayton.

Rosie, whose interest had instantly been sparked by the foreign stamps and return address on the fat legal envelope, raised a single eyebrow as she handed it over to Holly in the doorway of her parents' house. '*Well*,' she said. 'You don't think it might be. . . .'

Holly glanced up before she could look hard at the envelope. 'I don't know.'

'If it's something big, you'll tell me, right?'

'Sure. But I'm sure it's – nothing.' Refusing to look now, Holly shoved the letter into her bag.

A few seconds later, Mrs Ortega and Corinna appeared in the kitchen doorway.

'Mom!' Corinna shouted. She bowled down the hall, straight into Holly's legs. 'Going home,' she said.

'That's right. Home.' Holly struggled to disentangle herself. Tonight was one of her late nights, when she went to lectures after work. By the time she got Corinna home, it would be nine, and it always took at least an hour to get Corinna calmed down and into bed before she could even think about relaxing, herself.

Or not relaxing, as the case might be. The very knowledge of that letter's presence in her handbag made her stomach clench into a knot.

'Are we going to Mr Tong's?' Corinna jumped up and down and pulled on Holly's skirt. Mr Tong's was the Chinese restaurant a few blocks away where Holly took Corinna as a treat most Friday nights.

'Mr Tong's,' she told Corinna, 'is tomorrow. Tonight we go home. I'm beat.'

A little after ten, Corinna safely in bed, Holly carried a plate of leftover spaghetti to the dining table, and got out her envelope. She recognised everything about it: the thick creamy paper, the address at Lincoln's Inn.

Dear Lady Carr,
    We are obliged to inform you . . .

She forced herself not to look ahead, but to read slowly

through to the end. And then she thought, *It can't be true. Was that all he wanted? There must be some trick.*

Tyrconnel, who had sworn he would never allow her to end their marriage, was suing for divorce.

'Mom?'

She turned. Corinna was standing in her pyjamas in the bedroom doorway.

'What's that?' she said, padding over. 'From Rosie?'

'No, not from Rosie. It's nothing, honey.' Holly shoved the letter away and shepherded Corinna into the dark back room, where she groped amid the menagerie of soft toys on the bed. 'So now. You're going to stay put this time. Aren't you? What does Mr Turtle say?'

'Go . . . to . . . sleep!' Corinna chimed in as Holly tucked the big stuffed turtle in beside her. 'That's what he always says,' she mumbled, her voice growing drowsier. 'Why doesn't he . . .'

Holly stroked her daughter's back until she drifted off.

Back in the living room, when everything was quiet, she stared at the typed page. Tyrconnel couldn't be letting her go as easily as that. There must be some catch. What was it?

The next afternoon at the office, she waited uneasily for Leonard to be free. She had never talked to him about anything as personal as this before. Though they had worked together now for two and a half years, they still knew barely more than the basic facts about each other's domestic lives. Holly knew that Leonard had a wife and two sons, aged thirteen and eleven, out in Scarsdale; he knew she had a daughter, whom occasionally he teased her for spoiling rotten.

He often teased her; he seemed to find her amusing, for reasons that had puzzled her at first. He had taken to calling her his 'English secretary', because, he said, she must have picked up an English accent, since she certainly didn't sound like a New Yorker. Holly told him that she never had, but he took no heed; the nickname suited his image of her – choosy, ladylike, unversed in New York's ways or its ethnic diversity. Leonard, a Jew who adored hot, spicy food and ate almost exclusively in Asian restaurants, flattered himself that he embodied that very diversity. The first time he had expounded on his eating habits – 'Cheese,' he said, 'in food, is an abomination' – Holly had asked him innocently if this was something to do with keeping kosher. He had hooted with laughter.

'Kosher!' he said. 'No way. I'm about as secularised as they come.'

He described himself as an 'Alabama Jew' – a contradiction in terms, or so Holly had first thought. 'Heck, no,' said Leonard. 'There's a whole gang of us down Montgomery way. We've even got our own country club.' After serving at the Pacific end of the war, he had settled in the north-east – Harvard, then Columbia Law School – and remained a devoted New Yorker ever since.

And so it was thanks partly to Leonard, and partly to her own initiative, that Holly was learning the city's essentials. That you always ordered pastrami with mustard on rye. That you hung on to quarters, for laundry and the buses. That you answered the phone with a name, yours or the office's – never with such time-wasting pleasantries as 'Good morning.' Holly even said her own name now when picking up the phone, which she knew was a badge of status, of sorts. It meant that she had her own place in the establishment. Many of Leonard's clients had come to realise that she could deal with their routine business as quickly as Leonard could. Gradually more and more everyday chores were ending up in Holly's lap. 'A great way to learn the law,' Leonard would say genially, as he passed her overcrowded desk. 'Hands on.'

But Holly knew that often he worked far harder than she did. He did indulge in a few two- and three-hour lunches, surprisingly often with women, whom he introduced to Holly as 'old friends'. Usually these were the wives of clients. 'Got to keep 'em sweet,' he said. 'Half the time their husbands won't tell me what the hell they're really up to. I've got to find out somehow.' For most of the last year he had been trying to work out a compromise in a shipping dispute between a Texan oil magnate and a Greek billionaire; the Texan's wife, suntanned and glamorous, was one of Leonard's more frequent luncheon guests.

It was part of her rapport with Leonard, Holly realised, that she asked no questions – at least not about the wives and the lunches. About the cases she did ask, and learnt as much as she could. Within a few months she could see that she had made a real difference at Lyall, Kravitz: no more boxes littering the halls and Leonard's office, everything neatly filed away, the phones answered. 'You're a godsend,' Leonard had told her once, and blown her a theatrical kiss. 'Tell me where they made you, Holly, and I'll send for a hundred more.'

The reward for efficiency seemed to be more work, but she didn't mind. She composed letters from Leonard's scrawled notes; she proof-read; she took on the excess work of the other two partners, Gordon Lyall and Abe Kravitz, and because no one else much wanted to or had the time, she trained the lost-looking young men who came to the office to work as paralegals, still dazed by their luck at avoiding Vietnam.

In return for all this, the firm had given Holly a generous rise last year. At last she could afford to pay Mrs Ortega properly for looking after Corinna. She could also afford a few new outfits, though she shopped mainly at the sales and the discount stores in Brooklyn. Her taste in clothes, she had to admit, had grown more conservative. Sometimes she looked at her own reflection with a certain detachment: short, bright-coloured suits, gold clip earrings, her hair brushed silky-straight into a French twist. She looked, she realised, almost like the perfect secretaries in the ads in *Vogue* and *Glamour*.

The only difference was, she had no intention of remaining one.

At five o'clock on the day after Tyrconnel's letter came,

she tapped on the frame of Leonard's door. 'Can I talk to you?'

'Sure.' Leonard stretched back in his chair, hands joined behind his head. It was characteristic of him, Holly thought, that although his window offered a panoramic view of Park Avenue, Leonard planted himself with his back to it, focusing instead on the comings and goings of the office.

'Can I – close the door?' Holly felt furtive.

Leonard gave an expansive shrug.

'It's this,' Holly said, holding out the letter from Tyrconnel's solicitors. 'It came in the mail yesterday. I guess I should explain before you read it – I know I let you think I'm divorced, but I'm not really.'

Leonard's dark eyebrows rose and fell.

Holly explained as best she could, without going into the background. She had wanted a divorce, she said, but without Tyrconnel's co-operation there could be no divorce under English law. 'So then,' she said, 'in the end – '

'You just left?' Leonard's eyes widened as he unfolded the letter. 'Doesn't that leave things a little messy? I mean, supposing you wanted to remarry.'

'I don't.' Holly spoke abruptly. 'I mean – when I left, that didn't seem to be an issue.'

Perhaps, she thought, she was already learning to talk like a lawyer. Using the precise-sounding terms that were still, in effect, evasions. . . .

Leonard took a minute or so to read the letter. 'Well,' he said. 'It seems pretty clear. I don't know about English law, but desertion for a specified period is grounds in most countries.'

'Three years,' Holly said, 'in England. I've been away nearly that long. The thing is . . . this isn't like my husband, to give me what I want. It seems to me there must be something behind it.'

'Well.' Leonard studied her, his dark brown eyes unflickering. 'Of course I don't know your husband. Maybe he thought you'd come back before, but now he's finally given up. Or is it possible he's found someone else he wants to marry?'

'I doubt that.' Holly's mouth twisted into something like a smile.

'Well, then.' Leonard shrugged. 'I guess he's conceding.'

'But he's offering me what I wanted all along.' Holly frowned. 'He would never do that. That was – I think – one of the reasons he wouldn't co-operate in the first place. Because that would have meant giving in. It isn't *principles* that matter to him, it's, well – winning.'

'Then I guess your ex-husband and I have something in common.'

Holly was too distracted by her own sudden realization to respond to the quip. 'Unless – ' she said.

'Unless?'

'Maybe he thinks he's winning now.' Holly fell silent. Suddenly Tyrconnel's behaviour made sense. *His* decision, *his* divorce.

'So,' Leonard said, 'are you happy with your financial arrangements?'

Holly laughed. 'Financial arrangements! There weren't any.' She told him about the legal wrangles before she left London; the custody threats; her father's will.

'Wow,' said Leonard at last. 'You got screwed.'

'Thanks. That's encouraging to hear.'

'You could probably take him to court, of course. Risk the whole custody thing coming up again. Hard to estimate your chances. He'd probably try to use the desertion against you. You know, irresponsibility.'

'That's ridiculous!' Holly felt her face growing hot.

'I know. I'm just saying what he'd try.'

'You should have gone into divorce law.' Holly forced a smile. It was not, after all, Leonard's fault if he happened to be the bearer of bad news. He was trying to help her.

'Divorce law's a con. No one wins. I don't believe in divorce, basically.'

'Neither did I.' Holly took back the letter, suddenly

feeling awkward again. 'Thanks, Leonard. Sorry to have taken up your time.'

Leonard shrugged; then he smiled, for a longer time, she thought, than she had seen him smile before. 'I wonder – ' he said. 'I mean, would you consider coming out to dinner with me, Holly?' His gaze grew suddenly intent.

For a moment she understood – or thought she understood – what he meant. 'No,' she said. 'Thank you. But I can't.' She smiled to soften the blow. 'I have to get home to Corinna. I take her out every Friday. You know, to Mr Tong's.' She shrugged.

'I understand. Say no more.' Leonard smiled and raised his hand in salute as she walked out.

He'd never asked her out anywhere before. That sudden question of his perturbed her as she rode home on the subway. She was sure it was better that she'd said no. Relations at the office were tricky, and she'd seen enough feuds at Lyall, Kravitz: not always based on sex, in fact hardly ever, since almost everyone there was male. But even friendships could form too quickly, and easily go awry, when people spent so much of their waking life together. That was why she was pleased with the way she got on with Leonard Green. They were friends, but not familiars. She found him attractive – of course she did, he had a presence that was undeniable. Charisma. The time when she had gone downtown to watch him in court, it took her breath away. She saw the way he used his voice, his walk, his gestures – now gentle, now sharp and sudden – to catch witnesses off guard. She watched him sum up before the judge as if he hadn't a grain of doubt – when she knew for a fact that the day before he hadn't been certain of the ground he stood on. She had been impressed, and thought, *if only one day I can do the same.*

Yet, for all that she felt his particular magnetism, she was not sure that she wanted Leonard Green so much as admired him. She did not, these days, think very often about that kind of want. She had grown used to her closet-bedroom lined with bookshelves; and used to telling herself – and, for the most part, believing – that she did not need or want a man there.

So she resolved now not even to contemplate it. A married man: she had made that mistake before. If she wanted any man, then, yes, it must be Leonard. But he was also utterly and permanently forbidden.

The subway creaked from side to side and she eyed the advertisements lodged in the curve between window and ceiling, some in Spanish, for rice and cockroach poison.

At the back of her mind she knew that her life could, perhaps should, be different. *You got screwed*, Leonard said. And it was true. One day she would have a big score to settle with Tyrconnel Carr. But the question was: now? Did she want it now? She imagined flying to England, launching a financial claim, defending her right to custody of Corinna in court. And she knew the answer.

She was doing all right as she was. Slowly but surely, she was getting what she wanted. A few months after she had joined Lyall, Kravitz, she had signed on for night courses at Hunter College, a compact, sooty city campus a few blocks north of the office. Thinking of law school, she had chosen political science as her major, and struggled to keep her grades up, studying for most of her free nights and weekends and taking her vacation weeks from work just before exams. In her first term she got an A and a B; last year she had all As. Leonard egged her on. 'You need those As,' he would say, 'to get into your choice of school. So what's it going to be? Harvard Law? Yale? Columbia?'

Half the time she knew he couldn't possibly be serious; but then sometimes, when she least expected it, he was. 'I know you're going to do it,' he had said once, with a perfectly straight face. 'You want it enough. I can see it. It'll happen.'

She did not mind being busy. In fact, she had grown so used to it that she felt restless with time on her hands. Over one holiday weekend, she had painted the apartment; over another, finally fed up with eating from tins, she had bought *The Joy of Cooking* and taught herself to cook. Knocking on the door and finding Holly in a steaming kitchen, Rosie told her she was crazy. 'What are you doing? You've got to get out of this place!' she said. 'Have some fun! Meet men.'

And Holly couldn't say exactly why she didn't want to. Corinna's company was enough for her, somehow; she really enjoyed their Friday nights, and hated it when she was delayed in picking Corinna up for any reason.

Corinna knew that, too.

'You're late,' she announced tonight when Holly appeared at the Ortega's front door.

'Not very.' Holly got out her chequebook to pay Mrs Ortega.

'Yes, you are! It's seven. You showed me, on the clock . . .'

'*Carina!*' Mrs Ortega issued a reprimand in Spanish.

Corinna answered in Spanish. Holly looked up, surprised. She had known Corinna spoke a few words of the language – she was bound to pick it up at the Ortegas', and if she did, so much the better. It might be useful to her one day.

But there she was, arguing, apparently fluently, with Annamaria Ortega. Holly couldn't even guess what she was saying. 'Corinna,' she said, 'don't talk back to Mrs Ortega.'

'*Yaya* says it's OK,' said Corinna, turning to her confidently. *Yaya*, 'Grandma', was what Rosie's two children called Mrs Ortega.

'Why don't you show Mama what you did this afternoon?' Mrs Ortega led the way through to the back room: a large, steamy kitchen and playroom, the carpet strewn with toys. At Mrs Ortega's urging, Corinna headed for the kitchen table, kneeling on a chair to look at a copy of New York's Spanish newspaper, *El Diario*.

'*Ayer y hoy*,' she said, and, running her finger along a headline, read straight on. Then she pointed to another block of dark print and read it, and another.

322

'Corinna, honey!' Holly was too taken aback to show how pleased she was, at first. 'Did you teach her?' she asked both the Ortegas; Jorge was sitting nearby in an easy chair.

'No.' He smiled back at Holly. 'She teach herself. Every morning I read to her, show her the big words. And today – ' He shrugged. 'She does it for the first time by herself. You better watch, Mrs Clayton! When this one goes to school, she gonna run away before all the others.'

'She's a smart girl,' said his wife. '*Muy inteligente*. I say to Rosie, if only hers would learn to read so quick.'

'Ay, all in good time,' said Jorge Ortega.

'Of course they will, they all do,' said Holly, feeling abashed by the comparison. Rosie's two – Ray and Luisa, four and five – were sitting transfixed by the television. 'Well!' she said briskly to Corinna. 'Mr Tong's?'

'Yeah! Mr Tong's!' No sooner had Corinna shown off her reading than she had forgotten it. And at Mr Tong's she wailed when her soup was too hot, and seemed more interested in figuring out how the fortune got inside her cookie than in trying to read it. Soon after that, she overturned her water and started to cry; and it seemed to Holly then that she was a normal three-year-old again, her suddenly revealed ability no more than a quirk.

Only Holly knew deep down that it was more than that. Corinna had been talking, stringing whole sentences together, since she was barely two; and now it seemed that, if the Ortegas weren't exaggerating, she might be a sort of prodigy in Spanish as well as in English. For the first time Holly felt daunted by her own child – or at least by the challenge of nurturing whatever spark of genius she possessed.

A week later, when they happened to be alone together in his office, Leonard Green asked Holly if she intended to contest Tyrconnel's divorce.

'No,' said Holly, 'I decided to ignore the letter. After all, it's what I've wanted all along.'

'So you're not going to go after any money.' Leonard held his voice steady, but his watchful expression told Holly that restraining his curiosity cost him an effort.

'I decided it's not worth all the trouble.'

'So you're going to forgive and forget, eh?'

'Oh, no.' Holly looked straight back at him, startled. Then she gave a crisp smile. 'I have no intention of forgetting.'

It was then that Holly began her files. They took shape, at first, in an informal way: her notes from her African politics course, clippings from the *Economist* and *Fortune* recommended by her professor. She started to read the newspapers more carefully, especially *The Times* and the *Wall Street Journal*, making cuttings from the office's discarded copies on the rare occasions when TCI or the African branch of its operations or its South American subsidiary, were mentioned.

She wanted to learn about TCI: learn as she had not managed to in all the years she had been married to its chief executive. Then, she had had an inkling of wrongdoing but felt powerless. Now, though perhaps still powerless, she was a little wiser.

And she had plenty of time.

'Mommy,' said Corinna, 'do I have a father?'

It was bedtime, but she had a bad cold and could not sleep. Mr Turtle, matted and misshapen, trailed from her hand.

Holly had known the question was bound to come, but how strangely, when it did: *Do I have a father?* Abstract and precise at once. 'Yes,' she said. 'You did have a father. All little boys and girls do.'

'Where is he?'

'Was Mrs Ortega asking you about this?' Holly was suspicious. If Mrs Ortega was stirring up Corinna's curiosity, she would have to warn her off it.

Slowly Corinna shook her head.

'Come on,' said Holly, bending down to hoist her up in her arms. 'Back to bed. You've got to try to sleep, bunny-kins, even if you feel bad. I'll bring you a hot lemon.'

'So where is he?' said Corinna again, obstinate.

'Now, Corinna, that's a long story. But he's gone. OK? Some people's daddies don't live with them. Yours doesn't. There's just us.'

Corinna was silent then, but as she sipped her hot lemon a few minutes later she still looked dissatisfied. 'Can he come back?'

The questions had come sooner than Holly had expected, and she was unprepared. 'No,' she said, ruffling Corinna's hair, 'he can't come back.'

'Why?' Corinna demanded.

'Because he can't. You'll have to take my word for it. He's just gone. Gone for ever.'

IV

The year Corinna turned five, Holly finally gave in to her demands and bought a television. It didn't strike her until she had watched the small black-and-white set for a few evenings that every programme on it seemed to be about families – *The Partridge Family*, *The Brady Bunch*, *Bewitched*. It should have reassured her that every family was different, but instead she found herself worrying. Would everything Corinna saw make her more aware of her lack of a father? But at least when she probed the subject with Corinna, Corinna seemed not to have noticed.

The real problem with the TV was that Holly couldn't seem to wrest her daughter away from it, especially the morning cartoons. Even today, when Corinna was sup-posed to be setting off for her first day at school.

Holly stood by the door. 'Come *on* bunnykins.' Corinna couldn't be afraid, could she? When Holly had taken her to the local primary school a few weeks ago to register, Corinna had seemed intrigued. 'Will I get to paint pictures on the wall like these?' she said. 'Will I be here all day instead of at the Ortegas'? Ray and Luisa go to school already. Ray hates it.'

'Well, you won't hate it. I'm sure you're going to like it.' Despite her words, Holly faced the preliminary interview with some trepidation. The important thing was to convince the school, if she could, to register Corinna under the name of Clayton.

Corinna had been sent to play in a corner while Holly explained the situation in a low voice. It did read 'Carr' on Corinna's birth certificate; but, since Holly had been divorced and gone back to using her maiden name . . .

The principal's secretary was sympathetic. 'I see. Well, I see no reason she couldn't be put down as "Clayton", in the class register at least.'

Last weekend Holly had taken Corinna shopping for school clothes; Corinna had tried them on every night since. No, it couldn't be that she was afraid of school.

'Enough.' Holly marched over to the TV. The cartoons were just ending, giving way to some jangly music.

'*Help!*' said an announcer's voice. 'The Beatles are breaking up. Help stop the Beatles from breaking up! Write to *Save the Beatles* now. . . .'

For a moment Holly froze. *The Beatles.* What an age ago it seemed. Vaguely, over the years since her first infatuation with them, she had registered the existence of their further albums, their transformation from good boys to psychedelic clones to hard rockers. She hadn't known they were coming to an end. How old it made her feel.

For a second the fancy took her to note down that address. Then she shook her head. 'Come on, honey.' She took Corinna's hand and switched the set off.

For the most part, Holly had been too busy in the last few years to pay much attention to music, or even to U.S. news. When she did read the papers, she felt angry and impotent. The police were shooting students in Ohio; the country was being torn apart by Vietnam. No one wanted the war, or so it seemed to her. The artist who used to bounce his basketball on the floor upstairs had run away to Canada to avoid the draft. Even Leonard thought the 'police action' had gone completely out of control. 'Hell, I was *in* one war,' he said, 'but if I were one of these young guys, I wouldn't want to get drafted into this mess, either.' His normally cynical view of the world – 'Sue or get sued,' he always said, 'eat or get eaten' – mellowed when it came to the issues of the day. 'I was,' he avowed, 'a communist at twenty-five. And I wouldn't want anyone to try to deny me the right to be one again.'

On a small scale, perhaps, when things were going wrong, people could get together and force changes. When Holly and her neighbours in the building had grown worried about the way the landlord was letting the place go to seed, they had formed a residents' committee, and knocked on doors. It turned out the same landlord, O'Hara, owned buildings on Joralemon and Henry Streets as well as Clinton, and that he was up to his neck in debt through his involvement in a property scheme that had gone bust.

'It figures,' said Rosie, rolling her eyes, when she heard that. 'The whole of New York City's broke, anyway.'

Perhaps through her tenuous connection with the law, Holly had been chosen as the tenants' organiser. With Leonard's help she was looking into the background of the case. If the worst came to the worst, they could even sue O'Hara.

However, all that was far from her mind as she walked the few blocks to school with Corinna. Looking at the front of the small, square school with its fenced-in asphalt playground, where the boys with their lopsided home hair-cuts and the girls in their short skirts and ankle socks played tag and waited for the bell to summon them in, Holly could almost forget that this was 1970 – the end of an angry, unsettled decade. At least schools and small children, she thought, had not changed. This one, for all that it was an ordinary inner-city state school where the children came from different neighbourhoods and races, and even spoke different languages, had an order about it which reassured her as she waited alongside the other mothers delivering their children.

A smiling, dark-haired woman at the door was welcoming the new pupils. 'Hello,' she said, shaking Holly's hand when her turn came. 'I'm Denise Lorenzetti. And your name?'

'Holly Clayton. This is Corinna.'

'Ah, Corinna.' Mrs Lorenzetti ticked off the name on her list. Then she bent down and pointed at the door. 'You go ahead, Corinna. Straight in there.'

Corinna sprang free from Holly's grasp, waved, and in a few seconds was out of sight.

'I know,' Mrs Lorenzetti regarded Holly, sympathetic. 'Sometimes the first day is harder for the moms. She'll be just fine.'

'Oh, I'm sure she'll be.'

'Will we see you back this afternoon?'

'I'm at work until six. Her babysitter will be picking her up. Mrs Ortega.'

'You work full-time?' Mrs Lorenzetti sounded surprised.

'I have to.' Holly had steeled herself against the question, as she had learnt to, but still felt faintly ashamed.

'Good for you!' Mrs Lorenzetti smiled again, brightly; she looked about Holly's age. 'Well! Hope to see you again.'

Corinna, as Holly had predicted, had no trouble adjusting to school. Some of the other children, she reported back at the end of her first day, were 'crybabies'.

'Not you?' said Holly, serving up that night's spaghetti.

'Nope.' Corinna looked disdainful. 'I told them they were being stupid and they ought to stop crying. But they wouldn't listen.'

Holly skipped a lecture to make it to parents' night in November. Mrs Lorenzetti was all praise for Corinna.

'She's a very grown-up little girl,' she told Holly. 'A good example for the others. Where did she learn to read?'

'She kind of taught herself. She speaks Spanish, too,' Holly couldn't help boasting.

'Does she.' Mrs Lorenzetti registered the fact, impressed. 'And so where do you work, Mrs Clayton?'

'In the city. In a law firm.'

'Wow. It must drive you crazy, juggling all that. I mean, your daughter – do you have any other kids? No? And your job, and men. . . . Men! That's a whole 'nother kettle of fish.'

Holly smiled. She wouldn't know.

'I got divorced last year. Crazy custody battle. But now my ex-husband's moved to California so I think we're in the clear. My daughter's a little younger than Corinna – just two.'

'Is she?' Holly's interest was piqued.

'Hey, you ought to come to one of our meetings. Some of my friends and I are getting a group together – a women's discussion group. I'll let you know.'

Holly forgot about the invitation until a note came home to her one day, carried by Corinna. And then she thought she might as well go along. She didn't really have any women friends except Rosie. Maybe at the meeting there would be others like her, balancing work and children and an education. Denise Lorenzetti was right; sometimes it *was* like juggling.

'What I wonder,' said a heavy woman, crouched on her knees, waving a cigarette, 'is why they think we *enjoy* it. I mean, I went to Vassar. I'm supposed to spend my life cleaning the bathtub and mopping floors?'

'Yeah,' echoed a few of the others, and, 'I know.' The air was thick with the fumes of cigarettes and cheap red wine, as well as a few incense burners dotted around the living room. Denise Lorenzetti's home had a studenty feel, with white walls where big Abstract Impressionist posters blended surprisingly well with her daughter's fingerpaint art.

'How 'bout you Holly?' said Denise. She was keen to bring everyone into the discussion.

'I don't know. I like things neat but I can't seem to keep them that way.' Holly shrugged. 'When our feet start turning black from walking barefoot, I sweep.' She got a few chuckles.

'Hear, hear!' said the first speaker, Vassar woman, with a genial wave of her cigarette. 'Cleanliness is *not* next to godliness. Cleanliness is slavery.'

'I think the point we're trying to make here,' said a more nervous woman, thin, with curly hair, 'is, equality's not just about being *able* to work. It's about being liberated from "woman's work". After all, if you've got a husband who comes home and complains if the place is dirty – '

'I want to talk about work,' said another woman suddenly. 'Women's jobs. Why should we be secretaries?'

Holly felt the blood rushing to her face and had to suppress her annoyance. Vassar woman had started again.

'I want to know why we *shouldn't* work the same jobs as men. We're just as smart. We're just as able. Why should we be stuck with second place?'

And it seemed to Holly then that she knew everything that anyone was going to say; that she had understood it all years ago. She agreed with these women. She had nothing against them. But right now she felt desperately tired, and all she wanted was to get home to Corinna.

She told Denise Lorenzetti politely that she didn't think discussion groups were 'for her'. Denise didn't mind; in fact they met for coffee several times in the next few months. As when they had first met, Denise was full of admiration for what Holly was doing; when her own daughter, Emma, got a little older, she wanted to take her Master's in education.

She talked extensively, and without much prompting, about her love life. 'Problem is,' she said, 'there are no free men in New York. Everyone says it, but it's true. Look, I dated this guy for three months, right? Nothing spectacular – your basic short baldy with glasses. At the end of it he tells me he can't "find the mental space" for commitment.' Denise wiggled her fingers for emphasis. 'I mean, do you meet guys like that?'

'I guess I do.' Holly really couldn't say for sure. A few of the men in her politics class had asked her out. She had put them off as politely as she could, saying that she liked to spend all her free time with her daughter.

They seemed to understand. One of them, better intentioned, perhaps, than the others, had explained that he had a son, too, and lived with his mother, and would she like to bring her daughter over for dinner? Holly had gone, and it had been an easy, friendly evening; but at the end of it Corinna complained because she'd had to miss *Bewitched* and the little boy had stuck putty in her hair. 'If you're trying to find me another daddy,' she said, 'it's OK. I don't need one.'

Lately her interest in daddies had grown worryingly acute. She asked about her own – 'Did he wear a suit? What colour hair did he have? What did he look like?'

Holly kept the answers as vague as she could, and encouraged the past tense when talking about Corinna's father. Oddly perhaps, she always thought of Tyrconnel when forming her answers. 'He was a sort of businessman,' she said. 'A banker. He lived in London.'

'But what did he *look* like?'

'Oh, I don't know. Nice enough. He was kind of tall and had blond hair. He was ordinary looking, really.' It was Holly's first deliberate lie.

'Where is he now?' Corinna asked once.

'Oh – far away.'

But at last there was no avoiding it.

'Will he ever come to see me?' Corinna asked, one day just before her kindergarten class broke up for Christmas. There was a yearning in her eyes which it pained Holly to see. Perhaps they had talked about fathers at school;

perhaps Corinna was beginning to idolise her own absent one.

'No,' Holly said carefully, 'he's not going to come to visit.'

'Why not?' Corinna's blue-green eyes were piercing.

'Because – because he's dead.' Holly had not known she would say that until she did.

She felt instantly guilty. As Corinna, the issue of her father temporarily forgotten, launched into a series of questions about dead people and dead animals and where they all went, Holly answered every one of her queries with scrupulous honesty. She wanted, somehow, to atone for the lie.

Yet it had already been told. She knew she must decide how to deal with further questions. The simplest possible explanation was best. *A car crash*, she thought. She would tell Corinna that after the divorce – for she and Corinna's father had been very unhappy together – Corinna's father had died in a car crash.

And so that was what she told Corinna, gradually, elaborating when necessary, over the next few months and years.

Denise Lorenzetti applauded her; said she was brave for going it alone and still aiming for the top, for law school. Yet Holly knew she wasn't brave. She had lied. She had taken the coward's way out. Nor was she even, as Denise seemed to imagine, especially clever, or gifted with special reserves of energy. What she had was endurance. Corinna had become so used to seeing her bent over the dining table, studying, that one day she had simply started to join her. She would kneel on a chair to reach the table – poring, at first, over *Madeline* or *Frog and Toad are Friends*, then, eventually, over books that were well advanced for her age, or even Holly's cookbooks and magazines.

Holly wondered sometimes if Denise Lorenzetti might be right; Corinna was advancing too fast for her own good. She ought to relax and play *with* her friends, instead of leading them into every game. But that was just her way. Twice Corinna had invited Doreen, her new friend from school, over to play at weekends. Doreen seemed to Holly a meek, malleable little creature, hardly Corinna's equal in spirit. But Corinna insisted they were best friends.

Like Rosie, Denise was always asking Holly about her love-life. Holly was evasive. In fact, she did not think very much about men, except when she thought about Leonard.

And that was more often than she liked to admit.

The Texas oil billionaire's case had wound its way to the New York State Court of Appeals, and at last Leonard won. He claimed he had scented victory all along.

Only Holly had her doubts about that. She had seen him pacing his office before she went home at night, and found him there, wearing the same rumpled clothes, first thing the next morning. She had learnt not to venture a 'Did you go home?' because sometimes the answer was no: Leonard had only dozed off for a few hours on his office couch.

On those mornings, she made strong coffee, and fetched him a bacon sandwich from the deli around the block. She took messages when his wife, Rebekah, called, because when Leonard was working full-out on a case, he did not like to be interrupted – or that was how he explained it.

The day before a hearing, he would ask Holly, 'The grey or the pinstripe?', 'Red tie or purple?'

It did not strike her as odd that she knew his wardrobe by heart. It had become part of the job.

The day after he won the Texas oil case Leonard asked her out to a proper lunch, for the first time – not just a sandwich at the deli, which they had shared many times before.

'I'm going to take you to the Four Seasons,' he said, 'and I won't take no for an answer. I assume you're free?'

'Sometimes I feel,' said Holly, smiling, 'like Miss Money-penny. Always here – just waiting for your call.' She knew Leonard rushed to every new James Bond film with the eagerness of a twelve-year-old boy.

He grinned. 'Will Miss Moneypenny condescend to accompany her grateful employer to lunch?'

'I think she has no choice.' Holly rose. 'I suppose you've made the reservation?'

She was reluctant to admit it to herself, but she revelled in that lunch: the food, the service, the sense that, there beside Leonard, she was one of a privileged few. She knew such things, in the great scheme of life, did not matter. And yet. . . .

She had to admit, part of the appeal her work held for her was the sleek, carpeted hush of the office. She liked to hear the partners and associates talk, if only to experience their lives vicariously: their ski vacations in Vermont and Aspen, their business trips to Geneva, the Hague and Paris. They stayed in the best hotels and ate in the best restaurants; in the winter they took their families to the beach at St Maarten or to St Lucia.

At home in Brooklyn, the central heating gurgled and belched and sometimes Holly, studying at the table, had to wear two dressing-gowns and two pairs of socks for warmth; she did not feel glamorous then, but she did at the office. And she did now.

Leonard was ebullient over lunch. 'I still can't believe it,' he exulted, sipping his Krug; he rarely drank during the working day, but, just this once, he had ordered a bottle. 'Well. In a *sense* I knew it was coming all along. . . .'

'Every one of those nights in the office, you knew it?' said Holly drily.

'Hey.' Leonard nudged her arm. 'How could all those lunches with Blanche O'Donnell not pay off? Hideous cow.'

'I thought you liked her.' Holly's answer was careful; she remembered Blanche's blonde hair and suntan, and the apparent relish with which Leonard had escorted her out of the office.

'She had the character of the Goodyear blimp. You don't think I was taking her out for fun?'

'I had to assume so.' Holly smiled. It was easy now that Leonard had said that about Blanche O'Donnell.

'Completely and totally brain-dead,' said Leonard. 'I'd have liked to get you two together just to see if you could find *any* common ground. Blanche, with her boats and interior decorating and shopping. . . .'

'I *have* been known to shop in my time.'

'And with a hell of a lot more taste than she does. Do you know, she hated my purple tie?'

'No! The lavender one?'

They gossiped on about the O'Donnells. By the time the bottle was half finished, Leonard had mellowed, stretching back in his chair like a contented cat. 'Tell me, Holly,' he said, 'have you thought any more about the law biz? Divorce versus international?'

'I waver,' Holly admitted now. 'I figure I won't have to decide for sure until I get to law school.'

'Ah, but it pays to know. Could make the difference where you decide to go.'

'Wherever I can get in, I expect!'

'Don't be so sure. I bet you'll have more choices than you think. You been working on your LSATs?' *Elsatz*, Leonard pronounced the word. Law school admissions tests: hundreds of multiple-choice logic questions, electronically marked – the bugbear of anyone applying to law school.

Holly shook her head; they seemed years off.

Leonard leaned forward, intent. 'It pays to start early. Look, a lot of those preparation courses are garbage, but you can do the same thing yourself at home. Take a lot of practice tests. Sure, we all know Hunter's an OK place, but you'll need to stand out.'

Holly giggled. 'I thought this was supposed to be a *non*-working lunch.'

'Yeah. I know. But with excellent LSATs . . .' Leonard was eager; his eyes were fixed on his prey and nothing would distract him. So, Holly thought, she might as well make the best of his expertise. They talked long and hard about New York law schools: NYU versus St John's versus Brooklyn, versus Leonard's own alma mater, Columbia. And then they returned to specialisations.

'You've got to think,' Leonard said. 'Do you really want to end up in some schmoozy firm in the 'burbs handling divorces? You've got to at least think about corporate.'

' "Got to at least think"?'

'Yeah. What?'

'You've done it again. Split infinitive.' Holly smiled.

'So what?' Leonard looked disgruntled, then gave a bearish shrug. 'Hey, I guess that's what I pay you for. Ignore me, Holly. Don't let up, OK? I'll learn.'

'I won't let up,' said Holly, sipping her champagne. 'For one thing I'm not at all sure you international corporate types aren't just a bunch of charlatans. Don't you ever think about the rights and wrongs of the cases?'

'What rights? What wrongs?' Leonard tapped on the tablecloth with a restless index finger. 'All right, you want rights and wrongs, I'll give you an example. Charlie O'Donnell had a shipping grievance, fair enough. But do you know where he got that oil he was shipping? He dug it up out of the south of Texas *after* showing the owners a faulty survey that said there was no oil underneath there. So what do I say in his defence? I say my case is about shipping – where he got the oil's another matter. It's all I can do. Sure, O'Donnell's a schmuck. But try telling anyone you're defending Anandakis.'

Holly recognised the name of O'Donnell's Greek opponent. 'I suppose,' she said, 'the problem is, both sides are equally guilty, one way or another. But what if one isn't?'

Leonard grinned. 'I'd try to work for him.'

'And if the other side paid you more?'

'Hey. There's a right side to most companies if you look hard enough.'

'You're just amoral!'

'Hey, what is this? Character assassination?' Leonard

spread his hands in protest. 'I give to the library, I give to Children's Aid, I vote Democrat.'

'You do?'

'Sure. I told you about my socialist days. Anyway –' Leonard grabbed the bill when it came to the table. 'I choose my cases, any lawyer does the same. And not just because I want to fight for the less reprehensible side. I don't like losing.'

It was hard to corner Leonard, because he never conceded. Trial lawyers, he had told Holly, gained ground by forcing admissions of uncertainty – of weakness – from their witnesses. 'If we didn't have any lawyers,' he said now, leaning forward to look intently into Holly's eyes, 'are you saying there'd be more justice in the world?'

'Of course not. I mean. . . . People would have to be their own lawyers, and some people are cleverer than others.'

'Right. So maybe we're just a way of redistributing the brains. Making the system fairer.'

'Brains for hire?' Holly raised her eyebrows.

'Sure. I keep the system working. If I worked to less than the best of my abilities, that'd distort the outcome. Not to mention cheat my clients. You might say it doesn't matter who I represent: they deserve a fair hearing.'

Holly threw up her hands, in retreat under the onslaught of words.

'Then again,' said Leonard with an amiable grin, 'I might just be a charlatan.'

That was what she liked about Leonard, she thought later: his refusal to seize the moral high ground, except in court. He knew his own weaknesses – his tendency to bluff, to dominate, to take over a conversation or a room – and he was always knocking them. 'Hey, shut me up, OK?' he would say to Holly.

In some respects, he was unabashedly vain. Every time he went to London, he ordered new suits from Savile Row. He liked hats, especially slightly outrageous ones with broad brims and decorative feathers, which he would adjust in front of the glass of a picture on the office wall

337

before he went out; but then, he always admitted they covered up his receding hairline. He worried about his weight and had a habit of patting his stomach and sucking it in. 'But, wow, I love food,' he said; as he did now, to Holly, breaking into his *crème brulée.*

'I thought you didn't like French food.'

'True,' he said. 'Too many flavours confuse the tongue. But I knew *you'd* like this place. I can cope.' He licked his spoon. 'Hey, what's your favourite restaurant, Holly?'

'Mr Tong's, maybe.' She smiled. 'You wouldn't know it. It's on Atlantic Avenue.'

'So you like Brooklyn?'

'I'm having problems with my building. The landlord's not doing any maintenance. The boiler's nearly kicked the bucket. We've started this committee. . . .'

As she started to tell Leonard about their troubles, she shrugged off the unease that had come over her for a moment. Just then, with his questions about her home life, Leonard had broached the possibility of friendship, of confidence. And did she want that?

As things were, she was on an even keel. Leonard was a sort of mentor, no more. And if she had memorised his schedule and his suits, if she learnt by heart what hotels he had stayed at and where he had eaten and what he had argued in court on what day – all that could be put down to the diligent pursuit of her duties. No more. She was a super secretary: everybody said so. Gordon Lyall made jokes about poaching her.

But she could not deny there was a difference in her feelings for Leonard and, for example, Gordon. The difference being that she never thought about Gordon outside the office; never dwelt on his remarks, never worried that the occasional work she did for him wasn't good enough. She never thought about the existence of Gordon's wife, or wondered if she made him happy. She never noticed if he looked as though he'd slept badly. Whereas with Leonard, she always noticed. Too much. So much that she had to stop herself from asking, 'Did you and Rebekah have an argument?'

For that would be going too far. She had rules: she would listen more than she talked. She would hear Leonard out, but never impose her feelings upon him. He must never guess that she was living through what had become almost a cliché: she was falling in love with her boss.

V

On an unusually quiet June morning at Lyall, Kravitz, Holly spread her papers out on her desk – the application forms of eight New York law schools.

Leonard sauntered out of his office. 'Jeez, is that the material? Look at all those forms. It's sure changed since my day.'

'I bet it's gotten more expensive.' Holly smiled up ruefully.

Leonard had picked up the forms for Columbia. 'Six thousand dollars! Hell, it sure has.'

'Well. I don't expect I'll be allowed the privilege of paying $6,000 for Columbia. But Brooklyn and NYU cost nearly as much.'

Holly had been putting off this moment, to tell the truth: the moment when she finally faced the issue of money. She had leafed through the back sections of a few course catalogues, each detailing an array of scholarships, loans and special programmes. Only half the schools she was considering allowed students to attend part-time. If she couldn't work while she went to law school, she would have to take out loans, and she was leery of the idea.

'You old Yankee!' Leonard said when she told him this. 'Everyone in this country's deep in debt, except you children of the Mayflower. Come on. Lunchtime. Let's get out of here.'

He beckoned, and Holly knew they would be heading straight to Vinnie's, the deli round the corner, for a sandwich and a long planning session. They rode down in the elevator with one of the firm's junior associates, who asked them over-eagerly, 'Heading off for lunch? Oh, yeah, where? They do a fine pastrami at Vinnie's.' He watched them both with an unreadable expression as they left him behind in the lobby.

'Do you think we should have invited him?' asked Holly as she pushed through the revolving doors.

'Nah.' A blast of summer heat hit them out on the street, and Leonard raised a hand to shield his eyes from the sun. 'The guy gets on my nerves.'

'I think he's still watching us.' Holly glanced back through the glass.

'Let him watch. I'm not having my lunch hour blighted by the likes of him.' Leonard took Holly's arm as they rounded the corner. 'Besides, he's from Boston, and up there they don't know pastrami from buffalo's backside.'

'You're mean.' It struck Holly, not for the first time, that Leonard made few allowances for the other members of his firm. 'You know,' she said, 'I don't think I'd like to work for you. Not as an associate.'

'What do you mean?' Leonard gazed at her in mock-affront; at least it seemed so to Holly. She could never be entirely sure when his visible emotions were feigned, theatrical.

'Come on. Haven't you ever noticed? You're totally unforgiving with the associates.'

'Hey, but you'd be different. You know Lyall, Kravitz inside out.'

They squeezed into a cramped table at the back of Vinnie's. 'Seriously,' said Holly, 'I know Abe and Gordon are sympathetic about my going to law school and all that. But I'm not sure they're as open-minded as you are. Especially Gordon. Whatever you say, I doubt they'd be so keen to welcome back one of their secretaries as a lawyer.'

'Oh, well. The times they are a-changing, like they say.'

Leonard scanned the laminated menu, unperturbed. 'Those two'll have to change, too. All kinds of women are starting to go to law school. We had a woman associate last year. Why should they mind your being the next one?'

'Because they know me already. As something else.' Holly found it hard to explain, but she was sure her instincts weren't wrong. Besides, she didn't want to grow too dependent on the cosy atmosphere of Lyall, Kravitz.

Or too dependent on Leonard. That was what she was really afraid of.

They went back to discussing law schools, and costs.

'I don't know.' Holly shook her head. 'With the rent and babysitting for Corinna and everything – I'll need about $6,000 a year just to cover living expenses.'

'At least you got that landlord of yours to cut the rent.'

'Yeah.' Holly smiled. She was proud of what she had accomplished there. Under the formal threat of a lawsuit – phrased by Holly, in her final warning letter on behalf of the tenants – O'Hara, unable to pay for repairs, had frozen the rent. However, that did nothing to improve the state of the roof, the damp or the peeling paint on the stairs. 'I just hope,' said Holly, 'the boiler holds up till I finish school. It's pretty miserable trying to study when your nose is dripping icicles.'

'Maybe you could move out.'

'Nah – ' Without quite realising it, Holly had picked up some of Leonard's habits of speech – 'Corrina's settled into school there. It's convenient. And, frankly, I've done so much painting and hammering in that place that it feels like home now. Faults and all.'

'I'll tell you,' said Leonard, reverting to the main subject, 'you shouldn't be too afraid of taking out a loan.'

'I was wondering, though,' said Holly. 'If I studied law at night school, and kept on working . . . I've got a little money from my mother's estate that could pay the tuition. Or almost.'

'But look, Holly! Part-time, you'd be talking six years. Don't you ever want to finish school before you retire?'

'Thanks a lot!'

'Look, you know what I mean. If you take out a loan, I promise you, the repayments are going to look infinitesimal once you're working.'

'Sure! If I get a job. But if I don't – '

'Of course you'll get a job!' Leonard laughed. 'Whoever heard of an unemployed lawyer? I'll tell you, Holly, you're the craziest mixture of confidence and insecurities I've ever seen. You're a crackerjack secretary. You're smart, you're pretty – '

Holly felt herself starting to blush. 'You know that doesn't make any difference to how I'll do as a lawyer!'

'I don't know.' Leonard's gaze was disconcertingly direct. 'A lot of things affect a court. Appearance – it's all about hitting them with something unexpected. A woman lawyer who has her act together, who has style – heck, who's good-looking – '

'Stop!' Holly protested.

'Why should I stop? It's true.'

'You shouldn't say those things.' Holly's face heated with annoyance, as well as the awareness that Leonard's flattery had worked on her in spite of herself. 'Can't you see – if you talk that way about me, you're treating me just like you'd treat some decorative receptionist. Like an object! Whatever her profession, a woman's looks shouldn't matter any more than a man's. We're here, just like you, to do a job. And – '

Leonard looked across at her, chagrined. 'OK,' he said. 'You're right. A hundred per cent. But you know – ' His smile flickered – 'you're going to have to stop losing the ends of your sentences. Always complete a thought. It's crucial in court.'

'I *was* in the middle of a sentence. If you'd let me finish.'

'Hey, what do you expect from me?' Leonard grinned. 'You tell me I split my infinitives, you hate my psychedelic ties, now you tell me I'm a – what do you call it? – a male chauvinist. . . .'

'That you most certainly are.' Holly was trembling even as she tried to keep her reprimand lighthearted. She was not sure whether it was because she was so keyed up – as she always seemed to be lately around Leonard – or because, for the first time in one of their arguments, Leonard had conceded.

And so the summer of 1972 wore on, punctuated by good-natured debates with Leonard about loans, and practice LSATs. Holly sat that exam so many times at home that she thought she was beginning to know the questions backwards and forwards. On her last two tries in August, her scores leapt up: 730 points out of a possible 800. Not in the genius bracket, but good. She might be able to nudge them even higher.

Corinna joined a summer programme for school-children, and brought home three new friends. She seemed to be growing more and more gregarious. Her first-grade teacher had remarked on her report card, 'Corinna sails through her schoolwork and seems to be a natural leader. She does, however, tend to dominate the shyer children. Corinna must learn to *share*.'

Corinna had greeted the report with a sniff. 'Anyway,' she said, 'I got all As. What did she give me all As for if she doesn't like me?'

Besides, as far as Holly could see, when Corinna bossed her friends around, they let her; they seemed to expect it. *A natural leader.* That was a good thing to be. Maybe Corinna's first-grade teacher was just an old-fashioned sexist.

Holly worked through until September without a break.

'You should take some time off,' said Leonard.

'I will.' Holly kept on typing as she talked. 'I'm taking two weeks before LSATs.'

'Two weeks!' Leonard was incredulous. 'Holly, seriously, you practise two weeks for those things, you'll go nuts. Go nuts or score 800.'

'The second option, I hope,' said Holly coolly.

Leonard walked away, shaking his head.

Holly kept a file for every law school to which she applied, with a checklist at the front: deadlines, scholarships applied for, interviews attended, references sent. She sat the LSATs, and got her score a few weeks later: 750.

'Wow!' Leonard thumped her on the back in celebration. 'Wait till I tell Abe and Gordon.'

'No, don't!' Holly jumped up in alarm to grab Leonard and stop him. 'Don't say anything. Not yet. I'm not even in anywhere.'

'Sure! But with a 750, you will be.'

'I'm just not counting on anything.'

During the course of the spring months of 1973, Leonard was gradually proved right. Holly *was* in, almost everywhere she had applied. She had to admit that he had probably been right to pester her about her grades and test scores. Without all those As and the 750, she probably wouldn't have stood a chance against the aggressive Ivy Leaguers competing for places.

The letter from NYU came last of all. She hesitated, pulling it out of the mailbox. It felt thin. That meant nothing, of course, really. But she decided to take it upstairs.

If only . . . , she thought. NYU was her first choice. It had an excellent reputation, a programme in international law; and it was only a short subway ride from home, in Greenwich Village.

Corinna glanced up from her cornflakes. 'Another one?'

Holly nodded. *Please*, she thought. *Let it be . . . .*

A minute later, she was crushing Corinna in a hug.

'You're in, right?' said Corinna. '*Mom!* Let go, you're messing up my hair.'

'Eight-year-olds shouldn't be so vain.' Holly displayed the letter, pointing to the part which began, *We are pleased to inform you that you have been awarded . . . .*

'A Hilda Coggins Memorial Fellowship?' Corinna wrinkled her nose. 'What's that?'

Holly herself could hardly remember at first, she had applied for so many scholarships and fellowships and prizes. But if she recollected right, this one meant. . . .

'*They* pay your fees?' said Leonard.

'That's right. And half my living expenses. That means hardly any loans.'

'So who is this Hilda Coggins?'

'Pioneering woman lawyer.' Holly couldn't help smiling a little smugly. 'Practised before the war. When she died she had an awful lot of money and no family, and to her dismay there were still almost no other women lawyers. So she set up this fellowship to encourage some.'

'Must be a bit more competition for it these days than there used to be.'

Holly nodded.

'Quite a tribute.' Leonard actually sounded subdued, a rare state for him. It must mean, Holly thought, that he was impressed.

He soon rallied, squeezing her shoulders and bearing her down the corridor to announce the good news to Abe and Gordon.

'So,' said Abe Kravitz, 'will we be seeing you next summer?'

Holly smiled and didn't answer, because next summer, with any luck, she would have a real legal job, as Abe probably knew. It would be hard enough sticking out her last few months here as a secretary.

She invited Leonard out to lunch. 'And I don't mean Vinnie's,' she said.

'Where? The Côte Basque? The Four Seasons?'

'No. Your choice. The food *you* like.'

'Korea Pavilion?' Leonard shrugged. 'But really, I'm open. . . .'

Leonard had been mad about Korean food ever since he got back from his last business trip to Seoul. If the food at lunch, thought Holly, was as eye-stingingly hot as he usually liked it, she would just have to bring tissues for her streaming nose.

'Sorry. I'm not – ' she snuffled, after her first two bites of *kimchi*, 'very dignified.'

'Hey, it's just us. Good thing we've got no clients here.' Leonard patted her on the back. 'You OK now?'

Holly nodded. 'We're getting like Jack Sprat and his wife. "Holly Clayton could eat no hot – " '

Leonard grinned. ' "Leonard Green could eat no *haute cuisine*." '

For Leonard a big bowl of soup arrived, full of fish heads and shells; Holly had ordered pepper steak, which came raw, to be cooked at the table. While Holly fiddled with the miniature grill and tongs, smoke billowing up, Leonard told her about his latest case, involving Filipino and Hong Kong banks.

'I don't know.' Holly shook her head. 'All that money going into *your* pocket. From the Philippines! As if they didn't have better things to do with it.'

'Hey, they're America's allies. And if they didn't have me they'd just hire some other guy who'd probably charge them twice as much. Anyway. Now you're going off to NYU when'll we see you again?'

'You'll have me around till September,' Holly reminded him drily, 'every day. Monday to Friday.'

'You know what I mean. Next summer. Like Abe said. "Holly Clayton, Summer Associate" – ' Leonard grinned, irrepressible – 'Can't you just see it, the sign on the door? Wouldn't you like that?'

Holly looked at him reflectively. 'A summer associate? Are you sure that's what Abe meant?'

'Sure! We've talked about it.'

Holly was taken aback. 'Well,' she said.

'So what about it?'

Holly smiled evasively. 'I don't know. Maybe I should sample the competition for a while. Or do something useful. Work at the public defender's.'

'Hey, don't look at me.' Leonard spread his hands. 'I did my stint at the public defender's back in the fifties. My advice is, avoid it. Dingy places, fourth-rate people. All the real idealists burn out. Look, you don't have to abandon your principles. Join a good firm, you can do some work *pro bono*. Work for those Third World countries, those agencies you're always talking about.'

'I don't know.' Holly shook her head. 'You talk a smooth line, Leonard Green.'

'Seriously.' Suddenly Leonard's hand had clasped over hers, on the table. 'We'd be glad to have you back next summer, Holly. Abe and Gordon and I – we all agree. Just say the word.'

'Thanks.' Holly kept her hand still. She could feel the heat of Leonard's against it, dry yet warm. How many times had she touched him in all these years? Once, twice . . . not many. Not deliberately. And she knew why now. The temptation was too strong. 'I – appreciate the offer,' she said. 'Believe me.' A smile cracked her face. 'And, hey, if I don't get any other offers I may have to take it up. But the point is, I've been with Lyall, Kravitz for so long. I need to break away. For my own good. See other . . . places.'

She realised she had almost said *people*.

She took Corinna out to celebrate their good fortune. Now that she knew where she was going next year, she felt she could liberate a little of their savings. She made Corinna a proposal: they could each have whatever they most wanted, Holly a new outfit, Corinna her choice of the toys in F.A.O. Schwarz. Afterwards, they would go for tea at the Plaza.

Only it didn't quite work out that way.

Every one of the peasant-style dresses Holly tried on in Saks drooped like a quilt which had lost its stuffing. Corinna, faced with the whole interior of Manhattan's biggest toy store, was totally at a loss. She ran backwards

347

and forwards, long golden hair flying, her face alternating between eagerness and indecision.

'Oh, Mom,' she said. 'Does it have to be just *one* thing? Let's make it two.'

'You know the rules! I said one.'

Just as they were giving up and heading out, Corinna caught sight of a bin of glittery rubber balls. 'There! I'll have one of those.'

Holly paid at the till: 50 cents. Outside, Corinna tested the ball on the pavement. It bounced heavily, sideways. Corinna thumped it down again with the same result. 'This is pathetic.'

Holly giggled. She didn't know why. Her suppressed laugh turned into a snort.

'Why are you laughing, Mom?'

'Look at it!' Holly burst into laughter. 'Both of us! We can't make up our minds, we can't buy a ball. . . . What would Hilda – ' She snorted – 'Hilda Coggins think of us?'

Corinna covered her mouth and snorted, too.

'We're not – ' Holly struggled to breathe evenly – 'not being nice. I know I should – be very grateful to Hilda Coggins. . . .'

Corinna picked up the ball from the pavement; one side had gone flat. Suddenly her snorts exploded into open-mouthed laughter. It was so rare to see her that way – her mouth wide over perfect teeth, her blue-green eyes crinkling – that Holly, astonished, started to laugh again, too. She no longer knew why. 'We're hopeless,' she gasped. 'Totally hopeless! Do you still want to go to the Plaza?'

Corinna tried to cover her mouth, and her whole body shook. 'Mom – can I just have a hot dog instead?'

So much, thought Holly, for the high life.

'So are you taking your vacation in August?' said Leonard, halfway through July.

'Yeah, I guess I'll save it up till I leave.' Holly was ploughing dutifully through a backlog of mail. 'I could use

348

a couple of weeks to get ready for school. Buy books and things.'

Leonard planted himself in front of her desk. 'I said *vacation*, Holly. You know, like beach, water, sunshine, fun? Somewhere away from New York City?'

Holly shrugged. 'I can't really afford it.'

'Come on,' said Leonard. 'What about old Hilda Coggins? Your money worries are over, remember?'

'From what I've read about her, she didn't approve of vacations.'

Leonard shrugged and strolled away, but Holly wondered about the look on his face. He was hatching something, she could be almost certain.

A few days later, he strolled out of his office with the words, 'What would you say to a vacation, Holly, if it didn't cost you anything? Or anything much.'

'I'd say, sure.' Holly looked up. 'What exactly do you mean?'

'I've got a proposition for you.'

Holly looked up warily. She saw a gleam in Leonard's eye.

'Last two weeks in August. Beautiful house in East Hampton. Three bedrooms. Just the size for you and Corinna.'

'What, exactly,' said Holly, 'has this house got to do with me?'

'Belongs to friends of mine and Rebekah's. They'll let you have it for free. I've already talked to them.'

'What on earth are you talking about? Houses in the Hamptons cost a fortune to rent in August. What's the gimmick, Leonard?'

'No gimmick.'

Holly tilted her head and studied his face, suspicious. 'Is this a real house? Not a boat or somebody's garage? Or – I know. They've got about four attack dogs and eight cats and all they want me to do is look after them.'

'No! The Weinbergs are just picky, that's all. They don't need the money, and they don't want strangers staying at

349

their place. But they like having housesitters. Friends of friends. . . .'

'How well do you know these people?'

'Our summer place is right along the beach from theirs. We've known them for years. Honest, Holly. They'll be glad for you to take the house. They almost did have someone for these two weeks, but he fell through.'

Holly hesitated; and that was long enough for Leonard to go to work on her again. He grinned, leaning forward on his piled-up mail. 'Holly. Come on, think about it. Are you going to put off enjoying yourself until you're fifty years old?'

He had struck a nerve. 'Look,' Holly said. 'I don't even know how I'd get around out there. You know I don't drive.'

'Train goes all the way out to Long Island from Penn Station. Cab to the house. It's right by the beach, and you can walk to the stores.'

Leonard, Holly realised, was simply not going to give up until she said yes.

Not that refusal held any particular attractions. The last two weeks of August, in the sweltering heat, in Brooklyn. . . .

'Leonard – you know, my boss,' she told Corinna that night, 'says he might be able to get us a house on the beach for two weeks.'

'*Yeah!*' Corinna let out a shout. 'Really? When are we going to go?'

Holly spoke to Leonard, who said he'd get on the phone to the Weinbergs. At the end of the small drinks party in honour of her last day at work, he handed her a set of keys, and directions.

Two whole weeks on the beach: it seemed too good to be true. On Saturday morning, Holly and Corinna took the earliest train out. Corinna drummed her legs on the seat with excitement, and gaped out the window.

'Wow!' said Corinna when they pulled into the small, semi-rural station. 'It's *big*.'

'What's big?' They stood on the platform with their suitcases. Holly saw trees, a white clapboard house. Grass waved in the wind.

Corinna spread her arms. 'Everything.'

Holly knew what she meant. So much space. So much sky. It was hard to believe that eight years had passed since she had been in the country; that Corinna, who had grown up entirely in the city, hadn't even known till now what country was. But she stilled the apology in her throat; Corinna was unaware of having missed anything. She was charging into the parking lot, ponytail flying. 'Hey! Are you a taxi?' she shouted to a man sitting in a car.

'Yeah.' The man laughed. 'You gonna bring your mom along? Hop in.'

Three bedrooms: that might have been the official description, but to Holly the house looked big enough to house three families. It was a modern chalet-style building, all peaked roof and wood and glass, sheltered behind a hedge of trees from the sand dunes and the Atlantic. From the window of her bedroom upstairs, Holly could see the waves furling and crashing into the shore.

She and Corinna hurried into their bathing suits and padded down the stairs of the wooden deck. It was a perfect day: sunny, not too windy, the water lapping and glistening. The beach, with its wide stretch of grey, soft sand, seemed too big ever to be crowded. Holly lay back on her towel and let the salt breeze invade her nostrils.

'This is nicer than Manhattan Beach,' said Corinna judiciously. 'Are there any jellyfish? If there are, I want to find one.'

'If you do, then you're the only one.' Before Holly realised it, she was drifting off to sleep. Some time later Corinna poked her.

'You'll get sunburn.'

Holly thought then that she would rejoice in sunburn, it had been so long since she had been sunburnt. But, sensibly, she went back inside to cover up. She had two weeks here, after all. Two immeasurably long, blissful weeks. . . .

351

The next day Corinna scouted out the nearest children her age, and was soon leading expeditions up and down the beach, joined halfway through the first week by Ray and Luisa, who had come out with Rosie, as well as Denise Lorenzetti's five-year-old daughter. Holly, Rosie and Denise made daiquiris in the kitchen blender – the kitchen, all chrome and steel, was a wonder, with every available gadget – and at night they struggled with the barbecue.

Rosie and Denise's presence made the time fly faster, and the end of the first week vanished in a series of shopping trips and swimming championships. Corinna stayed outdoors all day, only coming back to the house to change her swimsuit or stoke herself up with food. At the beginning of the second week, Rosie had to go back to New York. She was in secretarial school now, and had to fit her cleaning jobs in part-time around it. 'Grrr,' she said, baring her teeth as she packed away her orange bikini. 'I'm so mad I've got to go, probably tomorrow when I'm cleaning for Mrs Caulfield, I'll end up vacuuming up her chihuahua.'

Holly laughed at her expression. 'Good riddance.'

Denise, who had to get ready for the start of school, left a few days later. The house was unaccustomedly silent. Holly tried to savour her last few days, but the vacation was already painfully near its end.

On Saturday morning the phone rang: a voice she did not know, asking if she were Mrs Green.

'Excuse me?'

'Well, is Mr Green there, please? I'm calling from Tyler's, the agency. About the keys.'

'Tyler's . . . I'm sorry, I don't quite. . . .'

It took a few minutes for Holly and the woman on the other end of the phone to sort things out.

When she hung up, Holly walked out to the beach, her mind in confusion. In a selfish way, she was glad that she had not found out anything till now, because she could not have enjoyed the holiday had she known – could never have accepted it in the first place.

Of course he meant well, she thought. But still it was all wrong. She walked along at the edge of the waves, so oblivious to the faces around her that she did not even notice the figure far off in the water to her right, until she heard a shout.

'Hey!'

She saw a broad wave; Leonard grinning, his beard glistening with drops of water.

'Hi.' She waved back. But her heart sank as she walked further into the water. 'I didn't know you were going to be here.'

'Last-minute trip.' Leonard strode out to meet her. 'Finished up early Friday. Didn't know I'd be free. Our house is just down there.' He pointed along the beach.

'That's nice.' Holly backed away a little from Leonard. He was dripping, and she was still wearing her sundress from indoors. He looked, she noticed, more wiry and muscular in his swimming trunks than he seemed in a suit, and taller. 'I just,' she said, 'found out about the house. A woman from the agency called.'

Leonard nodded.

'I'm going to have to pay you back. You know I can't accept . . .' Holly glanced up and met his gaze.

Leonard looked hurt. He didn't answer for a moment.

'I know you meant well. I appreciate it. I've had a wonderful time. But – '

'You weren't supposed to know,' Leonard said, a little gruffly. 'God. Those *idiots* at Tyler's. That's the last time I have anything to do with them.'

Holly tried to inject some lightness into the situation. 'What, are you in the habit of treating other people to vacations without telling them?'

'I just wanted to give you something you'd enjoy. I thought you deserved it. I thought of all those years you'd been working, and – '

'Yes, I know. And I do appreciate it. But how am I

supposed to react?' Holly shifted her feet nervously. '*You* made a decision without consulting me, you paid for something that you know I wouldn't be able to afford.'

'That's not the way you're supposed to feel.' Leonard looked at her hard, his dark brows nearly meeting, then away. 'I only wanted. . . .' he shook his head, 'to give you something. I didn't want you to know. I *wanted* you to have it, because – Holly, this is hard to say – '

'Then better not say it.' Holly looked up steadily.

'Are you sure?'

Their eyes met. After a second or two, she nodded.

'Look,' she said after another awkward silence. 'I'll pay you back. It might take a little while.'

'No.' Leonard smiled. 'Absolutely not. A gift's a gift.'

'Oh, well. OK.' Holly smiled in return, thinking, as she did, of credit card bills and Rebekah seeing them; finally deciding that a great deal about Leonard's marriage was beyond her knowledge.

'I'd better go. Rebekah should be coming along soon. I don't suppose. . . . Do you want to meet her?'

'Maybe not just now.'

'I'm going to miss you,' said Leonard.

'I know. Me too.'

Holly walked away first, and gave a smile; a little, secret wave. Leonard smiled back as the sand buried his feet. He looked oddly bereft.

VI

On her first day of classes that September Holly arrived early at the Georgian-style building, Vanderbilt Hall, that housed New York University Law School. For most of the last week, she had managed to keep herself from thinking of Leonard: of how he would want to know what this first day was like for her, of what she would tell him.

Because she would not be seeing him. If she was going to try to forget him, now was surely the time.

She clutched her notebook, suddenly feeling very old for a first-year student as she wandered through the corridors. The students here looked, on the whole, more conservative and serious than at Hunter; there were fewer jeans, fewer men with ponytails – though there were some, all the same. The posters on the noticeboards displayed the concerns of the times: 'Radical Law Group', 'Down with Neo-McCarthyism!', 'Free America vs. Militarized Zone – An Open Debate'.

There were so many things to join, so many choices. Would she try for the *Law Review*? *The Journal of International Law and Politics*? The society for women lawyers – for public interest law – for the arts?

Right now she was just trying to find her way to her first lecture. She thumbed through her course list to check the room.

'Can I help you find something?' A young man with a lean, smiling face and black hair swung to a stop by her side.

'Sure,' she said. 'Contract law? Is that this way?'

'You a first-year?' The young man pointed the way down a corridor. 'It's thataway. Good luck. Contract's the worst, it's all downhill skiing from there. By the way, I'm Michael Jones.' He held out his hand.

Holly shook it, mildly amused that he had introduced himself. 'Holly Clayton.' She wondered if all law students were so eager to impress.

'I'll probably see you around.' The young man nodded and spun away again.

Holly headed off to her first lecture, by the end of which two fellow-students had introduced themselves. One had given her his card. She wondered if the preponderance of men in her class had anything to do with it.

She wondered also if these men, who couldn't be more than twenty-five or twenty-six, had any idea how old she was! Not that she saw any need to tell them.

By the end of the first week she had gone to introductory meetings for two law journals, including the international one, and three societies. She would have to choose carefully: most of them met at night, and she had hoped to have more time at home with Corinna now that she was studying.

Michael Jones was at the second law review meeting she attended. He asked her out to lunch. When she hesitated, he backed off, spreading his arms in mock self-defence. 'Strictly working,' he said. 'We could meet up in the library.'

'OK.'

Why, Holly wondered, was she so wary? Michael was young, good-looking, polite – she should be flattered. Why did she treat every date like a proposal of marriage?

She would change, she decided. She would try. These were the swinging seventies, after all. People were making free love in parks and fields; there were all-nude plays off-Broadway; Denise had dated fifteen men in the last year and *she* seemed none the worse for it.

She was too hung up on Leonard: Holly knew it. And that had to stop. She hadn't seen him for almost a month now. It would get easier. She was starting a new life, she reminded herself, meeting new people. Her days were full.

So why did she always feel as if something was missing?

Corinna had entered the third grade. As usual, her teacher had plastered gold stars on her first essay, and she had scored 100 per cent on her first maths test. But somehow, this year was different. Corinna's teacher, Mrs Simoni, disliked her; or so Corinna thought.

'Mrs Simoni made me stay after school,' she complained to Holly one night, 'just because I wouldn't clean out my desk! I said it was already clean, and she said to do as I was told 'cause I wasn't getting any special privileges. It's not fair!'

'I'm sure,' said Holly, trying to be diplomatic, 'she's trying to be fair in her own way. You'll get used to her.'

'No, I won't! She hates me. I heard her talking in the hall.'

'What did she say?' Holly closed her civil procedure text. She knew she shouldn't encourage Corinna to eavesdrop, but she was curious.

'She said something about – ' Corinna scanned her memory – 'children from broken homes always getting into trouble. What's a broken home? Does she mean our landlord and how he won't fix things?'

'No,' said Holly, 'she means that you live with just me, and no father. But that's a silly thing to say, about getting into trouble. Don't even listen to her.' She hugged Corinna, who retreated to her bedroom, which was, no doubt like her school desk, neat as a pin. Holly never had to nag Corinna to clean up. The only messes she created were piles of clothes when she couldn't decide what to wear in the morning. For her age, she was very style-conscious.

Holly assumed the trouble with Mrs Simoni had gone away until, one night in October, Corinna glumly handed her a stapled school note. 'Please come to see me,' it said. 'Corinna is being disruptive.'

Holly stormed into the school the next afternoon, ready to take on Mrs Simoni. What was she talking about – disruptive? All the other teachers said Corinna 'set a good example'.

Mrs Simoni was fat and fiftyish. 'I don't,' she said, 'believe in any of this new-style, do-your-own thing kind of teaching, Mrs Clayton. My pupils sit in rows, and we go at the same pace and wait for the slower ones to catch up.'

'Fine,' said Holly, bewildered by the teacher's confrontational stance. 'So how is Corinna causing trouble?'

'She is very inconsiderate,' said Mrs Simoni crisply. 'When we read as a class, she whispers things in the background, like, "Hurry up", and "I can't believe you're so stupid." '

'She can't! I don't believe you.'

'Why don't you ask your daughter for yourself? As far

as I understand, you are away from home all day, and since Corinna has no father there to discipline her –'

'None of that,' said Holly heatedly, 'has anything to do with you, or this school.' After a few more minutes' futile conversation, she walked out.

When she confronted Corinna with Mrs Simoni's accusation, Corinna squirmed uncomfortably. 'I didn't say *that*,' she said. 'Well . . . I said the first thing, "Hurry up", but I only said it once or twice . . . I was getting so fed up, Mom! We were reading *Puss in Boots*. That's a baby book!'

'I know, honey. I told Mrs Simoni you were reading more grown-up books at home, but she just said everyone in her class goes at the same pace.'

'That's stupid.'

'I know it's stupid, but you'll just have to go along with it. And you shouldn't say mean things to the others.'

'OK, Mom.' Corinna looked sulky but resigned. 'It's 'cause I don't have a father,' she said. 'That's why Mrs Simoni doesn't like me.'

'That's got nothing to do with it, honey.' Holly had the depressing feeling that Corinna was right.

'Well, if I have a father, where is he?'

'I've told you, Corinna, he's dead. It's too bad, but there isn't anything we can do to get him back.'

'Well, why don't you have any pictures of him, or anything?'

'Because,' said Holly patiently, 'I was unhappy when I stopped being married. We'd had so many fights. I threw them away.'

'Well, that's not fair. What if I'd wanted to see them one day?'

'Darling –' Holly shook her head. 'It doesn't do any good, seeing pictures. He's still gone.'

'Why did you marry him?'

Holly fell silent, startled. 'Because . . . I was very young. I thought I was in love. Now come over here, bunnykins, and give me a hug. We're going to forget all about that nasty Mrs Simoni. All right?'

Corinna nodded silently as she nestled against her mother.

In Michael Jones's room, the radiator clanked, and Holly shifted nervously against it.

Michael kissed her again: softly, slowly. 'You're tense,' he said.

'I guess I'm a tense sort of person.'

He smiled as if she had made a joke he did not quite understand, and pulled off his sweater.

She supposed she was meant to do the same. A small voice started up in her head again. *What are you doing?* She tried to silence it.

She had known Michael for exactly two months, since he introduced himself to her at Vanderbilt Hall on the first day of classes. They had gone out for coffee a few times, and tonight to a French film. He was twenty-six. She didn't know what his parents did, or what kind of food he liked, or even why he wanted to be a lawyer.

She told herself now that none of that mattered.

Michael leaned over her. 'Are you on the pill?' he said softly.

'No,' she stammered.

'So should I use something?'

She nodded.

When, a startlingly short time later, they were both naked and he extended himself on top of her, she tried to enjoy what was happening. Her body welcomed the kisses, the stroking, the warm contact and attention of another.

He thrust into her and the desires of her mind and body jarred. She tried to ignore it. This was a strange, narrow bed. She heard footsteps on the other side of the wall, and remembered that Michael had a roommate she hadn't even met.

And then suddenly it all seemed to have gone out of control without her noticing the build-up, feeling the tension. Michael's hips rammed against hers. He bent his head, intent on the motion, and he seemed to have forgotten the kisses, the talk. *Stop*, she wanted to say, *you're invading me, you don't know me.*

But then it was over.

'You didn't come,' Michael said accusingly.

'I don't – always.' Holly shrugged. 'Really, it doesn't matter. It was fine. Great.' She smiled and wondered if he could hear the lie.

It wasn't fine at all. What had she done?

'Do you do this a lot?' she asked, trying to bridge the gap between them.

'When I meet a neat lady like you. That's not all the time.' Michael smoothed his hair. 'Do you smoke dope, Holly?' Without waiting for an answer, he reached into a drawer and began methodically to roll a joint. It occurred to Holly that he paid the same careful attention to licking the edges of the paper as he had paid earlier to licking her neck, her ears. She lay back against the pillow and wondered if he would expect her to sleep here. Michael lit the joint and extended it towards her; she shook her head.

'Maybe it'd mellow you out. Be good for you.'

'Maybe.' Holly let out a nervous laugh. 'Michael, I've just been thinking, maybe I'd better get home.'

'OK,' he said. 'You can stay if you want, we could put on some music.' He sat sprawled on the floor in his bathrobe now, absorbed in his joint. 'Whatever.'

'Thanks.' Holly tried to be polite. 'I'd probably better get home. I only really sleep well in my own bed.' She hurried into her clothes, wondering if it seemed to Michael, as it did to her, an undignified scramble.

A few minutes later she stood at Michael Jones's bedroom door. 'Good-night.' She gave an ineffectual wave. 'Guess I'll see you – in class.'

'Cool.' He nodded. 'Catch you later.' He did not rise to see her out.

Holly crept into her own bed that night feeling furtive. The apartment was quiet and dark because Corinna was staying overnight at her friend Doreen's. At least she would never know.

What a disastrous experiment.

Holly knew, even before she saw Michael in class the next Monday, that she wouldn't repeat it. She didn't even feel particularly like boasting to Denise about it – her sexual liberation. She had never felt more repressed in her life. She wondered at first, on Monday morning, how Michael would behave. Sit next to her? Act as if they were a couple? Ignore her?

It came closest to the last. As he entered the lecture hall he gave her a casual wave. After the lecture he stood talking to a cluster of students, and after that, whenever he and Holly passed each other, it was with only a brief nod of recognition. A few days later Holly saw him deep in conversation with a girl in the library: dark-haired, caftaned, closer to his own age. And she did not mind.

In the second semester a few other men asked her out on dates. She found ways to refuse them. When they seemed sincere about wanting to talk about coursework, she would go to a coffee shop with them and pay her own half of the bill. It was not impossible, she discovered, to be friends with men. Her fellow-students seemed different to most of the men she had known before – men of her own age and older. These younger men were less courtly; they never opened doors first or waited for her to pass in front of them. They seemed relaxed with women, willing to take them either as friends or lovers: if lovers, she could not help suspecting, then without much passion.

Whether all her comparisons harked back to Leonard was a question she wasn't even willing to ask herself. She hadn't spoken to Leonard; hadn't heard from him, except as a signature on a Christmas card sent by all the staff at Lyall, Kravitz. But, as the year wore on, despite all her promises to herself, she still missed him. She missed his ebullience, his showmanship, his good-hearted concern. In an odd way, after various 'dates' and misunderstandings at NYU, she missed the relatively clear footing on which she had stood with him, acknowledging rules and restraints which, for her classmates, didn't seem to exist.

But still she did not call, or write, or drop by Lyall, Kravitz. She put her name down for the round of interviews for summer associate jobs at New York firms. To her surprise, the first that made her an offer was a large and prestigious one on Wall Street.

It was a relief, she realised when she walked into Tate, Marshall, that first morning in June, to be accepted at once, on equal terms with all the other associates. No one thought of her as a secretary here. Most days, the summer associates were treated to two-hour lunches in which to 'get to know' the partners. Holly found these rather gruelling, as was the enforced fun of company picnics at partners' homes or country clubs in Westchester, with obligatory tennis and golf.

The work, however, was another matter. Tate, Marshall seemed to have a hard time coming up with anything for its summer associates to do. Holly's office, like all the other associates', surrounded a fluorescent-lit central floor space occupied by an ever-changing bank of secretaries. The fellow-associate who shared it spent his mornings doing the *Times* crossword, while Holly spent it reading volumes on tax law from the library, thinking that if she had nothing else to do, she could at least get ahead on next year's coursework. No one monitored her progress; sometimes she wondered if the partners even knew her.

She began to wish she had, after all, gone to work at the public defender's office, where at least she would have been given some real work to do. Or that, despite her better instincts, she had gone back to Lyall, Kravitz. . . .

For the end of August she rented a house up on Cape Cod. 'Why can't we go back to East Hampton?' Corinna demanded.

'Don't you want to see someplace new?' Holly put the simpler reason out of her mind: way up in Massachusetts, they stood no chance of running into Leonard.

After two weeks at the beach, she returned to NYU with

renewed enthusiasm. All the more senior students she had known the year before said the first year of law school was the worst, and it was true. The toughest required courses were out of the way – tort and contract, property, civil procedure – and now she had more time for her chosen activity, the school journal of international law. All the same, twice a week she made sure she was home by the time Corinna got back from school; on Wednesdays she finished at noon.

She was walking out of Vanderbilt Hall one Wednesday, a crisp, cold early March morning, when she saw a familiar, bearded figure in a dark coat, waving, waiting for her across the pavement.

'Leonard!' She ran up. She wanted to hug him, but her arms were full of books. He hugged her instead.

'Hey. Forgive me for coming down here to find you?'

'Sure.' Holly looked up as Leonard's hold loosened. 'It's really great to see you. I've missed you.'

VII

They went to a small Japanese restaurant near Washington Square and ate sushi. It was a lunch like many of their others before, and yet, Holly thought, graced somehow with extra sunlight and spice and savour. Perhaps it was because they hadn't seen each other for so long; their conversation rattled along all the usual lines, but at twice the speed.

Holly wondered if she should have let Leonard persuade her to order the seaweed rolls. As she looked at them doubtfully, Leonard said, 'Go on! They're good for you. Did you know two ounces of seaweed contain as much calcium as a pint of milk?'

'That sounds like one of your factoids.' That was Leonard's term for any dubious assertion.

363

He pointed at Holly with his chopsticks. 'Look it up in a book about nutrition.'

Holly laughed. 'I didn't know you read books about nutrition. In fact – have you lost weight? You look thinner than I remembered.' She almost thought Leonard looked *too* thin. His slight paunch, never very noticeable, had gone, and the skin of his face seemed to hang too loosely. Though he smiled and joked and gestured as much as ever.

'Maybe.' Leonard shrugged. 'I've been fending for myself these days.'

'What do you mean?'

'I've moved into the city. Rebekah's . . . left me.' It was a rare hesitation.

'She has?' Holly studied him. 'When?' She wanted to ask, *Why? How?*, but knew she couldn't.

Leonard shrugged and forced a smile. 'All these years she'd been putting up with me – always complaining I never earned enough, I never took any vacations, why didn't we have a better car, a better house? She racks up my credit card bills, and then who does she go off with? Her dermatologist. This is the great man she's been waiting for all along. I just can't believe it.'

'Oh, Leonard, I'm sorry.' With some surprise, Holly realised she meant it.

'I mean – ' Leonard let out a laugh that seemed nervous, almost out of control – 'if she'd have left me for some nicer, richer guy, I could have understood. A better lawyer, more successful. But a *dermatologist*?' He laughed again. His chopsticks hung over his uneaten sushi.

'I'm sorry,' said Holly again. 'I wish you'd let me know. I know it's hard – '

'Three years they'd been sleeping together.' Leonard shook his head. 'I can't believe how dumb I was. There she was, always accusing me – this woman, that woman. Heck, Holly, I can't pretend I was always Joe Pure but they never meant anything. I would never have let them hurt Rebekah. And so now she's the one who's really gone and done it.' Leonard stared off into space for a moment as if he had forgotten what he was saying.

'Does she want a divorce?' Holly ventured.

'You bet. She wants the house and a fat load of alimony, which I can tell you she's not getting. If she wants to move in with Leslie Blumenthal, MD, he can support her, I've told her that. I'll take care of the boys, see them through college. . . .'

'Where are they? Where are they living now?'

'Jake's twenty, he's at Harvard, so that's OK. Jonathan's with *her*.' The fact evidently rankled. 'I guess she's got a point. He's got one more year of high school.'

'And you're living in the city?'

Leonard shrugged. 'I got my own place. It's OK. I'm getting along. I'm coping.'

Perhaps, Holly thought, he protested too much.

Leonard changed the subject. 'Hey, how about you? What are you up to? Still living in that hole out in Brooklyn?'

'Don't knock "that hole". The Heights are very fashionable these days, in case you hadn't noticed. Our landlord sold the building, so now it's in better shape.' Holly told him briefly about law school – her courses, the note she was working on for the *Law Review* – even though she wondered how much it could interest him, given all his current problems.

Still, it seemed to take his mind off Rebekah. 'Have you thought yet about next summer?' he said.

'Next summer?' She knew exactly what he was getting at, but she stalled.

'You know your second summer's crucial.' Leonard was eating now, more at ease. 'Thirty-five per cent of law students end up working at the firm where they did their second summer associateship.'

'Another factoid?'

'*Journal of the American Law Association*, September 1974.'

'You probably just made up that whole reference. And,

hey, even if it is true, then 65 per cent *don't* end up working where they spend their summer. So what does it prove?'

'Let's stop beating around the bush. We want you back. We'd be crazy not to. You were with us eight years, we know you practically better than anybody except each other, Abe and Gordon and me – '

'Maybe Abe and Gordon had better talk to me, then.'

'Hey, why so coy? Other second-year students would give their eye teeth – '

'Other second-year students wouldn't have to worry about whether you were doing them special favours.'

Leonard relented. He said he would talk it over with Abe and Gordon, and then maybe *they* could convince her.

'OK.' Holly smiled warmly. If only Leonard knew how glad she was to see him: she couldn't say it. Nor could she say how desperately she wanted to go back to Lyall, Kravitz. In all fairness, they had to want her as much. Maybe, she couldn't stop herself hoping, Gordon or Abe would come to her.

'Holly? Gordon Lyall.' The telephone voice of the firm's unofficial senior partner was friendly. 'Leonard tells me you've been thinking about coming back to us.'

'Oh, no. Has he?' Aware that she sounded dismayed, Holly shifted the phone to her other ear. Corinna and her friend Doreen were making a racket in the living room. 'The thing is, Gordon, I don't want special treatment. Of course, I'd like to come back to Lyall, Kravitz – '

'Great, then. What's the problem?'

Holly was stumped for a moment. 'None, except. . . . Are you sure Leonard didn't push you into this?'

'Totally sure. Shall we call it settled? Starting in June? I know you may get other offers.'

'That – ' Holly was momentarily lost for words. 'That doesn't matter. I'll be happy to start in June.'

'Terrific. All systems go.' Gordon Lyall was fond of a

'hip' computerese which jibed strangely with his otherwise old-money East Coast manner.

'OK, then. Great,' said Holly. 'And – thanks, Gordon.'

'No thanks necessary. We'll be in touch.'

They offered her a salary which sounded exorbitant for a summer associate, but she knew it would seem unprofessional to protest. Corinna was clamouring to go back to East Hampton where the beach, she claimed, was miles better than on Cape Cod; with all this money, Holly could afford it. Maybe she could even rent the 'Weinbergs'' house again. Or whoever's house it really was.

She and Leonard met again for lunch, near the end of the school year. Leonard was looking better, she thought, than before; his hair and beard were trimmed and the gaunt hollows in his face had filled out again.

'I joined the Racquet Club,' Leonard explained when she remarked on it. 'I'm working out.'

Holly stifled a laugh. 'Working out? Aren't you just a little too old for – '

'I'm only fifty.' Leonard looked hurt. 'What, is that suddenly so old?'

'No.' Holly had known his age from his office records. 'Of course not.'

'Honestly.' Leonard still looked hurt, but Holly could tell he was play-acting now. 'Miss Moneypenny's the cruellest secretary I know.'

Holly smiled. 'Hey. You know she's gone.'

'So who's replaced her?'

'Oh, some hard-nosed, seasoned professional.' Holly's mouth twitched as she smiled, for that image seemed to suit her as little as the former one. She would never be as hard-nosed or self-assured as half her twenty-five-year-old classmates. Perhaps because of the long back route by which she had come at the law, she would always remain a little sceptical of her own abilities.

Not that her clients would need to know that.

*

Summer at Lyall, Kravitz began with the expected round of corporate lunches. By the end of the second week Holly felt stuffed to the gills. She was sick of wandering aimlessly through the company library with Jim Hutcheson, the other summer associate.

'I want work to do,' she told Abe Kravitz when he asked her one day how she was getting on.

'What? Aren't you having fun? You know my wife and I are having a party on Friday and we were hoping you and Jim would come along.'

'Thanks.' Holly felt chastened. 'I'll try to. It's all been very nice, but . . . it's a little otherworldly, if you know what I mean. I know what the work's like here. I want to *do* something.'

'All right.' Abe Kravitz's round face wore an amused but tolerant expression. 'I'll tell you what. There's a case of Leonard's, Chemical Electric. He hasn't gotten on to it yet. We'll send you the files and why don't you and Jim see how you'd approach it?'

Jim agreed, with a good-natured groan, when Holly told him what she had arranged. But he was unprepared for the gusto with which she threw herself into Chemical. It was a complicated defence in an antitrust case, with international angles because the firm was largely owned abroad. Holly spent her first lunch hour hunting for precedents.

'Hey,' said Jim, bringing her back a pastrami sandwich from Vinnie's. 'Did you see that lady Leonard Green was taking out for lunch? That's the third one this week. Is he some kind of a player or what?'

'I don't know.' Holly shrugged and kept her eyes glued to the index of *International Legal Materials*.

'Don't you know him pretty well? I thought you used to work here.' Jim was very young – only twenty-three – and sometimes he could be a bit obnoxious.

'I did,' Holly said, 'but his private life's a mystery to me.'

'Hey.' Jim backed off. 'Sorry. Don't take it personal.'

'Never mind.'

Holly was glad she and Jim occupied an office at the opposite end of the floor to Leonard's. It made her former connection with him less obvious; it also meant that they didn't cross paths more than once or twice a day. Yet she had seen some of the women Jim talked about. One had even looked familiar, and greeted Holly by name: one of the lunch-time wives Leonard used to pump for information.

Or so he had said at the time.

One day Holly found herself riding down in the elevator with Leonard and a gorgeous Asian girl who looked all of twenty. When they reached the ground floor Holly walked outside swiftly, ahead of them. But on the way out that night she was trapped with Leonard again in the elevator.

'Hey,' he said, 'you know that girl I introduced you to at lunch-time. . . .'

'Yes?' Holly's voice was frosty.

'Well, it was like a blind date. I felt pretty stupid, to tell the truth. I didn't know she was so young. There's this friend of mine, Sam, he's always trying to fix me up with girls.'

'That's nice,' said Holly. What the hell was she supposed to say?

'And so Mila was one of them. That's all.'

'How nice for you,' said Holly again. She couldn't quite suppress the hostility in her voice. When the elevator doors opened on the ground floor, she edged out quickly, before Leonard could try to say anything else.

On the way home she realised how silly she had been. She didn't know anything about the women Leonard was seeing. Perhaps it was all innocent, as he seemed to be trying to tell her.

Fat chance. She remembered how, once, when they were talking, he had virtually admitted to having affairs when he was married. 'I can't pretend I was always Joe Pure . . .'

For heavens' sake, this was 1975. People met up in bars; they slept around. Just because she had tried it once and disliked it didn't mean she could pronounce judgment on everyone else. And besides, Leonard was divorced now. He wasn't deceiving anybody. It wasn't as if he needed to explain to her.

And yet, evidently, *he* felt he did.

To take her mind off Leonard, she threw herself into Chemical and by the end of July she had a potential case ready. She and Jim Hutcheson presented it at a meeting with Leonard and a few of the associates; Leonard looked uncomfortable as she laid out her strategy.

'That's fine,' he said at the end. 'But we can't pretend it's to any great extent an international case.'

'What about *US* v. *Ross Mining*?'

'That company was wholly South African owned.'

'Chemical's 45 per cent Swiss owned.'

They fired arguments back and forth while the others in the room sat, strangely silent.

At last one of the associates broke in. 'I think what Holly's trying to prove here, with respect, Leonard, is that there'll be some judicial room for manoeuvre. . . .' He rambled on.

Holly and Leonard glared at each other.

He's angry, Holly thought. He's annoyed because I've figured out his case just as well as he could.

For the first time, Leonard was silent that night when she ran into him by the elevators. They rode down as far as the fifth floor before he spoke.

'Sorry,' he said gruffly. 'You deserve an apology, Holly. I shouldn't have laid into you about the case like that.'

'You didn't lay into me.' The elevator stopped on the ground floor and Holly moved through the doors, waiting for Leonard to follow.

Leonard's feet shifted on the black-and-white tiles of the lobby. 'Well,' he said, 'I wasn't all that polite. At least not up to your standards. I guess I'm just not used to arguing with you . . . like an equal.' He gave a sheepish smile.

'That's OK. Anyway, you're still the boss. I'm just a lowly associate.'

'I get a worrying feeling you won't be for long.'

They moved out through the revolving doors.

'Well. Good-night.' Leonard gave an awkward wave as he dived for a cab.

'Good-night.' Holly was walking east to the 59th Street subway stop. She realised halfway there, what was odd. Almost habitually, this summer, Leonard had finished their occasional conversations with some casual reference to the next time they would see each other: lunch, the office, the next meeting. This time, he had not bothered. As if he had other things on his mind.

Another date? she wondered, and hated herself for wondering. If she cared so much where Leonard was going and whom he was seeing, why was she waiting on the sidelines? Leonard was a catch: a rich, handsome older man. As Rosie's and Denise's moanings made clear, available men were all too scarce in this city. Leonard wouldn't need to stay single for long.

The thought chilled Holly. To imagine that once – no, twice – she had had her chance. When he had rented her that house – perhaps his marriage had been on the rocks even then. And last year, when he was first on his own. Probably all she would have had to do was give him some sign. . . .

She had lost her nerve. Perhaps she had been in love with him so long, it had turned into a kind of paralysis. She knew she would always compare any man she met to Leonard. No one she had met in ten years came anywhere near him. If she wanted him enough, she would simply have to take the initiative. The trouble was, she was terrified of failure.

The firm gave her two more interesting cases to research after Chemical; but it was with that first case, she guessed, that she had made her mark at Lyall, Kravitz. Jim Hutcheson sent occasional barbs winging her way. 'So have they asked you yet to come back next year? Guess they will, after your big hit with Chemical.'

In fact, no one had spoken to Holly about it; but she tried to put the suspense out of her mind. She had arranged for two weeks in East Hampton at the end of August. To celebrate the end of her stint at Lyall, Kravitz, she invited Leonard out to dinner.

'Sure.' Leonard looked surprised.

'Is Friday night OK? That's my last day.' Holly felt nervous, standing in his doorway.

'For you – ' Leonard spread his arms wide, magnanimously – 'I wipe my calendar clean.'

Holly made her arrangements. Rosie agreed to have Corinna to stay overnight. The restaurant Holly finally decided on was an Indian one, known for its plush, otherworldly tranquillity, up at the top of a building overlooking Central Park.

More elevators, thought Holly. She and Leonard rode up in silence.

'Exciting,' said Leonard. 'I've never been to this place before.'

'Me neither.' Holly wondered: what if it was *too* sumptuous? *Please, let it be all right.*

From the elevator a waiter led them to a table surrounded by dark tapestries. Drums tapped in the background: a gentle, lulling beat.

'So you go away tomorrow, right?' Leonard said.

'Yes. Do you know where?'

He shook his head innocently.

'I'm borrowing this house,' said Holly, 'from some people who don't seem to care very much about rent. Called the Weinbergs?'

Leonard's face broke into a grin. 'You're kidding. You're really going back to that place?'

The wine was beginning to relax Holly. She could feel a warm glow working its way up to her face, but it did not feel like the wretchedly embarrassing torrent of a blush – just a welcome pinkness. Her dress was a bright orange-red, a shade she hardly ever wore, because it clashed with her hair. But she thought that perhaps tonight the bold-coloured folds of silk suited her after all.

Leonard was openly envious about the Hamptons. He had lost his own house there in the divorce settlement with Rebekah.

'But that's terrible!' said Holly. 'You love the water so much.'

'So does she.' Leonard was rueful. 'That house was our most hotly contested piece of property.'

'Oh. Sorry I brought it up.'

'No, no. It's OK. To tell the truth it's a relief to be able to talk about Rebekah.'

That wasn't exactly Holly's choice of conversation, but she remained diplomatically silent while Leonard aired his gripes and worries. The kids, the beach house, the money.

'Come on,' she teased him after a while, 'you know divorce these days is practically a status symbol. It shows you can *afford* all this stuff you're talking about. Sort of a consumer durable.'

'Or non-durable.' Leonard made a face.

'Or unendurable.'

They both grinned.

'No,' said Leonard after a while. 'That's marriage.'

'Well! Glad to know you feel that way.' Holly's face, she knew, was growing pinker still. But she didn't mind.

'So, are *you* getting married again?'

The question startled Holly. Then she realised it was a joke, like all the rest. 'Good Lord, no.'

'You know, you really keep yourself to yourself. All those years you worked for me, I used to wonder. . . . For all I knew you could be seeing dozens of guys.'

Holly rolled her eyes. 'Hardly.'

'But you were the mystery woman of the office. I figured you had all kinds of secrets.' Leonard smiled.

'I wasn't aware,' said Holly lightly, 'that I was being mysterious.'

'Well, you seemed that way to me. You know it took

months before I stopped being scared to ask you out to lunch.'

'No!'

'It's true! You had this air about you, like, "Don't touch." Always so ladylike, so calm. . . .'

'And do I still?'

'I don't know. Maybe. Different. I'm not scared of you any more.' There was a twinkle in Leonard's eyes.

'I think you're exaggerating.'

'OK. A little.' Leonard was still smiling, his face earnest and warm; it seemed to Holly that he had lost his forlorn look of the springtime. 'Jeez,' he said, 'do you realise how long we've known each other? Ten years.'

And for a moment she feared the worst. He was about to tell her that he had known her *too* long. That he would always think of her as a friend. . . .

The moment passed. 'Sometimes,' Leonard said, 'when I've been with these girls, you know, at lunch or whatever, I've just wished I was with you. I don't know what the hell I'm doing – ' He spread his hands helplessly.

'Don't you?'

The waiter came with their first course. Holly was glad. For the moment, she was saved: saved from hearing that she was as comfortable, and about as exciting, as an old pair of shoes. Saved from knowing that she had waited too long, and it was hopeless. She was glad when Leonard did not return to the old subject, but asked after Corinna; he talked a little, then, about his two sons.

'Jake's like me,' he said. 'He's at Harvard now. Wants to go to Harvard Law School – the works. I say to him, "Jake, but what do you really want to do in life?" And he says, "Go to Harvard Law School." Like that's the be-all and end-all. Like he's got it all figured out.'

'So?' Holly smiled. 'Maybe he has.'

'And maybe he'll crack up in middle age like his old man.'

'Come on. You're not cracked up.'

'Well, I'm leading a hell of a crazy life for a fifty-one-

374

year-old guy. Bachelor pad – I can't cook, I'm taking my own coats to the cleaners. . . .'

'Aww.' Holly moaned in mock-sympathy. 'It sounds like you're advertising for a wife. Or a housekeeper.'

'Is that so terrible?'

'*I* don't think you mind being a bachelor at all. In fact, I think you rather enjoy it.'

'Oh, do I?' Leonard smiled and then, chewing on a chilli pepper, let out a yelp. 'Jesus! These things are hot.'

'You ordered it.' Holly laughed as she regarded the segregated serving dishes on the table: the plain breads and mild coconut dishes for her, the red and hot ones for Leonard.

'Jeez.' Leonard looked up, puppy-doggish. 'You have no pity.'

'Have some of my water.'

They sank back in their rattan chairs, replete. The drums still tapped in the air, hypnotic; not a whisper of the noise of the city could be heard.

'You look great in red, you know,' said Leonard.

'What?' Holly had been lulled into relaxation by their old, familiar ways: the teasing, the gossip.

'You heard what I said.'

Holly could see the whites of Leonard's eyes, of his teeth.

'So, that's dinner. What now?' He smiled. But it was not his benign smile. Rather, his near-predatory one.

'I go on vacation.' Holly spoke lightly and shrugged.

'Before that.'

'Home. Of course.' Holly did not say whose. She reached into her purse for her credit cards so that she could be ready before he snatched the bill.

They went downstairs and when Leonard put his arm around her, walking out into the street, it seemed almost friendly. She forgot to be nervous, to tense against him, until he spoke again.

'There's a cab,' he said, signalling into the street. 'Where are you heading for? Brooklyn?'

'I don't know. Not necessarily. I've never seen your place.'

For a moment their eyes locked. Leonard's face was intent, almost stern. But he did not comment, and when he had ushered Holly into the cab, he said only, '548 East 88th Street.'

They travelled in silence, side by side. Slowly Holly's hand crept across the seat, reaching for Leonard's. She did not dare speak. She was afraid. What if, after so many years, it proved disastrous – horrible – embarrassing? She had wanted to take charge – she had taken the leap, invited herself – but now she was on the edge of losing her nerve.

She looked over. Leonard was watching her. Slowly his free hand moved toward her face. Without speaking, he brushed back a lock of hair from her forehead. She had not expected the delicacy of the gesture.

Slowly she leaned towards him. His fingers combed through her hair again, teasing it out, weighing it. And then he kissed her. When he reached round her shoulders and pulled her against him his strength surprised her. She felt the softness of his lips, his tongue: not invading her, no, more sophisticated than that – exploring, appreciating. His hands encircled her face as he pulled back, his eyes shining as if in victory.

But also, she thought, in something else. Wonder.

She knew from that moment that it would all be all right. 'I've never,' she said, 'kissed in a cab before.' She said it inconsequentially, just to say something.

Leonard's answer was to kiss her again.

When they reached the tall glass tower on 88th Street, they both feigned a decorous interest in their surroundings. That did not last long. The apartment, plate-glass-win-dowed, was not very big. The living room held an angular lamp and a black leather sofa, one glass wall giving a view of the surrounding towers, reduced by the night to black and indigo abstract shapes.

Holly spoke of the view; Leonard did not answer. He rested a hand on her shoulder, but for a moment did not move further. She knew why. He wanted the suspense to build and to last. She held still, let him take his time. His hand slid to her neck, brushed her hair aside, stroked her skin slowly.

'I think I know you too well,' he said, 'to ask the usual questions. You know the ones.'

Holly gave a brief nod. She had prepared herself this time: gone to the doctor. She might as well, she had admitted, stop pretending to herself that this would never happen.

Leonard smiled. 'Do you have to get home tonight, Holly?'

'No. Corinna's staying with – '

'Good.' Suddenly abandoning self-restraint, Leonard reached round her and kissed her. She realised now, even more than in the cab, how young, how almost wiry in its strength, his body felt. His embrace seemed to absorb all of her, from her ears to her toes. He was not afraid to hold her tight: to shout out, in exultation, 'Hey! Finally.'

Holly giggled at the outburst. 'What?'

'We've finally done it. Are doing it. My oh-so-ladylike love.' Leonard untied his tie and her sash, and half-danced, half-carried her into the bedroom next door.

'What,' she said teasingly. 'Did you think it'd never happen?'

'I didn't dare think it would.' He grinned.

'Nor did I,' she half-whispered.

He reached for a switch, but, instead of turning the lights off, as she expected, he put them on.

It was the first of several surprises.

They stayed dressed, or half-dressed, for quite a while longer. 'I don't want this one to go quickly,' Leonard said. 'When I've waited this long. . . .'

'*You've* waited this long! Do you know – ' Holly felt

bold now, stretching out on the crumpled sheets beside him. She reached and slowly shed her bra. '*I've* waited almost ten years.'

'You're kidding.'

Holly nodded solemnly.

'Hey, well, I must have waited nearly that long. You know, I think I liked you . . .' Leonard narrowed his eyes, reflecting back; he had drawn her close and was rubbing her back, her buttocks; his erection jutted against her, disregarded but disturbingly close. 'I remember – ' he grinned and kissed her – 'when I first saw you. In that suede suit, and those boots. I heard that little bit of an English accent, and I thought, "Hey, this isn't just some secretary I've got here. This is Diana Rigg." '

'I don't have an English accent!'

'Nah. I know that now. But you've still got the clothes.'

'No more suede suits, though.'

Leonard's hands moved to her breasts; the heat inside her intensified. Then he tugged her panties down and off, and then, before she expected it, he had entered her: a quick stab.

She let out a surprised cry. Sideways, the first time. Like equals. Leonard moved against her; she could feel his steady gaze on her, his lion-mouth smiling.

'Did I startle you?' he said. 'Is this OK for you? Or would you rather . . .' He shifted, quickened his pace.

'Do you always,' she gasped out, 'talk while you're having sex?'

It did not take her long to discover that he nearly always did.

VIII

Leonard followed Holly out to East Hampton the next morning and did not go back to New York until nearly the end of her holiday. When she teased him about taking leave of Lyall, Kravitz with scarcely a word of warning, he told her he'd been saving up vacation days just for something like this.

'Something *like* this?' Holly raised her eyebrows. They were sitting out on the sun-deck on their third day together. 'And if some other woman had come along?'

'But she didn't.' Leonard gave an amicable shrug.

'But if – '

'That's hypothetical. I don't deal in hypotheses.' He grinned, as Holly continued to frown, perturbed. They sat for a few minutes. 'Do you think Corinna knows?' said Leonard.

Holly shrugged. 'I think she guesses.'

In fact, Corinna had taken it remarkably smoothly when Holly told her that Leonard – 'my friend from the office' – would be joining them for a few days.

'What about Rosie and Ray and Luisa?' was all she asked.

'They'll come out later, maybe.'

Corinna had nodded, with a look of almost deliberate indifference. But she studied Leonard, when she thought no one was looking, with undisguised curiosity.

Holly had given Leonard the bedroom next to hers, at least to put his luggage in; it was also unavoidably near Corinna's. Holly could only hope that by the time she and Leonard went up to her own room, around midnight, Corinna was asleep. They whispered and giggled in the dark; sometimes she had to stifle Leonard's sounds of exultation.

'When do I get to spend the whole night?' he murmured.

'Soon. Once I've broken it to her.'

With luck, Holly thought, she wouldn't have to explain anything. But if Corinna did guess what was going on, she pretended she didn't with all a ten-year-old's obduracy. She hung around downstairs until long after her bedtime, demanding game after game of chess with Leonard; he had just taught her the game, and she took to it like a fiend.

Even once she went off to bed, she would pop downstairs two or three times more for things she had 'forgotten'.

But during most of the day she was away on the beach, where she had traced a few friends from two years ago. It was hard, then, for Holly to keep her distance from Leonard, because to curl up against him on the sand, to touch him, to hold his hand at least, seemed the most natural thing to do.

'Who cares?' He hugged her close when half their bodies were underwater. 'So what if she sees us?'

'You know what.'

'You spoil that kid rotten.' He released her a little as they both jumped to meet a wave.

'Do you think so?'

He nodded. 'Typical only child. But far be it from me. . . .'

'You're right.' Holly gave him a playful shove. 'Far be it from you.' Taking a look at her arms, which were beginning to redden, she announced that she was going back to the house. Leonard followed her.

'Hey. You know what? I love you.' He came up behind her on the sun-deck and enfolded her. His legs rubbed against hers, gritty with sand.

Holly looked up and saw only the implacable white grin below his dark glasses. 'Shall I return the sentiment?' she said. 'Or are you joking?'

'Of course I mean it,' Leonard said – but lightly. So lightly she knew this was not the real declaration: the one to pin any hopes on.

'Me, too.'

They edged, together, into the living room. The sliding doors stood wide open but Leonard didn't seem to care. This was stolen time – salty, hungry, hurried – and afterwards they took a shower and lounged, barely touching, on the canvas sofa.

'I'm still not used to it,' said Holly, shaking her head. 'Half the time I wonder if you're hiding your amazement at my inexperience.'

'What inexperience?' Leonard grinned.

Holly told him. It relieved her to think she would no longer have to pretend: to act like a woman of the world, perfectly at her ease in bed, when the last time she had really felt that way was eleven years ago.

'Eleven years!' Leonard raised his eyebrows, but Holly could tell he was not shocked. 'Well,' he said, 'I don't suppose the essentials have changed in eleven years. Maybe the frills. And you don't seem rusty to me, OK? So there.' He paused again. 'Do you really mean that? Eleven years?'

'Well, there was this one time . . .' Holly could feel her face redden. 'This younger man from law school. It was awful.'

Slowly Leonard coaxed more detail from her. 'I think one-night stands,' he said, 'are colossally overrated.'

'Do you mean that? I thought men went for them.'

He shrugged. 'OK. Guilty. Sometimes. So what about this ex-husband of yours? What went wrong?'

The question caught Holly off balance. 'Well . . .' She let out a long breath of air.

'Is it hard to talk about?'

Holly made a wry face. 'It's a long story. It'd help if I had a stiff drink or two first.'

Wordlessly Leonard moved off, and returned a minute later with a bottle and a bucket of ice.

When it was all over Holly was glad she had told him. Leonard was a good listener; he made no judgements, only letting out occasional noises of sympathy. 'So what about Corinna?' he said. 'Does she know all this? That the man she thinks is her uncle is really her father?'

'She doesn't actually know Jamie exists.' For the first time in many minutes Holly felt uneasy. 'I haven't really told her anything about that family.'

'So what have you told her?'

Still uneasy, Holly recapitulated the old story: the divorce, the car crash.

'Short and sweet,' said Leonard.

381

'Not very sweet.'

'But this guy Tyrconnel's still alive, right? As far as you know.'

Holly nodded, and twitched her shoulders in a nervous shrug. She had stood up to walk off the anxious tension that had suddenly come over her.

Leonard said, 'So if she ever decides to go to England . . .'

'I don't see why she should go to England.'

'But if she does – '

'There's nothing to find. Her father has no living relations. That's what I've told her.'

'But that's not true. Do you think that's right, to lie to her?'

Holly turned on Leonard; suddenly she found that she had to contain her anger. 'You've known about all this for all of fifteen minutes, Leonard. Don't you think you should reserve judgement – at least for a day or two?'

Leonard looked chastened. 'Sorry. Sorry. I guess all I mean is – don't you ever feel you're denying Corinna something she has a right to?'

'No.' Holly's face turned uncharacteristically hard. 'I'm trying to save her.' She gulped the rest of her drink.

'You're angry.'

'Yes, well.' Holly gave a false laugh, and tried to unclench her muscles. 'Now you can see what even thinking of the Carrs starts to do to me.'

It was to Leonard's credit, she thought later, that he didn't leap in then and try to soothe her. He poured her another drink – a small one – and turned on some music. Gradually she grew calmer; after half an hour or so had passed, she had unwound enough to apologise.

'Hey,' said Leonard, pulling her close. 'Forget it. That's my advice. Forget I even brought it up.'

Since she had already invited Rosie and her children to come and visit at the beach, Holly didn't like to renege. And it also occurred to her that guests might prove a distraction for Corinna, who was beginning more and more to dog her and Leonard's footsteps.

When she came out, Rosie needed no explanations. She looked Leonard up and down; out on the sun-deck, while Leonard was busy in the kitchen, she whispered to Holly, 'So how is it?'

'Shh!'

'Come on. This is, like, the guy you used to work for? So how old is he? Fifty-one? You're kidding. He's pretty good-looking then.'

'Rosie!' Holly shushed her again, turning red. But she had to give her friend credit. She knew exactly what was needed to keep Corinna busy and out of Holly and Leonard's hair. She organised excursions for ice-cream, and to distant beaches. She got the barbecue going, and on the last night, after dinner outside, everyone went chasing fireflies. Leonard scrambled around in the bushes and scrub grass of the yard, shouting encouragement.

'Hey, Corinna! Got you another. Open up your jar, here. She's a beauty.'

Her hair tangled and her nose peeling, Corinna beamed in the glow of her flashlight just as if Leonard were talking about her.

'I like Leonard,' she told her mother while Holly brushed her hair in the bathroom, later. 'He's pretty good-looking, for someone that old. Are you going to get married?'

'What?' Holly was genuinely taken aback.

'I don't mind, if you want to. Would that make him like my father?'

'Well, yes. I guess.' Holly hesitated. 'Do you want a father?'

'Maybe.' Corinna shrugged as she covered her toothbrush with paste. 'At least to find out what it's like, having one.'

'Well, I'm sure Leonard would be glad to know you like him.'

'Don't tell him,' said Corinna suddenly, a look of alarm, almost a glare, in her eyes.

'No,' said Holly, amused. 'I won't, if you don't want me to, bunnykin – '

'I told you not to call me that. It's icky.' Corinna finished her teeth and spat out methodically. 'You didn't answer my question.'

'No?' Holly smiled.

'So are you going to marry him?'

'I don't know. He hasn't asked me.'

'Do you want me to ask him for you?'

Holly laughed.

'No! I mean it, Mom. Maybe he feels shy, and so if it came from me . . . I could just give him like a hint. . . .'

'I think you'd better not.' Holly shook her head, smiling.

'Really. I don't mind.'

'I think not just yet, honey. But thanks for the thought.'

Corinna walked through to her bedroom, evidently still unsatisfied.

How easy it would be, thought Holly, if she could just have delegated the asking to Corinna. But she knew it was still too soon. *Patience*, she told herself. But it was hard, when she felt so in love – happy, restless, invigorated. She was afraid even to tell Leonard the whole of how she felt, for fear of scaring him.

For that was the odd thing about love, these days. It had become almost a forbidden word, no longer a gift, but something akin to a demand – for commitment, even for marriage – at a time when fewer and fewer people seemed to be marrying. When Holly was young, there had still been engagements, long white dresses and wedding cakes. Now all of that seemed to have gone by the by, as had 'fidelity' and its wicked opposite, 'cheating'. No one used those words any more. Couples 'swung' and got dissatisfied and divorced. All over America married people like Leonard and Rebekah Green were splitting up, some-times in anguish, but sometimes – as, Holly suspected, in Leonard's case – dropping a whole baggage of troubles in the process, as well as, apparently, years.

Which was why she couldn't feel sure of Leonard. When they returned to the city, she to law school, he to Lyall, Kravitz and his bachelor apartment, she couldn't be sure he wasn't seeing other women; she couldn't bring herself to ask. He called her nearly every night, which should have been reassuring. But instead it made her fret. When he *didn't* call – when she couldn't reach him – where was he?

Sometimes he volunteered his plans. 'Tomorrow I'll be out at the Kravitzes'.' 'This weekend I'm going up to Boston to see Jake.' And Holly heaved an inner sigh of relief when he did. She counted up the days about which she knew, and the nights she saw him; she tried not to think about the others.

She had an arrangement with Rosie for Friday evenings, which she spent up on East 88th Street. Rosie took Corinna, and Holly tried to be home by midnight.

'Cinderella,' Leonard grumbled when she climbed out of bed. 'At midnight the subway's going to turn into a pumpkin. Or maybe a cucumber, that's more the shape. Why don't you just tell Corinna you're spending the night here?'

'I will,' said Holly. 'When she's ready.' *Or*, she thought, *when I'm ready*. Perhaps she was worrying about ructions that would never come.

Sometimes she prolonged her stay at Leonard's, and took a cab home. Thanks to her well-paid summer at Lyall, Kravitz, she could afford a few indulgences. She treated herself to some new dresses – thank goodness, she thought, dresses were coming back in, after years of synthetic ruffles and flared pantsuits. Leonard was less oblivious of fashion than most men. 'That one of those Diane von Fursten-bergs?' he would say as she showed off a new dress.

'It is. How do you know that? From one of your other girlfriends?'

Leonard refused the bait. 'My secretary. She gets the catalogue of every department store in Manhattan.'

'Not like your old secretary?'

'No. This one can type.'

Holly stuck out her tongue.

Leonard laughed at her 'unladylike' behaviour. But he provoked it in her, too. 'You've got to laugh more,' he was always telling her. 'You work too hard.'

He didn't know the half of it, she thought. Not only did she work on her courses these days – she worked on *him*. Every Friday night, and some Tuesdays and Wednesdays, when she could get free, she rushed home from her classes or the library, to bathe and shave and shampoo and scent herself. Shalimar was her new perfume. Heady, sexy, unashamedly spicy and powerful, it billowed out of the bathroom when she emerged for Corinna's inspection.

'Phew.' Corinna would wrinkle her nose. 'What are you all dressed up for? You've got on too many necklaces.' Or, when she was in a more forgiving mood: 'Hey, you look nice. Just like Lauren Bacall.'

She knew what to say, thought Holly: the all-American look was in these days. So was the 'natural look', which actually meant taking more trouble with makeup than ever before. At thirty-five she had a few shadows and lines to hide, especially around her eyes, and more freckles – the price of her weeks of summer sun. Yet, she realised, she was in many ways better-looking than she had been when she was younger. She had given up the absurdities of false eyelashes and straightened hair; now, she just had hers cut all one length and let it dry into waves, however it fell. Waves were in now. She bought new lingerie: silk and satin, bronze, green, purple, black. Every colour appeared in the shops now, as if the staid glass counters of the underwear departments had finally given in to liberation. Holly bought things she hadn't thought of in years: camisoles, high heels, silk stockings. It tickled Leonard to see her in new guises. And her, too, she had to admit: to become – almost – someone else for a few hours. As the weeks wore on, their Friday nights became more like a fantasy – a dream, towards which she worked through the week: their meetings in his smoky-walled rooms, the sushi they would go out for or the meals she would cook in Leonard's wok – wild improvisations, pasta with caviare or scrambled eggs with hot Tabasco sauce, the only condiment Leonard possessed.

He didn't know that on her nights at home she huddled in her bathrobe over a table of textbooks; he didn't know about the mornings when she ran for the subway in jeans, her eyes sticky with sleep. Sometimes she told him, but even in the telling it took on a romantic air. 'I want you *too much*,' Leonard would say. 'Can I help it if I want you to stay?'

'Mm,' she would agree sleepily.

She was, in short, the perfect mistress. It was a role she crafted out of her own longing and determination. No one could be better for Leonard than she could. She understood him: they did the same work, spoke the same language.

Leonard, though he did not know it, was her project. He would become all hers, eventually. Just give it time.

Early in November she got the call she had been awaiting from Lyall, Kravitz.

They wanted her. For good, starting next summer.

'We spoke to Jim Hutcheson too,' Gordon Lyall told her, 'but I'm afraid he's already accepted another offer.'

Holly was secretly relieved. She would be the only new entrant to the firm; she wouldn't be compared with anyone. She was on the verge of declaring her delighted acceptance, when she remembered. 'There's something,' she began tentatively, 'I'm not sure you and Abe are aware of.'

'You mean you and Leonard?' Gordon Lyall was frank. 'Do you think that'll be a problem? I'll tell you what, maybe you'd better come in and we can talk it over.'

When Holly did go in to see Abe and Gordon, however, they seemed almost blithely unconcerned.

'Problems?' said Abe. 'Come on. You and Leonard won't be fighting.'

'It'd be good to see Leonard settled down again,' said Gordon.

'So,' said Abe. 'I guess what we're saying is, go on and go for it, Holly! Marry him.'

Abashed, Holly said, 'I'm not sure it's so easy.'

'Ah, use your feminine wiles,' said Abe. 'Oops. I guess I'm not supposed to say that these days.'

'No, you're not. But I'll let it go.' Holly smiled.

'Yes, well – ' Gordon extended a hand. 'That's all settled then. Are you coming online?'

Gordon, Holly observed, was still wedded to techno-speak. 'Yes,' she said. 'I'll be delighted to.' Her voice sounded firm, controlled. Inside, she felt exultant.

So in that year, her last at law school, she didn't bother applying for jobs. Instead she concentrated on the international law journal, and on her grades: it would please her to finish with a flourish of As.

With Leonard, with a job for the next year, she coasted towards Christmas. In fact, the only cloud on her horizon was Corinna.

She came home one afternoon after classes to find Corinna sitting glumly at the dining table, looking out of the window.

'What are you doing here?' said Holly. 'You know you're supposed to wait for me at the Ortegas'. I was just going out again to do some shopping.'

'What, can't I come home just for once? Can't I be on my own? You gave me the key.' Corinna looked over; her face was puffy. She sniffed as she looked away again.

'Have you been crying?'

'Leave me alone. It's none of your business.'

'Corinna . . .'

As Holly approached from behind and put a hand on her shoulder, Corinna batted her away. 'I said leave me alone!'

'Damn it. I'm not going to leave you alone! I want to know what's wrong.'

'Oh, just forget it. You couldn't do anything anyway. You're never here when I want to talk to you. You're always with Leonard.'

'That's not true. I see Leonard two nights a week – not even that. And you know you can always talk to me.'

Corinna only shook her head, her back to her mother.

Holly sat down in the chair next to her. 'Honey.' She reached out and touched a lock of hair: soft and deep gold, with hints of red, of brown, of pale yellow, it seemed to Holly ineffably beautiful in the sunlight. Though of course Holly never spoke of it, that hair reminded her of Jamie's.

Yet, strangely, Corinna's face, when she turned her head, defiant, reminded Holly of someone else.

Tyrconnel. The slight arch in the bridge of the narrow nose, that had developed over the last year or so. The fine bones covered in porcelain skin; the slightly cleft chin.

Perhaps because she was so beautiful and, what was more, tall and apparently mature for a ten-year-old, Holly tended to forget that Corinna was still a child, and could have a child's troubles.

'Come on,' she said now, meeting Corinna's wary gaze, 'it's never too late to tell me.'

Corinna began to pick at her nails. She sniffed, and then said in a collected voice, 'I hate school. I don't want to go there any more.'

'What do you hate about school?'

Corinna only shrugged. After a few seconds, she mumbled, 'Everything. No one talks to me.'

'What do you mean? Of course they do. They must.'

Corinna shrugged again. 'At recess. After school. No one talks. I told you.' She picked at her nails again. 'It's because I'm out of the club.'

Holly vaguely remembered Corinna talking about a club: a group of girls in her class who would meet up at break, and gossip or play house or whatever it was girls did. Doreen, Corinna's timid friend, was one of them.

'Wait a minute,' she said. 'I thought you and Doreen *started* the club.'

'Mm. Well, she's still in it. She's president now.'

'You mean you're not president any more?'

'I told you! They kicked me out.' Corinna's voice took on a high, whiny note. 'I want to move, Mom. I want to go to a different school. I hate it here.'

'Corinna, honey.' Holly hesitated, on the edge of indulgence, as well as honesty. It was true, she had thought of moving next year when she started at Lyall, Kravitz. Either back up to the East Side to be closer to work and to Leonard, or out to the suburbs. Corinna would be starting junior high school soon and Holly wasn't sure she wanted her to attend one in the city. To tell the truth, she was getting sick of the city herself: the smoke and the fumes, day in and day out, no trees, no space. . . . And if Leonard –

But she stopped herself from going down that path. She wasn't going to let her future wait on Leonard. 'We might,' she said, 'move next year when I get my new job. But that's a long way off, so if there's a problem here we'd better sort it out.'

Slowly at first, and then in a rapider and rapider stream of confession, Corinna blurted out everything. The club. The children who picked on her for being teacher's pet. Even Ray and Luisa hated her.

'Come on,' said Holly. 'I'm sure Ray and *Luisa* don't hate you.'

'They do. Ray won't play chess with me because I always win, and Luisa doesn't care about anything but her boyfriends and her stupid clothes and stupid makeup.'

Holly sighed. Rosie's children were several years older than Corinna, so this was bound to happen. 'Well,' she said, 'maybe that's just the way things go. But I'm going to go and see Mrs Bruno about this business in your class.'

'No, Mom, don't –'

Holly took Corinna out to Mr Tong's that night to comfort her; and, despite Corinna's protests, she went to the school the next afternoon and spoke to the fifth-grade teacher.

It was what she had expected; had prepared herself for, by now. Mrs Bruno sighed and squirmed. Corinna was a bright pupil – a brilliant pupil, really. But she had no patience with the other children – no tolerance of their failings. 'The trouble is,' said Mrs Bruno, 'she doesn't know what it's like not to be the best. When the children were building haunted houses for Hallowe'en, Doreen Malone came to me complaining that Corinna wasn't letting anybody else in their group do any work, because she said they didn't know how to build anything.'

'So? How do you know she's telling the truth?' Holly's conscience forced her to make a stab at exonerating her daughter.

Mrs Bruno sighed. 'I know it's difficult to accept,' she said apologetically. 'But maybe Corinna's going to have to learn some of these lessons for herself.'

Holly supposed the teacher was right. Perhaps she should have seen this coming, after those problems a couple of years ago with Mrs Simoni. But she had been able to dismiss that teacher as prejudiced and inflexible. This time, nothing was so clear.

She went home and told Corinna everything would get better in time.

'Who says?' said Corinna. 'It's still the same, Mom. Nobody talks to me.' Suddenly her eyes filled up with tears. 'Sometimes I think it's going to be this way *for ever.*'

'Oh, honey.' Holly pulled her close. 'It won't.'

'Can I go to a different school, Mommy? Please?'

Holly couldn't help but soften. 'Yes, honey, you can. We'll probably move next year. Like I told you.'

Corinna sniffed. 'Leonard said he was going to take me to a play. He still hasn't.'

'He's been busy. I'll remind him.'

Corinna sniffed and fell silent.

The next morning Holly woke up to find a big home-made card on the breakfast table. 'THANK YOU, MOMMY,' it said. It was decorated with blocklike flowers and squiggles: art had never been Corinna's strong point.

'Oh, Corinna.' Holly reached out to hug her daughter, who stood by, looking on anxiously. How, she thought, could anyone's heart not melt at the sight of her? How could anyone say she had not learnt her lesson, when this time she so evidently had?

Christmas marked an unwelcome gap in Holly's meetings with Leonard. He had promised to take Jake and Jonathan skiing, and since Holly and Corinna didn't ski, this once, he thought, he ought to spend some time on his own with the boys. Holly had to accept Leonard's reasoning; still, she resented it when she had to cancel several Friday nights in January and February, usually on the boys' account.

'For heaven's sake,' she couldn't stop herself saying on the phone, 'they're grown up. Can't they keep themselves entertained on weekends?'

'That's unfair,' said Leonard. 'You know I hardly ever see them any more, thanks to Rebekah and Dr Dermatology. You see your daughter every day of the year.'

'Yes, and I still make time for you. Even though she's jealous and doesn't like it.'

Leonard was silent and for a moment Holly was terrified. She had promised herself never to make scenes.

'I guess you must miss me,' he said at last, in a neutral tone. He sighed. 'Look. It's the same here – '

'Of course I miss you.' Holly's voice cracked and softened. 'I damn well miss you! That's what I've been trying to tell you.'

An hour later, Leonard turned up on her doorstep with an armful of flowers.

Holly was in her bathrobe, with wet hair. She panicked when she heard Leonard's voice over the buzzer. Even when she had let him in, kissed him hello and fixed him a drink, she could not keep still; she moved back and forth across the living room, stacking up books, straightening curtains.

'So this is what you're like when you're at home, relaxing,' Leonard laughed from the sofa.

Holly shrugged and sat down beside him. 'You know you shouldn't have come,' she said. 'I appreciate it, of course I do, but I've got a meeting up at NYU in two hours.'

'What meeting?'

Holly found her heart was pounding unnaturally fast as Leonard took hold of her hand to stop her fidgeting. 'Women in Law,' she said defensively.

Leonard chuckled. 'How about Women in Love? Can the meeting and stay home with me.'

'I've got homework.' Holly didn't know, herself, why she was fending Leonard off. Was it because they had argued? Or because, whenever she thought too much about where he spent his time, she was eaten up with jealousy. . . .

'Can the homework, too.' He wrapped her in a bear hug. 'Like I said, I used to wonder what you were like when you relaxed. Now I know what the answer is. You don't.'

'That's not true!' Holly protested. Yet perhaps it was.

'If I can cancel everything to come over here, so can you.'

'What, did you have to cancel one of your blind dates with a twenty-three-year-old?'

'My God, Holly. You still remember that?'

'Of course I remember it. I remember *all* of them. I'm sorry. Sometimes I can't stop myself wondering. . . .'

'About what?' Leonard spoke sharply; his face was so close to Holly's that she couldn't see whether he was cross-examining her or laughing secretly.

'You know.' Holly tried to speak lightly. 'About all those twenty-three-year-olds out there.'

'Why? What the hell would I want with a twenty-three-year-old? What is she going to have to say to me, or me to her?'

'I don't know.' Holly squirmed.

Leonard chuckled, then let out a deep, full-throated laugh. 'Honestly, Holly, I've never heard anyone so paranoid. I'm not seeing any other women – is that what you thought? Why on earth would I want to?'

Holly graduated from law school with honours in June, 1976. She had arranged not to start work until September; that way she would have the time to look at apartments and houses and get herself and Corinna moved by the new school year.

Leonard had rented a small house near East Hampton for the whole summer, to use whenever he could get away from the city. He drove Holly and Corinna out there for the Fourth of July weekend.

To Holly it seemed an echo of the summer before: a different house, a different beach. And, with Leonard, something easier, richer, deeper. On the night of the Fourth they walked out along the shore. Fireworks still exploded in the distance.

They held hands; they made no effort not to, now, even with Corinna. Leonard trailed a long stick of driftwood in the sand beside him.

'So,' he said, 'we'll have to decide what we're doing next year, now you're coming to the firm and everything.'

He sounded so matter-of-fact. Holly gave an inward sigh. She had hoped for something more romantic. 'Well,' she said diplomatically, 'what do you want to do?'

'Well, we could move in together.'

'Oh, Leonard.' Holly's voice was disappointed, wary. 'I don't know.'

'What, don't you want to?'

'I don't know how I feel about living together.' Holly separated herself from Leonard a little. 'I know I'm silly, that my ideas are stuck back in the 1950s. But I'm just not sure it's right.'

'Well, what do you want, then?' Leonard grinned, bemused.

Holly didn't answer. She took the stick from him and

started to draw a big heart in the wet sand: 'H. C. + L. G.'. . . .

'You don't want to get married, do you?' Leonard sounded aghast.

'Yep.' Holly nodded. 'I'm afraid those are the terms. Though I could do,' she added, looking over, smiling, 'with a more romantic proposal.'

She watched, then, while Leonard hesitated, while emotions crossed and crisscrossed his face. When he looked back, and took both her hands and spoke again, the words this time were everything she could have wished for.

IX

In March 1979, the Conservative Party sent James Carr to America, along with other prospective Tory ministers, to work up goodwill towards a prospective Thatcher government. He spent four days in Washington meeting politicians, and two in New York meeting journalists.

This was the first time he had seen New York, and it rather overwhelmed him: the long straight streets, the sheer drop of glass walls to pavement, the battered, elongated yellow cabs whose horns seemed to echo from one block to the next. The quiet of his first Sunday in the city took him unawares. He found himself wandering from the Plaza, where he was staying, over towards Sutton Place; he had to ask directions.

He told himself he had no purpose in going that way. He looked curiously up and down the rather bleak avenues he had to cross, and it was with something like relief that he first saw the gracious, mainly pre-war buildings of the last block of 57th Street before it came to an end at Sutton Place and the river. The buildings all had awnings, doormen. River Towers, he noted, was the tallest and newest-looking of them, quite near the end of the block.

He spoke to the doormen in the lobby. And then he told himself he should not have been surprised when they said they had not heard of a Mrs Clayton, or a Mrs Carr.

Perhaps one or both of them had moved away. She might have moved away long ago, to somewhere more peaceful, more suitable than this city. With Corinna.

Corinna would be fourteen now.

He walked back to his hotel, telling himself that must be the end of it. He knew of no further address. He scanned the people he passed on the pavement: women in their sixties strolling their tiny dogs, long-haired girls jogging in T-shirts. A few of them looked him over with idle interest, as he did them. He had a more or less accurate idea of what they saw: a figure in a well-cut dark coat, a bit formal for here, for a Sunday. He was aware that these days he often received strange looks, as if people had seen him, perhaps on television. Though, of course, here they hadn't.

As he looked at the women he realised he had absolutely no idea what *she* looked like now.

Against his own better instincts, he found himself searching the phone directory in his hotel room. Clayton, Clayton, Clayton. Carr, Carr, Carr. There were so many.

Finally recognising that he was not going to give up the search, he pulled out his address book. Helen English was in it; he had met her at a party a few months ago, slimmer than he remembered and rather obviously without her wedding ring. They had exchanged cards but he had never phoned her. She would think it odd that he was doing so now, transatlantic. Perhaps she would even be annoyed.

Helen picked up on the third ring.

'Jamie!' She sounded pleasantly surprised.

'It's an odd reason I'm ringing,' he said. 'I'm in New York, actually. I was thinking I'd look up – Holly.' He spoke more quickly now, to cover the awkwardness. 'I don't seem to have her current address, and I was wondering. . . . Do you still keep in touch?'

'Yes.' Helen sounded cool. 'She writes at Christmas. Let me just look. . . . You know she's remarried.'

'No – no, I didn't.'

'A couple of years ago. She lives in Connecticut now.'

Jamie found his heart was pounding absurdly. As Helen read out the address he made agreeing noises as if he were taking it down. In fact, the place-names came and went, and when they were gone, he couldn't remember them.

'Thanks,' he said. 'Thanks a lot.' After a few more politenesses he put down the phone.

Connecticut, he told himself as he headed out for a walk in the park, to clear his head. He didn't have time to go out there, anyway. Too far out of town.

Though of course that was not really the reason.

X

On a Friday at the end of April 1982, Holly Green realised as she was driving home from the station that this was Corinna's election day. She had been running for president of her senior class at Greenwich High School, and if this election went like all the others, she would win. Her victories had come to seem so easy and inevitable that Holly had let herself forget.

She tapped the wheel, suddenly impatient to get home, and took off with a start when the traffic lights changed to green.

'Easy!' said Leonard. 'That one nearly knocked the wind out of me.'

Holly glanced over with a knowing smile. 'I bet you've forgotten. I just remembered. It's Corinna's big day.'

She cruised at a more sedate pace through the suburban streets: tree-lined, their green grassy banks surmounted with large Tudor and Italianate and stucco Spanish-style homes – many of them more like mansions. She anticipated the next few days with satisfaction. For the first time in a month, they would all be together for the weekend: no entertaining, not even any work in her briefcase, or Leonard's. And they deserved it. Leonard had just won a case which had dragged on for nearly four years; Holly herself had clocked up two victories and a successful negotiation in the last two months, involving trips to Paris, the Hague and Geneva. She still didn't travel as much as Leonard, partly because they both agreed one of them should be at home for Corinna; but she could imagine that in a few years' time, things might be different.

Their house on Highbury Avenue lay about two miles from the station. Sometimes the temptation of home was so great that Holly lurched through the red lights and stop signs, earning Leonard's reprimands. She liked driving. Having learnt it at the belated age of thirty-seven, she was still, she suspected, going through a teenage phase of speeding and racing around curves, shaving fractions of seconds every day off her home-to-station record. When she was alone in the car, she liked to open the windows and turn up the radio, usually left on one of Corinna's rock stations. It was her secret vice.

The car climbed up Highbury and then Holly slowed as she turned in between the brick gateposts that framed the driveway. It still bowled her over sometimes, this house she and Leonard had earned – were still earning. They had not paid for it yet. It was too big for them, really: three storeys of red brick 1920s Georgian, with a garage wing and servants' quarters above, and a large glassed-in conservatory. It stood on the crest of a hill, approached by a long upward sweep of lawn. The ground sloped gently down again at the back, where there was a fenced-in area for the dogs – two springer spaniels – and a sunny terrace with a swimming pool.

Holly adored the pool. She had fallen for the house as soon as she saw it, and her enthusiasm had pulled Leonard in its train. Their wedding, performed by a judge out at

East Hampton, had been so unostentatious that their house could be a little showy. Why not?

Every day before breakfast, from May to September, Holly swam. She and Leonard held barbecues around the pool, where they invited their neighbours, and Corinna her schoolfriends. For Corinna, moving up here had started a whole new life.

Holly could still remember when she and Leonard first brought her here. She had been eleven then, and she ran from room to room and slid down the long banister of the main stairs with unselfconscious glee. She located every secret cubbyhole and opened every door. 'Wow,' she said at last. 'Are we really going to live here?'

'You bet.' Leonard's eyes twinkled with amused indulgence.

'I'm going to have all my friends here,' said Corinna. 'I'm going to have so many friends – ' She broke off, running outside to test the water in the swimming pool, which had been green and slimy then, due to the last owners' neglect.

Holly and Leonard had the house repainted. Luckily everything else was in good repair, because they couldn't have afforded much more than the mortgage. 'Live dangerously,' Leonard liked to say; and they did, in the sense that they spent nearly all their money even though, between them, they made quite a lot. In fact, it was largely Holly's salary that paid the day-to-day expenses, because so much of Leonard's was tied up in the house and in putting his sons through law school. Jake was at Harvard, as he had always planned, and Jonathan at Columbia. 'We're getting to be a regular legal dynasty,' Leonard joked, not bothering to hide his pride.

Corinna wanted to go to law school too, though her ambitions changed with disconcerting frequency. She had gone through phases of wanting to be a doctor, a physicist – even a model. 'They make lots of money,' she told Holly defensively; she had been fifteen then, and already five foot eight.

Holly didn't doubt that she had the looks for it, but she tried to dissuade her. 'What do you want to do that for? You have too good a brain.'

'Models aren't stupid, you know. If I made enough as a model, I could pay my way through college. And maybe marry a rich man, too.' Corinna grinned; her smile was dazzling, white, infectious.

Holly laughed. 'Leonard and I can put you through college. And feel free to marry a rich man, if you want. But since when was that so important?'

Corinna shrugged. 'I want to be rich enough that I don't even have to think about it.' Once again, she grinned, defusing the aggression in her tone. And Holly thought it would be mean to come down too hard on her.

She was probably just going through a materialistic phase. Holly knew, from the way she talked at other times, that she was proud of the life her mother had made for them even before they had money. She was a feminist; she talked earnestly sometimes about running for Congress, 'because we need more women in politics, Mom. Because I could change things.' And she had rejected the idea, when Leonard had raised it, of switching from her state school to a private one.

Of course, that might be on account of what she had achieved for herself at Greenwich High. Popularity: she had set out to gain it with single-minded determination.

They had moved to Greenwich at the start of Corinna's last year in primary school. 'I'm going to have lots and lots of friends,' she announced, just before her first day there, in September.

'Are you?' said Holly placatingly. 'That'll be nice.'

'No, really. I am. I've thought about it – ' Corinna's face was earnest, serious – 'and all those things you said, and Mrs Bruno said. I'm going to be nice to people. And I'm never going to say anything mean, and even if they're really dumb I'm just going to act like I don't notice.'

'Well, that's good! You'll be doing very well if you can follow through on *all* your good intentions.'

'Well – ' Corinna was examining herself in the hall-closet mirror, straightening the collar of her new coat. 'I figure it's important to be popular.'

'Not the most important thing in the world,' Holly reminded her.

'No. But *pretty* important. When people like you, you can have lots of friends. And it's horrible when people *don't* like you. . . . OK.' Corinna had beamed. 'I'm ready.'

As far as Holly could tell, ever since that day Corinna had stuck to her resolution. She did have lots of friends. It helped, Holly suspected, that she was so pretty and had a big house and swimming pool to bring them home to. But Corinna seemed to have learnt the trick of being liked, by both boys and girls. She was friendly, but direct, not particularly flirtatious; she had boyfriends, too many and too often changed for Holly even to keep track of them all. She had joined the Honours set at school, and routinely brought home report cards full of As, dropping them on the dinner table with a casual flourish.

She had also started running for office. In the ninth grade she was elected class secretary; in tenth, vice-president and last year, finally, president, which, for her final year, she had every hope of becoming again. Holly still remembered her first campaign posters. Printed on otherwise blank bright green paper, they read only, 'VOTE . . . FOR SECRETARY.'

'Aren't they great?' Corinna had waved one at Holly. 'They'll act on people's subconscious. Vote Green!'

Everyone knew her as Corinna Green, since Leonard had adopted her in the first year of his and Holly's marriage. He had pulled all the strings he could to speed the paperwork through court, but a nagging doubt still remained in Holly's mind that all was not exactly as it should be. No attempt had been made to locate Corinna's father, though of course Holly's own statement to the effect that she had had no contact with that father since birth was completely true.

Anyway, Leonard's application had been accepted. Corinna was his daughter now.

To Holly's relief, Corinna's interest in the question of her 'real' father virtually vanished after the adoption. Leonard became, in every sense, the father she had been looking for. He helped her with her campaign speeches and drove her to dances and had, Holly suspected, given her several sessions of long, earnest counsel about 'boys'.

And so Corinna, though she had known of the name 'Carr' for years, seemed to be too busy to think of it much, or of England. The one alarming exception to this had been two Octobers ago, when out of the blue the Greens had received a visit from Helen English.

Holly hadn't seen Helen in over fifteen years. At first she had been frozen with shock when she heard that familiar, half-insolent drawl over the telephone. Helen was in New York, on a buying trip for the antique shop she owned now. Could she come up to Connecticut? Her shock already melting into a belated delight, Holly had managed, 'Of course.'

She had been immensely curious to see Helen, who, she knew from their annual exchange of Christmas cards, had separated from Nige English four years ago. When she did lay eyes on her, she was surprised by her friend's transformation. She knew she herself must have changed – 'You look *marvellous!* So tanned! Such wonderful curly hair!' Helen cried as they embraced on the platform of Greenwich Station. But that might be flattery, while the new Helen was positively *different.* Chic and almost thin now, she had given up her long print skirts and bangles for Japanese-designer black. Her cheekbones showed now, accentuated by short bobbed hair, but she still wore the same dangly earrings. And she had the same attitude. She called everyone 'darling': Leonard, Corinna, Holly herself. She smoked normal cigarettes now, instead of the old, foul-smelling French ones. She used adjectives like 'sumptuous' and 'splendiferous', but always in mockery. 'It's the junk trade, you know,' she said. 'I've had to learn to flatter.

Oh, not people, darling, not people. I flatter the stuff I *sell*.'

She and Holly drank tea in the conservatory, while Corinna sat by, not overly friendly but, Holly could tell, intrigued.

'What do you sell?' said Corinna.

'Oh, old rubbish. Bed frames, coffee tables, rugs. Anything that doesn't have woodworm. I draw the line there. You'd be surprised how fast a whole shop can be infested by one dodgy buy at a country house sale.'

'What's a country house sale?' said Corinna.

'Oh, well, you know. It's these people who own houses far too big for them – not my problem these days! I live in a broom cupboard in Fulham. Would you believe it, Holly, Fulham's moved up, those little terraces are getting positively des. res. these days. Anyhow, Corinna, when the old folks die and the young Honourables want to get their hands on the dosh. . . .'

'Oh, Helen,' Holly giggled. Her friend was just the same as ever. Like most of Holly's other friends – Rosie, who had become a Wall Street secretary, and Denise, now head of a school – Helen had found her professional niche, and more satisfaction there, perhaps, than in her personal life. She and Nige had divorced amicably. 'If the word can be said to apply.' Helen grimaced. 'Way of all flesh, I suppose. Nige wasn't coming home from "work" till midnight. His PA, of course. I should have twigged. I told him it was really very tacky and *obvious*, but he didn't take any notice.'

'That's too bad,' Holly said. 'I always thought you were such a good couple.'

Helen shrugged. 'Who's to tell a good couple from a bad? Maybe we were, at twenty-five. At forty-five I honestly couldn't say.' Her pride injured, she had stuck up her nose at alimony, though she regretted it now. Her son Frederic was at boarding school: Marlborough. 'It's a shame,' she said, 'how one loses touch with them. You're lucky to have Corinna at home.'

Helen spent a weekend in Greenwich, doing the rounds of the antique shops in Mystic and Danbury with Holly. For much of the time, Corinna tagged along with them, which surprised Holly; usually her interest in shopping was strictly confined to clothes. Her constant presence made Holly nervous, too, in case Helen might let something slip.

But, having been forewarned by Holly of how little Corinna knew, Helen handled the situation expertly. She reminisced in a vague way about London in the 1960s: about shopping on Carnaby Street and the time she and Holly had seen the Beatles, 'and all the clubs. The Establishment! Good Lord, it *was* years ago. Do you remember it?'

Corinna was enthralled. 'You saw the Beatles! Were they good live? Did you see the Rolling Stones?' Fortunately, she seemed more interested in Helen's general recollections than in anything she might know about the Carrs: they were just a name to her, introduced casually by Holly long ago. Her father's boring name, 'John Carr' on her birth certificate, was of no particular interest.

And besides, as Helen explained to Holly in private, 'I really couldn't tell you much about *them*. I'm hardly their circle these days. Oh, I did see Jamie.'

'Did you?' Holly hovered, tense, over the dishwasher. 'I'm not – sure I want to know. How is he?'

'Doing all right. Still married – '

Greta, the Greens' housekeeper, came in then, and Helen wisely changed the subject. They never went back to it.

Helen spent a good deal of time with Corinna, who seemed, in three days, to develop an extraordinary interest in antiques. When the Greens dropped Helen off at the train station, Helen shouted in farewell, 'You must visit, you know, all of you. Or Corinna – you're old enough to come on your own now. Do come!' She waved from inside the train window with a broad smile and a flurry of kisses.

'Can I?' Corinna demanded that day, and many times over the next few months.

'Now, I don't know if she really meant it,' Holly told her. 'It sounded as if her apartment's very small. And she has a shop to run. She'll be busy.'

'But I want to go. She said I could go!'

'I don't think it's a good idea just now. You know we're all going out west next summer –'

'But I could go in August! When we come back.'

'We'll see.'

Holly hoped the idea would die down, and, thankfully, it did. By the time summer came, Corinna still talked intermittently about England, but she ended up taking a job as a camp counsellor in August. To Holly's relief, by the autumn she had too many other things on her mind – college admissions, her class presidency – to think about England at all.

Holly pulled the car into the garage. As she and Leonard got out, Corinna ran from the kitchen door to greet them.

'I won! I won!'

'Aw, honey. We knew you would.' Leonard swung her up in the air in a hug. She was almost taller than him now, but still light enough for him to lift her, though the effort made him grunt.

'Hey! Put me down, Dad.' Landing, Corinna ran to hug Holly. 'I got 75 per cent! You know, I think the posters really helped, Dad. And Greg got vice-president and Laurie's going to be secretary. . . .' She led the way into the kitchen, bubbling over with her victory.

'Hey, smells good in here,' said Leonard.

'I made dinner for you guys.' Corinna hopped ahead to check the cooker. 'Swedish meatballs. Greta's out on a date. Have we got any wine, Dad?'

'Swedish meatballs.' Leonard gave the bubbling casserole a doubtful glance.

'OK, OK. So it won't take the roof of your mouth off. Dump some of your Tabasco on it, if you insist. *Mom* will appreciate it.' Corinna and Holly exchanged a conspiratorial look as Leonard stumped down to the cellar in search of wine.

Holly switched on the TV in the big eat-in kitchen while they waited for dinner. She had to admit, she enjoyed not having to cook these days. An hour's commute, while it had its rewards – a pool, grass and space at the end of the journey – didn't leave time for much at the end of the day, besides dinner and a few minutes' talk and bed.

'Anything I can do, honey?' Holly was glad when Corinna said no. She kicked off her shoes and collapsed gratefully into the torpid state the evening news usually induced in her. Farm prices, missiles, the deficit: the seven o'clock news was relentlessly domestic, American. To find out anything about the wider world, you had to read the papers.

Suddenly a face caught her eye, up at the corner of the screen. She leaned forward to turn the sound up.

'Samuel Hrere, the leader of the coup which last week ousted President Willem de Vriet from Manangwe, today stated that he intended to nationalise many foreign-held industries in that country. Marcus Johnston reports.'

Holly was suddenly attentive. She had read the news about the revolution in Manangwe with interest. Hard to say, yet, how it would affect TCI.

The TV screen flashed brief shots of dilapidated streets, with background noise of gunfire; idling soldiers. Then a face filled the screen: dark, round, smiling with a genial irony. *Gen. Samuel Hrere*, said the caption. *Interim President.*

'No.' Hrere smiled in answer to a question. 'I would not call it illegal seizure if the properties of which we are taking possession belong legally to us.' He spoke with an oddly English accent.

'General Hrere,' the reporter's voice broke in, 'was for over twenty years a personal assistant to the deposed President, Willem de Vriet, until last week's coup swept him to power – '

'Mom!' Corinna complained. 'Can we turn that off? I

thought you said dinner's supposed to be a civilised meal where people talk to each other.'

Leonard stood by with the wine bottle. 'Just give your mom a minute, Corinna, honey. Maybe she wants to know what's going on down there.'

'Nope. It's over anyway.' Holly switched off the TV. 'Corinna, that smells delicious.'

She hoped no one noticed any oddness in her composure. For the truth was that inside she felt strangely shaken. She must not say anything now. This was Corinna's night. She could tell Leonard all about it later.

Leonard was already buried under the patchwork quilt, halfway through an Eric Ambler, when she came to bed. He could get through a mystery a night when he really got going.

Holly switched off their bathroom light. 'Leonard?' she said. She waited until she had his full attention. Then, settling into bed beside him, she said, as casually as possible, 'I had the funniest feeling when I saw that piece on the evening news. You know, about Manangwe?'

'Mm-hm?'

'I'd seen the articles in the papers, of course. But I felt so stupid just there, on the news, when it hit me.' Of course he had looked different. Twenty years older; some fifty pounds heavier. 'Samuel Hrere. The new President. I think I know him.'

XI

It took a long time to get through. Holly had expected that. The phone service there had never, from what she remembered, been reliable, and now lines would be down and exchanges out of commission, due to the fighting. Even once she managed a successful connection, she did not know what stratagems, what names she would have to use.

She had not asked her secretary to do the phoning, or fetch the files, because those she kept in a bottom drawer of her desk. She did not regard them as the firm's property, but her own: the record she herself had built up of events in the countries where TCI had holdings.

To be honest, she had lost interest in those files as the years passed. Leonard, when she had told him how for years she had been waiting for the chance of revenge, had warned her, 'I wouldn't pin too many hopes on it, you know. In my experience, revenge is sweet for about two seconds. Then you'll wonder, "What's next?" '

She wondered, though, if he had any way of knowing. As if to confound his predictions, she had tried to keep the files going, the vengeful fires burning. But she found that they went out despite her. She had so much else to do, so many cases. Sometimes she wondered what she would even want from the Carrs now. Corinna was safe with her, almost grown up; she didn't need their money. And yet. . . .

The phone rang in Manang: a distant bleat.

'Hallo. Chief office.' The man who answered spoke English, but in such a low voice and heavy, lilting accent that at first Holly could not make out the words. Then she realised: after ten calls to the operator, she must have got through.

'Hello, yes, I'm calling from New York,' she said. 'I am an old acquaintance – old friend – of General Hrere.'

'Who is this?' said the man, suspicious.

'Can you tell me how to get through to the General?'

'One moment.'

Miraculously, the line did not go dead. She reached another man, who passed her on again, and a third, who made meticulous enquiries. She was forced to draw on the name of Tyrconnel Carr.

'Lord Carr,' she said, 'of United Manangwe Mines. His ex-wife.'

She was made to hold again. A phone buzzed somewhere.

'Hello. Lady Carr?'

She recognised the warm, round, mellow tones. 'General
Hrere? Sam?'

'Lady Carr. Why on earth do you call me?' Samuel Hrere
did not sound hostile. As with the television reporters on
the news the other night, he was jovial, in control: a
friendly lion, baiting his audience.

And if she had had fleeting doubts, she was sure now
that this was Sam. The same Sam. The President's assistant. . . . He couldn't have been more than eighteen, back
then.

'Do you remember me?' she said.

'Surely! I always remember such a charming lady. You
telephone from England?'

'No. America. I'm not married to Tyrconnel Carr any
more. We got divorced.'

'Oh.' Samuel Hrere sounded momentarily perturbed.
'My condolences. I am affectionate to England, you know.
I was at Oxford.'

'Were you?' Holly had the feeling that she ought to be
directing this conversation more clearly. But then again,
she had learnt over the years not to hurry clients. Potential
clients.

'I attended your husband's old college,' Hrere went on.
'Magdalen.'

'Did you? That's great.' Holly still wondered just what
Hrere was leading up to.

'I think your husband was right about Oxford, you
know.' Hrere's voice sounded suddenly ominous. 'University taught me to think. When I came back to Manangwe
I was not the same. I still worked for the President, but as
you will understand. . . .' He paused, as if to let Holly
interpret.

'I always wondered,' said Holly, 'if you were as loyal as
you seemed, Sam.'

'That is it exactly.' Sam laughed. 'I know how to be

patient. I see Malawi, Tanzania, Zambia – all becoming independent. And yet I wait, because for Manangwe, the time is not yet right. I see Mr Ian Smith – up in smoke. Yet I wait. I need the people to follow me. Twenty years.'

'So,' said Holly, 'you were always planning this?'

'Yes.' Hrere chuckled again. 'I was with the revolution always.'

It was the oddest conversation, Holly thought, that she had ever held in her life. And yet, though she had not made her message clear, Samuel Hrere seemed in no hurry to get rid of her. 'The reason I'm calling,' she said cautiously, 'is that I think I can help you.'

'Help me?' Hrere sounded more amused than suspicious.

'I'm a lawyer now. I qualified when I came back to America, and I've been working in international law for six years. I've read that you are interested in reaching a settlement with the governments making claims on . . . Manangwean property.' She chose her words carefully.

'Are you working for Lord Carr?' Hrere was suspicious again.

'No. Just the opposite. I want to work for you. You've said that you wish to see any complaints against you settled under international law . . . to remain a full part of the international community.' Again, Holly had chosen her words carefully.

'Yes.'

'I'd be prepared to advise you. To act as your counsel.'

'Ah!' Hrere broke into a laugh. 'I see what is up. You are soliciting for business. And against this Lord Carr, who is no longer your husband. Now that is a puzzle.'

'I could help us both.'

'How is that?' Hrere was still amused.

'Let's just say, if you let me I could clear Manangwe's name and win a case against my ex-husband. Both of which I would be very glad to do.'

Hrere, almost to her amazement, seemed to be taking her seriously. She had never made a call out of the blue like this before. He was a tough customer. They discussed

410

hourly rates and fees and terms – Abe and Gordon, not to mention Leonard, would be livid if she took on a case involving so much work for free – and in the end they settled on a compromise.

'I think,' said Hrere, again with a pleasant laughter in his voice, 'you must fly to Manangwe to see me.'

'Are there flights?'

'Next week there will be. I guarantee you. By the end of this week, I can tell you, Lady Carr – excuse me, Mrs Green – this country will be at peace.'

He was as good as his word. By the end of the week an almost deathly hush settled on Manangwe, which included a news blackout. Leonard was nervous about Holly's flying there alone. He had been little enough pleased when she told him what Hrere was paying her. 'What? Are you nuts?' he had shouted.

'I *need* to do this. I need it for myself. Because of Tyrconnel.'

'You and your goddamned ex-husband. Well, I'll tell you this much. I hope this is the end of it. Once this case is over, *finito*. End of Tyrconnel Carr.'

She had been shaken by Leonard's anger. Leonard was hardly ever out of control.

'All right,' she said. 'I'd hoped you would understand.'

Leonard had come back to her later that day, apologetic. And now, while she got started with her research, he pitched in with advice. By the time she flew, Holly needed to know the history of Manangwean mining as well as be able to interpret the well-hidden meanings of TCI's annual reports from the year 1963. Before then, when it was a private company, there were no annual reports, which made things even more difficult. In the end, Leonard had started helping and stopped worrying. But he still wanted her back home soon.

The sea sparkled invitingly outside her hotel window by the Manang ocean-front, but Holly had no time, on this visit, to swim. She spent the days, from ten in the morning sometimes until nearly midnight, at the presidential palace; but she had thought it wiser to return to sleep in a place of her own choosing than to accept Samuel Hrere's offer of a room. She needed a space into which to retreat which would be hers alone.

Sam had also offered her a military escort up to the north to see the mines. With some trepidation, she accepted. The fighting was over, after all: Manangwean television news declared so every night, though sometimes it was interrupted by unexplained silences and power cuts. Willem de Vriet and the other members of his government had given up opposition and fled to South Africa.

Holly's hotel, the old-fashioned, rococo Manang Majestic, seemed disconcertingly empty. The smashed windows of the restaurant had been boarded over, but there was little other visible damage. According to Sam, it had been a bloodless revolution. She wanted to believe him.

She wanted to believe him, too, when he said he would create a better Manangwe, democratic, free of debt – that he would not repeat the mistakes of his African predecessors. Because to doubt him would be to side with Tyrconnel.

Sam swore he would change nothing about the country but the ownership of its resources, and a few wrinkles in its tax and land laws which favoured whites. He did not want to drive the white population out. He wanted peace.

He said much, on the afternoons when he and Holly met, which she thought justified his revolutionary stance. But finally she had to ask the question.

'Why,' she said, 'did you feel you had to nationalise? I know what all the UN resolutions say – control of resources. But at the cost of goodwill, and of foreign investment – '

Samuel Hrere's answer was abrupt. 'Have you seen the mining country? No? Then you must go up tomorrow, I think.' A smile played on his lips. 'After all, one's chief counsel should know, I think, exactly that against which she is fighting.'

Not until midnight was Holly able to get through to Leonard to tell him where she was going. At six a.m. a military convoy was due to pick her up in front of the hotel.

'Are you sure you want to do this?' said Leonard. She could tell he was suppressing his feelings. Worry? Anger?

'You went to Kabul in 1979,' she said defensively.

'You know damn well that's different.'

She could only repeat Sam's words, for she sensed he was right. She had to know what Tyrconnel had done with the mines: *that against which she was fighting.*

At twilight the military van bumped up on to a bleak, deserted plain.

'We sleep here,' the driver told her, pointing to a shack in the distance.

'Here?'

There was not a tree, a bush, a blade of grass in sight.

'Yes. It is suggestion of the honourable General that tomorrow we tour mining encampments and drive home at the evening. If that pleases you.'

Holly was getting used to the formal language of her military entourage. She smiled and acquiesced.

It was a short and uncomfortable night. When they drew closer to the shack she could see that it was in fact the near end of a whole complex of humped constructions in mud, breezeblock and scrap metal. A team of women inside were cooking rice and a thin soup.

'Workers eat here,' Holly's driver, Sese, told her. 'Of course – ' he shrugged – 'with the revolution, some have run away to join the army, and of course so have the guards who would keep them here.'

'The guards?' Holly wondered.

'You know.' The driver, a tall and handsome man, smiled. 'No man would stay here if it weren't for guards.

Like an army. Paid by the old mine owners, of course, TCI. They had very big guns. Rumour was, they would shoot for desertion.' He smiled again, as if it were a joke.

It was five o'clock and men were lining up already outside the hut with tin bowls in their hands. Some of their heads were shaved clean, others covered by a thin, fuzzy stubble. To Holly, all of them looked horrifyingly thin.

Sese took her back for second helpings, but she did not notice the men getting any.

Perhaps this was what Hrere had wanted to show her.

It got worse. In the morning Sese took her to the mines. To her surprise, these were not underground tunnels but deep, dusty basins dug into the hills. Dust seemed to be everywhere: underfoot, blowing lazily from high-piled heaps, creating a fog that turned the sunlight a sulphurous yellow. The air echoed with the noise of bulldozers, excavators and water pumps.

'Is it all strip mining?' she asked Sese, who relayed the question to one of the foremen, who laughed.

'Yes,' Sese translated the answer, 'he says there would be no other kind here. For the owners, too expensive.'

The black rock dug out of the hillsides and loaded on to barrows looked, to Holly, dull and unmetallic. Transforming the ore was the job of the smelting plants further down the hills. It seemed to her that they, and the mines themselves, gouged out of the land, made this northern section of the country far uglier than anywhere else she had been. Sese drove her a few miles north and west, beyond the mines, where, by comparison, the land was green and tranquil and beautiful.

They descended slowly, by winding roads. Here and there, Holly could spot the edge of the blight, again: bare patches of land, piles of grey rock refuse; that yellow dust.

They passed through villages bordering on the stream that trickled downhill from the mines. The villagers, slow-moving and listless, and their livestock, looked even thinner than the miners had.

'Poison,' said Sese succinctly. 'Comes from water.'

Holly looked more carefully at the stream now, and saw that its bed was yellow with algae. No plants grew on its banks.

Blight, thought Holly, was the only word to describe it. Tyrconnel's mines had blighted the land. And now she wondered. Were they doing something far worse – killing the people?

Late in the afternoon, Sese drove her back to Manang. She arrived at the President's palace the next morning sunburnt and short of sleep.

Hrere waited for her alone. 'You have seen.'

She nodded. 'What's wrong with the water up in the hills? I saw some villages – '

'Ah,' said Hrere. 'Run-off from mines.'

'I asked my driver what it was, but – '

'Driver would not know. The water is pumped from the mines, you know – highly toxic? Full of metals. Mine-owners should dig pools, I have learnt, to let that water filter before going into rivers. But that is too expensive for Lord Carr.' Hrere's eyes gleamed in mockery at the name.

'Sam?' Holly looked up. There was certainty in her gaze.

'Yes?'

'You don't need to show me any more. Let's get started.'

There was much work: searching through UN resolutions on natural resources, World Court decisions and treaties. Each new discovery, whether made by Holly or the junior Manangwean lawyers working with her, led to hours of discussion.

Halfway through the third day Hrere broke in on their meeting. He was grinning.

'Guess,' he said, 'who is just ringing me?'

The lawyers were respectfully silent.

'Tyrconnel Carr,' said Hrere. 'He wants to do business. Him and us. Leaving out the British government. I think

415

we are in luck.' He rubbed his hands together in gleeful greed.

The Manangwean lawyers were similarly jubilant. Only Holly had doubts. She knew exactly why Tyrconnel wanted to do a deal. The chances of his breach-of-contract suit reaching a world court were slim. If the British government took up his case, it would lump it in together with those of other dispossessed companies, and put it in the hands of diplomats. And diplomats, as Tyrconnel Carr would know from his acquaintance with Hywel Campbell, had their own agenda. They wouldn't bargain nearly as hard as he could for himself.

Operating alone, he could hire his own negotiators: high-powered, aggressive, the best legal minds he could pay for. If he did, Holly thought, then perhaps this case might be way out of her league after all.

She flew home. She knew from past experience that this kind of negotiation could drag on for years. It wasn't too late to back out; to advise Hrere to recruit someone else more experienced.

But that meant admitting she wasn't up to it.

'I don't know. I just don't know.' She paced the conservatory of the house on Highbury Avenue. Leonard stood by, hearing her out, while outside, Corinna and a gang of her friends splashed in the pool. Right now they seemed to Holly to inhabit another world: unreal, idyllic. 'It was so horrific, what he'd done there. The mines were like a concentration camp. People in the villages were being poisoned.' She shook her head. 'I don't know. Tell me I was seeing things. That human beings don't let other human beings be treated like that in the late twentieth century.'

'Well, you've seen poor countries,' Leonard reasoned. 'India – '

'At least those people are free.'

'So are your miners, now. They can run away.'

'I don't think they have the will left to. Sese said they stayed because they were superstitious. They believed if they tried anything the guards would come back after them. Like ghosts.'

'Maybe.' Leonard laughed and tried again to hand Holly her drink.

She took the glass from him distractedly. 'Oh, I don't *know*!' she said. 'I could screw up so badly. Should I tell Hrere to get someone more experienced?'

'Think about it this way,' said Leonard. 'You have six months, right? At least. Maybe a year. Maybe two before this thing settles. If you do well out of this it'll make your reputation, for certain. So, OK, no multinational will hire you ever again.' He laughed. 'But there are a lot of countries out there like Manangwe. This could be your big case – hell, I know it's not really a case. Big *negotiation*. But, still. Do you want to give that away? *I* know you can do it.'

Holly decided at first that she would give it a few weeks' thought. Gordon Lyall, Abe Kravitz and, needless to say, her husband, relieved her of her other work for the time being. They seemed to agree that, as Leonard had said, a Manangwean property deal could make her reputation – and, by association, enhance the firm's.

So she kept on researching. Hrere rang her every week. His main aim was to stall negotiations for as long as possible. Summer lapsed into autumn with no change.

'I thought,' Holly told him finally, 'you wanted to clear your name, Sam. I know you can drag this out for years, but frankly I don't see what you've got to gain from it.' Sam started to speak, but she intercepted him. 'The money. I know. But, look, you stand to lose as much in foreign aid if you drag this out, as you would by making a reasonable settlement.'

'So.' Sam's mellow voice rang down the line. 'You are saying you *want* to settle? You are ready?'

'Yes. I think I am.'

'I have heard Tyrconnel Carr has chosen his representative. Thurso.'

The name sent a shudder down Holly's spine. Everyone had heard of Thurso; he was English international law's

417

best-known name. A barrister at a prestigious Inn of Court, he also taught at Cambridge, where his professorial salary amounted to less than a tenth of what he earned every year in legal fees.

'Thurso,' she said as coolly as she could. 'Well. That shouldn't be a problem, seeing as how, when we get to the bottom of everything, TCI's possession of the mines is basically illegal.'

Tyrconnel's contract with the Manangwean government, she had realised, violated the country's laws on foreign control of resources. But that had been overlooked in 1959, and for over twenty years since. Holly could not be sure she had such a trump card as she pretended.

The negotiations were held in Geneva just before Christmas. It was funny, Holly thought as her taxi swept her across the Pont du Mont-Blanc and she checked into her hotel, the Metropole, how the representatives of all countries, no matter how hard up, favoured meetings in a city which had to be one of the most expensive in the world.

She was relieved, anyway, that she didn't need to go to England. She had avoided that country for seventeen years. She wondered now whether, tomorrow at this time, she might be facing Tyrconnel.

No, she told herself. He tended to distance himself from his company's public activities; to keep his hands clean.

Trying to distract herself, Holly laid out her clothes for the morning. She ate the chocolate on her pillow, set her alarm and phoned Leonard. After that, she knew, she must try to sleep. She didn't expect to sleep well.

The first day of meetings, held in a neutral blue chamber in the depths of another, larger hotel, crawled nowhere, very slowly. Tyrconnel Carr was not in sight. Thurso niggled over minuscule points. He looked like his pictures: distinguished, with a bushy white head of hair and a pompous demeanour. He came accompanied by three fidgety legal underlings, and when he was not himself speaking, he looked bored. Perhaps, Holly thought, she would eventually be able to exploit that.

When she returned to her hotel that night after dinner, a message awaited her at the desk. 'Mr Thurso,' said the clerk, 'is waiting for you in the bar.'

'When did he come in?'

'Twenty minutes ago.' The clerk smiled up from her watch, the picture of fluent Swiss efficiency.

'Thank you.' The last thing Holly wanted was to meet Thurso one to one, away from the negotiating room. Yet if she didn't, he would think she was afraid. She slung her camel coat over one arm and walked through to the bar.

Thurso was sitting at a corner table reading the *Financial Times* and drinking a cognac.

'Ah, Mrs Green,' he said, rising to shake her hand. 'A pleasant end to the day. I didn't have time to look this morning, but my shares seem to have gone up.'

'Well,' said Holly noncommittally, sitting down. She was suspicious of Thurso's small talk.

The waiter brought the sparkling water she requested, while Thurso settled back in his chair, in no hurry. Holly studied him, comfortable and plump in his expensively inconspicuous suit. His fawn and blue spotted tie was echoed by the spotted handkerchief in his breast pocket; it was his only dandyish touch, and it reminded Holly unpleasantly of England – of a particular type of Englishman about whom she would rather not think.

'I expect you know why I am here,' said Thurso finally. 'At least, dealing with a woman of your well-known advance preparation, I should be surprised if you did not.'

'Well, I'm afraid you'll have to enlighten me.' Holly gave him a chilly smile.

'I'm quite aware of your previous connection with my client's chairman and principal shareholder.'

'I thought you might be.' Holly's heart thudded; she had hoped that TCI's lawyers would not have figured out this connection. Futile, perhaps; still, she had to show Thurso how unimportant she thought it.

'Well.' Thurso studied his near-empty glass. 'If you don't mind my saying so, Lady Carr, I don't think that's quite fair play.'

'I haven't been known as Lady Carr for seventeen years,' said Holly frostily, 'and as they say, all's fair in love and war. Only, thank goodness, this isn't war, and it isn't even arbitration. It's only a private negotiation, and about those there are very few rules.'

Thurso looked her directly in the eye now. 'If you have taken up this case out of personal pique. . . .'

'Certainly not. As you yourself have, no doubt, I have come on this mission in the interest of justice.' Holly rose to leave.

'Well, I must say I regard it as remarkably dirty poker. As you Americans might say.'

'I don't see why. Everything I know about TCI I learnt as an outsider. I know as much, or perhaps as little, as you. Good-night, Mr Thurso.' She nodded and moved away.

Thurso looked after her with an amused gleam in his eye. He had woken up, she thought. She only hoped his interest would flag again in the course of the next few days.

She dressed the next morning in her second Armani suit. In shades of grey, black and camel, the three she had brought were virtually interchangeable. By the time she had given them all a couple of airings, she hoped she would be on her way home. The English lawyers, surely, would get restless as Christmas approached.

She spent the next few days talking until her voice was hoarse, and listening until she wanted to keel over with fatigue and frustration. The negotiators agreed to take Sunday off. Holly spent it searching for an open shop where she could buy a few fresh clothes.

She trudged wearily to the meeting room the next morning. The blue chamber was beginning to make her claustrophobic; since when had she thought she could wind up this business quickly? Hrere's whole interest was in prolonging proceedings, while TCI's was in crippling the Manangwean

420

economy with debt, until, Holly supposed, they were virtually invited to come back in and take over.

On the afternoon of 21 December, Thurso broke from a long harangue about compensation, to make a flat offer. TCI would settle for £250 million.

Startled, Holly said, 'Is that a formal offer?'

The English lawyers conferred and nodded. So did Holly's team. 'This is not so bad,' said one of them in a low voice, near her ear. 'The General will approve.'

Holly turned to Thurso again. 'Out of the question.'

The murmurs in the room grew louder.

Thurso rose and clicked his briefcase shut. 'If you will excuse me,' he said, 'I shall return when I am convinced I am dealing with reasonable people.'

Bluff, Holly thought. She said, '100 million.'

Thurso leaned on his case: glanced around at his colleagues.

If he can act, thought Holly, *so can I*. 'I have,' she said, 'a document here you might like to consider.' She took her time to circle the table, photocopied page in hand. 'Statute Law (1926)', it read. 'Foreign ownership of mineral rights.'

She was not sure how seriously anyone would take it now: the Manangwean 'constitution'. It had been broken many times before, and would be again.

But Thurso looked shaken. He suggested they adjourn.

The next day, Holly began to use her real ammunition – the evidence she and her team had gathered: human rights abuses, environmental damage. The illegal maintenance of quasi-military forces within Manangwe, paid for by TCI.

On the morning of the 23rd Thurso greeted her with a grim face and a round number: he was demanding only 60 million more than the original, flat offer she had made.

Holly glanced back at the others on her team, who nodded. Her face broke into a smile. 'I think that's done.' She shook Thurso's hand. They spent the rest of the day pinning down details. Suddenly everything was moving very fast.

She had won. In so far as it was possible to 'win' a negotiation. At any rate, she had managed to secure the mines for Manangwe at a fraction of their value.

That afternoon she walked down the Quai du Général Guisan to where she could see the white plumes of the fountain jetting from the midst of Lake Geneva, and for the first time she looked at the city, white and serene as a coasting gull above the water. She found a souvenir stand and bought a postcard. Never mind that she would get home to Leonard before it did. WE WON, she scrawled across it, and dropped it in a mailbox.

She had exactly a day left to do her Christmas shopping. When she phoned Leonard, he said, 'Is it sweet?'

'What?' she said laughing, already knowing the answer.

'Revenge.'

'Ask me tomorrow. Right now I'm too tired to be sure.'

But on the plane home she made a mental note to tell Leonard: yes, despite the fact that her adversaries could have been any men, the representatives of any corporation. She had never seen Tyrconnel's face, but by now he would know that he had lost – and lost to her. The United Manangwe Mines turned in almost ten per cent of TCI's annual profits, and, try as the accountants might to negate that on the balance sheets, it would make a serious dent, and for years to come. Tyrconnel would never get his hands on another Manangwe.

She must let Leonard know he was wrong about revenge. Because it was sweet indeed: she was only beginning to savour it.

XII

Soon after her return from Geneva, Lyall, Kravitz and Green made Holly a partner. She had almost come to expect it, though of course Leonard could only hint. In the last few years the firm had expanded to include four other partners besides the original founding three; so Holly would be the eighth partner, and the first woman.

'Ah, who cares about *women*,' said Leonard. 'It's not just any old woman who's getting this, it's you!'

'Thanks,' said Holly drily. 'This old woman is glad to hear that.'

'Hey, you know what I mean.' Leonard squeezed her around the shoulders, then picked up the phone to book a table at the Korea Pavilion to celebrate.

Lyall, Kravitz were planning to redecorate their offices. Sixties functionalism, they had finally agreed, was out; they needed something more in tune with the new traditionalism. Something more old-fashioned. At their first meeting to look over plans, the other partners turned to Holly.

'Why ask me?' she said. 'I don't know anything about interior decoration.'

'Well – ' Gordon Lyall harrumphed, evidently feeling awkward.

'We just thought we'd consult you,' said Abe Kravitz diplomatically, 'since we don't really like anything these designers have turned in. We were thinking if we hired another, you could maybe give him – or her – some guidance. . . .'

'A woman's touch?' Holly gave him a pointed look.

'No, no, no,' all the men variously averred, shaking their heads.

Redesigning the office was, Holly had to admit, like a vacation after the months of hard work she had put in on the Manangwe case. At the beginning of the new year, more similar work had come her way when the head of a small South American country contacted her for help with negotiations. She supposed this proved what Leonard had said: that word would spread about her work. More developing countries – more Manangwes – would start queuing up for her services.

The notion seemed absurdly out of tune with the sedate,

423

expensive opulence which the partners wanted for their new offices; Oriental rugs, dark panelling, pictures in time-worn frames. In search of antique maps and prints, Holly rang Helen English, who put her in touch with a dealer. Money was not an issue; the practice was flush. How much it had changed from the day Holly had first walked in and seen boxes piled up everywhere. Now the place hummed along like a high-performance engine, and Holly wondered from time to time if this meant that Lyall, Kravitz would inevitably grow more like the padded corporate world it was increasingly serving. If so, then maybe Abe and Gordon were right when they joked that she was their 'conscience': working for clients like Manangwe who couldn't pay so well. It ought to be done.

Yet sometimes Holly felt that she and her ideals were alone in the world, even in her family.

'But, Mom,' Corinna would say, 'of course I'm proud of you. You're right to have faith in reformers like General Hrere. Somebody has to.'

Holly gave her a long, hard look. 'You mean you don't?'

'I've been thinking,' said Corinna, dodging the question, 'maybe after college I should move out to the Midwest. Nebraska, Wyoming, Montana. . . .'

'What on earth would you do there?' Holly was bemused.

'Well, obviously I'm never going to get a Senate seat in an overpopulated state like Connecticut.'

'So you think you'd stand a better chance out in the West?'

'Two senators for every state, no matter how small.'

'You'd have to be a Republican.'

'That's just party. Who cares?'

'And you think it'll be easy to go out there and win them over? As a northeasterner? And a woman?'

Corinna had shrugged again. Her plans were as fluid as ever. Sometimes they included law school, sometimes business school. Holly enjoyed sparring with her if only to test her eighteen-year-old's certainty. For, despite their disagreements, she was proud of Corinna – glad she was so confident. She had grown up with feminism and took its achievements for granted; all the universities to which she was applying had been male-only preserves when Holly was her age: Harvard, Yale, Princeton, Brown. Holly only hoped Corinna wouldn't be disappointed, because she had no fallbacks, no second choices. When Holly questioned her on it, Corinna just shrugged. 'If I don't get in, I'll take a year off and reapply to more places.'

Just last summer she had talked of applying for a Rhodes scholarship to take her to England after college. Holly had felt her whole body go rigid as her daughter spoke; yet she knew she had to conceal the tension within her. 'Oh,' she said. 'Why?'

'Well, England's part of me after all,' said Corinna defensively. 'Shouldn't I take an interest in the place? I was born there.'

'As far as I'm concerned,' said Holly, 'it was almost an accident that you were born in England.'

'How can you say that, Mom? You spent seven years of your life there. You were married to my father there.'

'You know your father's dead. And you shouldn't fool yourself that if you go over there you'll find anything to do with him. I've told you, he only had one aunt and one uncle, and they both died before he did.'

'Why do you get so uptight every time I even mention my father? OK, so he's dead and I won't find him. I don't want to find him!' Corinna paced the tiled kitchen floor, her hair flying.

'Corinna, calm down. I didn't mean – '

'What difference does it make to you if I go to England? I want to see the place. OK? I'll only know once I get there whether I feel anything special about it or not.'

Corinna had wound down and Holly tried to keep control of herself. Corinna wasn't going, not yet. She was only talking about a remote possibility, years away. 'Sorry,' said Holly. 'Sorry I flew off the handle.'

'Bad day at the office?' Corinna threw her a twisted,

roguish smile, which for a second reminded her exactly, indelibly, of. . . .

'No,' Holly said, 'not really. Odds and ends. Leonard was tied up at a meeting but he should be home on the six forty-nine.'

'Want me to pick him up?' Corinna had already reached for the car keys on the hook by the door.

Holly had sent her off, relieved that the worst was over, and they had not discussed the Rhodes scholarship or England again.

In April Corinna's acceptances came. Brown, Princeton, Yale, Harvard.

'Now, don't think you've got to say yes to Harvard just because of me,' said Leonard. 'Of course I'd be thrilled if you went there. We old alums are loyal. But think it over.'

Corinna had already chosen. All the schools that had accepted her had big names, but Harvard was by just a fraction, she thought, the biggest: the oldest, the most renowned. She wrote off as soon as her parents would allow her, accepting a place in the class of '87.

She would coast through the rest of her last year of high school, now. Holly felt she was coasting, too. And it seemed to her that nothing could disturb the peaceful stream of her life when, one weekend in mid-May, the phone rang and an unfamiliar voice asked if it was speaking to Holly Clayton.

'Yes.' Holly answered warily. Most people knew her as Holly Green these days.

'This is Christopher Deakin,' said the voice: a raspy southern drawl. It took Holly a second to recall the name.

'Chris Deakin! How are you?' How on earth, she wondered, had he managed to find her? Through the office? And why was he getting in touch, after all these years?

'Miz Clayton – ' Chris's voice came slowly, awkwardly. 'I'm going to have some difficulty saying what I've got to say, but I thought it was . . . important I call you. The reason I'm calling is, the programme says we've got to make our amends.'

'The programme?' Holly was mystified.

'I don't know,' said Chris laconically, 'if you were aware that I was addicted to heroin.'

'No. No, not really.' This was getting weirder and weirder, thought Holly.

'So I joined the programme last year. It's saved my life.'

'That's good.'

'I've learnt to let the Lord into my life.'

'Mm-hm?'

'And so you see, the final step, Miz Clayton, is we've got to take account of all the people we've hurt over the years, and make amends. And for a long time I couldn't do it, Miz Clayton, I just couldn't talk to you. Because you're the worst.'

'What do you mean?'

'I killed your father, Miz Clayton.'

Everything seemed to Holly to have gone silent, except the phone.

'Out on the boat. It wasn't an accident.' Silence, again.

'Chris?' Holly tried to keep her voice low and calm. 'Can you tell me more?'

'It was the habit. I needed the money.' Chris paused. 'There was this guy, one day, came cruising around the harbour. Big sort of guy with an English accent. He asked me these questions, like did I work for your father and how well did I know his boat. Then about a week after that I got this call. A lady. She was English, too. She said – would I be able to make an accident happen to Joseph Clayton.'

'What did she sound like?' said Holly.

'Kind of . . . a low voice. Older, maybe. Kind of sexy.' Chris stopped, abashed.

'Did she identify herself?'

'No. But she said she had the money for me, if I did it. A thousand before, a thousand after. A week later I got the first thousand in the mail.'

427

'Was there any address on the envelope? Any postmark?'

'No. I didn't see none.' Chris seemed to be breathing faster. 'So – like I said, it was because of the money. I needed the money so bad, Miz Clayton. I'm sorry – '

Holly felt her chest clench up tight. 'Go on. Tell me the rest.'

Chris dragged the words out now. 'What I had to do was – get him out one day on the water when the weather was bad. And, honest, your dad was a good sailor, I didn't even know how I'd do that. But. . . .'

'But you did.'

'It was, like, one of those halfway days. We had a couple of drinks by the shore. It was clouding up but your dad didn't seem to notice, so then we went out . . .' Chris's breath seemed to catch. 'The lady on the phone – she said to shoot him. But I lost my nerve.' Chris spoke faster now. 'So when he was trying out the engine, like, I hit him. On the head. There were these weights we used, for the fishing . . . I tried to be quick, Miz Clayton . . . I put the body overboard.'

'And then what happened?' Holly heard her own heart beating; her voice, a hushed monotone.

'When the storm came in bad, then, I thought I'd die. I knew I'd done wrong, I didn't care if I died. I let the boat go over like I knew I had to. Then they picked me up. I lied about the engine to the Coast Guard. And to you. She said I had to. She told me they'd – get me, if I didn't.'

'Yes,' said Holly, trying to soothe, trying to keep Chris on the line. 'Chris, can you tell me where you are just now?'

'I'm on the Key. Oh, my God. You're not going to tell on me. Please, Miz Clayton. God bless you. Please don't tell on me.'

There was a sob; the phone clicked and the line fell dead.

Holly couldn't sit still. Somehow, she couldn't stop shaking. She put on a sweater, then another, and still she huddled, her arms clenched around herself for warmth.

Leonard and Corinna had gone out shopping. *Please*, she thought, please let them come home. She needed Leonard more than she ever had before in her life.

As soon as he and Corinna came in with the groceries, she drew him aside.

'Yeah?' he said. 'You look cold, honey. Are you all right?'

'I've got to talk to you.'

They retreated to the conservatory.

'Where was this guy?' said Leonard, when she had told him about the conversation. 'Was he still down on the Keys?'

'He started to say so, but then – that's when he hung up.'

'He's probably still down there. We'd better go as soon as we can get a flight out. Oh, hell.'

'What?' Holly felt warmer now; calmer, for the feel of Leonard's arms around her.

'Hell,' he said again. 'I've got that Warne and Telford meeting on Monday morning.'

'That's OK, then,' said Holly, as calmly as she could. 'I can go down on Monday. I can . . . manage it. I'll talk to Chris – maybe it's better if you aren't there. After all, he knows me.' She wished Leonard could come, too, to reassure her, but it seemed there was no way around it.

'I'll call the agents, get you a flight,' said Leonard, giving her a reassuring squeeze and a kiss on the forehead. 'And I'll tell you what, I'll fly down the minute I get free. Do you want to take that shuttle down from Miami to the Keys?'

'No.' Holly shuddered. 'I took it in 1965. It was a real rattletrap of a plane.'

'Probably improved in the last twenty years or so.'

'Still. I think I'd rather drive. Maybe it'd calm my nerves.'

She was beginning to feel easier at the prospect of going. Leonard was right. She couldn't just leave that phone call hanging. She needed to know the whole story. And if it was a case of murder. . . .

A contract killing. Planned by . . . it had to be Imogen. Murder, only a few months after her father changed his will. She couldn't even begin to think about that now.

Sleep wouldn't come. They were both pretending. Leonard snorted and shifted under the covers. The bed grew hot. 'Leonard?' she said at last.

'Yeah, I know. I can't sleep either.'

'I can't stop thinking about it.'

'Me neither.'

'I thought I was done with them.' Holly gave a shallow laugh. 'I know a lot of people these days don't believe in evil, but I always have. Because of them. And now it seems ironic. The worst thing they did, I never even knew about.'

'Yeah.' Leonard's voice was hushed. 'It seems too – surreal. Murder.' He was silent for a moment. 'All these years in the law, and I've never been anywhere near a murder before.'

Holly gave a dry laugh. 'There's always a first time.'

They lay quietly, both thinking.

'So,' said Holly. 'My flight's at noon on Monday, right?'

'Yep. Are you going to tell Corinna?'

'Corinna?' Holly had not even thought about it. 'Oh, no. I don't want to. Not now.'

'If this gets really big we're going to have to.'

'What do you mean?' Holly's voice trembled.

'I mean if we're dealing with a serious crime here. Conspiracy to murder. You want to get these people prosecuted, right?'

'If we can. I guess – I just hadn't thought about Corinna.'

'She's going to have to know, some time,' said Leonard reasonably.

'You're right,' said Holly. 'I know you're right. When I get home I'll tell her. OK? But just let me deal with one thing at a time.'

After that they pretended to sleep again.

Corinna kissed Holly goodbye before she left for school. 'So where are you going this time?' she said. 'Florida? Lucky you. Sometimes I don't believe you *really* work at all!'

Holly forced a smile and waved as her daughter, all long bare legs under a Norma Kamali minidress, ran off down the drive.

On Tuesday night Leonard had to work late, and so Corinna came home to an empty house, except for Greta. She rang up her new boyfriend, Greg, but Greg was grounded and so she read *Forbes* in front of the TV until her father came in. He said hello in a distracted way and, when the telephone rang, ran for it like a shot.

There was nothing unusual in that either. Leonard liked his wife's business trips less than he let on; in fact, he often seemed adrift in the big house without her there.

Corinna heard his voice in the kitchen.

'Christ. Is he?'

Then Leonard ran past her towards the upstairs extension.

He came down a few minutes later. 'Honey? I'm going to have to go to Florida tomorrow. Your mother's running into trouble with some of these people she's dealing with.'

'Mm-hmm. When are you coming back?'

'Couple of days. Will you and Greta be all right on your own?'

Corinna smiled up, unconcerned. 'Sure, Dad. We'll be fine.'

By Wednesday night Holly thought she would go mad with waiting. She had arrived late on Monday; yesterday morning she had driven down to the harbour, looking for Chris Deakin.

'Chris?' said a lackadaisical man repairing a boat in dock. 'He's gone. But he should be back. Yeah, he should be back. Sometime later.'

'Any idea when?'

The man shrugged. 'This afternoon?'

Holly hung around all that morning and early afternoon, in sight of the boathouse. She drank one iced tea after another in a nearby café. The glasses dripped with condensation. May was the wrong time to visit the Keys; the weather was hellishly humid and hot. She shed her jacket, then, surreptitiously, her tights.

Chris never came. A few more enquiries led her to the house he was renting, a few streets back from the harbour. The door was locked. His car was gone, but none of his neighbours had any idea where he was.

'Chris, he always turns up again,' said the man back at the boathouse, tinkering away now with an outboard motor.

Holly asked around. By the end of the day she was asking everyone in the local shops, anyone she could find – but no one knew where Chris had gone. Last night, at the end of her tether, she had called Leonard. And she had been ashamed at her own relief when he said he was coming. He would take the burden of worry off her shoulders. He would take care of everything. . . .

He told her to wait at the hotel because he couldn't be sure what flights he would be catching. He would take the shuttle from Miami for the sake of speed.

'Are you sure?' Holly said on the phone. 'That plane always made me nervous.'

'Nah, no problem. You're just a scaredy-cat. I'll be there by tomorrow night and Thursday we're going to find that jerk Deakin. OK?'

Holly remembered the whispered 'good-nights' – the sweet affection that still took her by surprise sometimes, after so many years of necessary separations and practical partnership. As she finished the last of the bottled water from the mini-bar, she wished Leonard would hurry up. Surely nothing in New York could have been so important as to keep him in the office past three.

At six, she flicked on the local news for some relief. And then the image that took over the screen froze her.

'*The mid-air collision of an Oris Air flight 999 and a private aircraft kills thirty-three and injures eleven. . . .* '

The last words echoed in her head. *Kills thirty-three and injures eleven, kills thirty-three and injures eleven.* And she could not seem to make sense of them.

But Leonard would not have been on that flight. Would he?

No, of course not. He was late. Held up at the office.

She tried to reason with herself. To panic, just because of what she had seen on the screen. . . . It would be absurd. He had caught a later flight. There were several a day. Maybe he didn't even catch a plane in the end. He could be driving. . . .

He could be one of the injured.

No, no. She would not even think that. He had probably not been on the flight at all.

Several minutes passed before the cold paralysis that had seized her loosened, allowing her to move and switch off the TV. She must phone. She flipped through the phone book, searching for a listing for Oris Air.

Please, she told herself, *let anything else happen, but don't let it be Leonard.*

When, after several tries, she heard the voice of a telephonist answer at Oris Air, the rest seemed almost mechanical. She heard her own voice. 'My husband . . . on the list of passengers? Could you check?'

There was a long silence. Then a new voice came on the line: more stilted, more formal. 'Mrs Green? We are very sorry. Nothing has been confirmed yet. . . .'

She knew then. They didn't have to tell her any more.

This, she thought later, when the worst had come and gone, this is how we are parted from each other in the modern world. No funerals, no bodies, no slow decay. It is never real.

First her father, now Leonard. Both of them. They just disappeared.

Leonard hadn't even been old. Fifty-eight. They had only been married seven years.

There were odd facets to losing a loved one to the air. The muddled conversations with the airline: yes, let us check the injured list. No, he doesn't seem to be on it. Let us check the list again. Wait. . . .

There were the photographers, the TV interviewers, even though she made no attempt to approach the barriers that surrounded the wreckage of the two planes. They still picked her out, by her height or her clothes, perhaps by her obvious appearance as a grieving widow. She had nothing to say to them. She never knew whether she ended up on the news that night.

There was the impulse to tell Corinna, when she called her, 'No, don't fly down.' She didn't want anyone she cared for to fly ever again. Yet everyone did.

She herself did eventually, when there was nothing more she could do or hope for on Key Isotro. She sat in a central seat, lulled by tranquillisers, Corinna holding her hand.

Odd parcels arrived at the house, even months later: objects retrieved from the wreckage that the airline somehow imagined that she would want. Several – a scorched, vinyl-covered Bible, a gold signet ring – were patently not Leonard's, and she wanted to hurl them back at Oris Air in her anger. *Is this your pathetic compensation? Is this all you can do?*

And then, incomprehensibly, the sight of those pitiful objects, not even Leonard's, made her cry. Objects could do that: his ties, his feathered hats in the closet, his giant bottle of Tabasco in the kitchen cupboard.

She learnt to put away his things, one by one. Just as she learnt to fly again, because she had to. Sometimes, still, she would wake up at night drenched in sweat, and realise that she had had that dream again. She had been in Leonard's place, sitting on a plane. Something jarred; lights went on; nothing had happened yet, but it was about to. She knew it was all over: that she was going to die.

For a moment, she felt inseparably close to him.

She found she could talk to Corinna about more than she expected, that in these worst of times her daughter could be strong and unselfish. Corinna insisted on deferring Harvard for a year: she would go next year, and stay with her mother now, while they needed each other.

She wouldn't listen to Holly's protests. 'Forget it, Mom,' she said in that brusque, blithe way that masked her moments of kindness. 'I've already fixed it. Anyway, it'll probably be good for me to get a job – see the real world for a change.'

She got two jobs, in fact, one in a real estate office and another waitressing in a local Italian restaurant. And when, in mid-June, Holly had forced herself back to the office only to find that it was all too much for her – Leonard's presence was still too strong – it had been Corinna's idea that she should take a few months off and write a book.

'A law book,' she said, logically enough. 'How about one on the Manangwe case?'

So Holly wrote her book, over that year which would have been Corinna's first at Harvard, and, perhaps appropriately, it was Harvard University Press which eventually published *Compromise in Cases of Nationalization*.

At the end of that year Corinna helped her mother move back to Manhattan, for the house out in Connecticut was really too big now; besides being too much inhabited by memories. She gave the two dogs, elderly now, away to neighbours, too numb, still, to mind the loss of them very much. She sold most of the furniture and the car, and stopped commuting.

At the end of that summer, just before Corinna went off to Harvard, they made a whirlwind tour of the Far East together: Bangkok, Java, Bali. They posed together for pictures taken by strangers, fellow-tourists, and when Holly went through them afterwards it seemed to her that in them she looked, to all appearances, happy. Recovering.

'You're coping so well,' everyone said, but if only they knew: every day of her life she missed Leonard. Even in her compact, single woman's apartment, the sense of his absence would not leave her: the feeling that she was incomplete now, alone, always waiting for a warm voice to answer her call; homecoming steps on the other side of the threshold. And beyond the loneliness lay the sense that, whatever the logic or the facts, a further injustice had been done.

The Carrs had killed her father, and got away with it. In the attempt to punish them, Leonard had died. The plane crash had been an accident: no one had questioned that.

But they might as well have killed him, too.

1989

I

'I'm not telling you this,' Tyrconnel continued, 'to shock you. Although I suppose the desire for an excuse to take out a pretty young woman did cross my mind.' He smiled, the recitation finished. It had been astoundingly brief.

Corinna, who had not yet absorbed it all, took a few seconds to reply. Automatically she had registered the old man's flirtation, and almost automatically she answered in the same vein: if only to stave off recognition. 'Of course,' she said with a shaky smile, 'it could still be an excuse. If it is, it's a pretty elaborate one.'

The earl gave a teasing, V-shaped smile. 'I do hope I haven't alarmed you.'

'No.' Corinna was still reeling. Looking down, she saw that her trout was going cold on her plate. Between snippets of his story, the earl had been tucking into his *entrecôte* with enthusiasm.

Suddenly the fish, with its solitary, soggy eye, seemed too much for Corinna. She started on her vegetables instead. 'If it's all true,' she said, 'why are you telling me now? Twenty-four years went by, and you didn't try to find me.'

'Is that what your mother says?'

'Well, it's true. Isn't it?' Corinna looked up. Her eyes, usually hazel with a strong dash of green, had a way of going dark and mutinous when she was challenged.

The earl sipped his water again. He had hardly taken any wine. 'I wrote,' he said, 'a few months after your

437

mother left this country. All my letters were returned. I could only assume that she had moved. It would have been very difficult to trace her.'

Corinna held his gaze. He could be lying about the letters, she knew, but somehow she believed him.

'Even if I'd found you,' he said, 'your mother would have tried to keep me from seeing you. She was quite possessive of you. My only alternative would have been to put her – and you – through the trauma of court proceedings.'

'But my mother told me you were dead. Why would she say that?'

'Goodness knows. I expect, to evict me as effectively as possible from your thoughts. Your mother, as no doubt you know, can be very determined. What she did, in fact, when she decided to leave me, was walk out without saying a word to anyone. We were very worried. Your nanny – '

Corinna let out a sudden, incredulous laugh. 'I had a nanny?'

'Of course.' Tyrconnel looked bemused. 'Everyone in the family does.'

'I'm sorry. It's just – so different from the way I grew up.' Corinna's face turned serious. 'Well. I guess you wouldn't know. For a long time we didn't have *anything*. We lived in this one-bedroom apartment in Brooklyn. Mom worked all day and went to school at night. That was how she became a lawyer.' Corinna stopped for a moment. When she looked around at the well-dressed luncheon crowd in the restaurant – when she thought to herself that this was Tyrconnel Carr's everyday world – she felt more confused that ever. 'I just don't understand. If she had so much – servants and everything – when she was here, why would she have wanted to give it up?'

Tyrconnel remained tactfully silent. He had sketched the outlines for Corinna, not filled them in. That would be too cruel. It would be better to let her understand gradually. 'Your mother,' he said smoothly, putting down his napkin, 'seems to have changed a very great deal since I married her.'

Corinna and Tyrconnel – she supposed that she ought to call him 'Father' now, or even 'Dad', but she couldn't get used to it – parted on the promise that she would call him in a week's time. He wanted to have her up to Stad-hampton the weekend after next, business permitting.

Only once she was on the train back to Oxford did Corinna realise there were all sorts of questions she hadn't asked. If Lord Carr was her father, she must have uncles, aunts, cousins. . . . She wondered how many, and who they all were.

Soon after her arrival in England, she had gone to stay in London with Helen English – her mother's old friend, who had always promised to show her around. During a whole weekend, Helen had not mentioned the Carrs once. She must, Corinna knew now, have been told not to say anything. She must have been in on Holly's lies.

Yes, lies. That was the heart of it. The plain 'John' of her birth certificate, the ordinary banker, deceased, had never existed. Tyrconnel Carr, the earl, the entrepreneur, was very much alive.

Corinna had not heard of TCI, but she would look it up in the shares pages once she got back to college. She wanted to learn more about it – this company her father had started up from nothing.

He was handsome, too. And charming. Her mother's defection must have hurt him badly. Corinna remembered how, with an ironic twist to his mouth, he had described his as a 'fairytale wedding'. Yet her mother had abandoned it and him; and, years later, built a whole tower of lies to cover up the fact. *Why?*

However much Corinna thought, she seemed always to keep coming back to that same question.

She hurried into college just in time for late dinner, wanting to burst out with the truth but holding it in: watching the students around her. They suddenly seemed as plodding and terrestrial as the potatoes they were shovelling up from their plates.

But she, Corinna, was different. She knew who she was now. It had not taken her long in England to recognise the subtle differences between those born to a privileged self-assurance and the larger, benighted bulk of British humanity. As an American, and a woman, she knew she was fortunate, because, though Americans weren't prized here, women, through relative scarcity, were. She was glad to fall outside the system; for, when she admitted the truth to herself, she knew that the alternative was to be one of the have-nots.

Now she was the daughter of an earl, and all that had changed.

Justin Lucas-Jones caught up with her just as she was making her escape from dinner.

'C'rinner. Did you get my note?' He sounded uncharacteristically out of breath.

The earl, she remembered – her father – had pronounced her name properly, not sticking an 'r' on the end of it the way Justin always seemed to. Suddenly Justin seemed rather lower-class: the flashy, old-money way he dressed, the way he talked – everything. 'What note?' she said uninterestedly. She hadn't had time to check her pigeonhole.

'The OUCA drinks party. You know, the Conservative Association –'

'Yes. I know what OUCA is.' Corinna avoided Justin's beady, suddenly over-eager gaze.

'So are you coming?'

'Oh, I don't know.' She headed out into the cold air of the front quad, with its sixteenth-century leaded windows and gargoyles. 'To tell you the truth, I feel like staying in. I have some things to think about.'

Justin didn't take the bait, and she was a little disappointed in him. Evidently his only concern was to find a girl to drag along to his party.

'Oh, well.' He tossed his head and looked aloof.

'Besides,' said Corinna, softening, 'you've got to remember, I'm not a Conservative. I'm a Democrat.' She flashed Justin a smile as she turned through the archway towards the back quad.

In the middle of the next week she rang Lord Carr – Tyrconnel, her father – at the office number he had given her. He had given her two home numbers as well, one in London and one in the country, but he warned her not to use the second one just yet as her call, out of the blue, might alarm his mother. 'Not,' he said, 'that I would expect anything truly to shock her. She's ninety and has probably seen more of life than most of us.'

Corinna got through easily, not to Lord Carr but to his secretary, who seemed well versed in his comings and goings. He was in Singapore, she told Corinna, but would be back by the weekend and expecting her at Stadhampton on Friday night, if she could come. She would be met at the station.

And so, as the late-afternoon train to Birmingham pulled out of Oxford station, Corinna sat back, comfortable in the knowledge that her fate for the next few days was in other hands than her own. She would be met; she would be taken care of. It was a nice feeling.

She bent her head over a volume of Rawls but ended up staring at the same page for half an hour. Across the aisle, a gang of teenagers in leather were spilling beer on their table and emitting snorts of laughter.

England was such a strange place. Some of the people here made her feel positively misanthropic, and this was new to her. For until now she had always believed what they taught in high-school history class – that all men, all people, were created equal. . . .

Not here. While she despised discrimination in principle, she was beginning to see that it had its purposes. People who grew up in England could label anyone they met in a matter of seconds: place of origin, attitude, class, likely politics. It helped them to mark out their potential allies.

How else had she and her father zeroed in on each other so quickly?

They had understood each other, read each other's subtle signs. They were alike, really, different nationalities or not. Tyrconnel's world was the one she belonged to. It was one she could easily recognise as exclusive, in effect a series of first-class compartments: Belgravia, the Ritz, a chauffeured car, a private plane. She could see, now, why he stayed in that world, where he belonged. If she ever got the chance, she would do the same.

When the train pulled into Stadhampton Station, Corinna had to scan the empty platform for several seconds before she spotted an old man in uniform waiting at the far end, where the first-class carriage would have dropped her off.

It seemed to prove the rightness of what she had been thinking.

The chauffeur, recognising her, loaded her overnight bag into the boot of the Rolls-Royce in the car park and drove her, without comment at first, through the nondescript outskirts of the town of Stadhampton: ring roads leading to roundabouts among a mass of nearly identical yellow brick sixties housing.

'Don't have to go through the centre,' he said suddenly. 'Thank heavens for that. Traffic's terrible on a Friday.'

'I know,' said Corinna. 'Like Oxford.' She peered out again. 'Is it far?' She had no idea what to expect. For all she knew, Stadhampton House might be right in the middle of all this.

'Oh, 'bout fifteen minutes.' The chauffeur lapsed into silence.

When they emerged into country, it took Corinna by surprise. The land was flat: winter-brown fields edged by a dark smudge of trees, the division between earth and sky barely visible in the twilight.

'Pity we can't take the ring road,' said the chauffeur. 'Goes straight past the house, it does now, but there's no exit here. So this here's the back way, the B4133.'

'Oh.' Corinna wondered what she was supposed to make of all that.

The Rolls's tyres crackled on gravel as it turned in sharply between a pair of golden stone pillars.

'Not the same as it used to be,' said the chauffeur. 'Quiet, now it's only my lord and the Lady Imogen staying.'

'Mmm,' said Corinna. 'I see.' She had thought servants talked that way only in *Masterpiece Theatre* costume dramas. Now she knew that they did in real life, too. It made her feel honoured: important by association.

The car drove up a gentle slope and through some trees, and then the house rose into sight. With its pillars, its glittery tall windows and its dome, it looked forbidding, almost defiant in the waning winter light. As if its day was waning, too: as if it knew it was nearly done.

Corinna felt almost sad for the house – maybe, like the chauffeur, it regretted its emptiness – until she reminded herself houses didn't have feelings. In fact, buildings were something she rarely paid attention to. It was odd that this one should have roused in her such a sudden stab of emotion.

At the bottom of the drive that formed a loop at the foot of the front steps were two discreet, green signs: 'Coach Parties' and 'Car Park', each accompanied by arrows. Neither coaches nor cars seemed to be visiting the house today.

The chauffeur braked and hopped out to take her bag. She felt odd, ascending the steps; she wanted time to take it all in, the whole façade of the place, her father's. So many windows, so many possible rooms. And yet there seemed to be no vantage point, except from way back in the drive, from which she could see it all. She looked down at the navy coat and checked miniskirt she was wearing: suddenly they seemed far too subdued for the occasion. This was the sort of house one ought to enter either in a ballgown, or in jeans. She had miscalculated.

Her father ambled down the front steps. 'Corinna! Glad you could make it.' He pulled her close for a kiss; he smelt of some rare orange liqueur. 'Shepley, you can take that up to the Rose Room.'

'Yes, my lord.'

'I thought,' said Tyrconnel, with a glint of amusement in his eyes, 'that you might like to have the bedroom where your mother used to sleep. It's been done up since then, of course.'

The tall front doors led into a cavernous yet surprisingly bright hallway. Looking up, Corinna could see that tiny windows and a skylight in the dome admitted what seemed like hundreds of slivers of light.

'I'd take you upstairs first,' said Tyrconnel, leading her past the foot of the stairs, 'but Mother's so eager to meet you. She doesn't have much to entertain her these days. She's hardly stopped talking about your visit.'

This would have daunted Corinna had she had time to think about it, but when she entered the grandly proportioned, yet warm and cosy library, her eyes lit immediately upon an old woman in a wheelchair. This must be her grandmother.

'Ty?' A frail voice rose, and a hand.

'Yes, Mother. She's here.'

'Corinna?' The voice seemed at once to have lost its frailty. Something buzzed, and the chair, evidently motorised, approached them. The old woman's hair was sleek and quite white: a contrast with the round, dark, acute eyes which fixed on Corinna now.

The old woman extended a hand; her left, the same one she had used to buzz the chair forward. 'Forgive me if I don't get up,' she said with a wry, one-sided smile. 'I can't. Can't do much of anything these days.'

'I'm sorry.' Corinna shook the offered hand, which was cool and bony.

'Don't be sorry. Happens to us all.' The old woman was brusque, obviously making the effort to enunciate despite the immobility of the right half of her face. 'Stroke, last summer. Paralysed me, all down the right side. Physios thought I'd never get out of bed again.' She gave a smile which had a hint of intriguing menace in it; or perhaps, Corinna thought, just mischief. 'You look like your mother.'

'Do I?'

'I would have said she looked more like me,' called Tyrconnel from over by the fireplace, where he was pouring drinks. 'What are you having, Mother?'

'Whisky,' said Imogen.

'You're not allowed it.'

With a sudden look of determination on her face, Imogen jabbed at the buttons on the arm of her chair, wheeling round to charge at her son. 'I haven't reached the age of ninety,' she said, 'just to take orders from *you*, thank you.' She reached out with a shaky hand towards a bottle of Glenlivet. 'I think,' she called back towards Corinna, 'a woman has a perfect right to die of drink at my age, don't you? Tell your father.'

Corinna laughed. 'I'm not getting caught up in that,' she said. 'I'm too new here.'

Eventually Tyrconnel, as she rather expected, conceded.

Her grandmother, she had time to note, *knew*, then. She had called Tyrconnel 'your father'. Discovering new relations seemed not to faze her.

She was, Corinna had had time to observe, a remarkably stylish old lady. No support tights or sensible shoes for her. That looked like a Chanel she was wearing: a purple, square-shouldered jacket and black skirt, matching her low pumps and jet clip earrings. It fitted, Corinna noted, rather loosely, though she must be all of a size eight. Like most thin women, she had aged not in the body but in the face; her cheeks, when she talked, were a mass of shifting fine lines. And yet her skin was white and unblemished and, on the whole, tighter than any ninety-year-old had a right to expect; her knotted, arthritic hands showed her age rather more.

If Corinna had examined her grandmother surreptitiously, her grandmother was forthright in examining her.

'Here, come into the light,' she said. 'I can't see your face. You're so tall. How tall are you?'

'Five foot ten and a half,' said Corinna, a little abashed, though usually she found her height useful: she could see over crowds.

'Just like your mother,' Imogen clucked. '*She* used to slouch, though. I'm glad you stand up straight.' With her good hand Imogen lifted her whisky for a sip. 'So,' she said, 'I suppose it's all rather a shock to you.'

Tyrconnel, notably silent, had settled in one of the easy-looking velvet chairs in front of the fire; Corinna perched on the matching sofa. The whole room, despite its tall shelves of leatherbound books and cabinets of what looked like rare and exquisite china, had a homelier air than she had expected. The seats of the chairs sagged slightly; a large television sat, incongruous but prominent, in the corner. A whole occasional table seemed to be devoted to Imogen's medicines.

'I suppose,' said Tyrconnel, 'you've had time to get used to it, haven't you, Corinna?' He tossed back the strand of sandy-grey hair that had flopped in his eyes. 'After all, that's the essence of success in the world today. Adaptability to change.'

'Oh, don't give us that business-school rubbish,' Imogen snorted. 'You sound like a company prospectus.'

'I'm getting used to it,' Corinna interposed. 'In fact, I always wished I had a bigger family. So I'm glad, now, to find out that I do.'

'I don't think,' said Imogen, 'that you'd have much in common with your cousins.'

'Why? How many are there?'

'Three,' answered Tyrconnel disdainfully. 'Dropouts, every one.'

'Jamie's girls aren't academically minded,' said Imogen more diplomatically.

'Now it's your turn to talk rubbish,' said Tyrconnel to his mother. ' "Academically minded." There's not an A level amongst them. But never mind that.' He turned to Corinna. 'We want to find out about *you*.'

Normally that announcement would have unnerved Corinna; put her on exam-day, college-interview guard. But the warmth of the room, the unexpectedly friendly reception she had had from her grandmother, and perhaps the large gin and tonic Tyrconnel had poured her, all served to put her at her ease. She found herself answering their questions – Harvard, Oxford, the Rhodes scholarship – with, even for her, unaccustomed fluency.

They talked on easily about politics and the British economy, and it surprised her to see that it was already eight o'clock when Tyrconnel, checking his watch, said, 'Well, may I suggest we adjourn? Mother,' he informed Corinna, 'likes everyone to dress for dinner.'

He escorted Corinna up the main stairs to the first floor and down a corridor to the Rose Room. The house was enormously large, Corinna thought, but she would soon learn the lie of it: it was very symmetrical. What amazed her was the idea of Ty and Imogen living here all alone. In fact, Imogen must stay here by herself a great deal of the time, if Ty's last week's travelling schedule was at all typical.

She was relieved that in the middle of their conversation her father and grandmother had suggested together, spontaneously, that she call them by their first names. ' "Father" and "Grandmother" are so much to get used to at once,' Imogen had said, 'and so formal.' Tyrconnel had agreed. All the close family called him Ty, he said, so why shouldn't Corinna?

Corinna had accepted happily, more at ease now that she didn't have to force them into a compartment into which they didn't really fit. For most of the evening she had felt more as if she were visiting old family friends than actual blood relations; now she could continue to think that way.

She changed into a crêpe blouse and grey flannel skirt – one of many outfits her mother said were 'too old' for her.

But then they often disagreed about clothes, avid shoppers that they both were. She wondered, looking around the room, with its dusty rose damask walls and half-tester bed with what looked like brand new rose hangings, whether her mother could ever have felt this room really belonged to her. It seemed to Corinna, despite its obvious renovation, to belong more to the eighteenth century, to some long-vanished inhabitants, than it could to any current occupant. No matter how many knick-knacks and photos you imposed on it, this room would overwhelm them.

Perhaps that was how it felt to live in a house like this: however long you stayed, you were never more than a tenant.

Perhaps her mother had felt that way. Not that she cared desperately about furniture; in Brooklyn she had lived with a mishmash of things, and, out in Greenwich, went along with what a decorator chose. But still, for everything to reek of the past this way. . . .

Perhaps it had got to her.

Perhaps that was the beginning of an explanation.

Imogen, to Corinna's amazement, had dressed for dinner too: or been dressed, by unseen hands. Her purple jacket had been changed for a bright deep-red silk blouse which echoed the shade of the rubies in her ears. She extended a hand to Corinna and smiled up engagingly. 'My dear,' she said, 'come and give me a kiss. You look wonderful.'

'So do you,' said Corinna. And, even discounting the fact that her grandmother was ninety and half-paralysed, she realised that she was not lying in the least.

They ate in the informal dining room which lay across from the library on the ground floor; Corinna was beginning to gather that her grandmother, in her wheelchair, did not go upstairs, though in this house that seemed hardly limiting. The small dining room's sea-green walls and ceiling were sculpted, in the Adam style, around Wedgwood medallions; the round walnut table laid for three in the centre of the room seemed far too small for the space surrounding it, though it allowed the servants – there seemed to be two, a man and a woman – to move around easily. Both halves of the double door were left open to allow Imogen to pass through.

'One advantage,' she said, 'of an old house. No trouble with a wheelchair.'

Corinna suppressed a laugh, and her grandmother, catching sight of her expression, smiled.

'We had to give up on the London house for Mother,' said Tyrconnel, passing a dish of Parmesan to accompany some delicious *capelletti* in cream and tomato sauce. 'In the end it was just too small.'

'So here I am. Marooned.' Imogen pulled a face, or half a face. 'You shall have to congratulate Niccolo, Ty. And you too, Corinna.' Her eyes sparkled at her granddaughter. 'I never thought we would be able to replace my old chef, Eduardo. Keeled over of a coronary at sixty-three. It still makes me sad to think of it.'

'But Niccolo's got the right touch, I think, Mother. Apart from a few infelicities. . . .'

There followed a conversation which astonished Corinna in its detail: Niccolo's *scallopine*, his risottos, his broths, his choice of cheeses. Tyrconnel seemed to be up on every fine point of Italian cuisine; his mother the same, though, eating left-handed, she barely finished half her *capelletti* before motioning the servants to take it away.

Corinna wondered what it was that surprised and almost amused her about the relations between Ty and Imogen. Was it the way they talked like an ancient husband and wife? The way they argued petty points, and at times seemed so wrapped up in each other that they forgot her presence?

Tyrconnel broke off the two-way conversation at last. 'Corinna,' he said, 'we're being unpardonably rude. Forgive us. What sort of food do you like?'

Corinna explained that the cooking at home had varied. Her mother's was basic American; her stepfather had loved Far Eastern food.

'Oh! Do tell us about your stepfather,' said Imogen.

It was natural, Corinna supposed, that they should be curious. Still, she felt on a tightrope answering their questions, precariously balanced between friendliness and disloyalty. For it did feel somehow disloyal, discussing Leonard with the Carrs. She was relieved when, once she had given a brief description of Leonard's career, Tyrconnel turned the conversation to other topics.

'Tell Mother,' he said, with a gleam of amusement in his eye, 'what you're studying at Oxford.'

'PPE,' said Corinna. 'Philosophy, politics and economics.'

'The same as Ty.' Imogen beamed.

'And Jamie,' Tyrconnel reminded her.

'Yes,' Imogen said, 'but don't let's spoil our dinner by talking too much about Jamie. So, tell me, Corinna, what about the ERM – in or out? I have to confess I'm torn.'

Once again, the sense that she was being interviewed returned to Corinna. Yet she felt that Imogen and Ty took more than a perfunctory interest in what she had to say. It was no wonder, perhaps, if they stayed alone in this place, starved of company. What a strange existence.

She, too, learnt a good deal that evening. So much that by the time she retired to bed she could not even begin to sort it all out in her mind. She learnt about the history of the house; about the extensive renovations the Carrs had carried out in the 1960s and 1970s, which, in return for state grants, had obliged them to let in visitors: although they did that only in summer, and then as little as they were allowed to get away with.

'I don't see,' Imogen had said, 'why we couldn't pay for it all ourselves and tell Heritage or whoever it is to bugger off with their grants and their *hoi polloi*. But Ty disagrees.'

'This house,' Tyrconnel explained, turning to Corinna, 'would be a bottomless pit, if it could, swallowing up all our money.'

Imogen snorted. 'We can afford it.'

'That's not the point. The grants exist – we ought to

take them up. If we don't, other people will. We pay enough in tax.'

'I never thought,' Imogen finished with a smile, 'the Carrs of Stadhampton would end up on benefit. But there you are.'

Even later, she had revealed to Corinna that she was dyslexic. 'Can't read. Never could,' she said. 'For fifty years I had no idea what was wrong with me. Then one day I saw this actress woman on television – talked about her trouble reading, letters jumping about. She said she had the worst time telling left from right. . . .' Imogen blinked, as if still struck by the surprise of recognition. 'I never knew it had a name. So that was that. I rang her up, and we started a committee. Raised money. There were articles in all the papers.'

'Mother's still honorary chairwoman,' Tyrconnel added proudly.

Imogen had sat on other committees, too. In fact it sounded to Corinna as if the two of them – in London, and out here, too – had led an incredibly busy life until Imogen's stroke. And led it, to a great extent, together.

That was odd, of course. A middle-aged man, and his mother. . . . Perhaps it was by default. After Holly left, when Ty hadn't married again. No more family, no children. It made Corinna feel momentarily sad for him.

Of course, there were other children: Jamie's. They hadn't talked about Jamie much – hardly at all. Even though, these days, he led the most interesting life of them all.

Curling up under the covers of her chilly rose-covered bed, Corinna made a mental note to ask them about Jamie in the morning.

However, as it turned out, the morning was already fully booked. Tyrconnel took her out for a ride – she had to borrow some old clothes and boots from the stables – and after that there were luncheon guests, a self-important old lady called Bullenden and a meeker, fortyish Lord Farnham, apparently the son of an old friend of Imogen's.

When the guests had gone, they had tea in the library, where Imogen had Tyrconnel search out the old *Sunday Times* colour supplement with a feature on Corinna's christening.

Only mildly curious at first, Corinna flipped through the pages: ads for Crimplene frocks, for cheese-boards, for sunny winter cruises whose prices were advertised in guineas and shillings. 14 February 1965. And then the headline, above a full page of pictures:

STADHAMPTON'S NEW GENERATION
Lord Carr opens his house to our photographer
on the day of his daughter's christening

Corinna did not speak. There was her mother at the centre of the main photograph: slim legs crossed, smiling shyly in a pink coat and hat, holding a baby.

That baby was her.

'She looks pretty, your mother, doesn't she?' said Imogen amiably. 'She was rather a wild dresser in those days, ordinarily. Though perhaps not at your christening.'

Corinna recognised Imogen in the photos without much trouble, even though her hair had changed completely from the jet-black it had been. She did not know many of the other people: only Tyrconnel, standing with a jaunty smile, one hand on Holly's shoulder, and another man whom she recognised instantly as a younger, longer-haired Jamie.

She flipped through the pages. Mom did look pretty, she thought, and so young. And somehow – afraid. It didn't seem to fit her.

Encouraged by Corinna's interest, Tyrconnel and Imogen got out their albums of photos, naming all the relatives in them: weddings, Christmases, christenings. Holly, still nearly a newlywed, peeped hopefully from the christening of Jamie's second daughter – but not that of his third.

'Why isn't my mother in this one?' Corinna asked. 'Was she away?'

Ty and Imogen exchanged glances.

II

It did not shock Corinna, so much as hurt her. The thought that her mother had never trusted her enough to tell her the basic truths about her early life: her marriage, her unhappiness. Her nervous breakdown.

That kind of thing happened to lots of people, Corinna thought, but it was typical of her mother that she should want to conceal it: to maintain an aura of impregnable perfection. Holly didn't like to confess to weaknesses. In the weeks after Leonard died, she had insisted, glassy-eyed, 'I'm all right, I'll be all right.' Eventually, that resolve had got her through.

But not, perhaps, when she was twenty years old.

A lot of it could be explained. She was young, she was homesick. Tyrconnel had admitted that perhaps he had been selfish to marry her so quickly, before she was used to the shock of a new country and separation from her parents. 'But,' he told Corinna with a sad smile, 'I was in love. In love one is ultimately selfish. One doesn't always think.'

The truth explained so much. Not, perhaps, the years that had elapsed between Holly's spell in hospital and her final decision to leave England – wanting, Corinna supposed, to put her weakness and the memory of it behind her. But it explained why she took so long to remarry. Tyrconnel and she had not even been divorced until 1968.

Holly had always said they divorced before she left

England. Another lie. The truth was that Ty had kept on hoping, waiting for her. Because he loved her.

'I have to concede,' said Imogen, tilting back her glass, 'I do believe you're right. I didn't, at first. When you told me you'd met her, I thought, "Dear Lord, he's getting his hopes up over nothing. She'll be just like Jamie's." '

Tyrconnel half smiled. 'Blood doesn't always tell. She seems to be the proof of it. Top marks all through school, the best colleges.'

'You're sure you don't want to leave it a little longer?'

Tyrconnel's jaws clenched. 'There may not be that much time.'

'Nonsense.' Imogen looked away. 'I won't listen to you being defeatist.'

'Mother, I'm a realist.'

Imogen's gaze returned to her son, softened slightly. 'Yes. I know. So am I.'

The next afternoon, Corinna and Tyrconnel stood on the south terrace, just outside the green and gilt resplendent chamber the Carrs called the summer ballroom. Though its moulded plaster ceiling and delicate paintwork had been restored, at great cost, to their original perfection, almost no one saw or used the room now, except for the tour guides and groups who paused there before passing through to the gardens.

Corinna leaned on the balustrade and gave an expansive sigh. 'You know, I wish I wasn't going! Oxford will seem so dingy, after this.'

'Well, you must come again.'

'Oh, any time.' Corinna grinned over, showing white teeth.

'I am glad we met,' said Tyrconnel soberly. 'Because there are many things we should talk about. In fact, we've barely begun.'

'Such as?' said Corinna brightly. She was convinced that all the difficult revelations were over; Tyrconnel had hinted at as much this morning, when he told her he was sure she would adjust to her new situation.

'You know,' Tyrconnel said, 'I have no heirs.'

Corinna's heart thumped. The golden stone of the balustrade, the dim green of the grass, the sky and expanse of land before her seemed for a second to take on a preternatural glow.

'It seems, therefore,' Tyrconnel went on, 'that the earls of Stadhampton will barely outlast the twentieth century. When I die my brother will succeed me, but of course he has no son.'

'I think it's totally unfair,' said Corinna. 'Why shouldn't a woman inherit from you?'

'Well, she can,' said Tyrconnel, 'as far as the property itself goes. And the company, TCI, which is what effectively supports all this.' He spread his hands to indicate his surroundings. 'Once upon a time – ' he gave a wry smile – 'a little allowance from the Queen would have done it. But our good socialist governments have taken care of that. I had to start a company to keep this place. Little did I know that it would grow into something far greater than Stadhampton itself.'

Corinna waited, caught up in fearful expectation. She was afraid even to admit her hopes to herself.

'So,' said Tyrconnel, a slow smile dawning on his lean face, 'while you cannot inherit any titles, Corinna – unfair as it is, I am afraid there is nothing I can do about that – you can possess Stadhampton. You can take my place. What I should like is to train you to be the next head of TCI.'

'But I don't know anything about business.' Corinna's heart was pounding fast.

'Neither did I, when I started. Neither do these absurd management consultants who go about telling companies how to hire and fire, on the balance of an Oxbridge degree! You can learn.'

'I've thought about going to business school,' Corinna admitted. 'I'd probably join an investment bank first – '

'Well.' Tyrconnel spread his hands. 'You can join me. I don't believe any of that rubbish about starting from the ground up. You'd start in the executive offices. Travel – get a feel for the various economies. We operate in thirty-one countries. You'd be making operational decisions by the end of the year.'

Corinna gulped. 'The end of – the year?'

'You'd have to leave Oxford, of course.'

'Couldn't I . . . wait, until I finish my degree?'

Tyrconnel twitched his head. 'I'm afraid not.'

'Why not?'

Tyrconnel's fingers clenched on the balustrade, his knuckles whitening. 'Because – time is short.'

'What do you mean?' Corinna searched his face. It was impassive.

'Only what I say. Time is short. I should give you a good deal of independence – it's the only way you'll learn. But all the same it will be years before you're ready to take over.'

'Well, if I finish at Oxford that would only be one more year.'

Tyrconnel shook his head. 'You don't need Oxford. Too much education ruins people's minds. Even a good one like yours.' He smiled. 'Think about it. Do you really need to spend another year slaving over books – taking exams? Exams are a very poor predictor of future success.'

Corinna wondered. She had always been quite good at them.

'And besides,' Tyrconnel continued, 'I have my other managers to consider. It so happens that there is a vacancy on the team now. In a year's time there would be rather less space for you if you did change your mind.'

That sounded to Corinna strangely like a threat: take it or leave it.

But then, warming again, leading her down from the terrace for a walk across the great lawn, Tyrconnel talked of benefits: a flat in Knightsbridge, the use of his private plane, a company car.

'You'd be making,' he said, 'rather more, I imagine, than any of your contemporaries. And of course, eventually the whole investment group would be yours. Mother's shares come back to me when she dies; when I die, it could all go to you. A controlling interest.'

Corinna frowned as they walked past the still, baroque fountain. 'But why?' she said. 'I mean, a month ago you didn't even know me. You must have had plans for what to do with the company then.'

'My current will,' said Tyrconnel neutrally, 'leaves everything to my brother and his daughters.'

'Couldn't they succeed you?'

Tyrconnel gave a sharp laugh. 'My brother's a politician. He has no experience of this kind of thing. And his daughters. . . .' He laughed again. 'Not a hope.'

'Why not?'

'They'd be useless. They're all horse-mad, just like their mother was. The eldest's married, the next one's a groom, the youngest runs a stud farm in Wales with her intellectually subnormal boyfriend.'

Corinna giggled at Tyrconnel's sudden vituperation.

'So.' He smiled and reached for her hand. His wrapped around it, smooth, large, warm – *fatherly*, Corinna suddenly thought – as they stood in the shadow of the fountain in the afternoon sun. 'You see,' Tyrconnel said, 'why I am quite serious when I say there is no one else. Even if any of my relations were capable – for a number of reasons I would not want to give them what I am offering you. I suppose when I was younger I never would have thought a woman could do the job.'

Corinna bristled slightly.

'But so much has changed in these years. Look at what your mother has done. I admire her a great deal, you know.'

'Me, too,' said Corinna in a small voice. For some reason she felt guilty discussing her mother with Tyrconnel.

'And she's done a splendid job of raising you. Perhaps better, after all, than I could have done. I was always so busy. I suppose it may be selfish of me, but, meeting you now, I want to claim you. I want to make up for all the years we lost, Corinna. I want to give you what I have.'

'But it's all by chance,' Corinna said in a small voice. 'If you hadn't found me, if you hadn't figured out who I was – '

'Then,' said Tyrconnel, still holding her hand, 'we must simply have been meant to find one another.'

Three weeks later, Corinna made what she thought had to be the hardest phone call of her life.

It was impossible that she should make it from college: standing in a queue for the pay phone, other people hearing.

So, having confided in a limited way in Justin, she made the call from his room, which had everything: telephone, refrigerator, bar. He had agreed to leave her alone for half an hour.

She punched the numbers for her mother's office, because she knew that, although it would only be nine o'clock in New York, her mother, who had worked ferociously hard ever since Leonard died, would probably be in.

She was right. Holly picked up on the second ring.

'Mom?' said Corinna baldly. 'I've got a few things to tell you.'

III

For several minutes after Corinna had rung off, Holly felt as if she were still talking to her, trying to reason with her. With sudden ferocity she picked up the receiver again, only to remember that she had no way of reaching Corinna directly.

She let out a long sigh and stood, fingertips poised on

her bookshelves, looking out her plate-glass window. A bright winter morning on Park Avenue.

Perhaps it had been bound to happen, ever since the day Corinna first set foot in England. It was such a small place. Holly had told herself her fears were silly, and yet she had been right all along. Tyrconnel and her daughter had met at last.

She barely heard the knock on the door, and then, when she turned, ready to greet whichever of her colleagues appeared, it turned out to be only the mailboy.

'Thanks.' She gave him a mechanical smile and shoved all her letters, even the ones marked 'Personal', into a pile for her secretary to deal with.

Well, she thought. There was nothing else to do. She would just have to go to England.

When she sat down again to buzz Gordon and tell him she would be taking a week or so off, the air felt cold against her forehead and palms. She was sweating all over.

Justin came back into his room just as Corinna was hanging up. He deposited a bottle of Pimms on his bar shelf and wiped two glasses.

'Thanks for the phone,' said Corinna. She knew she ought to go, but somehow felt too drained to move.

'How'd it go?'

'My call? Oh, fine. Like I said, thanks.' Leaning forward, Corinna made a distracted effort to gather her belongings into her handbag.

'Drink?' Justin offered.

'Oh. No thanks. Too early in the day for me.'

Justin gave a small frown of disappointment, or annoyance.

'So,' said Corinna, standing. 'I've got to go.'

'And you aren't even going to tell me what you're being so mysterious about.'

'Oh, nothing. Really. I just needed to call my mother in private. Let me know how much it costs and I'll pay you back.'

Justin swung round to the door before she could get there, arching one arm up against it.

'What's wrong?' Corinna's nose wrinkled in distaste. She didn't like having her way blocked.

'Don't you ever wonder,' said Justin, 'what exactly we're doing? You and I. Because I do.'

Corinna tossed her head, annoyed. 'Justin – '

He backed off, nodding at her to go on out.

'Justin, we're friends. Aren't we? Are you mad at me?'

He opened the door. 'You little tease.'

Corinna did not have time to think about Justin. She put him right out of her mind.

It disconcerted her, the way her mother had not been angry, but only asked her a few reasoned questions. *Do you know what you're doing?*

'I don't think,' she had also said, 'that Tyrconnel Carr is the kind of man to offer anyone a good deal unless there's even more in it for him. Is this really what you want?'

Corinna had exploded. Of course she knew what she wanted. She was twenty-four. She had heard her own voice growing louder and louder, and in the end she had put down the phone before her mother could.

Now, she supposed, she should call Tyrconnel, and tell him the answer was *yes*. But something stopped her.

Holly's Concorde flight to Heathrow landed just after 4 p.m., and already the sky was getting dark. She had forgotten the peculiar gloom of the winter nights here: the urge she used to feel to rush indoors to light and warmth before the darkness could overtake her.

As her cab drove her into London, it was raining, too.

'You here on holiday?' said the driver, and his cockney accent gave her a tremor. An unexpected thrill rushed through her suddenly, like the memory of good times. Afternoons, out on the road with Jamie.

Jamie. Of all the people in the world he was the last one she should think of now.

460

She answered the driver belatedly, 'No. Business.' It was her automatic answer and usually served to forestall conversation. And yet she found herself, instead, wanting to ask the driver questions. Had London changed? How much? She didn't remember this stretch of highway at all. *I haven't been here for twenty-four years*, she imagined herself telling the cabbie, but she suppressed that notion, too.

She had booked herself a suite at Brown's Hotel. Its cloistered, slightly gloomy atmosphere, she thought, would suit her mood. She was disappointed, when she checked in, to find the lobby lightened and polished. She noticed from a plaque on the wall that Brown's was now part of a chain. Her suite, with thick curtains and dark wallpaper, was reassuringly chilly. As she sat on her bed, thinking her way through the next few days and what they held, unconsciously she hugged her leather briefcase closer.

She had brought them with her, of course. Her files on TCI. She had let them lapse after Manangwe, but then, after Leonard died, she had set to work again, in a whole new way.

TCI operated in thirty-one countries. In twelve of those countries it ran what were, in effect, its own armies: to keep the peace; to discipline workers in outlying regions; to sustain shaky governments. In seven more countries the company channelled funds direct to military dictators. In nineteen countries it enforced illegal labour contracts; in eighteen, its unlawful disposal of effluents had poisoned whole tracts of land and their inhabitants.

She had spoken to witnesses – ex-employees, doctors, victims of torture. She needed more, of course, just as she needed to travel to all the countries involved to see conditions for herself. She had been too busy, in the last few years, with other cases; but now she would set her mind to this one, and win Abe and Gordon round to letting her give it first priority.

After all, collectively, the lawsuits would exact the biggest damages from a multinational in history. If she won,

461

she could destroy TCI. Even then, it would take years for countries to undo the damage it had done.

She was willing to compromise. If Tyrconnel backed down, so would she. TCI could reform itself. It would be costly. It would make the group a less inviting prospect for investors, for its own employees – for Corinna.

If Corinna, she thought, still wanted to work with Tyrconnel after everything she was about to learn, then she must be greedier than Holly had ever guessed.

The next morning, she took the train out to Oxford. As her cab from the station dropped her outside the front gate of Corinna's college – the tower above, if she remembered correctly, had some association with T. S. Eliot – Holly reflected to herself that, yes, this was the sort of place Corinna would choose: large, assuming, parading its history. Corinna had always pursued the cachet of labels, from Harvard and Oxford right down to the tags on her scarves and sweaters. Holly remembered some of their trips to New York museums together, when she was younger. Corinna had always glanced at the name on the plaque, before looking at the painting.

At the porter's lodge she asked directions to Corinna's room, and was pointed across the broad front quad to a smaller one, where, at the top of Corinna's staircase, she knocked. No one was in.

She settled down at the top of the stairs for a long wait.

'*Mom!*'

Corinna stared up from the landing below.

Holly stood. Her knees felt creaky and stiff. 'I didn't think it was any use trying to talk to you any more on the phone. So I came.'

Corinna walked past her mother, at the head of the stairs, with a wary look. No hug. She got out her keys. Her skin looked pale, Holly thought. Perhaps the effect of the English weather. Her eyes looked greener, too.

A few minutes later, Corinna handed her mother a mug of nearly black tea. 'You look tired.'

Holly perched on the arm of a chair. 'I've had a lot to think about. I've been worried about you.'

Corinna tossed back her head, or flinched: Holly wasn't sure which. 'About me! That's silly. I'm fine, Mom. Do you want a biscuit? These are kind of old. . . .'

'No, thanks.'

Corinna drummed her fingers on her cup. Suddenly, before Holly could speak, she burst out, 'You know, you're wasting your time if you think by flying over here you're going to change my mind.'

'So.' Holly put down her cup. 'You think you know everything there is to know about Tyrconnel Carr. You trust him.'

Corinna's eyes narrowed. 'Shouldn't I? He *is* my father.'

Holly let that pass.

'Besides, we get along really well. He's a nice man. I like him.' Corinna waited for the words to sink in. 'In fact, the one thing I just can't understand is why you never let me know about him. Why you always lied to me and told me he was dead.'

'It seemed the best thing to do at the time. Since I knew you weren't going to see him again.'

'Why? Why shouldn't I have seen him again?'

'Because he was across the ocean! Because of the arrangements – '

'Ty says there weren't any arrangements. He says you just ran away and for all these years he had no idea where I was.'

Holly felt her heart pounding and knew she had to regain her calm, or an appearance of it. She forced herself to sip her tea before she spoke. 'Frankly, Corinna, whatever he says now, I don't think he cared where you were.'

'How do I know that? How do I know you're not just lying again? Because it suits you – '

'I lied to protect you. All right. Maybe I was wrong. . . .'

'And you lied about other things. Or didn't tell me.'

Corinna looked away from her mother, towards the low, gabled window. 'Like the way you had a breakdown before I was born. You were in a mental hospital.'

'No –' The verbal reaction came before Holly could stop it. 'All right, yes. I was.' She stood and tried to approach Corinna; the room was so small that she felt absurdly caged – both of them, with their outsized emotions. We should be outdoors, thought Holly irrelevantly. Like duellists. 'I was in –' she began with difficulty, 'that kind of hospital, for – a long time. But it was a mistake. Tyrconnel and his family were able to put me there because they had connections. Because I'd threatened to leave Tyrconnel and because they wanted me out of the way. And while I was in that hospital. . . . This is what you need to know, Corinna, most of all. They killed my father.'

Corinna's head snapped round. 'That's ridiculous.'

'It may sound ridiculous, but it's true.' Holly paused. 'The Carrs have killed people. They are capable of doing it. There may not be many people in the world these days whom one could call truly evil. But they are.'

Corinna was smiling. 'Uh-huh, sure, Mom.'

'Look at me that way if you like. But I'll tell you. . . . Do you remember the time I flew down to the Keys? Your father – Leonard – was due down to join me.'

For a second the smile vanished from Corinna's face. *The crash*, thought Holly. *She remembers*. And now, reassured by Corinna's listening attitude, she began to talk.

A few minutes later she stopped. Corinna, she realised, was simply staring at her, mute, a tolerant half-smile stiffening her lips.

'That's what the Carrs did,' finished Holly.

'Uh-huh.'

'I didn't think I'd tell you at first. But perhaps it's best that you should know.' She decided on one more twist of the knife. 'Since, after all, you never did get to meet your grandfather. Now you know why.'

'Uh-huh.'

Holly realised then that something had gone wrong. The truth had failed to take. 'Don't you believe me?'

Corinna squirmed and looked away. 'Well, if you want to know – no. Not really.'

'There's proof. I never followed up the case because – well, you know perfectly well. Leonard was gone. I had other things on my mind. And my witness had disappeared. I'm quite aware it may be impossible to prove that Tyrconnel and Imogen are murderers. In that one instance.'

'Why stop at Tyrconnel and Imogen, Mom? Why not Jamie? Why not Jamie's kids? Why not throw all of them in? A whole family of gangsters! The Corleones of Stadhampton.' Corinna grinned.

'Don't you dare make jokes, Corinna. This is serious.'

'Well, there's one slight problem, Mom.' Corinna paused. 'I just don't see how you'd know anything much about how my grandfather died. As you said yourself, you were . . . *away* when it happened.'

'And I only found out the truth afterwards. As I told you.'

'Mom.' Corinna stepped forward. 'I don't want to be mean. But people make things up sometimes. It happens to all kinds of people. Mental illness is very common. I was reading in the paper just the other day – '

'I am telling you the truth!' The words exploded from Holly's mouth. 'Don't you dare tell me that I don't know what I'm saying. Because I do. Far more than you can ever be aware of. I'm trying to help you, Corinna. I'm trying to warn you – if you decide to trust Tyrconnel Carr, you will be getting involved with a dangerous man. Not only the man, but his company. I don't intend to let either of them go on as they're doing. In fact – ' Holly backed towards the door – 'I intend to meet Tyrconnel quite soon to discuss a lawsuit which will probably do so much damage to his company that he'll be forced to forget about hiring you, or anyone else, for quite some time.'

Corinna only blinked. 'Come on, Mom. Lawsuits come

and go. You think some rinky-dink case is going to hurt us?'

Us. Holly heard the word, and it hurt. She grasped the doorframe as she stepped out on to the slippery landing. 'Believe me,' she said, 'this one will.'

'Well, I'd work for Ty anyway.' There was a taunting note in Corinna's voice. 'Whether or not he paid me. That doesn't really matter, does it? Since I'm going to inherit everything from him one day. I'm his only child.'

Something in Holly's face froze as Corinna spoke again, and kept her from speaking the last few words in her mind. *He's not your father.*

'Thanks for coming by, Mom. You know, I think you've helped me make up my mind. Ty said I could start at his offices next month. I think I'll just give him a ring now and tell him I will.'

Holly turned her back on her daughter.

On the train back to London, she wondered why she had failed. The conclusion was inescapable.

As the train moved among the anonymous towers of Reading and out again, towards Paddington, she stared through the muddy, shatterproof glass. For a moment, instead of seeing the rows of houses beyond, she saw the men in white coats and the nurses, inspecting her.

The window of her room in Norfolk. Unbreakable glass. She had tried to break it, and then they sedated her so that she could not move.

She remembered them coming in, prodding her, studying her, as if she were an inert lifeless lump; then injecting her again despite the scream that lay unformed in her throat. The urge to fight – succeeded, finally, by a deeper understanding that whatever truth she tried to tell them they would think a fantastical lie.

The powerlessness.

It was funny, she thought, how at the end of it all, facing Corinna, she had felt powerless all over again.

*

She went back to Brown's and sorted through her papers again – and her thoughts. She would call a meeting: herself and Tyrconnel. There she would lay it on the line: her class-action suits, her evidence. Corinna could go ahead and join TCI. Within a year or two there would be nothing left of it to belong to.

Or Tyrconnel could back off on all fronts. Reform TCI. Let go of Corinna.

She could not force Corinna never to work for him, but she could at least insist that he allow her the time to wait. To judge for herself.

How Corinna might eventually decide in that case, she had no way of knowing. She was a Carr, after all. Sometimes the resemblance unnerved Holly. Especially today, as she stood, her skin paler, in the light: the clean bones of her face, the long, arched nose, the cleft chin.

She did not look like Jamie, so much, or her mother. She looked like Tyrconnel.

'I think,' said Helen English as she twirled her *linguini* around an oversized fork at her favourite new-wave Italian restaurant in Soho, 'you're making far too big a drama out of it all. A sensible girl like you.' She shot Holly a mocking look through brown eyes no longer suited to strong, spidery black eyeliner – though she still wore it, along with pale powder and lipstick.

Holly heaved a sigh. 'I'm just relieved to have someone to talk to. After two days like this – I thought I was going crazy.'

'Look.' Helen nibbled at a black olive from her sauce. 'Maybe she was bound to find out about her father. I mean – ' she waved a hand at the gaffe – 'about the Carrs, at least. It's only natural. They are a part of her past.'

'You sound just like Corinna now.'

'Well, she's a sensible girl, too. Look – she's probably had her head turned, that's all.' Helen thrust a nervous hand through her ash-blonde hair, and an earring rattled.

'Maybe having it out with all of them's the best thing you can do.'

'I know. But I'm dreading it.'

'Well, what did you expect? Vengeance in the abstract?' Helen laughed. 'I can tell you it's never so good as the real thing. Do you know what made last year for me? Running into Nige and his new wife Mona in the middle of Heathrow, having a blazing row. The kiddies were screaming and she'd put on at least three stone.'

Holly laughed, and then, for no reason, felt a tear trickle down from each eye. She wiped them as best she could with her napkin. 'Oh, dear,' she said. 'I don't know what's wrong with me. Stress, I guess.' She laughed again, helplessly. 'I feel as if ever since I got here I've been putting on this act – the invincible woman, telling it straight to everybody, to Corinna. . . .' She shook her head. 'I'm just afraid that once I see Tyrconnel again, I'll lose it.'

'No, you won't.' Helen was firm. 'You'll handle him. I know you will. When are you two meeting?'

Holly paced around the sitting room of her suite, as nervous as if she had never conducted a meeting like this before. Well, in a sense she never had. Not with her own ex-husband.

She knew she would have to fight to keep her distance. Already, on the phone, Tyrconnel had turned on the charm.

'Holly!' He managed to inject varying shades of warmth into the mere pronunciation of her name. 'You astound me. After all these years. Are you back in London?'

'Yes.' Holly decided to be sparing with her words. 'I need to see you.'

'Well, this *will* be interesting.' For a second, Holly expected him to mention Manangwe: their contest over the mines six years ago. But he did not. 'Would you like to come to my office?' he said. 'No, I'll tell you what – come to Chester Square, for a drink. Around seven?'

'No.' Holly knew she had to hold her ground. 'I'd like you to come to me. If you don't mind. I'm at Brown's.'

'All right.' Tyrconnel grew more distant. Just before he signed off, his voice had warmed again. 'You know you have a lovely daughter. Or should I say *we* do? It's been a pleasure to meet her after all these years.'

'No – ' Holly's voice was hard – 'I wouldn't use the word *we*, if I were you, and in fact Corinna is the reason I want to talk to you.'

She wondered now if she had made a mistake giving away the game; especially since a few hours later Corinna herself had rung her.

'Look, Mom.' Holly could hear the familiar hubbub of students' voices in the corridor behind the pay phone. 'What's this about you getting together with Ty to discuss *me*? Don't you think I have any say in what goes on here? I don't exactly like being discussed behind my back.'

'We're not discussing you,' Holly had answered, knowing she was on thin ground. 'We're discussing Tyrconnel's company. Legal matters.'

'Oh, yeah, right, like this is nothing to do with me. Like your coming over here was just out of the blue – nothing to do with Ty offering me a job – '

'Believe it or not, Corinna, yes.' Holly was rapidly losing patience. 'This whole thing does not *entirely* revolve around you.'

'Well, if Ty's coming to see you, so am I.'

'Fair enough.'

So now she had both of them coming. *Two against one.* She didn't like to think of it that way, but she couldn't help it. If they were both on the same side – as it seemed inevitable now that they would be – then she would just have to face up to both of them.

With a sudden, sharp pang, she wished Leonard could be with her.

Someone knocked. She rushed to answer the door, then slowed her steps. She composed her face, smiled.

'Hello, Tyrconnel.' She extended a hand. 'Corinna.' She did not know what to do with her daughter – kiss her?

469

Shake her hand as well? And so she backed away to let them both in, without doing either. She felt momentarily daunted by their mutual height, their shared, lionish features. Only now, as she made a show of pouring drinks, did she risk a surreptitious study of Tyrconnel's face. It had aged disconcertingly little. She wondered for a moment if he had had plastic surgery; it had occurred to her before that Imogen had probably done so. And his hair had, surely, a touch of the artist about it: carefully blended shades of gold and charcoal and white.

Irrelevant, all that, really. But she couldn't help noticing his good condition; envying it a little, as she moved towards him with a glass in her hand. She had gone out this afternoon and bought a bottle of malt, to avoid the indignity of pouring tiny drinks from the mini-bar; Tyrconnel, similarly, had chosen a straight-backed chair with an eye to stature rather than comfort. Corinna, less experienced, was leaning forward in an easy chair, struggling not to fidget.

Petty manoeuvres, Holly thought. And yet every move counted. This was psychological warfare.

She sat down on the edge of another straight chair. 'I think,' she said, 'you may both be under some misapprehension about the future worth of the company that you – ' she nodded at Tyrconnel – 'own, and that you – ' she looked at Corinna – 'are considering joining.'

'Oh, no, I doubt that.' Tyrconnel looked amused; then he waited.

There was no drawing him on; she should have known that. 'You won't have been aware of it, of course,' she said, 'but there are a large number of class actions in preparation against TCI, on behalf of its employees in twelve of its operating countries.'

'That's utter tosh.' Tyrconnel gave her an irritated glance. 'People try that kind of rubbish on us all the time. It gets thrown out of court.'

'Not this time.'

'I suppose you've got documents – witnesses.' Tyrconnel's mouth twisted into a sneer. 'That is, assuming that you're the agitating party behind this so-called suit. Well, I might as well warn you, Holly, these Third World monkeys who are so eager to complain when they think there might be a few dollars in it will start lying through their teeth when – '

'Wait a minute.' Corinna's glance crossed them both. 'What are you talking about?'

'Your mother's making threats – ' Tyrconnel began, dismissive.

'I am trying to explain to you,' Holly began at the same time, but continued, 'exactly the sort of operation you are proposing joining. A company which rapes poor countries of their natural resources, which employs its labour under conditions we in the West would never tolerate – '

'Good Lord, Holly.' Tyrconnel snorted. 'We've certainly heard this one before. We're hardly talking about Palm Beach, are we, or Bognor Regis. These are countries in which the average wage, the average standard of living – '

'And I'm not talking about just wages, Tyrconnel. If the wages your companies paid were merely inadequate, I'll admit, I wouldn't have a case – '

'Hold on!' Corinna's shout pierced the air. 'What is this all about, here? Does somebody want to tell me? I came along here thinking this was supposed to be about *me*, and – '

'Of course it's about you,' Tyrconnel said. 'Your mother's only making threats.'

'Then doesn't she think I should have a say – ' Corinna's voice had become high and whiny.

'This isn't just about you,' said Holly, in a deliberately low voice. 'Yes. I admit it is, in part. But even if I'd never known Tyrconnel – never met him before – I wouldn't want you to have anything to do with his filthy operations. And if you decide that *his* company and his family are what you want to be part of, I would have no hesitation in blowing them both to kingdom come.'

'Is that a threat?' Tyrconnel smiled. He glanced towards

471

the door. In the moment's silence that ensued they all heard a distinct knocking.

'Come in,' said Holly, annoyed that the hotel staff had to decide to disturb her now.

Jamie walked in.

'Hello,' he said, with a glance at his brother. And then he walked towards Holly – his old, sauntering step, she would have recognised it anywhere – and stretched out both his arms. 'Holly.'

He reached for a kiss, and she could only stand and accept it.

'Hello, Jamie,' she said in a small voice, trying to recover from the shock.

'Don't let me stop things,' said Jamie agreeably, backing off. 'I've only dropped by for a minute. I'm on my way out to dinner. Tyrconnel told me you were in town.' He glanced down and seemed to notice Corinna for the first time. 'Say.' He addressed her. 'Have we met before?'

'I don't know,' said Holly, taking a deep breath. Suddenly everything became clear and easy. 'Well. If you haven't met, I suppose someone ought to introduce you. Jamie, this is Corinna. Corinna, meet Jamie. Your father.'

IV

For a moment, after she had finished, everyone seemed to talk at once. Except Holly. She picked up her room key and waited by the door.

'Well,' she said, 'I'm sure you all have a lot to say to each other, but I'm afraid that, like you, Jamie, I have a dinner appointment. So if you don't mind I'll just leave you here. The door will lock behind you when you go.' She turned and, for a moment, heard raised voices. Then the door clicked neatly shut behind her.

Of course she had no plans for dinner. She had nowhere

else to go at all, except away from the hotel. So she started walking, as fast as she could in her high heels, down Dover Street.

She did not dare think of Jamie. Not yet. His entrance had disconcerted her more than she liked to admit. Planned by Tyrconnel, no doubt. It was a clever trick, and so easy: she should have thought of it herself. How better to embarrass his ex-wife than to haul in her one-time lover on the pretext of a social visit? She could imagine Tyrconnel on the phone to Jamie, dropping a casual invitation. Jamie wandering along to Brown's for an unexpected reunion. Without a clue. . . .

Tyrconnel hadn't needed to bargain on Holly's own shock. He could be sure of that. But what he wouldn't guess – what she had concealed, she hoped, from all of them – was the way her knees had turned to liquid when Jamie's cheek brushed hers. Just for a second. The effect, she supposed, of the unexpected touch of his skin, his scent. She got the better of it quickly.

She was still trying to get the better of it now.

She heard steps behind her, and, not looking back to see if someone was following her, quickened her own pace.

'Holly!'

At the sound of the voice, she turned.

'For Christ's sake, Holly. You turn up after twenty-five years and then run off like that? No.' Jamie looked pink in the face, disarrayed. 'I'm not going to let you do that.'

Holly couldn't help smiling. 'I thought it was worth a try. A quick escape.'

'You don't have any dinner appointment,' he said accusingly.

'No. But I seem to remember you do.'

'Yes.' He smiled. 'As of right now. With you.'

'Well, all I know – ' Corinna's voice rose – 'is, it's pretty dishonest. Stringing me along, offering me goodies as if I were a child – '

'Well, stop acting like a child and maybe people will

473

stop treating you like one.' Looking harassed, Tyrconnel paced over to the cabinet and poured himself another whisky. 'How did I know your mother was going to drop a bombshell like that? We've lived with the polite fiction for twenty-four years. Hell, Corinna.' He turned to face her. 'I *think* of you as my daughter. Try thinking that way about someone for twenty-four years and see if you don't get pretty damned used to it.'

'Oh, well, that's great,' said Corinna sarcastically. 'You think of me as your daughter. There only happens to be this minor little complication. . . .'

'Well, at least you've hit on the right word there. It is more complicated than you think.'

'That's what everyone's been telling me for about the last week. What I want to know is why you've all been telling me a pack of lies.'

Tyrconnel stood back then for a moment, and thought. About changing times: different generations, different mores.

'All right,' he said, relaxing a little, coming to sit down on the sofa opposite Corinna. 'I'll tell you the whole truth. But it will take a while. And you'll have to try to understand.'

Corinna supposed it made sense. It fitted in with the other bits and pieces of Ty's character that had never seemed to mesh before. His failure to remarry, despite his obvious attractiveness; his fierce attachment to his mother; the odd loneliness that seemed to face him as he approached old age.

'You don't mind?' he said now, questioning. A long strand of hair had flopped down over his left eye, and he brushed it back with long thin fingers.

'No.' Corinna answered in a small voice. 'I don't mind. Lots of my friends are gay. You could have told me before.'

'Still.' Tyrconnel shrugged. 'When a man introduces himself as your father – '

'Well, maybe you're right. Maybe you *are* my father in

474

a sense. I mean, when I met you, I thought we were alike. That something . . . ran between us. You, and the business, and all the things I've wanted to do.' Corinna spoke with growing conviction.

'Perhaps.' Tyrconnel gave a helpless, appealing smile. 'I suppose I felt it too. I *wanted* you to be mine.'

'Then that's OK.' Corinna smiled. 'We'll still be friends.'

'I'm a rotter, you know.' Tyrconnel rested his chin on his intertwined fingers, looking over at her. 'I've done a lot of rotten things. Including, I suppose, to your mother. In the effort of concealment. It becomes second nature.'

'But you don't need to conceal anything now.'

Tyrconnel shrugged. 'I'm hardly going to come "out of the closet" at this late stage.'

Corinna gave an understanding smile.

'You know, all those things I proposed to you – the house, the business – that still stands.'

'Thanks,' said Corinna. For a moment the thought of Jamie's daughters, her cousins – her sisters? – wafted through her head, bringing a flicker of guilty conscience.

She suppressed it.

Holly and Jamie sat on either side of a smooth, white-clothed table, in a restaurant whose plushy, expensive silence reminded her oddly of Vignola's, long ago. She kept wanting to reach out to touch Jamie across that expanse of white; to reassure him that she was still there. To reassure herself that he was real.

'I *knew* I'd seen Corinna before,' said Jamie. 'Now it comes back to me. When I went to speak at the Oxford Union, she stood up and asked the first question.'

'That sounds like her.'

'She was impressive. I wondered if she was from one of the television stations at first. Very cool. Very organised.' Jamie sipped his wine. The restaurant's service was leisurely, but they were in no hurry to eat.

'And your daughters,' said Holly. 'What are they doing now?'

He filled her in.

'It sounds like they've all got Daphne's horsy interests,' said Holly politely. Then she remembered. Daphne hadn't even crossed her mind until now. 'How is Daphne, by the way? I mean, are you still – '

'Daphne's dead.'

Jamie spoke the words straightforwardly, but not coldly.

'Oh. I'm sorry.' Holly swallowed hard. *What had happened? Daphne was still young. . . .* 'I know,' she said, 'what it's like, I guess, because – my husband died, too. Six years ago.'

Jamie told her how it had happened. Holly could tell that it was still difficult for him. She wanted to spare him, and yet she could also see that he needed to speak, if only to explain to himself. Because he was still angry.

'We never divorced,' Jamie said. 'In fact, after you . . . after you left, Holly, I pretty much resigned myself to sticking with Daphne. It's an awful thing to say, but that's how I felt at the time. Resigned.'

He went on. He'd been an imperfect husband; in the political ins and outs of the 1960s and 1970s he never rose any higher than parliamentary private secretary, a humiliation after having served as chief whip. However, he cosied up to the right patron, Margaret Thatcher, and when she got in in '79 he was rewarded with a Treasury post – the ideal position so far as Tyrconnel and his interests were concerned, right at the centre of power.

And then came Brighton. 'Do you remember the Brighton bombing?' he said. 'Was it in the news in America?'

Holly remembered it, not as well as she should, perhaps, because when the pictures of the wrecked resort hotel had appeared on the news she had switched off, overcome by her visceral aversion for anything British.

'It – disgusted me.' Jamie posed his elbows on the table, looking straight at her. 'There'd been bombings before, but I realised at Brighton that all those pictures were only two-dimensional. That was all they could be. Ordinary

476

people were risking this all the time. I hadn't known – what that was. Not at all.' He paused. 'I was on a lower floor, so I was lucky. But I saw everything. The smoke – it was chaos. We didn't know who was alive or dead.'

He spoke on the news that night, denouncing the terrorists, and when the next round of resignations came in, he volunteered for the post of Northern Ireland Secretary. Everyone thought he was crazy, foolhardy. Especially Imogen. He had given up a plum job at the Treasury, a likely shot at the Department of Trade and Industry next time round. TCI had no interests at all in Northern Ireland. Jamie's position there was useless.

'And so that was when – ' Jamie hesitated, choosing his words – 'relations in the family grew uncomfortably strained. Daph and I decided to move out of the big house. We bought a farmhouse with paddocks. Daph was quite pleased with that, and, oddly enough, she didn't mind my taking Northern Ireland. Not that she'd actually *go* there. She didn't like to travel much to anywhere, and leave the horses. But, as she put it, she could see that I was doing something useful for once. It surprised me, her saying that. But anyway. . . .'

About five years ago Stadhampton City Council started making plans for a new road: a bypass, to ease congestion in the city. The only practicable route which didn't involve knocking down houses cut through the southern parklands of Stadhampton House. After a year of virtually no communication, Tyrconnel and Imogen approached Jamie, expecting, naturally enough, that he would block the development. He refused. His constituents wanted and needed the road.

'Wow,' said Holly. 'Imogen and Tyrconnel must have been furious.'

'They were. But there wasn't much they could do.'

'Are you sure you didn't refuse them just to spite them?'

Suddenly Jamie's face cracked into a grin. 'No. I'm not at all sure, if you want to know. But it felt good. Finally

477

having them off my back. I didn't need them. That's what I realised. I really didn't need them at all.'

'And so – ' Holly lifted her glass, smiling – 'the rise to power of James Carr, QC, MP, *not* so much of Stadhampton.'

'More or less.' Jamie gave a lopsided smile and dug a fork into his *frisée*. Both of their first courses had been sitting in front of them for several minutes now.

His face grew serious again.

'Then – ' said Holly, 'what happened?' She meant about Daphne, though she did not venture to say it.

'The IRA,' said Jamie, almost without expression. 'We were living in our new house. We had round-the-clock protection. We . . . one has to. They send in people to watch the house, keep an eye on the premises, check the car. . . . Well, anyway. Somewhere they – somewhere we slipped up. Daphne went to take the car out one morning, and. . . .'

'Oh, no.'

Jamie nodded. 'Don't know whose fault it was. It just – blew up. It was all over in . . . less than a second.' He gulped his wine and glanced away. 'It's been three years now, but it's still hard.'

'I know,' said Holly. *Six years*, she thought. Even six years made it no easier.

'I still – ' Jamie spoke more quickly now – 'still blame myself, in a way. It must have been one of those last-minute changes of plan – Daphne never was any good at remembering. She must have popped in the car without warning the security people – but still, it was their fault too. That was their job. And mine . . . I should have watched out for her.' His mouth contorted and his eyes looked fearfully into Holly's, then away. 'I'm – not saying we had a particularly happy marriage. It was one of those things. . . . We learnt to rub along. But the worst part was, I missed her so much, once I knew I could never have her back. More than I'd missed her before.'

'I know,' said Holly.

'Do you miss him?' Jamie asked suddenly, then smiled in repentance. 'This is mad. Here I am asking you questions and I don't even know your husband's name.'

'Leonard.' Holly looked up from her plate, and as her eyes met Jamie's she wanted all at once to tell him everything – to pour out her soul.

And so she did: or began to. It surprised her how easy it was, even when, in the telling, she felt herself reliving all the emotions – the fear, the anger. Again she remembered the initial reaction, in her grief. *It was the Carrs' fault.* She had someone to blame – an enemy – just as Jamie did. But that had not seemed to help either of them get over the loss.

'Do you mean,' Holly asked as they were eating their main course, 'you're supposed to have bodyguards with you, all the time?'

Jamie shrugged. 'They say Northern Ireland is a job for life.'

'But that's awful. Never to be on your own. . . .'

'I slip away sometimes. Like tonight. Though if tonight's lot are any good they'll be outside this restaurant by now. Anyway, they're most worried about the house – and the cars, of course. Anywhere they might plant a – '

'God, I'd be afraid.'

'You learn not to be. Or you learn not to think about it. I wouldn't have taken the job if I thought I was going to let every day be dogged by fear.'

'Still.' Holly's eyes were wide. 'I'd worry.'

'You have to take the days as they come.'

Holly wondered at his answer. It sounded fatalistic – too much so.

She railed in her thoughts. 'I suppose,' she said, 'you're right.' She smiled. 'But still. If *I* had any say about it, I wouldn't let you take chances.'

Then she blushed. Foolishly, deeply. Why on earth had she said that?

Holly woke up late in her hotel bed the next morning,

with a stripe of sun across her. For a moment she just lay there, savouring the hazy, slightly hung-over memories of the night before. How was it, she wondered, that she had met up with Jamie?

And then it all came back to her, making her head ache and spin almost instantly as she sat up. The problem had not gone away. She had postponed it for a few hours, that was all.

Last night when Jamie had dropped her off at Brown's, he had promised to ring her to arrange another meeting. Now she could see that that was the worst possible idea. Where on earth could it possibly lead? How could it help?

She moved to the bathroom and gulped down some water. She had left nothing but loose ends last night, with Tyrconnel and Corinna. She didn't know if they had argued – how Corinna had taken the revelation.

Good grief, how could I do that to her?

She needed to go out and find Corinna again, to try to explain, to make up for her thoughtlessness. Corinna might have said some thoughtless things to her, too, but still. . . .

As it turned out, while she was still getting dressed, Corinna came to her instead. She knocked and then entered without waiting for a summons, her face pasty and wary.

'Hi,' said Holly, inadequately. 'How did you get here so early?'

'I stayed in London.' Corinna was slowly circling the edge of the room. 'With Ty.'

'Oh. At Chester Square?'

'Yeah,' said Corinna shortly. 'So, Mom, haven't you got anything to say to me after last night?'

Holly's answer was terse. 'I'm sorry.' She edged towards the window, her hands clenched. 'I didn't know Jamie was coming.'

'My uncle Jamie?' Corinna's voice was heavy with sarcasm.

'I meant to explain. It's very hard, Corinna. It was all –

480

a long time ago, and – I regret some of the things I did. The fact is, Jamie and I – neither of us was happily married – '

'Fine,' Corinna interrupted. 'So you screwed around. That's just fine. Is there anything else I should know?'

'Yes.' Her daughter's insolent tone angered Holly. 'There is. There's an awful lot. But if you want to know the truth about the Carrs, you're going to have to sit down and listen, because it'll take some time.'

'Oh, I'm willing to listen.' Corinna's nostrils flared. 'I've been willing to listen for years, if you'd have trusted me. Remember how I used to ask you about my dad, when I was little? And how you always shut me up, saying he was dead, that you didn't like to talk about it? Oh, I shut up all right. I learnt – '

'That's not fair. I didn't shut you up.'

'You made it pretty damn clear you didn't want to talk. So, OK. Maybe I can understand that. But what about the lies?'

'That happened by accident. I meant to explain, when the time was right.'

'But you never did, did you? When was the time going to be right, Mom? When I was sixteen? Eighteen? And all the time I had a father over here, wondering what had happened to me – wondering where I was. . . .'

'Your father – if, as I assume, you are still referring to Tyrconnel – never cared two cents about you when you were little. And if suddenly he's started to care now, it's beyond me why – '

'Because he needs me. He missed me. He has a lot he wants to give me, and you never let him. We didn't need to be poor. You always made out as if you had no choice.'

'I didn't.'

'Or maybe that was just your trip. Making it on your own, no help from anybody.'

'We were never poor. Yes, it's true, I did make it on my own. But we were all right. We had a roof over our heads and food on the table. When didn't you get anything you really wanted?'

Corinna tossed her head, avoiding her mother's eye. 'When did I get a chance to tell you what I wanted? I never saw you.'

'That's not fair. I made all the time I could – '

'Sure, like a few minutes in the morning and an hour at night.'

'I was doing what I did for *us*.' Holly could hear her own voice echoing, angrily loud.

'Or maybe for you.'

Holly was silent. She was too incensed, now, to answer. And what if, perhaps, it were true? She *had* chosen her path, for herself. But she had thought it was best for both of them. 'Fine,' she said, in a tight voice, after a silence. 'If that's the way you want to think of it. I never knew you were so greedy. Or so selfish.'

'No more than you.' The green of Corinna's eyes flared up at Holly. And Holly could see the hopelessness of denying anything, just now. Corinna was aggrieved. She was set on a course.

Suddenly Holly was fed up with pleading with her. *Let her go to Tyrconnel*, she thought. 'I can see,' she said, as coolly as she could, now, 'there's no point in arguing. But do one thing for me, Corinna.' She walked over to where her briefcase lay on a chair, and extracted a file. Luckily she had made copies. She held one out towards Corinna. 'At least,' she said, 'read this before you make up your mind.'

'What is it?' Corinna drew back.

'My evidence. For that case I was talking about last night. Look at it, before you decide TCI is the kind of operation you want to be involved in.'

Corinna took the folder, with a resentful shrug.

Holly closed the door as her daughter went out and let out an inaudible sigh. It was going to be a long time before she got her daughter back. If ever.

And if this – what she had seen this morning – was what Corinna was becoming, she wasn't so sure she even wanted her.

V

Corinna handed in her essay at her last tutorial before the end of term. Her life seemed to have become empty all of a sudden. Partly, perhaps, because she had spent so little time in Oxford over the last few weeks. This last essay had been a joke: she'd hardly looked at the reading. 'What's happened, Corinna?' her tutor had ventured, pursing his lips in an old-maidish way which indicated that he certainly did not want to hear about anything personal.

'Sorry. I've been busy.'

'Well, you'd better start putting your studies first for a while.'

Corinna hung her head and accepted the admonition, something she had not been doing much of lately, with anyone else. *Silly old coot*, she thought. Who cared about Heidegger and exams and a dumb old second BA anyway? One was enough.

Time hung on her hands. Justin, to her surprised pique, had started hanging around with *another* American girl. All of the other Rhodes scholars had gone off travelling for the Easter break. She kept expecting Tyrconnel to call – to propose a trip somewhere, maybe to visit one of the 'economies', as he called them, where TCI operated.

But he didn't. She had spent most of last week with him in London and Stadhampton, but when he dropped her off here they had made no plans to meet up again; Tyrconnel had mentioned a busy few days ahead.

She had no idea where her mother was. She didn't even know whether she was still in Britain – not that she was going to go chasing after her.

But Mom could call, at least. Leave a message with the porters, the way she used to. Corinna had thought she would at least do that.

So, as almost everyone vacated the college, she was left alone with her neglected philosophy books and a fat blue folder, her mother's. She ignored it. She wasn't going to pay any attention to her mother's cooked-up case. That was all Ty said it was: 'The imaginings of a desperate woman.'

Her books seemed the least threatening option. She read through the rest of the Heidegger, just so that her tutor wouldn't be able to accuse her – as he had almost done, the last time – of not understanding it. Then she started in on some of the work for next term.

Her tutor in the autumn had told her he thought she could get a first. She would like to, really. To come in at the top of the class here, as well as at Harvard – she had to admit she coveted the distinction. The truth was, she liked university: the brilliant abstraction of its subjects, the secluded quads, the hours to herself, reading.

Not that she didn't want to join TCI, of course. She couldn't stay at university for ever. Even if she went back to the States, went to law school, she'd have to come out some time into the real world. And surely it was better, as Ty said, to start at the top. . . .

She couldn't help wondering. Surely he would let her finish her two years here. He wouldn't be so hard-nosed as to insist she give up now: right away.

In the middle of the first week of break, she called him at his office.

'Corinna!' He sounded delighted. 'Where've you been?'

'In Oxford.' A little resentment crept into Corinna's voice. 'Where else did you think I'd be?'

'Nowhere,' said Tyrconnel lightly. 'Are you just getting your things sorted out, ready to move?'

'Well . . .' Corinna hesitated. 'That's just it. I'm not sure I'm ready to leave – just now. You know, like I told you, it would make me pretty unpopular with the Rhodes scholarship people . . .'

'I thought you didn't mind about that.'

'Well, I don't. I mean . . . of course it's not as important

484

to me as working with you. But I was wondering. . . . would it really make such a difference if I just waited until next year? It seems like such a waste. I'm halfway through my degree already.'

'I thought you'd made up your mind.' Tyrconnel's voice grew cooler.

'I have. I mean, I want to join you. I definitely do. It's just – '

'Well, it's no use to me your wavering. You'll have a lot to learn once you get started. I'll need to plan your time here. This isn't university, where you can drift in and out as you please.'

Tyrconnel had stopped talking, and now it seemed to Corinna that she could feel him clocking the seconds that went by before she answered.

'I'm sorry,' she said.

'Listen.' Tyrconnel was terse. 'I'll give you a few more weeks to make up your mind. That's more than I'd give any other prospective employee. Say, two weeks. I'll expect to know by then.'

'OK.' Corinna felt cornered; she did not like the sensation.

'Well, then. I'll look forward to hearing from you.'

'Yeah. Talk to you soon.'

Corinna was not sure whether Tyrconnel even waited for the end of her sentence before hanging up.

She walked out of the college and up St Aldates to buy some food for herself, distracted. Tyrconnel had not sounded very welcoming. In fact, he had treated her like some junior employee, some lowly peon – as if he had never shared his secrets with her a week ago.

Of course, that could be because she had called him at the office. He was probably busy. She struggled to find excuses – explanations – but none of them seemed to suffice.

A few days later, tired of solitude and of feeding herself while college Hall was closed, Corinna decided to call

Imogen. Surely offering to visit a lonely old lady wouldn't be seen as so crass an act as 'inviting oneself'.

'Hallo?' The woman who answered the phone sounded harassed.

'Hello. This is Corinna Green. I was wondering, is Imogen there?'

'She is, dear. But she's not at all well today. Perhaps you'd like me to tell her you've been asking for her. What did you say your name was?'

'Corinna Green. Are you sure. . . .' Was there no way of getting past this woman? 'I was just wondering if Imogen might like a visit.'

'*Corinna*, you said.' Evidently the woman was still taking down the name. 'You wouldn't be . . . are you Holly's daughter?'

'Yes.'

'Well! I've heard about you.' The woman sounded neither pleased nor disapproving. 'I suppose I should tell you, I'm Esmé.'

'Oh?' Who the heck was Esmé?

'Your aunt.' Esmé sounded impatient now. 'Or half-aunt, I suppose, to be correct. We're awfully busy up here, I'm afraid, Corinna. Mother's taken a bit of a turn. She's in her bed now. We're doing our best to keep the situation in hand.'

Somehow, Corinna noticed, this Esmé person made it sound as if she personally commanded an army. 'I'm sorry to hear that,' she said. 'I hope she feels better.'

'Well, it's a handful. My brother's never here. She shouldn't have been left on her own.'

'No. I guess not.'

'So. I'm afraid I must dash now, Corinna. Perhaps I should take your number, in case of . . . developments.'

Corinna gave the college number, which Esmé scribbled down.

'Good. Ring again, dear, if you'd like to know how she's doing. 'Bye.' Esmé ended on a cheery note.

Corinna wandered out with the vague intention of

486

buying a get-well card for her grandmother. But then she wondered: did you send a countess in Chanel suits a saccharine poem? A cartoon of furry animals? Nothing seemed quite right, so she settled for a note on college stationery.

That was the way her whole life seemed to be going these days. She had never been the sort of person to wander and debate and demur; yet now she was rapidly losing her sense of direction. Who was right? What did she really want? *Who am I?* Life became very confusing when you turned out to have two families instead of one.

She wondered about her mother. What if she'd flown back to New York still angry? She had better try and call her.

'Brown's Hotel.'

When Corinna asked to speak to Holly Green, the receptionist told her she'd checked out last week.

'Uh . . . what day exactly?'

Not immediately after their argument: four days later, in fact.

What had she been doing for all that time? 'Thank you,' said Corinna.

Mom was back home, then. Corinna dropped a handful of coins into the pay phone and dialled Lyall, Kravitz's number.

'Corinna! How are you?' Holly's secretary was the enthusiastic type. 'Your mom? No! She's not back. Did you think she was? Here, let me check her calendar . . . Oh, no! I remember. Abe told me she'd called in yesterday to extend her vacation through the end of next week.'

'Oh. Thanks.'

'So don't you know where she is?'

'No. Not exactly – but I'm sure I can find her. Thanks, Mimi.'

So now her mother had dropped off the face of the earth, too. That was great, thought Corinna. Just great.

'I can't help thinking.' Jamie stretched an arm round

Holly's shoulder as they watched the waves lap against the long, flat shore. 'So much lost time.'

'No offence – ' Holly smiled out at the wheeling gulls – 'but I never think of it that way. When I think over the whole of my life I figure I've been lucky.'

'Well, you were happy in your marriage.'

'Yes. I was. While it lasted.' Holly still watched the waves, even though she could feel Jamie looking down at her. Why was it always easier to speak the truth, looking away? Why should his eyes disconcert her? 'I suppose I haven't really spent much of my life married. If you add it up. Only six years with Leonard. I'm afraid I'm most used to being on my own.'

'Funny,' said Jamie, 'how you think when you're twenty or twenty-five that life's so full, you'll never be lonely – '

'Speak for yourself.'

Jamie looked down, guilt wrinkling his forehead. 'I wasn't there for you much, was I?' He pulled her closer, stroking her back.

She tilted her head up: took in the long creases in Jamie's cheeks, which had – or so it seemed to her now – always been there; the weathered, tanned skin, the square cheek-bones, the windblown hair, almost white in places. But she couldn't help drawing back. She needed, somehow, to put him in perspective, to try to remember that this was a man who had diminished himself in her memory. Whom she had had to fight from her thoughts for more years than she liked to admit.

So that, in fact, she had forgotten him: in the way one forgets even the most important facts of a life, when to remember means to risk not moving forward.

'Do you still hold it against me?' he said. 'The way we started.'

They had been over this before. And *no*, she had said that time. Jamie had described the past as a house of cards. *You think, I'll just nudge this one here, barely a touch, it won't make any difference. But as soon as you do it all the others start to fall, one by one at first, but in the end the whole house has fallen down round about you, and you think, 'What did I do to start all this?'*

Jamie said he had pursued her at first because his mother told him to; had gone on, despite his better instincts, realising that the woman he had seen starkly, as his prey, was needy and fragile; had kept seeing her even when he knew she had no intention of having a baby, because by then it was too late. He needed her, too. Love came slowly, and by the time you recognised it, it had shattered the whole house of cards.

Or it could have.

And then Diane had come along: another affair, a betrayal of Holly, for which Jamie couldn't pretend he was anything but guilty. There were explanations. A temptation which, at that age, he was unused to resisting; a bit of light relief which he imagined, perhaps, would ease the intensity of his affair with Holly. It hadn't.

I was stupid, Jamie had said – when was it? Yesterday? The day before? *Sometimes there are no excuses.*

'Do you still hold it against me?' he said now. Again.

'The past,' Holly said now, simply, 'is the past. I don't hold it against you. But I don't much like living in it either.'

Jamie smiled. 'Do you think that's what this is?'

Holly's mouth twisted, apologetic. She was not sure.

'Did you ever think about me, after you went off to New York?'

'Oh, yes.'

'I came to look for you, once.'

He told her about the Plaza, and searching out Sutton Place, and phoning Helen.

'You should have phoned us! Once you'd got that far,' Holly reproved him. But she wasn't sure that she meant it. She felt uneasy at the thought of her two worlds colliding. Her two loves. Leonard and Jamie.

No, she thought. Better to keep them apart.

'Too awkward,' Jamie said. 'And – you've never been back here?'

'Don't you believe me?' She smiled up.

489

'You've travelled just about everywhere else.'

'And avoided England. You know exactly why.'

'I would have liked to know what was happening to Corinna.' Jamie sounded wistful.

'I thought – if you knew, the others would, too. I was always afraid of Tyrconnel finding Corinna. Maybe it was silly of me.'

'And you thought I couldn't keep a secret? You didn't trust me.' Jamie smiled. He seemed to expect reproof. 'Maybe you still don't.'

'I do now. I think you've changed.'

'I've grown in your esteem.' He said it jokingly.

'Yes.' Because, joking or not, it was true. He had done more than she had expected: broken away from the Carrs, stuck with his parliamentary work through all the lean years, made more frustrating by an initial whiff of power; stayed the course of his marriage; taken enormous risks to confront what he saw as evil.

'Oh, well,' he said. 'With me, you know what you're getting. Bit of a wasted life. Unlike yours.'

'I don't think so.' She smiled; the wind blew her hair back, and she tilted her face and reached her arms up round his neck, because she was tired of talking. They had talked through what seemed like years.

It was time.

Later, she thought, no one would believe – she herself would not have believed – that she and Jamie had spent five wet days, alone except for each other, in adjoining rooms in a hotel on the north Norfolk coast, and remained, in all that time, utterly chaste, except for the occasional good-night kiss or accidental touch.

But it was true. They were afraid, perhaps. Jamie, despite his old womanising ways, to broach the question; and she, for her own mundane, silly reasons. Because her breasts hung lower than they once had and spidery veins showed in her thighs, and she feared that, once stripped of her coverings, with whose help she might still look glamorous, she would be revealed as old. She feared that once Jamie saw her like that, they could never regain the lost time: it would stand too clearly before their eyes.

She had not made love in a very long time, and the thought of it, like a lighted window on a dark night, warmed her spirit. She had known ever since they left London together that that was their inevitable destination.

But, she wondered, was it a mistake, trying to relive memories?

She caught Jamie's gaze and arched up against him. *I'm too old*, she thought, in a sudden panic. *We're both old.* But it did not feel that way when he reached down, his fingers curling round the nape of her neck as he kissed her. She felt his body press hard against her as his other arm snaked around her waist; and the blood ran through her, warming, responding. Her body had not forgotten. And when, after some minutes had passed, they pulled apart, she laughed meaninglessly, from relief, as if she were young and nervous and did not know what she was doing.

'I haven't done this for an awfully long time,' Jamie said, smiling. There was an unmistakable hunger in his eyes.

'I thought you politicians had worlds of opportunity.'

He shrugged. 'I don't know why, but these days I usually seem to stop at speculation.'

'You've gotten blasé. Too much of a good thing. You think you know exactly how it'll be even before it happens.'

'This time – ' he gave a canny smile – 'I do, and yet I don't.' He offered her his arm for the way back along the rocky path to their room.

It was cold, of course. 'All proper British hotels should be,' said Holly; and so they made a fire and drew the big red Victorian sofa up in front of it and lay there lazily, kissing occasionally, their arms curled round each other. When the fire began to roar they peeled off clothes, little by little.

'You've kept your long hair,' said Jamie. 'I'm glad.'

'Don't you remember? It was you that suggested it.'

That time, on the same Norfolk coast, so long ago. Perhaps that was why they had come back.

No, thought Holly. *Not perhaps. Certainly.*

She clasped Jamie's shoulders when she saw they were still the same, square and muscled; and if other things had changed, she did not notice. And so, she realised, a few minutes later when she lay back on the hearthrug beneath him, he must not have noticed either. About her. The years didn't matter.

She had imagined, somehow, from Jamie's restraint these last few days, the delicacy of his kisses on her cheek, that probably his style of making love had changed: grown slower, become an act of connoisseurship rather than lust.

But it wasn't so. He buried his face in hers and his fingers dug into her shoulders; they became an engine, pure energy, like the fire, forgetful of everything else.

And it went on, undiminishing, for a very long time.

Afterwards, she blinked and tried to refocus her eyes. Jamie leaned up on his elbows above her.

'I know you may think it's too late. But I mean this. Would you like to marry me, Holly?'

'What?' Her heart lurched and she blinked again.

'There's nothing to stop us now. Not that I can see.'

'Wait just a minute!' Her voice shook as she tried to sound lighthearted, and she could not seem to control it. 'I think there are. Just a few things. Like your family . . . my job. And the fact that that we live in different countries.'

Jamie only smiled. 'Minor impediments.'

'Jamie. Come on. You know they're *real* impediments.'

Jamie's mouth twitched as he glanced away. 'Oh, well. Just thought it was worth asking.'

'Thank you. It's a kind thought.'

'I didn't say it to be kind.' He got up suddenly, without warning, and left her.

He didn't bring up the subject again. She was glad, because they had a wonderful week together: that was what counted, to enjoy each other while they could. People in their fifties – she had to be realistic – didn't so often have flings like this; didn't, perhaps, always want those who wanted them. She and Jamie were lucky.

She wished Jamie would understand that. He had grown more distant – however barely perceptible the distance was – since he had brought up the idea of marriage, and she had rebuffed it. She didn't like to hurt him. Lord knew, it was tempting: there they were, two lonely people, remembering what it had been like to be in love. . . .

Give it time, Jamie had told her. *Don't say yes or no. I know you're right. We need a present before we can think about the future.*

There can be no future! she had wanted to answer: but held back, for fear of hurting him again. This week was an escape, a shared adventure, a retreat into the past – they could call it what they liked, but one thing was certain: it had no future. People in love didn't separate for twenty-five years and then get back together as if nothing had happened. And besides, things had gone wrong, back then. They would only have to spend enough time together, and then – Holly had no doubt of it – the old rough ground would start to get in their way.

But she preferred not to talk about that, and Jamie concurred. Time was short. They talked about everything else they could think of. There were only a few sore spots – like Corinna.

'She's a great girl,' said Jamie one morning as they lay in bed. 'I hope I'll get to know her.'

'She's . . . confused,' said Holly carefully, 'right now. I don't blame her. She'd just gotten used to the idea that Tyrconnel was her father – '

'Then I came along.' Jamie smiled, but his forehead wrinkled in a frown. 'Maybe we'd better not push her into changing her ideas too fast.'

'Well, at the moment, I'm not sure when she and I will be speaking again. Or if.'

'Oh, come on. I'm sure you will.'

493

'I don't know.' Holly frowned. 'He's really won her over. Anyway. It'll do no good my chasing after her when she's like this.'

'Did you ever want to have other children?'

The question caught Holly up short. 'Yes and no. I suppose I was too old by the time I decided I might like to. Leonard agreed with whatever I wanted to do. We tried for a little while, but the way it worked out. . . .'

'Riskier, having just one,' said Jamie lightly, to change the subject. 'I suppose I hedged my bets, with three.'

'Four,' Holly reminded him.

'*Four.*' He nodded and gave her a squeeze. 'Oh, well, that gives me one more chance. One of my offspring should still be willing to put up with me by the time I get old.'

'Lucky you.'

'She'll come round.' Jamie squeezed Holly's shoulder again, in reassurance.

'Hmm.' Holly had her doubts.

They drove back, via Stadhampton, on a day of March winds and rain, the security men who had shadowed Jamie so discreetly in Norfolk as to be barely perceptible, following in a car behind them. Before going back to London to catch up with work, Jamie wanted to show Holly his house. 'Just in case,' he said, 'you change your mind.'

'Jamie, please.' Holly tensed up, staring at the windscreen. The rain was covering it in thick, rippling sheets of water.

'Don't jump on me.' Calmly Jamie steered into the wind. 'I just want you to know I meant what I said. I still mean it.'

Holly's heart was pounding. 'I hardly think this is the time to talk about it.'

'What? Driving in a gale? Why not? I'm a good gale driver.'

Because, Holly thought, *I feel trapped*. The small space of the car's interior was starting to overheat. 'I thought we agreed,' she said.

494

'I don't remember agreeing anything.'

'Look.' She tried to reason. 'I don't want . . . to stop seeing you completely. But it's difficult. Transatlantic relationships are impossible to keep up. I've seen people try. The travelling's exhausting. . . .'

'I agree.' Jamie went on, unperturbed. 'That's why I'm talking about something more settled. A commitment. Look, I'll accept that we might not always be together. I couldn't insist on your living over here – '

'No. You couldn't. I happen to have a job in America, Jamie! I can't just fly off. And let's be realistic. You can't leave parliament.'

'All right, so we'll just have to commute. See each other at weekends. Bankrupt ourselves on Concorde.' Jamie smiled.

He wasn't taking it too hard then, thought Holly. At least he could joke.

'Or,' he said, 'there are things you could do, if you did decide to come and live here. Oxford, for instance. They're always crying out for Fellows in law.'

'They'd never have me.' Holly hated to admit it, but the idea tempted her. Just a little. She'd always wanted the time to write another book.

'Think about it.'

'No, Jamie, really. I can't.'

'Can't or won't?' The car jerked to a sudden stop. Jamie turned on her, his face heated.

'Look. What are you trying to do?' said Holly. 'Corner me? Where are we?'

'I want to know,' said Jamie, 'why you won't even consider it. It seems to me that when two people love each other, when they've missed twenty-five years of their lives together, the least they can do is try to make up for it when they get the chance again.'

'Jamie. . . .'

'Is it because of what happened all those years ago? God knows, I wish it were different. I've said I'm sorry.'

'No,' Holly said truthfully. 'It's not any of that.'

'Because I love you. I always have. I haven't forgotten you. Perhaps you don't feel the same.'

'Jamie. I do. I think I do, but I can't. . . .' Holly's words trailed away.

'All right. Fair enough.' Jamie sat silently for a moment, his face stony, looking ahead.

'Where are we? Aren't we going on?'

'We're there,' said Jamie curtly. 'This is my house.'

Everything was in an uproar at Stadhampton House. As well as Corinna, Esmé and three of her children and one of Jamie's daughters were there; Tyrconnel had come, and the only person they couldn't get hold of was Jamie.

'I'll go,' offered Corinna. 'I can at least leave a message at his house.' She had caught the first train up when Esmé called her.

She borrowed Esmé's Mini and got lost in the outskirts of Stadhampton before finding her way out to the western fringes of the town, where Jamie lived. It was pouring with rain. Finally she spotted the place, at the end of a village lane – a low, thatched stone house in wide grounds, surrounded by fences. Two cars were pulled up in the drive. One was empty, and then two people got out of the other.

Jamie, reaching for his house keys; and her mother.

So that was where she'd been all this time.

Corinna watched for a little longer, feeling a momentary admiration. Her mother and Jamie. Imagine that, after all these years.

Only the two people trudging up to the door didn't look particularly happy.

Corinna got out. 'Hey!' she called. 'Mom! Jamie! Everybody's been looking everywhere for you.'

Jamie turned a weary face to her first. 'Oh. Hello, Corinna. What's this? Who's "everybody"?'

Holly stared back at Corinna without speaking. She looked tired, too.

'Up at the house. It's – your mother, Jamie. I'm sorry to have to tell you this. She's had another stroke.'

'But she's all right?' said Jamie.

'Right now she is. She's resting.'

Corinna kept herself from telling him the doctor's verdict right away.

VI

Imogen's great-grandchildren scampered along the length of the summer ballroom and up and down the broad front stairs. They rarely visited Stadhampton, and after the limited confines of the converted stables where they lived with their mother, Clara, Esmé's daughter, in Oxfordshire, the enormous spaces, concealed doors and evident secrets of Stadhampton House came as a boundless delight.

Esmé and her children and grandchildren rather hoped to be here more often when Imogen went. Well – after all, as Esmé kept saying, with the appropriate degree of sad resignation, it was only a matter of time. At ninety her mother couldn't hope to last for ever.

In an age when death was so often stripped of ceremony, Imogen had insisted on the full formalities for hers. She was not going to hospital. She had made that clear to the doctor as soon as he came, after her night-time seizure. She had lost most of the use of her body but still clung to the remnants of speech.

Four trained nurses had come to occupy the hunt room and the library adjacent to the green parlour on the ground floor, which now served as Imogen's bedroom. The servants had quickly reached Tyrconnel and Esmé, and now three of Esmé's children as well as one of Jamie's – all being otherwise unemployed – had come to the house with a selection of their offspring: Imogen had seven great-grandchildren in all. It was the fullest the house had been for years.

Imogen didn't bother to try to tell all these people apart.

She dozed, off and on, in the narrow, incongruous hospital bed next to the marble fireplace in the green room, and blinked uncomprehendingly at her visitors. Except for Tyrconnel. She still made the effort to talk to Tyrconnel.

What they talked about, no one else in the house knew, because Imogen banished everyone else from the room when her eldest son came.

And though the others might have imagined mother and son conferring about the house, about TCI and the further manipulation of their fortunes, they did not, in fact, talk about anything so grand. Mostly they remained silent, Tyrconnel holding his mother's small, papery hand.

'I'm sorry,' Imogen stuttered from time to time.

'Don't be sorry, Mother. You'll be all right.'

'I'll be dead soon.'

'So you will.' Tyrconnel smiled, but had to twitch his head away so as not to look at her. 'So will we all.'

'That girl.' Imogen's dark eyes fixed on her son.

'What girl?'

'You know.' Imogen's wrist jerked. 'Don't let her. . . .' Her voice faded.

They had many such conversations. Occasionally Imogen announced herself willing to see Esmé, or Clara, or even the great-grandchildren, but inevitably by the time they came her eyes were closed, and her head twitched away when they tried to talk to her.

'Poor old thing,' Clara clucked, watching her from the door of the green room.

'I'm sorry I never got to know her better,' said Corinna.

Clara gave her a smile. 'Oh, well. I was always afraid of her, really, anyway. I look at her now and I don't know why.' Clara was thin, with lank, mousy hair and an ineffectual prettiness: the looks, in Corinna's estimation, of the sort of woman who preferred being married to working – who spent her days eking out alimony cheques in the country in the hope of landing a new husband.

My cousin, thought Corinna. The words were a novelty

to her; she had never had any cousins before. Now she had seven. Or really four . . . plus three half-sisters.

She didn't think of them that way, Jamie's children. It blew her mind when she tried to take it all in: *half-sisters.* So she thought of them as cousins.

Anyway, she couldn't see that she had anything at all in common with Davina, the slight blonde stable groom from Berkshire who was the only one of Jamie's daughters who had come, so far, to see Imogen. Esmé – she of the iron-grey hair, broad hips and martial manner – kept making excuses for Jamie's daughters – 'Well, they have commitments at home, I'm sure' – which were obviously intended to show up the superior virtues of her own children.

When Jamie and Holly first arrived, Imogen was sleeping. Esmé greeted them both briskly, bearing Jamie away to confer with the nurses while Holly was left standing by the library door, unsure where to go. Her first impulse was still to hurry back to London, before she got caught here with no possibility of escape. She and Jamie had left everything unresolved, and she didn't like it that way, but obviously there were going to be no proper farewells now.

Corinna came out of the library.

'Are you going in to see Imogen, Mom?'

'I don't know. I've avoided it for this long.' Holly spoke stiffly, not meeting her daughter's eye.

'Maybe you should. She's just a tiny old lady.'

'That's what she always was.' Holly gave a grim smile. 'Though she never seemed like anything so feeble.'

Corinna shrugged. 'I'll get Ty to tell her you're here.'

Before Holly could stop her, Corinna was off again. She was wearing the necklace, Holly noticed: the old baroque pearls, along with a silk shirt and scarf and suede jodhpurs. No doubt she had found out where the pearls came from by now. Holly's only piece of Carr jewellery: virtually worthless. She gave another grim smile, remembering.

The hours ticked by, and the house's small staff, rising as

best they could to the task of feeding nearly twenty, laid out a buffet in the small dining room at which the visitors nibbled, drifting in and out. It became clear to Holly that she was not going to get away unless she called a cab and just went; and where that would leave her and Jamie, or her and Corinna, not to mention Tyrconnel, she did not know. Eventually Esmé, sweeping through the small side parlour where Holly was trying to read, announced that the yellow bedroom had been made up for her.

Jamie, she supposed later, must have gone home, because she did not see him until the next morning.

Then, after breakfast, Imogen's doctor called a conference. Holly stood on its fringes, while Tyrconnel questioned and nodded.

'I see. . . .'

'We could still take her into hospital, but as she has expressed a clear preference – '

'No,' said Tyrconnel. 'It would be wrong to take her away from here. It's absolutely the last thing she wants.'

'In that case, we should be prepared. . . .'

Jamie turned away, disconsolate, before the doctor had finished.

Holly took a tentative step towards him; tried to meet his eye. He didn't seem to see her.

Later that morning, Imogen woke. She began speaking incoherently, continually, and the nurses, in a fret, ran to fetch Esmé and Tyrconnel and Jamie. Imogen wanted something; that was clear. Why else did she never stop talking?

More and more people crowded around the hospital bed in the green room. Imogen's head lolled to the side. Sometimes she stared, and at other times her mouth stretched into a leering grin and she let out a monstrous laugh, almost a cackle.

'This could be it,' said Esmé self-importantly to Clara, and anyone else who was listening.

Holly followed the others into the green room. She

watched from behind Esmé and two of the nurses as Imogen extended a hand to Corinna, who, Holly saw now, was standing close by Tyrconnel.

'*Holly.*' Imogen's voice forced itself out, slurred but quite loud. 'Holly!' She clutched at Corinna's hand and smiled with what part of her face she could still move.

Holly herself started forward. She wanted to say, *No. That's Corinna. Here I am.* But Imogen was already speaking to Corinna. And that stopped her.

'I want you to know. I want you to – '

'Yes?' Corinna squeezed Imogen's hand and bent close to hear her voice.

'The . . . necklace.' The word was barely audible. 'It's not old, or new, or borrowed – and it's certainly not blue.' Imogen smiled. 'But I wanted you to have it.'

'Thank you,' said Corinna, appeasing.

Imogen forced her head upright; her two black eyes met Corinna's. 'I killed your father.'

'What?'

Imogen laughed. 'In the boat! I killed your – father. No one – knows. Not even Ty. But I – got it done. I did it.' One side of her mouth twitched up in a hideous smile.

'What do you mean?'

'I did it. No one found me out.' Imogen's head lolled sideways and she began to laugh as her hand fell away from Corinna's. 'I did it! I did it!'

Holly felt her knees giving way. She clutched at the footrail of the bed to keep from falling.

'Holly?'

She felt Esmé's grasp round her shoulders.

'It's all right.' Holly forced herself to stand again. 'I'm fine.'

Murder, she thought. It was murder. And Imogen, after all these years, had confessed to it.

There was a commotion at the head of the bed.

'What?'

Tyrconnel's startled cry cut into Holly's thoughts. She heard the answering voice of a nurse, trying to be soothing.

'It's all right, Lord Carr, she's gone now. She went in peace.'

'Ty?'

Jamie ran after his brother, who had staggered from the room.

Tyrconnel glanced back, then waved a dismissive hand. 'It's all right. Go on back, Jamie. I want to be alone.'

He walked out to the terrace to breathe the air. For a moment he leaned on the balustrade, trying to keep his eyes clear; trying to remember. She was ninety. What had she said to him yesterday?

I'll be dead soon.

So will we all, he had answered. It was true, she was old, she was bound to die.

But she could have hung on. She could have waited.

Esmé found her half-brother sitting on one of the lower steps leading from the terrace to the garden, his knees drawn up, his face buried in his hands.

With atypical tact, she withdrew. Ty had been closer to Mother than anyone. It was only natural that he needed some time by himself to get over the loss.

The family ate lunch. Appetites were not much affected by the death of a woman of ninety; everyone murmured to each other that really ninety was quite old and at that age it was probably for the best. Imogen's bizarre confession was generally dismissed as a product of hallucination.

'Where's Ty?' Corinna asked Jamie at one point. She was worried about him, disappearing like that.

'He's – on his own. Esmé said she saw him out by the terrace. I think he just wants to be alone for a bit.'

Corinna nodded. She supposed she should go sit by her mother, who was by herself on one of the sofas by the window. She must feel awfully out of place here.

More out of place than I do, even, thought Corinna suddenly. For she had grown to feel almost at home here.

She went over.

'Hi.' Holly looked even more tired than yesterday. She nibbled at a sliver of cold chicken.

'You look beat,' said Corinna.

'Beat. Yeah, I guess that about sums it up.' Holly gave a thin smile.

'I guess it's pretty crummy getting dragged into all this. Not exactly what you bargained for.'

'I probably shouldn't have come to England.'

'What do you mean? Of course you should have come. I was glad to see you.'

Holly's eyebrows lifted. 'You didn't seem all that glad.'

'Oh, Mom.' Corinna pushed a stick of celery around her plate, afraid to meet her mother's eye. 'What was I supposed to think, when you came in on the warpath like that?' She paused. 'I want you to know. I read your stuff.'

'The papers I left with you?'

'Yeah. I . . . I see there's a problem.' Corinna looked up. 'I don't know. I'm not really sure about this whole thing – any more.'

'All I wanted was for you to think hard about it.'

'Oh, yeah?' Corinna ventured a smile. 'I don't believe you. All you wanted was for me never to have met Ty. And if I did, you wanted me to have nothing to do with him.'

'True, I guess.' Holly's face relaxed a little. 'Maybe I was wrong. At least for not telling you the truth.'

Corinna munched again; then she frowned. 'Mom? You remember what Imogen said in there . . . Do you think she thought she was talking to you instead of me?'

And then Holly knew that it was worth trying to tell Corinna the truth, again, about her grandfather.

It seemed to Corinna that she had spent many days at Stadhampton House, but in fact it had been only three. It seemed to her that her mother had been here for months, that she had known about Ty and the Carrs and TCI for years, at least. But in fact this whole thing had started less than two months ago.

She wondered if she wished it had never happened, and decided, *no*. Even if because of it she felt a whole lot older, and less sure of herself and her future than she had ever been before, she thought – and she believed she had even made her mother admit – it was always better to face the truth.

And that included the truth about her new family. The fact that TCI had been founded, in great part, on her grandfather Joe Clayton's grave.

Corinna was sorry she hadn't believed her mother earlier.

Because, imagine it: to have your in-laws murder your father and not even know it until more than twenty years later . . . Mom must have hated Imogen when she found out.

No. Hate was too small a word.

Corinna wondered if a company founded on murder, thriving on oppression and pollution and the wiles of dictators, could ever be reformed. Could TCI ever change its ways? Or would it, and Stadhampton, too, finally have to close down?

She thought she should see Ty. She wasn't sure what she felt for him now, after all she had heard and read. Pity, mostly. She wanted to help him turn his company around, if he was willing to do it. But on her own terms.

She walked out into the garden after lunch. She wasn't looking for Tyrconnel yet; she could understand his wish to be alone. The outdoor air was warm and moist. She walked down the terrace steps and on to the lawn; from the edge of the grass she could see the cars whirring down the long scar of the Stadhampton bypass.

When she headed back to the terrace, she noticed a door in the high stone wall projecting from the ground floor of the house. A secret garden, perhaps. She was curious enough to test the handle.

The door creaked open and she saw the rosebeds

encircled by gravel paths; the plants were still in their wintry, leafless state.

And then she saw Tyrconnel, by the far wall. He turned, beckoning.

'Come in, and close the door. I'm glad it's you. You've never seen this place before, have you?'

Corinna shook her head and went to join him. This hardly seemed the time for a tour of a rose garden. 'How are you doing?' she said cautiously.

'All right.' Tyrconnel spun on his heels, distracted, as if looking for something.

'I'm sorry if I've disturbed you – '

'No.' Tyrconnel glanced at Corinna for a second, with a fleeting frown, as if he couldn't quite place her. 'Anyway, I wanted to talk to you.'

'Sure. About what?'

Before he answered, Corinna had a feeling she knew.

'You know. The company. We can't go on without a decision for ever.'

'I'm not sure this is the time. . . .'

'Corinna, I'm getting tired of waiting.' Tyrconnel dug at the gravel with his heels. When he looked at her again, down his beakish nose, his expression was impatient, unfriendly.

'I know, Ty, but . . .' Corinna shifted on her feet. 'You have to understand, it was a hard decision to make.'

'I take this to mean you've made it, then?'

'Well . . .' Corinna took a deep breath. 'Sort of. I'm just not sure I can join you now. For one thing, I want to finish my degree.'

Tyrconnel let out a short breath. 'Oh, well, then, that's that.'

'No, but, I wanted to say – '

'I don't see that there's anything more to say. I made myself clear: two possible answers, yes or no. You've answered me. Fine.' Tyrconnel twitched his head as if to shoo her away.

'No. Wait a minute.' Corinna's voice grew more heated.

505

'It's not fine. It's not just that I want to finish my degree. I have serious doubts about what you're doing. I think if your company's going to survive at all it needs to change. Not just on ethical grounds – '

Tyrconnel cut her off. 'Thank you, Corinna. I can do without your petty moralising.'

'It's not petty moralising! I'm talking about peoples' lives – the kinds of things my mom was trying to tell you. . . .'

'Well, that's not too important to me now.'

'What do you mean? Of course it's important.'

'I have to think of myself.' Tyrconnel's voice was crisp, and he held his head high as he looked beyond Corinna, towards the pilasters of the great house. 'I have to think of *us*, and who'll carry on what I've done. I think you'll take what I'm offering you, in the end. You have to. Because you're the last one of us left.' He twitched his head.

'What do you mean? You have lots of family, not just me. There's Jamie and Esmé and their children. . . .'

'I'm a rotter – I told you.' Tyrconnel reached across to seize Corinna's arms. He smiled an eerie smile. 'All rotten inside. But you are too. We all are. Some rot sooner than others.'

'What are you talking about?' Suddenly Corinna was scared. She didn't like the look in Ty's eyes. It was too . . . otherworldly.

'We all shrivel up, and die.' Tyrconnel stared at her, and gave her a little shake. 'Yes, we do. It's true, Corinna. Some people talk as if it's God's vengeance. I never believed that. I've always known God loved me.'

Corinna stepped back carefully. 'Listen,' she said. 'Why don't you come inside? It's getting cold out here.' She slipped her hands free from Tyrconnel's.

He seemed not to notice. 'I need you,' he said, 'you see. You're the only one. Say yes, Corinna, and I'll change my will. Cut the other lot out. They don't deserve it.'

Corinna gave him a nervous smile and backed towards the garden door.

'I mean it,' he said. 'Without you, I don't have much – reason to go on.'

'Of course you do. You have lots of reasons.' Corinna stood at the door. She really didn't think Ty should be alone now, but she didn't know how to put it politely. 'Aren't you coming?'

'Aren't you?' He gave a ghostly smile. He looked suddenly frail. 'Think of it, Corinna. Just us. We could conquer the world.'

'I don't – want the world.' Corinna's voice broke suddenly, and she turned away.

She left Tyrconnel in the garden because there seemed to be no coaxing him out. His state disturbed her, and yet she did not tell any of the others about it, when she found them. She doubted, somehow, that they would understand.

'Have you seen Ty anywhere?' Esmé asked her at one point, and she shook her head.

Everything had become very clear to Tyrconnel. He knew he didn't want to wait any longer. *Today*, he thought. The same day as Mother.

He thought of the graveyard at Little Hampton, and the pious words that would be spoken over broken earth, over all their unrepented sins, shared, together. And he laughed.

And then he knew the pure joy that he would feel, leaving it all behind. No more thought of plagues then, or wondering how long he had left, before the symptoms started to show: before the rot moved outward.

He had never told anyone he was sick, and now they wouldn't know.

We're all bound to die anyway.

He had made one last trip to the house, but no one had observed him. And now it was time: before someone came. He curled his finger round the trigger.

*

Only two of Esmé's grandchildren, playing in the ballroom, heard the noise. They gave a gleeful shout.

'What's that?'

'An explosion.'

'Maybe a plane crashed! Let's go and look. . . .'

Clara heard them, and came in. When they told her about the sound, she was puzzled. 'Probably something backfiring,' she said; but all the same, she went outside to investigate.

Someone had left the door to the rose garden ajar. Clara found her uncle curled in the gravel, thrown sideways by the blast.

The dates of death did not feature on the two tombstones, when they were eventually set into the ground at Little Hampton. Nor was it widely known, beyond the family, that the post-mortem examination of Tyrconnel Carr's body had discovered antibodies in the blood that, in themselves, served to explain why someone in his position should choose to take his own life.

What amazed Corinna was that no one had known. No one at all. Tyrconnel had seemed in such good health; and only a few of his remarks, in retrospect, made her wonder. His hurry that she should join his company, learn to take his place.

And his last, strange words to her. *All rotten inside. Some people talk as if it's God's vengeance.*

Corinna mourned for Tyrconnel. She mourned in part because she felt to blame for his death, because she had left him only a few minutes before it.

And she missed him. She wondered if anyone else did. She had known, until the very end, only the kinder, courtlier side of him, and she had felt a kinship there. *Rottenness, perhaps.* She had to admit it. Tyrconnel's avarice and her own ambition.

But she liked to think there was something better in both of them; something they could have brought out in each other, given the chance. She would never know.

Jamie inherited everything: the title; the houses and lands; the company, although Tyrconnel's nieces and nephews all possessed substantial shareholdings in accordance with the will Tyrconnel had made several years before.

Jamie had become the Earl of Stadhampton, for what that was worth – not much these days, as he liked to joke, but the PM would be saved the chore of presenting him with a life peerage when he retired. Because that, in effect, was what he had, with no male heir. For a while he contemplated renouncing the title in order to keep his seat in the Commons. But then he thought, *why not?* If he left the House he would hardly be retiring. He had an enormous house to maintain, and acres of agricultural land. Most of all, he had TCI. Tyrconnel had been so possessive of the company that he had never really trained anyone to follow in his footsteps. Now, Jamie had to admit to himself, he was beginning to relish the job. It would be a challenge, overhauling TCI: changing its ways and forcing it to conform for the first time to ethical standards.

He had the power to do so now, and he was sure, with perseverance, it could be done. Corinna might even come to work with him, once she finished at Oxford. If only Holly. . . .

He had resolved not to think about that.

Two days after the funeral he had driven her to Heathrow. He watched Corinna wave her mother off from the pavement in front of Brown's Hotel; she and Holly were still feeling their way with each other, he could tell, but their relationship would mend, because that was what they both wanted.

And then he had let Holly go. It was, he thought, the hardest goodbye he had ever said. Perhaps Holly was right, and their lives were too separate ever to join again. They might believe, even with all their hearts, that they were still in love, but in truth they were only clinging to the past.

'I do love you,' she said. 'Remember that, Jamie. I love

you right this minute and that's all we can know. It's – a beautiful illusion. If we tried to stay together we'd only ruin it – '

She broke away. Turning her back on him, she walked quickly through the departure lounge, on to her plane. And so Jamie didn't know that as she walked down the carpeted alley, tears were streaming from her eyes.

She knew she was right. But just then she could hardly bear it.

What have I done?

VII

Corinna let the hem of her long dress trail on the floor of the ballroom in her father's house. *My father's house.* She liked the sound of that.

She had been wary of Jamie at first, afraid of committing herself and her feelings again so soon after losing Ty. Jamie had not rushed her. A month or so after the funerals, he had written to her at Oxford, inviting her to come up to Stadhampton if she weren't too busy. *I'm still learning my way around*, he wrote, *but I'd be glad if you could join me.*

And so she had gone up. They had not tried to talk about her mother, or about Ty; she sensed that those were touchy subjects with Jamie. But gradually she had realised how much else they shared. She remembered that first spark of recognition, when she had seen Jamie at the Union, and wondered if he were any relation of her father's. It seemed funny now.

So they talked politics and the economy, and at the end of summer term she went up to spend another week at Stadhampton, before going home to see her mother in New York.

Only then had she learnt all about her mother and

Jamie. The story came in bits and pieces, as was perhaps appropriate, for there were two stories – one from twenty-five years ago and one from just last winter.

'Last winter,' Holly had said, in a sad, dry sort of way, 'wasn't really anything of its own. It was only a sort of dream.'

Why? Corinna wanted to ask her. How could she be so sure?

But she knew enough not to say anything. It was hard enough for her mother, she could tell – trying to do the wise thing, the right thing, when her feelings fought against it. Her mother had had to struggle to think clearly: to come to realise that the obstacles – distance, different lives, the past itself – were real, and that nothing would make them go away. Life wasn't a fairy story.

Or hardly ever. Corinna walked to the window and smiled. The English sun stayed up so late in summer that it still had not set; and it must be nine by now. A dim pink light shone in the sky beyond the trees, beyond the fountain and fields and the long thin scar of the bypass. Corinna heard steps behind her and turned.

'How do you think it went?' said Jamie.

'Great. You look good in a tux.' She plucked playfully at the red rose in his buttonhole.

'I thought,' he said, 'this house needed at least one more great party in our lifetimes.' He smiled wryly. 'Whatever the excuse.'

'Who needs one?' Corinna grinned and they both glanced around them at the disarray of tables, some of them stripped of their cloths, some covered in abandoned glasses; the vases of flowers and the *chinoiserie* chairs still arranged where the musicians had played by the fireplace.

'Well, at least I talked you into getting a jazz band,' said Corinna. 'Otherwise nobody would have danced.' Jamie, she noticed, was looking restless. 'So where is she?'

'I don't know. It beats me what women get up to when they say they're "changing". She didn't need to. We're not going anywhere. Not tonight.'

Jamie sounded disgruntled, but Corinna knew he didn't mean it.

He was wrong anyway, because when Holly walked in a few seconds later, she was still wearing the same dress she had worn that afternoon. The golden creamy silk, embroidered with seed pearls, fell in rich folds to her ankles. Loose red curls tumbled over her shoulders, and now, as she saw them both waiting, her eyes lit up.

She looked even more beautiful than she had at the wedding.